JAMES BOND: DEATH IS FOREVER

JAMES BOND

DEATH IS FOREVER

JOHN GARDNER

PEGASUS BOOKS
NEW YORK LONDON

James Bond: Death Is Forever

Pegasus Books LLC
80 Broad Street, 5th Floor
New York, NY 10004

First Pegasus Books trade paperback edition 2014

ISBN: 978-1-60598-535-0

10 9 8 7 8 6 5 4 3 2 1

Printed in the United States of America
Distributed by W. W. Norton & Company, Inc.

And the eyes of the man . . . spoke to him and said: "Mister, nothing is forever. Only death is permanent. Nothing is forever except what you did to me."

—Ian Fleming, *Diamonds Are Forever*

One cannot rule out . . . that some adventurers might try to profit from their knowledge.

—Markus (Mischa) Wolf, former head of the East German Foreign Intelligence Service for over three decades, in answer to a question about the dangers which might exist from, as yet, uncovered East German agents (November 1991)

For John and Pam, who love joy and living.
Remember ''Lucky.''

Contents

DEATH IS FOREVER

1

The Deaths of Vanya & Eagle

Ford Puxley came face to face with death at exactly 4:12 PM on a chilly October Thursday outside the Frankfurter Hof Hotel in the heart of Frankfurt. In the last split second of his life, Puxley knew the arrival of death was his own fault.

During the iceberg center of the Cold War, Puxley had instructed many novice spies, and his watchword was, "Wear tradecraft like a good suit, or carry it like an American Express Card. Don't leave home without it, but use it automatically. If your tradecraft sticks out like a lion in a monkey run, it will kill you."

So, at the end, Puxley's tradecraft, or lack of it, killed him.

There was a convention beginning that week. Conventions and trade shows are a way of life in Frankfurt, and the locals do not care whether it is books, business machines or automobiles. Conventions and the like mean business, and the jingle of cash registers.

The lounges and lobbies were full. Once-a-year friends were being reunited; smooth businessmen, with wives or mistresses, were arriving smugly from the airport; a large aggressive woman tried to complain about her room—in execrable German, to a young man who spoke better English than the plaintiff—while bored conventioneers stood in line.

Ford Puxley hardly noticed any of them, for he was in a hurry. The telephone call he had just taken in his third-floor room had been a breakthrough. He stopped only long enough to make a quick return call. Now, the sooner he got out to meet his source, the faster he would be back in his neat little house in Greenwich, with its trim garden and his young wife. He had married late and that proved to be a boon. Nowadays he did not like being away from England.

He shouldered his way through the crowd in the main lobby, and out onto the street. After the failed August coup in Moscow, the imploding of the once Evil Empire, and the outlawing of the Communist Party in what used to be the Soviet Union, his subconscious had sent all of his lifetime security habits to sleep.

He barged out onto the twilight pavement, ignored the commissionaire, and waved to the trio of taxis waiting for trade. The first in line started his engine, but the Opel was faster. It was grey, splashed with mud and came scooting out from its hiding place at the end of the row; accelerating and cutting in front of the taxi which was only now starting to move slowly forward.

The whole thing was beautifully executed. The inside bumper of the Opel struck Puxley's hip, skittering him around. Then the vehicle fishtailed so that the whole rear weight of the moving car sideswiped the staggering man, throwing him into the air, crushed and dead before he even hit the pavement, scattering amazed and frightened bystanders.

In the moment before death, Puxley's mind registered several things. He realized the man near the row of taxis had raised his hand, and it was not to hail either a cab or bus. Classic. A signal to the Opel. He also took in the fact that the Opel's registration had been fouled with mud. By the time the car hit him, Puxley realized he was being flyswatted. That is what they used to call it in the old days, within the shimmering glacier of Berlin. His very last thought was how well it was being done. They were certainly experts, and he went into oblivion cursing himself and knowing exactly why this had happened to him.

They took Puxley home to England and buried him. M, who personally went to the interment, said later that it had been a very dull little funeral. "The widow didn't seem to be much bowed with grief," he told Bill Tanner, his Chief of Staff. "The sherry was undrinkable. Also, I didn't much care for the parson. He had a cold and was in an obvious hurry." But M was, of course, more used to Naval funerals, with the Royal Marine band playing a cheery march as the mourners left the cemetery, while the chaplain treated the deceased as one of his own. This cleric, he said to Tanner, could have been planting a tree. "Not right you know, Bill," he muttered. "Death is the last enemy and all that. You don't get another turn."

In the field, Puxley's cryptonym had been *Vanya.*

Exactly one week after Puxley's dull obsequies, Libby Macintosh arrived at a pleasant, unpretentious hotel in one of the many tributaries which flow off Berlin's Kurfürstendamm.

Ms. Macintosh, a lady in her late forties, had never stayed in this hotel before, though she knew the city backwards. If the authorities had taken the trouble to check up on her, they would have discovered that she had been in Berlin many times over the years, and, on this occasion, had already lived in the city for the best part of a month, though they would have been hard put to seek out the different addresses she had used: apart from the five alternative names.

Libby Macintosh was an American businesswoman, and it showed in the power suit—severe, navy with white trim—to the power briefcase she seemed to guard with her honor. Certainly, it was later said, she would not let the bellboy take it, with the two Louis Vuitton suitcases, to her room.

She quietly told the concierge that she was expecting a Herr Maaster to visit her. A Herr Helmut Maaster. He should be announced and sent up the moment he arrived.

She tipped the bellboy, and called down to room service

asking for coffee and *gâteaux,* which were duly sent up to her.

Herr Maaster did not materialize, and the next anyone knew of Ms. Libby Macintosh was when the chambermaid called agitatedly for the housekeeper who, in turn, sent for the Duty Manager.

In all, Ms. Macintosh had resided in the hotel for around two hours. When the chambermaid went in to make up the room for the night, she found its occupant spread-eagled on the bed, clad only in black silk underwear. Her seductive look—for Ms. Macintosh still had an excellent figure—was spoiled by the fact that she was dead.

The management was not overjoyed. No hotel is happy about death on the premises, and, rightly, they felt it was an affront. However, the business blew over, and nobody said anything about foul play.

In fact, the police released Ms. Macintosh's body after only two days, and the corpse was returned to the United States where it was buried—an Episcopalian service—in a small Virginia churchyard under its rightful name, Elizabeth Cearns. Among the family mourners were two senior officers from Langley, or, to be more accurate, from the Central Intelligence Agency.

Nobody could prove anything about Ms. Macintosh/ Cearns's death, but there were those in forensics at Langley who had a feel for these things. They suspected an old method, long out of date, last used, they thought, in the late 1950s—the cyanide pistol.

Death by cyanide inhalation is supposed to leave no trace, but the people at Langley had performed an autopsy on the victim's brain, where they found minute traces: enough to finger the method.

In the field, Elizabeth Cearns's cryptonym had been *Eagle.*

Three days after Elizabeth Cearns's burial, the two deaths were brought to the notice of Captain James Bond RN, just before he was summoned to the presence of his Chief—M, as he was known to those who lived, moved and had their being in the arcane halls of the British Secret Intelligence Service.

2

Death of Cabal

"Cabal died sometime between September 30 and October 6, 1990." M sat in his ultra-modern chair in the chrome and glass office on the fifth floor of the anonymous building overlooking Regent's Park.

"The week of Germany's reunification," Bill Tanner supplied in a quiet footnote kind of voice.

"Went dead, really," M continued. "Just closed itself down. Fragmented, if you like. No orders from either us or our relations at Langley, as Ms. St. John already knows."

Ms. St. John nodded from her seat on M's left. James Bond sat on the right, and Bill Tanner hovered near the window.

"And this is a concern to us now." Bond raised his eyebrows.

M's eyes flicked towards his agent: a small flash of irritation. "Should be obvious, Captain Bond." His voice reflected the sharp snap of annoyance. "You read the file this morning, and Ms. St. John's been dragged across the Atlantic from her hearth and home. I should've thought even a cretin could deduce that Cabal is a matter of unease."

"I was making a statement, not a query, sir. Haven't we left things to stew for rather a long time? I mean October 1990's two years ago."

"A lot of things've been left too long, 007. I know that and

17

you know it. Europe hasn't been the easiest operational continent since 'ninety." The Old Man was rattled, Bond thought, and when M was perturbed it was time to batten down against a storm. M was too experienced to be easily discomfited.

M grunted, and Ms. St. John gave a small, supercilious laugh.

James Bond had not taken to Ms. St. John. She was the kind of American woman to whom the old chauvinistic center of his nature remained allergic. Short and pert, Ms. St. John wore clothes which seemed to envelop her: a baggy pants suit with a checked waistcoat over a white shirt, under a loose coat which seemed too large for her small frame. She was, he decided, dressed more for a grouse shoot than the kind of field they would be beating. He also detected the stir of condescension in the girl's manner.

When Bill Tanner had introduced them in his office less than thirty minutes ago, she had given him a curt "Hi" and a handshake to match, while the pearl-grey eyes appraised him as if to say that all men were inferior, but some were more inferior than others. Bond had the distinct impression that, as far as Ms. St. John was concerned, he fell definitely into the latter category.

M continued to talk. "If you've read everything, you'll know that Cabal was, without any doubt, our most successful network running out of the old DDR, out of East Germany before the great thaw."

Bond nodded. At the height of its success, Cabal had sported over thirty active agents, including two deep penetrations within the old KGB headquarters at Karlshorst. Cabal had probed and listened, fed disinformation, and carefully lifted at least three solid defectors from within the ranks of KGB, the, now defunct, Stasi of ill renown, and the HVA—the Hauptverwaltung Aufklärung, the former East German Foreign Intelligence Agency.

Cabal had run every kind of operation in the book, from dangles to false flags, deceptions and even the odd honeytrap. Its history was the history of the Cold War, and its weapons had been classic to that time—the meat and drink of all the famous espionage novelists. If the CIA and the British SIS had their way, every member of Cabal would have been loaded with medals. Now nobody could be found. Not a single agent could have the Congressional Medal of Honor or the CBE pinned to his or her chest.

"Disappeared in a puff of smoke," M continued, "and when the original case officers went after them, they both wound up dead. One outside a hotel in Frankfurt, the other inside a hotel in Berlin. You've read the details."

"And both dispatched by outmoded means, sir." Bond looked at the ceiling, as though talking to himself.

"Everything's outmoded now." M sounded tired, as though the end of the Cold War had brought new horrors into his fiefdom. "Everything, including a whole network vanishing in broad daylight."

"Could someone be trying to send us a message?"

"Such as?" M remained seated, with his head bowed, as though in meditation, accepting the input of others and cycling it through his mind to find answers by a magic which only he possessed.

"The old ways. Antiquated methods for what the Russians used to call wet work. Using old cold warrior weapons. Flyswatting and the cyanide pistol. Flyswatting went out with the ark: too expensive; and as for the cyanide pistol, well, we all know they threw that out after one operation."

"Yes. Certainly it could be a message." M gave a Buddha-like bob of the head. "We, the Ancients, are still among you, that kind of thing, eh? But what about motive?"

"Revenge, sir?" Bond tempted, as though trying to draw his old Chief.

M shrugged sadly, commenting that there was certainly plenty of that going on in Eastern Europe these days. "One of the reasons we must keep active. The Joint Intelligence Committee's adamant that our Service will be required to remain fully operational in Europe for a minimum of ten years. One of the reasons Cabal was so important. Together with our American brothers, we had listed new targets for them: political, economic, para-military, terrorist."

In some ways, Bond thought, it must be like the situation directly after World War II, when the various secret agencies had their work cut out sniffing around for Nazis hiding in the woodpile of freedom. Now they looked for diehard Communists: people anxious to see the discredited regime regain its lost credibility; men and women whose lives had been dedicated to the Marxist-Leninist cause; persons now without rank, authority or political estate, who craved for a return to the norm in which they had believed down all their years. There was a lot of talk about underground Marxist terrorist groups; and the reorganization of secret cadres ready to infiltrate fledgling democracies.

"The two of you'll have to get out there and follow in the footsteps of poor old Puxley and Ms. Macintosh . . ."

"Cearns, sir." Ms. St. John seemed to come out of a daydream. It was possibly the jet lag. "Liz Cearns. She was an old colleague and friend."

"Yes, Cearns." M looked at the young woman, his gaze bleak. "Just as Ford Puxley was an old friend and colleague of ours, Ms. St. John. Your service does not have the monopoly on grief."

"Then it should make us all more determined, sir." She bit the words out, as though holding back a geyser of anger.

"Oh, I think we're determined enough already. Hope you're not too emotionally involved, Ms. St. John. Doesn't do to go off into the cold woods with anger and sentiment leading the way. Going into the labyrinth and plucking out what's left of Cabal's going to need cool, dispassionate minds."

Ms. St. John opened her mouth, then seemed to think better of it. M treated her to one of his embracing, avuncular smiles, warm as a spring morning. "Come," he said, his voice following up on the smile. "Let's get down to work. Play at being Sherlock Holmes for a while. Let's go through what information we have, and then deduce what went wrong for Ford Puxley and Elizabeth Cearns. *Vanya* and *Eagle*. That way lies more safety for you."

He rose and, uncharacteristically, removed his dark blue blazer with the anchored buttons, pulling back his shirt sleeves, like a man about to sit in at a round of high-stakes poker. "Roll up our sleeves, what? Get down to it." He turned to Tanner, asking him to organize coffee and sandwiches. "It's going to be a long night, I fear. Might as well make ourselves comfortable. Get out of that coat, Ms. . . . I refuse to go on calling you *Ms.* St. John. What do people call you, Elizabeth, isn't it?"

While Ms. St. John did not actually thaw, she visibly relaxed, slipping out of the voluminous coat to display that, even clothed in the tweedy pants suit, she possessed a body of neat feminine proportions. "Friends," she said, smiling for the first time, "call me Easy."

M did not even return the smile, and Bond felt his eyes crease into a twinkle.

"My initials," she nodded. "Elizabeth Zara. Eee Zee. By the age of fourteen I was the best arm-wrestler in my school. You know what kids are like."

"Indeed, yes." Bond took his cue from M and suppressed the laugh, drawing his chair closer to M's desk.

When Bill Tanner returned with the sandwiches and coffee, the trio looked like conspirators, hunched over the desk, their faces drawn into shadow outside the circle of light falling from the angled lamp which provided the only illumination in the room. M had switched off the overhead lights so they could more easily concentrate on the papers he had before them.

For over six hours they carefully put together the jigsaw of *Vanya*'s and *Eagle*'s last days.

From the final week in September until their deaths, within a week of each other, the two case officers had kept in constant touch: both with each other and their home base, which was a joint facility in rural Oxfordshire, separated from, but run under the auspices of, a small Royal Air Force Communications base hard by the village of Bloxham, a stone's throw from Banbury, famous for the nursery rhyme "Ride a cockhorse to Banbury Cross."

Using electronic wizardry, in the shape of short-wave transceivers little bigger than credit cards, but crammed with smart boards operating on a fixed frequency, every telephone call, and each report to *Moonshine*—the home base—had been monitored. The transcripts now filled a loose-leaved book almost three inches thick.

It was like reading a secret diary; or the vigilant correspondence of a pair of clandestine lovers. Both *Vanya* and *Eagle* knew each other's handwriting backwards. Single words spoken over insecure telephones could be transcribed as clear instructions or intelligence, while sentences of a dozen words were stuffed with volumes of information. They had their own shorthand, and their knowledge of Cabal's topography—its safe houses, letter boxes, and personal signals—was encyclopedic.

Both of the officers had covered all the ground they had worked with Cabal in the past. They followed each other through the well-known haunts of Hamburg, Stuttgart, Frankfurt, Munich and Berlin.

On two occasions they had slipped, separately, into Switzerland, meeting at an old safe house in Zurich where they left the minute transceivers on send while they talked.

Bond knew the place well, and as he read the transcript of the conversations, he could see the view from the window, out over the Sechselauten Platz to the lake, with its toy pleasure steamers coming and going. He remembered, from years before, eating dinner with an agent in a small warm café near the lake, and later, in that same safe house, briefing the man, who went directly from the affluence of Switzerland to his death behind the Iron Curtain. The agent had died because of incorrect information Bond had been told to give him, and 007's conscience had been scarred with the memory.

Now, as they read and discussed, other deaths were surfacing. Of the original thirty members of Cabal, only ten remained alive. Six had died from natural causes, six were irretrievably missing, presumed dead, and eight—*Vanya* and *Eagle* had discovered—had been killed in accidents which could not have been mischances.

The ten Cabal agents remaining in Europe had left some traces, and together *Vanya* and *Eagle* followed trails which went, by turns, hot and cold. On telephones, and at their two meetings in Switzerland, they spoke of the agents only by their exotic work names—*Crystal, Ariel, Caliban, Cobweb, Orphan, Tester, Sulphur, Puck, Mab* and *Dodger.* These names, which were folded into the conversations, had to be cross-referenced in M's office in order to finger the true identities, and, if this were not difficult enough, there was a set of street names used on some of the transcribed telephone conversations.

At one point the tenacious Puxley came very close to *Caliban,* while Elizabeth Cearns reported having had sight of, and then losing, *Sulphur.*

But the real action came almost as the two case officers met their deaths. Only minutes before Puxley was swatted by the Opel outside the Frankfurter Hof, he took a telephone call in his hotel room.

"Is that Dan?" asked on the pick-up. The voice was male and heavily accented, said the notation by the transcriber.

"Which Dan do you want?" The sudden excitement and adrenaline rush was almost tangible in the words lying cold on the page.

"Dan Broome. Mr. Dan Broome from Magic Mountain Software."

"Speaking."

"It's Ulricht. Ulricht Voss."

There in the darkened office, M cross-referenced what they already knew: the caller was using the identification code of Oscar Vomberg, in straight Cabalspeak, *Mab.* The sequence— "Dan . . . Dan Broome . . . of Magic Mountain Software"—was distinctive. "Only Vomberg would have used that sequence," M said quietly. "Which means that, if it is not Vomberg—and our voiceprint people swear it is—then it's someone using a sequence culled from Oscar, who's a pretty shrewd old scientist. Worked with the East Germans on drugs—mind control, that kind of thing."

Back on the page, Ulricht Voss, who was really Oscar Vomberg—*Mab* to any inhabitants of Cabal—asked to meet Dan Broome urgently. He gave the name and address of a notorious local clip joint and brothel, Der Mönch—The Monk. Then added, "To see *Sulphur*."

The transcript went on to show Puxley's fast call to *Moonshine*. "For the insurance," M said. "That's how fastidious Ford Puxley was. In case his little piece of electronics had not done the job with the incoming call, he wanted home base to know what was happening. 'Contact with *Mab*,' he had said, quickly giving the time and place, then adding, 'Meeting *Sulphur* now at Der Mönch.'"

So, with that final report, Ford Puxley, aka *Vanya*, dashed down from his room, threw tradecraft to the wind and went out to death from the Opel car in twilight Frankfurt.

The transcripts showed a similar series of events leading up to the death of Ms. Elizabeth Cearns, aka Libby Macintosh, aka *Eagle*.

Following the second meeting with *Vanya* in Switzerland, it was decided that she should go back to Berlin, where she already claimed to have had sight of *Sulphur*. "Now *Sulphur*, as you will see from the charts," M pointed out, "is, in reality, a Bulgarian. She joined Cabal in 1979 when she was only eighteen years old. KGB had recruited her from the Bulgarian service—the old and ruthless DS, the Dajnava Sigurnost. She worked at Karlshorst as a liaison officer between KGB and DS. We bought and paid for her." He gave a tiny smile. "I should say the American Service bought and paid for her, in 1982. She was fabulous. Hated the Russians, loathed her own people—or, at least the then controlling faction of her people. She gave us more than anyone. Very bright, a quick study as they say. The Americans even got her out for two weeks for a crash course. I

24

believe your people, Easy, used the term 'A Class Act.' I gather that's high praise."

"The highest."

"Mmmm. Well, if you read this passage you'll see that your Ms. Cearns considered that, should *Sulphur* surface, she would do so in only the best places. Puxley and Cearns decided that Cearns should show herself at the Kempi."

The Kempi is Berlin's fabled Bristol Hotel Kempinski. It has been said the fate and future of Germany has always been decided at the Kempinski.

"And her real name?" Bond's eyes narrowed as he leaned across the desk to peer at the classified lists of Cabal's assets.

"Praxi," M said quietly. "Praxi Simeon."

"A pretty name, Praxi," Bond muttered.

"You think so?" from Easy who wrinkled her nose as though she found the name distasteful.

"And there you go." M flicked over several pages of transcripts, then tapped down on a page with his index finger. "The incoming calls to *Eagle* at the Bristol Kempinski."

The first few were direct communications with *Moonshine*, and included a sobering conversation in which the *Moonshine* controller broke the news of *Vanya*'s death. There were several other *en clair* talks between *Moonshine* and *Eagle*, also between *Eagle* and *Duster*, who was, M explained, Liz Cearns's direct controller at Langley.

"Martin de Rosso," Easy said. "He's my controller also, as far as this is concerned. What happens next, sir?"

"Day before *Eagle*'s death." M flicked at another page. There was an incoming call at 3:26 PM. Liz Cearns picked up:

"Hello?"

"Can I speak to Gilda?" Female, the note said, speaking German with slight accent.

"You want Gilda?"

"Gilda von Glocke."

"Yes, who is that?"

"Ilse. Ilse Schwer."

"I'm sorry, do you represent a company?"

"Yes. We *have* met, Frau von Glocke. I work for Herr Maaster. Maaster Designs. You remember?"

"Yes, I vaguely remember you. I'm sorry. But, yes, I am very anxious to speak with Herr Maaster."

"And he wishes to see you, but he has a very full schedule. He doesn't want to come to the Kempi. You know what he's like, Frau von Glocke. . . ."

"Yes. Where would he like to meet?"

"He says tomorrow afternoon. Around three at the Hotel Braun." She gave the address.

"I'll be there. Tell him to ask for me at the desk."

"Nice to speak with you again, Frau von Glocke."

There, the transcript ended.

"And the sequence is right?" Bond asked.

"Everything's right. The voice analysts say it's definitely *Sulphur,* that is, Praxi Simeon. The Maaster Designs business was the identifier. The entire sequence is correct."

"And Herr Maaster was . . . ?"

"There is no Herr Maaster. For a face-to-face *Sulphur* would choose a place. It was always left to her. She has a great nose for the safest place. The Hotel Braun is nondescript. *Eagle* called it in, and informed *Moonshine* as soon as she had moved."

"And her transceiver?" Bond asked. "It wasn't on when she . . ."

"Two calls. Both to the United States." M pointed to the log. "Then it was as though she just switched it off. Something she would not do under normal circumstances."

"A lover?"

"It has crossed everybody's mind, but there's nothing to back it up."

"Her lover lived in D.C.," Easy supplied. She had been very silent during the past few minutes. "Unless she had met someone . . . No, that's not in character. Liz was the most faithful of women."

26

"Yet someone clobbered her with a cyanide pistol, and she was in the room dressed only in her underwear." Bond bit his bottom lip. "No sign of a struggle. Nothing odd."

M shook his head. "Teaser, isn't it? Well, you'll both have to go out there and find out exactly what happened." He pushed his chair back. "Before tonight's out I want you to memorize everything. Agents' cryptos, their street names, all the sequences, the word codes, the body language, the safe houses, letter boxes, street meets. Everything."

"That's an awful lot . . ." Easy began.

"I know," M said coldly. "I know it's asking an awful lot, Easy, but that's life in our business. As far as we can tell, there are ten former Cabal agents out there, and two of them—Oscar Vomberg, *Mab;* and Praxi Simeon, *Sulphur*—might be tainted goods. We've done the necessary. Put the ads in the local papers; broadcast on the correct frequencies at the right times; published in a couple of magazines Cabal used for contact. You, James, are the new *Vanya,* while you, Easy, must assume *Eagle*'s mantle. We'll all stay here for the night and work with you, but I want the pair of you on flights to Berlin no later than tomorrow night."

Bond already felt that strange mixture of excitement and fear fluttering and firing in his belly.

"I want both of you to learn, and then think, deduce, try to find the answer to the puzzle of your predecessors' deaths. Up to it, are you?"

Bond gave a grim nod, while Easy swallowed before saying "Yes," though the word stuck for a second in her throat.

3

||||||||||||||||||||||||||||||||||||||||||||||||||||||||||||||||||||||||||||||||||||||||||||||||||||||||||||||||||||||||||||

Responsible for a Death

From the moment he went through passport and customs control at Berlin's Tegel Airport, James Bond knew he was being followed. He arrived on the late afternoon flight from Heathrow—Easy St. John would follow on the evening flight—and at first it seemed that little had changed since he was last in Berlin, before the incredible events which had altered not only the landscape, but also the hearts and minds of a newly united people. Tegel, with its calm sense of Germanic order, did not appear to be any different.

As for Berlin itself, the Wall had gone; the city was whole again. You could almost touch the regenerated freedom in the air; but it was only when the taxi turned onto the Ku'damm that he saw the streets had undergone a subtle change, and that the glittering store windows had shifted infinitesimally.

In the old bold days, the sidewalks of the Ku'damm were filled with a mixture of affluent Berliners, military personnel and strolling tourists. Now, the crowds seemed larger. The Berlin matrons still sported their little hats with perky feathers; a great deal of fur and leather adorned people's bodies. But moving along, next to the familiar, there were other pedestrians, less well-heeled, shabbier, and with looks on their faces which reflected envy. The poor cousins of the old East Berlin

28

were slowly integrating with their more comfortable relatives. It was a fleeting message, and Bond did not linger on it for he was more concerned with the surveillance which had picked him up at the airport.

He had been particularly careful at Tegel. For one thing, he had only managed three hours sleep in the past twenty-four. In a profession such as Bond's, physical fatigue enhances the senses. It is as though the fear that exhaustion might cause some terrible error forces intuition to go into overdrive; eyes and ears seek out the unusual, as if operating on intensified perception; while touch and smell become almost painful.

He spotted a couple of possibles as he came onto the main level of the terminal. A man and woman talking beside the hexagonal information booth. The man, a mousy, pockmarked person, was short and fat, with restless eyes which took in Bond through one fast glance, leaving a strange sense of nakedness in its wake. The woman appeared wary and nervous.

Of one thing Bond was certain, they did not belong to each other. The pair gave off vibrations which said they had only recently met, and had yet to become comfortable as a pair. His intuition, though, said they were part of a larger team. They could be simple criminals—pickpockets—but he thought not. The way they stood, talked and moved spoke of a different kind of felony: the theft of political souls.

As he stepped outside into the queue for taxis, Bond spotted a tall man in a leather coat, pacing to and fro, as though waiting for an arriving passenger. This one held a rolled newspaper, which he thumped rhythmically against his thigh as though irritated by the delay.

Thoughts of Ford Puxley's flyswatting ran through his mind. How someone had raised his hand as a signal for the Opel to come hurtling out—a bullet on four wheels, deadly as a rocket—and he half expected to see Leather Coat go through the same performance.

He remembered a description in a novel: a target had been hit by a car. The victim had been holding a newspaper, and as the car struck the paper popped up in his hand, opening like a stage magician's trick bouquet of flowers.

Joining the orderly line of new arrivals, Bond saw Leather Coat turn away and go back into the terminal. A second later, the woman from the information booth came out alone and joined the taxi queue. Perhaps, he thought, this was early paranoia—and why not? To be in the field again meant putting on the invisible coat of suspicion: being aware of everything; seeing ghosts in shadows; threats in innocent loiterers; evil in a passing glance. It was that sixth sense which could turn blameless men and women into assassins or informers: the stuff of his dying art, the tools of a craft as old as time, the invisible card index a spy carries for life.

Then, as he entered the cab and told the driver to get him to the Kempi, he saw the movement, on the periphery of his vision. Not Leather Coat, but the young woman, placed two persons behind him in the line. A distinctive motion: her right hand coming up, clutching a cheap leather handbag, which covered her face for a second as she ran the back of her hand across her brow. It was the kind of body language beloved of watchers.

As the cab took him towards the Bristol Kempinski, Bond tried to watch the rear without alerting the leeches by shifting around in his seat. He leaned forward, craning to catch glimpses in the wing mirrors and, after a mile, thought he had made the surveillance vehicle. A maroon VW Golf with a driver and a passenger riding shotgun. The car nipped in and out of the traffic behind them: dropping back, then catching up, driving erratically. Not a trained pro, he considered, but certainly someone intent on seeing where he was heading.

When they arrived at the hotel the VW had gone, but whoever was interested certainly knew by this time where he was staying. Normally, Bond would have instructed the cabbie to take him to the Gehrhus, or even the Inter-Continental, so that he could dummy the shadows and hitch another cab to the Kempi. But M had said they were to play it out in the open.

30

"Puxley and Cearns both used all the angles," The Old Man had told them. "Yet Puxley and Cearns were fingered and put away, neat as butterflies in a killing jar. So let them see you. Whoever they are."

"Will you be backstopping us?" Bond asked.

"If we are, you won't see them," the Chief had snapped, meaning that any cavalry riding to the rescue would already know where they would be setting up headquarters.

M explained that people on the spot had put out every alert known to the old members of Cabal. "Any elements of the network still trying to make contact will know who to look for." He made a little grimace, as though signaling that the posted alerts—the newspaper and magazine ads, together with the whole gamut of chalk marks and similar physical indicators— might also be known to those who appeared bent on the complete annihilation of Cabal: whoever *they* were.

Both Easy St. John and Bond brooded over who *they*—the main enemy—could be, going through all the obvious questions. Had someone sold out on Cabal before the Wall came down, and the new order made itself felt? Had any Cabal op gone awry, leaving dissatisfied elements calling for revenge? Who was Cabal's most natural enemy?

To this last, M had said the obvious: Markus Wolf—known as Mischa to his colleagues—Spymaster General to the old HVA, the Foreign Intelligence Agency of the former DDR. But Wolf had truly come in from his cold, giving himself up in the hope that he had enough friends at court to allow him an old age untroubled by vengeance.

Then M had tapped out a little ruffle with his fingertips on the arm of his chair. "Of course, there's always Mischa Wolf's deputy." He gazed at the ceiling, his face hidden in the darkness outside the bright circle of his desk lamp. "Nobody writes about him. The newshawks appear to have forgotten his existence, but then they're all being a mite selective as far as the old regime's concerned."

He drummed his little tattoo again. "No, I haven't seen

Weisen's name in either the London or New York *Times*, let alone the *Washington Post*, or the news magazines. He's gone missing, joined the lost boys of the old regime. Perhaps . . . ? And then again, perhaps?" His face had come back into the light and his lips were now tilted into a sinister smile.

Wolfgang Weisen, Bond thought, my god, there would be an enemy and a half. It was claimed by some that Markus Wolf was merely a figurehead for the more fanatical Weisen, born in Berlin of mixed parentage—Russian mother and German father—moved into Russia as a child, and returned to his native Germany after World War II.

Just as there had never been a good photograph of Mischa Wolf, so there had never been even a good description of Weisen, only hearsay and double-talk. Weisen, the Poison Dwarf of the East German intelligence and security services. A man who had learned his trade at the knees of some of the most vindictive in the business. Moscow-trained, ambitious, ruthless, a confirmed and unyielding Communist, whose ties went back to Stalin himself. Weisen, the Communist zealot with the full, near-Jesuitical education from the true evil which had, at one time, overtaken the ideology of Marx and Lenin.

Bond had studied the file, which maintained that, as a boy, little Wolfgang had spent time, quite a lot of time, at the aging Stalin's strange villa at Kuntsevo: the house which was constantly growing, yet had a ground floor of identically furnished rooms—each a combined sitting room and bedroom—where old Joseph Stalin would eke out his days sending death by a look, or even a thought that someone had betrayed him.

As Bond recalled it, the evidence told of the boy Wolfgang sitting with Stalin to watch the grim old dictator's favorite Tarzan movies, over and over, again and again, the terrible man keeping up his own running commentary on the banalities. It was also said that Stalin had given the child private tuition on how to usurp power. Some, at that time, had seen this small, stunted boy as the crown prince of the macabre despot.

The file also had a number of notes, based on firm intelligence, that the child, Wolfgang Weisen, had been a favorite of the awesomely depraved, utterly implacable Beria, head of the pre-KGB service. The man who sent his hatchet men out onto the streets to pull in some fancied schoolgirl on whom the degenerate Lavrenti Beria would perform unthinkable sexual acts. Beria, the beast of Dzerzhinsky Square, Stalin's first minister of horror.

There were footnotes, not corroborated, that Weisen had inherited many of Beria's traits and warped desires, together with Stalin's illusory intuitions. What if Wolfgang the Terrible, as some of the experienced analysts called him, was loose and had Cabal in his sights?

The thought again crossed Bond's mind as he entered the pleasant luxury of the Kempi, with its restful tropical fish tanks and unhurried order. "Good day, Herr Boldman. It is good to have you back, Herr Boldman. Suite 207, Herr Boldman, if there is anything . . ." and all the usual smiling warmth and willingness to please.

Bond unpacked, stripped, showered—first scalding hot followed by cold—the bathroom door open and a view to the suite's door unimpaired via the mirrored wall. He then toweled himself vigorously and, wrapped in the crested Kempi robe, stretched out on the bed. Easy St. John was to go through a telephone code as soon as she arrived. Now he had nothing to do but think.

The 9mm ASP automatic, which had traveled in the specially lined briefcase, lay under his pillow, and, while he would have given almost anything to allow sleep to fold him up, Bond put his mind on alert. Then, for the hundredth time in the past twenty-four hours, he went over the facts again and tried to make some logical sense of the whole business.

First, he thought about Easy St. John. Though they had spent a great deal of intense time together, mostly in the company of M, and mainly poring over documents, Bond considered it would take a great deal longer for him to get used to her. Easy gave off the paradoxical characteristics of a career business-woman—a brusque, know-it-all outer surface which could change in a second to charm and understanding. It was as though having reached her relatively exalted position within the American Service by dint of her own talents, she now claimed a certain reverence as her right. Bond knew where that kind of thinking could lead—a power base of isolation, which did nobody any good.

He would have to work hard to bring her down to the full realization that life in the field demanded more than simply talent and good training. His concern was that she might well be living a fantasy where playing by the book, which she obviously knew by heart, was enough to survive. There had been one incident, in particular, concerning the death of *Eagle*—Liz Cearns—which had made him doubly unsure of her.

Before leaving London, he had even confided in M, who had shown a certain amount of irritation. "She's all we've got from the American Service," he spat, testily. "If necessary, you'll have to train her on the fly, 007."

"She's really a desk jockey who's simply done the right courses, isn't she, sir?"

"Possibly. They're reorganizing at Langley, you know that. Trying to give more people real field experience."

"Sir, with respect, you don't send a pilot who's only flown simulators straight out in a jet fighter for real."

"Apparently the Americans do, 007. You'll have to make the best of it."

M's whole attitude told Bond that his Chief was as leery of Easy St. John as he was. He had seen it before. M's only concern was really the British side of the business, which meant he was trusting Bond with the lion's share of the work.

Now, lying on his bed in the Kempi, he wondered how much extra stress would be added in trying to keep a somewhat ego-centric Easy out of trouble. In the end, he decided to worry at it instead of about it, taking things a day at a time, an hour at a time, even—he contemplated gloomily—a minute at a time.

From the Easy problem, he again went over the facts of Puxley's and Cearns's deaths.

Cabal's original case officers had both perished after speaking to supposedly loyal members of the network. The call from Oscar Vomberg, *Mab,* the scientist, had sent Puxley—*Vanya*—scurrying to his appointment with the Opel outside his hotel. The simple act of the telephone call had led, unmistakably, to the agent's death by an outmoded KGB method.

In Vomberg's case they had studied the voiceprints and looked over all the analytical evidence. The graphs showed that the caller was unequivocally Vomberg. So the only conclusion to be drawn amounted to him having been used, wittingly or unwittingly, as the trigger to the event outside the Frankfurter Hof Hotel. There was no room for any other theory.

The same applied to Liz Cearns's death. Just as Vomberg had pressed the button on Ford Puxley, so Praxi Simeon, *Sulphur,* appeared to have done the business with her old controller, *Eagle.* Once more, the voice analysts had been emphatic that Praxi's voice had been the one on the telephone. So, Praxi's call had prompted Cearns to change hotels, thereby setting herself up for what appeared to be a frankly old-fashioned, and tricky, form of death. A kind of death so precarious that even the old black heart of KGB had last used it in 1958 and 1959 against two targets in what was then West Germany.

On that occasion, the assassin was a young man—KGB trained for these special assassinations. His name was Bogdan Stashinsky, and the work was done with a clumsy-looking pistol, in reality a tube with a trigger mechanism at one end. The tube was seven inches in length, and made up of three sections. The trigger and firing pin, within the first tube, ignited a powder charge in the middle section which, in turn, crushed a glass phial in the third section. The phial contained 5cc of hydro-cyanide.

Fired a couple of inches from the victim's face, the cyanide killed instantly and, supposedly, left no trace. The assassin, however, was also armed with a pill, which had to be ingested before the kill, and a further antidote in a glass capsule. It was necessary for the murderer to crush his capsule between his teeth and inhale the antidote at the moment of firing the cyanide.

The method was used twice, against anti-Soviet Ukrainian Nationalists living in Germany. The first murder went undetected, the victim being Lev Rebet, editor of the Ukrainian exile newspaper *Ukrainski Samostinik*. On October 10, 1958, Stashinsky murdered Rebet as he was on his way to his office. The autopsy concluded that the victim had died of a coronary obstruction. Nobody suspected violence.

In the following year, Stashinsky used the same method on Ukrainian exile leader Stepan Bandera. But this time the autopsy yielded traces of poison in the brain. Eventually, Stashinsky—a reluctant assassin—gave himself up to the American Intelligence authorities. He was the center of what amounted to a show trial, drew only eight years, and now lived happily ever after with his wife and family somewhere in Germany.

After that there appeared to be no other murders using the cyanide pistol, until Liz Cearns took a faceful of the poison in her room at the Hotel Braun off the Ku'damm, and that worried Bond, who had studied the evidence and photographs with great care.

Certainly Praxi appeared to have lured *Eagle* to the place of death, but the forensic and autopsy reports showed no further marks on the body. She had died lying stretched out on the hotel bed, clad only in provocative underwear. From the photographs she looked like a woman prepared and ready for intense sexual activity, and there was no reason to believe she had been placed in this position after death.

It was as though she had eaten a piece of very rich cake, drunk two cups of coffee, let a lover into the room, prepared to make love to him, or her, and was then surprised as annihilation came to her, floating on a small cloud of vapor.

Both M and Bond quizzed Easy St. John for some time, for

she seemed to have been a particular friend of the deceased case officer.

"You said she had a lover in D.C.?"

"Yes. Liz and I were . . . Well, we shared each other's little secrets . . ."

"That was all, just girl talk? You didn't share any restricted information?"

"Girl talk." Easy's brow creased and her nose wrinkled into what was becoming a familiar gesture, used whenever she thought anyone was being unfair to her. "Liz was a first-class officer, and I pride myself that I would never have asked any question which might have made her uneasy. I would never have asked her about classified material which I had no need to know." This last spoken with an underlying confidence, as though she was saying how dare you even think I would have talked about restricted matters.

"Tell us about the lover," M prodded.

"He's a lawyer. The Agency uses him occasionally. He checks out. It was a great shock to him. I'd go as far as to say he was prostrate. . . ."

"Name?" Bond asked.

There was the slightest hesitation. Then: "Richards. Simon Richards. Robertson, Richards and Burns. A very old D.C. law office. As I said, it's Agency connected."

"And you say she was a faithful lady?"

"Utterly."

"You're sure?"

Again a pause. "Yes. I only remember . . ."

"What?"

"One small indiscretion. It must've been two years ago. She told me about it over lunch, in . . . oh, it must've been 'eighty-nine. I know we lunched at Maison Blanche. I know that for sure. Just as I know she really felt bad about it: the little fling, I mean. You see, Liz was a girl who longed for marriage. They were going to be married, Liz and Simon. No doubt about that. She told me . . . I mean the words she used . . ."

"She told you what?"

"She used the words, 'my conscience has been seared. I feel dirty.'"

"She felt dirty about one lapse?"

Easy nodded. "She even wanted to tell Simon. I advised her to keep it to herself."

M nodded, and, in the silence that followed, Bond asked if the incident had taken place in Washington.

"She had just come back from Europe. I suppose from her work with Cabal."

Bond and M exchanged looks which spoke entire encyclopedias of doubt.

"So the indiscretion took place in Europe."

"Oh, yes."

Bond sighed. "Easy, why didn't you tell us this in the first place?"

"Because it was one time. A one-off. It happened once, and she was upset about it."

"It wasn't one of those indiscretions some women claim were once, and it turns out to have been with the band of the Royal Marines?"

"That's offensive, Captain Bond. I find that most offensive."

"Okay, Easy, I'm sorry, but we have to know . . ."

"She said it wouldn't ever happen again."

"And you *believed* her?"

"Of course!" High dudgeon, and very defensive.

"Easy," Bond said quietly, "you don't know for certain. You can't know for certain."

"Liz was an honorable . . ."

"Honor has nothing to do with need, Easy. Have you never been faced with a situation like this—I don't mean sex—any situation?"

"No. If I say I'm not going to do something again, I don't do it. Liz was like that also."

"Did she mention the lover's name?"

"Not really. Hans, or Franz, something like that. No family name. He was German."

"Oh, my God!" Bond had sighed. This was yet another nail in Easy's coffin of inexperience, and it left him even more unhappy about working in a very dangerous area with her.

Yet Liz Cearns was very experienced. Would she fall for one of the oldest tricks in the game? The reverse honeytrap? The use of what was known, in the business, as the joy-boy syndrome. Bond just did not know, but the whole thing made him very dubious about Ms. Easy St. John and her conception of honor, not to mention her blind belief in people she liked.

He rose from the bed and walked over to the mirror, looking at his reflection: wondering, for a second, if death would come to him in some unexpected and absurd manner. For what could be worse than meeting your end as you reached up to enfold a lover in your arms?

He dressed. Razor-creased slacks, a Turnbull & Asser shirt with a Royal Navy tie, and a tailored blazer that did not even show a lump where he carried the ASP, tucked into his waistband behind his right hip.

Easy should have arrived by now. As soon as she checked in with him, he would go down and have dinner. They served wonderful smoked salmon at the Kempi, he remembered. Also the beef Wellington was out of this world.

He was standing in front of the mirror again, adjusting the set of his tie, when the telephone rang.

"Hello?" He expected it to be Easy, so was ready for her code sequence.

"James?"

"Yes?" Oddly perturbed because she was supposed to ask for Jim Goldfarb.

"I'm in 202. I think you'd better get over here quickly."

"What's wrong?"

She should at least give him the word "particular" if something was amiss. Instead: "Just come straightaway. It's urgent."

Her voice sounded level, and he detected no fear. Touching the ASP like a talisman, he left the suite and went down the corridor to 202, knocking at the door.

"It's open," she called out, and he gently pushed the door. "Won't be a moment, James." She only raised her voice slightly from behind the half-open bathroom door.

Then, as he kicked the main door closed behind him, she appeared in the doorway, her face grey with fear. A man stood behind her, his arm around her throat.

He was tall, in his early sixties, with thin grey hair swept back from his forehead. He wore thick pebble glasses, was unshaven and looked as though he had slept in the shapeless brown suit which hung off his body, making him look as if he had suddenly suffered a severe weight loss.

Easy St. John was held and pushed in front of him like a shield, his left arm pulling her head back, forcing her forward, while his right hand, thrust in front of her body, held a nasty little IMI Desert Eagle automatic—the 0.44 Magnum variety, Bond thought. Not that it would make much difference, as the Israelis had produced a handgun that would stop a target with either version at this range.

"Forgive me," the man said, looking oddly distorted by the thick spectacles which made his eyes seem huge. "You are the new *Vanya,* I understand."

"Don't know what you mean, friend. Why not let the lady go? It isn't easy to carry out a reasonable conversation when someone's waving one of those things around."

"I wish to remain alive." He had a thick accent. Originally Munich, Bond thought, though he was no Professor Higgins as far as German dialect went.

"I think we all want to do that."

"Then you will kindly sit down, please." The eye of the Desert Eagle flicked towards a chair. He knew how to handle the weapon, bad eyesight or not.

Bond obeyed and sat with his right arm across the back of the chair, a little repro Venetian 18th century, with a carved and polychromed back.

"So." Easy's captor had swiveled her to face the seated Bond. "So, you are the new *Vanya,* yes? And this is the new *Eagle?*"

"What did you tell him, my dear?" Bond forced a smile.

"Nothing!" She tried to shake her head, but the man with the bottle glasses and the Desert Eagle pistol pressed in on her neck made it impossible.

"Tell you what." He allowed his hand to drop behind him, casually floating down his back, feeling for the butt of the ASP. "Tell you what. You let us have your name and we might trade some secrets with *you.* How about it?"

He seemed to be thinking it over, opening his mouth and then closing it a couple of times.

"Okay." Bond smiled. His fingertips touched the metal under his jacket. "Let's make it easier. I'll tell you who you are. Right?"

He saw the man's grip relax a fraction.

"I think you're the world-famous mind-bending drugs doctor known as Oscar Vomberg; sometimes called Ulricht Voss, and using another alias—*Mab.* I also think you were responsible for the death of a friend of mine. You knew him as *Vanya,* yes?"

The gunman's mouth dropped open and Bond sprang from the chair.

4

||||||||||||||||||||||||||||||||||||||||||||||||||||||||||||||||||||||||||||||||||||||||||||||||||||||||||||||||||||||||||||||||||||||||||||||||||||||

Death Through the Mouth

As his fingers finally curled around the butt of the ASP automatic, Bond pushed off with his feet, swiveling slightly so that Vomberg would have to make an awkward turn in order to retain his grip on Easy and bring his pistol to bear on Bond.

He had pulled both his feet in, almost under the chair, giving him maximum purchase to thrust himself forward. His body was still in the air as he drew the pistol, but the weapon would only be a last resort. He wanted Vomberg alive and talking, for the last thing they needed was a pistol shot which might lead to the management calling the police. German cops would not take kindly to gunplay at the Kempi, while the German Intelligence Service would blow all its fuses if they found elements of British and American Intelligence operating on their turf. The BND are notoriously touchy about such matters, particularly since reunification.

As he moved to the right, his left leg curled at the knee, then shot out with all his weight behind it: a high kick of great force which brought the heel of his shoe smashing onto the hand that held the Desert Eagle pistol.

He heard the bone crack, then a whimper of pain, a muted scream from Easy, and the thump as the weapon hit the floor. He landed firmly on both feet, facing the pathetic myopic

Vomberg, who had released Easy and was clutching his damaged hand, whining with agony.

Bond kicked the Desert Eagle across the room with his left foot and grabbed Vomberg with both hands, wringing the man's tie and shirt collar tightly against his neck so that his eyes popped and his face began to turn blue.

"Get the gun, Easy! Lock the door and then sit over there!" He cocked his head in the direction of a stand chair near the door. Vomberg smelled of stale sweat and garlic as Bond lifted him off the ground, turning him around and pushing him heavily into the chair.

Vomberg still whimpered, clasping his hand and struggling for breath; finally he managed to get a lungful of air. He gulped, his face creasing with pain, then raised his head and gulped again, looking like a beached fish. He stared into Bond's furious eyes. "Get on with it, then." The voice rose, near hysteria, croaking from the bruised larynx. "Get on with it. Kill me. That's what you're here for."

Bond's voice came calm and quiet. "Why do you think I would do that, Oscar?"

"Why? Don't treat me like an idiot . . . er . . . I call you *Vanya,* yes? Until someone gives me a better name."

Bond nodded. "*Vanya* will do, but you can call me James if you have problems with *Vanya.* You probably *do* have problems with that name in particular, after all you're responsible for his death."

"What the . . . ?"

Bond dragged another chair over, so that he could sit opposite Vomberg. "Look, Oscar." He leaned forward, elbows on his knees, right hand still clutching his pistol, face grim and his voice dropping almost to a whisper. "Oscar, you're not really cut out for the violence, are you? You're more of a cerebral spy. I'm even surprised to see you with a weapon."

Vomberg shook his head. "Desperate times," he said, as though that explained it all.

"I promise you, Oscar, nobody wants you dead. In fact, we

want you very much alive. We want all of Cabal alive. Your original controllers, *Vanya* and *Eagle,* are dead. You know that?"

The elderly, shortsighted, now hunched, man gave a quick nod.

"Okay. We've come from London and Washington to replace them. To replace the original *Vanya* and *Eagle.* And we need you. All of you."

"Then why have your people been killing us off?" Vomberg appeared to have regained some of his composure. "One at a time, ever since *Sulphur* was told to stand everyone down and scatter. One at a time you've sought us out and killed us. Well, I'm not afraid to die. It's all over, so do it."

"I've no idea what you're talking about."

There was a long pause, then Vomberg croaked, "Okay, you claim to be on the side of Cabal. Then prove it." He leaned back, his face grey from the pain in his hand which had started to swell.

Bond gave a quick series of nods. Before leaving London they had been given bona fide codes. "These go very deep," M had said. "None of the members of Cabal know each other's personal word sequences. Even if someone has penetrated Cabal, it's unlikely they've ever broken down the IFF sequences. They're buried far too deep. Individuals wouldn't even share them with each other." IFF stands for Identification Friend or Foe.

Bond riffled through the words he had memorized back in London, and remembered that, when going through these IFF codes, he had thought it odd that Oscar Vomberg had been given three lines from a revered Irish poet. The answering three lines had been taken from the same poet, using a quite different poem. Goethe, he thought, would have been better for a German, then he realized that the Cabal agents were foreign to the English language, and had all been given British, American or, as in this case, Irish poets.

"Give me your IFF," he said softly, and Vomberg, stumbling over the words, quoted:

> *"Was it for this the wild geese spread*
> *The grey wing upon every tide;*
> *For this that all that blood was shed."*

Bond answered, and heard Vomberg's sudden intake of breath, watched his eyes widen, as he said:

> *"And pluck till time and times are done*
> *The silver apples of the moon,*
> *The golden apples of the sun.*

"There, Oscar. That good enough for you? Or do we have to go through some more mumbo jumbo?"

Vomberg swore an old German oath, his eyes still wide. "To know that, you must . . ."

"Yes, I must," Bond smiled. "Didn't anyone in this prime little coven of spies think of using their IFF exchanges before? Or did you take everything on trust, and then become angry when you discovered you were all being screwed."

Vomberg seemed lost for a moment. Then:

"Look, I kept the faith. I did what had to be done, and we were told *Sulphur* would always pass the word if it was an emergency. If *Sulphur* was not available, it would be *Hemlock*, then *Barnaby*. After that it was to be alphabetic. *Hemlock* and *Barnaby* are both dead now, but *Sulphur* lives, and . . ."

"And how many more are gone?"

"You don't know?"

"Only some. Those who went naturally. In London and Washington we counted another ten of you were still around."

"Which ten?"

"*Crystal, Ariel, Caliban, Cobweb, Orphan, Tester, Sulphur, Puck, Mab* and *Dodger,*" Bond rattled off, and Vomberg nodded.

"Until a week ago that was about right. We don't know any more. *Caliban*'s certainly gone. They shot him. In Rome. Broad daylight, in St. Peter's Square. It made less than half an inch in *Oggi,* but I'm surprised nobody picked it up in London or Washington. Two days ago I know *Orphan* was dragged out of the Grand Canal in Venice. That didn't even make the papers, but *Sulphur* told me." He stopped suddenly, as though second thoughts had invaded his conscience. "Tell me the true name of *Sulphur?*"

"Praxi Simeon."

He gave another quick nod, like an interrogator receiving the right answer and pleased with it.

"And Praxi was the one who gave the orders to scatter?"

"*Ja,* yes. Praxi telephoned each of us with the same signal." He gave a little laugh. "*Nacht und Nebel.* That was the signal to fold up and scatter. *Night and Fog,* like in Wagner. Like in Hitler also. You scratch Wagner and you find Nazis."

During World War II in 1941, Hitler had issued the infamous *Nacht und Nebel Erlass,* a directive which provided for methods to be used in occupied countries for suppressing resistance movements. People arrested under this order were to disappear into the "fog of the night." Even their deaths in camps or prisons were never to be divulged, and Hitler separated himself from the order, putting it out under the name of Wilhelm Keitel, his Army Chief of Staff.

"We thought it a little sick joke." Vomberg made a grimace which could have been a smile.

"So, you broke and scattered? You disappeared into *Nacht und Nebel?*"

"Of course. We all had places to go, but we did not share our individual locations with those who directed us: with the original *Vanya* and *Eagle.* It was thought to be unsafe. If it came to *Nacht und Nebel,* we felt all ties should be cut: even though the

46

main threat seemed to have disappeared with the reunification of Germany."

"And Praxi claimed to have received the order?"

"She did receive it. I was there. It came via a telephone contact. All the safety codes were correct. She checked and double-checked. I was there and heard it all."

"Yet you did keep in touch. The surviving members of Cabal kept in touch?"

"With each other, yes. More or less."

"Come on, Oscar, more than that. *You*, and *you* alone, telephoned the original *Vanya* in Frankfurt. You arranged a meeting place with him. He left his hotel, and died in the street, on his way to see you."

"He wasn't coming to see me."

"We have the tapes, Oscar."

"I called him, yes. *Sulphur* instructed me to call him and set up a meeting. She was going to see him."

"Praxi Simeon instructed you?"

"She telephoned me. My hideaway was in Frankfurt. I saw *Vanya* in the street and passed it on . . ."

"To Praxi?"

"In a way, yes."

"What d'you mean 'in a way'?"

"There was a number. You call it, what? An 800 number? Free call."

"An 800 number, yes."

"This was set up long ago. 1985, '86. It was one of the safeguards. Security. If we had to cut and run we could always call in an emergency to the number. It was, what you call it, a tape?"

"An Answerfone, yes."

"So, yes, an Answerfone. We simply gave our crypto and a number where we could be contacted. Whoever was holding things together—Praxi, as it happened—could get messages from the number. I think there was some device used, so that the messages were played back over another telephone . . ."

"That's common enough. The phones have special access numbers known only to the owner, or a beeper is used to reach the playback tape. You can get a message on a tape in London and access it from Washington or Timbuktu. So Praxi got the message?"

"She called me back, and she'd been doing some checking. Told me where *Vanya* was staying in Frankfurt. Told me to set up a meeting. It was a club . . ."

"Die Nonne," Bond tried.

"No. Not quite. You try to trick me, eh?" He gave a little humorless laugh, and some of his greying hair fell forward across his brow.

"Of course."

"It was Der Mönch. Not The Nun, but The Monk."

"That's right. She told you to call him and set up the meeting? Then what?"

"To get out of town. To find another hiding place and call her later. On the 800 number."

"And you did?"

"It was agreed we should trust Praxi. All of us."

"So you knew nothing of *Vanya*'s murder?"

"Yes. Three days later. I left my new number—here in Berlin—on the answering phone. Praxi called me and said what had happened."

"Did she tell you what happened to *Eagle?*"

"Yes. She was contacting anyone who gave their number to the answering phone. This time—when was it? Another three or four days later?—she called. Praxi sounded . . . how would you say it? In a state?"

"Concerned?"

"Not strong enough. She sounded agitated, dismayed, upset. She was weeping. Praxi was sobbing. She said nothing was safe anymore. She had set up a meeting personally, and she went for the meeting to find *Eagle* dead. It looked natural, she told me, but she thought it was something else."

"It *was* something else, Oscar. Did she get in touch again?"

48

"Oh, yes. The signals were posted first the day after *Eagle* died."

"Which signals?"

"That a new *Vanya* and a new *Eagle* were coming."

"The day *after?*"

"The day after *Eagle* was dead, we had the first signals. The alerts. They were in newspapers. In the classified advertisements pages. All major cities where old Cabal people might be. That was the arrangement. *Vanya*, can I see a doctor? My hand. You hurt my hand bad."

"In a minute, Oscar. I'm sorry about the hand, but you came on a little strong, waving that gun around."

"I'm sorry. I was full of suspicion. It was right I should be." He was half doubled forward in obviously severe discomfort. "How else does a spy survive?"

"I know. Just a few more questions, Oscar, then we'll get you to a doctor."

"I get to my own doctor. You have to prove your trust, *Vanya.*"

"All right. We'll do it your way."

"Good, so I'll bring someone back with me. Another Cabal. I bring back *Tester*. You know who is *Tester?*"

"Yes."

"Good. I bring him back when they fix my hand. Please, the questions. I can't last much longer."

"Right." Bond wanted to know about the so-called alerts. If Vomberg was telling the truth, M and the people at headquarters had jumped the gun, or been very sure of their ground, for it meant the alerts had been posted before the word had been passed on to Easy or himself. He asked what the safeguards were: how the alerts were phrased?

"All start with special words. But why don't you know this?" Suspicion had flooded into Vomberg's mind again.

"Because we were only just briefed. We'd never heard of Cabal, or its individual members, until yesterday."

The German thought for a minute then decided he had

nothing to lose. The alerts would appear in the classified advertisement section of newspapers in Berlin, Munich, Frankfurt, Stuttgart, Rome, Venice, Madrid, Lisbon and Paris. The notice would be a want ad, and the first sentence had to contain three words: Singer, High and Quality.

WANTED: MALE ROCK SINGER FOR A HIGH-QUALITY GROUP, would be okay. WANTED: FEMALE SINGER FOR AMATEUR CHOIR. SOPRANO OF GOOD QUALITY ESSENTIAL would not do. The bulk of the message would be a two-liner which divided exactly into groups of five letters. These could only be deciphered by the designated member of Cabal who was supposed to be looking after the scattered members. The groups were a simple book code. Secure because nobody else could unbutton them unless they had the book. Not just the book, but a certain edition. The final signal was contained in the last line which would read: REPLIES TO P.O. BOX 213112—or the same numbers in a different order—followed by the central post office of the newspaper's city.

It was as foolproof as you could get, Bond believed. "And how, Oscar, did you deduce that *Eagle* and myself had arrived here, at the Kempi?"

"We were told this morning."

"This morning?"

"Yes, Praxi called again. This morning's papers contained further messages. A man arriving on BA792 and a woman on BA782. Both coming straight to the Kempi. *Tester* and myself checked you out. It was quite easy . . ."

"You followed me in a maroon VW Golf?"

"No. *Tester* watched arrivals. Described you to me by telephone. I spotted you checking in here. We had decided to wait for the pair of you. Then I was to move in and telephone *Tester* when I had you both. After that we were to use the 800 number and inform Praxi. She told me to isolate you, so I became like a cowboy, and look at me now." He painfully raised the hand, which had become a very swollen claw.

"You'll have to wait a few minutes before you leave to get

that hand seen to, Oscar. I also have suspicions, so I must check you out."

He instructed Easy to watch over Vomberg while he went down to make a call to London. "I don't want to use the telephone here, in this room," he said, realizing that, should the rooms have been given ears already, whoever was dealing out death sentences to Cabal would know everything. It all concentrated his mind intensely, for he thought again of the VW Golf that had followed him from the airport. That Cabal had been totally penetrated he had no doubt.

"Only open the door to me, Easy. Only me. Anything funny, call the number we were given." He spoke of the Berlin Station number. The British SIS station in Berlin was still operating. They knew nothing of the current operation but would render aid on M's say-so, if required.

Down in the main foyer, among the tropical fish and leather, Bond sought out a public telephone, where he dialed the direct, no-charge international secure line that would put him in touch with either Bill Tanner or M personally.

It was M who had stayed in his office in the hope of some contact that night. The conversation was brief, but Bond learned quickly that Vomberg appeared to be telling the truth about the alerts. "We had no doubt that we could get you in pretty quickly." M sounded weary at the other end. "It was just that we wanted to give as much warning as possible. Yes, all *Mab* says is true, and, yes, we gave them your flight numbers and hotel this morning. The Chief of Staff telephoned the newspapers last night while we were still working."

Upstairs again, he asked Oscar Vomberg exactly what he would do. "You think you can get to a doctor on your own?"

"Sure. Sure I make it on my own. I call *Tester* first. He'll meet me. Expect us two hours. Three at most. We'll call this room from the foyer. Give you a set of clear signals so you know I'm not playing games with you."

Bond admitted that he was unhappy about the man leaving on his own, but at least, providing he was playing it straight, another member of Cabal would be returning with him. Two would be better than one every time.

As soon as Vomberg left, Bond turned to Easy, who now looked much more unsure of herself. Her face, which had been so hard and full of confidence in London, was noticeably softer, and she began to speak before Bond could get in the first shot.

"I know, James. Don't even say it. I screwed up just about as badly as I could."

"You can say that again." He crossed the room to the mini-bar, found what he was looking for and made himself a vodka martini. They did not have all the ingredients he would have liked, but that could not be helped. He did not even ask if Easy wanted a drink.

"What in hell's name did you think you were playing at?" he snapped. "I know he had a gun on you, but that's never stopped a trained field officer from slipping in some kind of warning."

"I froze. Please, James, don't get mad at me. I just froze. He had that damned great gun in my ear. I've had no field experience. I'm a desk jockey: analyst, control hand-holder. Not really up to it. Vomberg said he would know if I tried to warn you . . ."

"Did they teach you nothing at the Farm? Or did you go there a thousand years ago? The way you behaved was not simply unprofessional, it was criminal. And how did you let him in? You didn't use even the first lessons in security. Easy, I really don't know if I can work with you. In the field we have to count on each other, and you've already proved you cannot be relied on. I, for one, want to come out of this alive, and, if you've learned anything from the past hour, you'll know this is all damned dangerous stuff. People are getting killed."

"James, I . . ." The heavens opened, and she began to weep. Real tears, nothing phony. You can tell the synthetic variety because a woman's nose does not go red when she turns on crocodile tears. Easy's nose went several shades of red. It also poured superfluous liquid so that Bond had to pass over his handkerchief.

Between the sobs and the rivers, Easy pleaded. This was her first time in the field. She wanted to make a good impression. With things as they were in the American Service, what with the recession and all—"They're firing people by the office load . . ."—she stood to lose her job. If Bond sent her back in disgrace, that would be it. "My whole career down the tubes . . ." she shuddered. "And I know nothing else. . . . Please, James. Please give me another . . ." And so, and so, and even more so.

James Bond liked weeping women as much as he liked having his teeth drilled. His nerves were as strong as the next man's but a weeping woman made him cringe. He could never abide by the old proverb which says "It is no more pity to see a woman weep than to see a goose go barefoot."

He went over to her and put a comforting arm around her shoulders, muttering soothing words and sounds—stroking her hair, which, he realized, had the texture of heavy silk.

"You're going to have to learn how to operate, Easy. You have to remember everything they taught you. I'm certainly not going to sacrifice myself because of some idiocy on your part."

"Yes, James," she said meekly. It was a complete turnaround from the tough, power businesswoman who had sat in M's office.

"You understand that, should you jeopardize things, I can't help you?"

"Yes, James. You'll let me stay on?"

"For the time being. If matters get really rough, or if you completely louse things up again, I'll have to turn you in and go it alone, okay?"

She lifted her face and kissed him gently on the corner of the mouth.

Bond could taste the salt, and, oddly, Ms. Easy St. John became much more attractive than she had at first appeared.

Two hours dragged by. Easy went off into the bathroom and put on a new face. She also changed into a striking green dress, all sheer and with floating panels. You could see her small, but perfect, body move under the material as it swirled. The color contrast with her hair was startling and, for the first time, James Bond realized that for a shortish woman she had exceptionally good legs—particularly in high heels.

"Looks as though friend *Mab*'s taking his time. You hungry?" he asked.

"Ravenous, but we daren't go down to the restaurant."

"I'll get sandwiches sent up."

He called down to room service and ordered three rounds of cold chicken and smoked salmon, plus a bottle of Riesling Spätlese—a Kreuznacher '73. "Clean, fresh and racy. Particularly well-balanced," Bond declared. "That should keep the pangs at bay, until *Mab* returns with *Tester*. What do we know of *Tester*, Easy? Come on, let's test you on *Tester*." His smile gave the impression that all was forgiven and that he was providing her with the opportunity to shine.

"Okay. *Tester*. Old Cabal hand. Name, Heini—'Harry'— Spraker. Recruited when he was twenty-two—some ten years ago. Born Leipzig. In the first year of service with the Army they marked him for intelligence. Did the codes and ciphers courses and ended up with the Stasi, then transferred to Karlshorst, where he worked on clandestine communications of the HVA. Recruited directly by Praxi. Puxley *and* Cearns put him through the mill while he was supposed to be on his annual leave in 1979. Found him exceptional, strong anti-communist views, a whiz at electronics. Provided steady flow of Grade One communications intelligence."

"IFF?"

"Auden. Three lines from Part One, verse three, of *Letter to Lord Byron*. Answerback, first three lines of *May*."

"Good. Now, physical description."

"Exactly six feet; well-built; muscular; full dark hair; complexion dark; eyes black; very piercing look. Small scar, in the shape of a bracket, just to the right of his mouth."

"How'd he get that?"

"In childhood. His cousin threw a glass at him in fun."

"And what else?"

"He is supposed to be very attractive to the ladies. Became Monika Haardt's lover in 'eighty-four when she ran the Karlshorst Seven."

"Who were the Karlshorst Seven?"

"Moscow joy-boys. Did much damage with Emily operations in Bonn."

Bond nodded, pleased. Monika Haardt was still on the run, like Wolfgang Weisen; and, like Weisen, Fräulein Haardt had the killer instinct. "Now, if you get as good as that in the field, things'll go well," he said to Easy, who smiled a stunning smile. Again, for the first time, Bond noticed how the grey eyes would sparkle when she was happy. In M's office they looked as inviting as the North Sea in mid-winter. Now they were all summer evening, the glow suffusing a pearl-grey sky.

The Emilys she had spoken of were unmarried women, sometimes unattractive, who worked for the FRD government in Bonn: the former West German Government. During the latter part of the Cold War, many had been seduced and compromised by agents working directly from Karlshorst, much to the disarray of the FRD. The most successful of these had been Monika Haardt's so-called Karlshorst Seven.

A quiet knock at the door heralded the arrival of a slim young waiter, wheeling a trolley heavy with a large oval platter, its contents hidden by the usual silver domed cover. The wine was chilling nicely in a bucket, and there was a good supply of the normal accessories.

The waiter lifted the dome for a few seconds, speaking immaculate English, showing the sandwiches arranged on a bed of lettuce—"The smoked salmon are on the left, the chicken on the right." He returned the cover, uncorked the wine and asked if he should pour it. Bond declined. "Let it breathe for a moment." He signed the bill and added a tip.

The waiter left, pleased, with much bowing and the knowing smile of all waiters who think they have caught a man in the wrong room with the right woman.

"Doesn't need to stand long." Bond poured for Easy, then for himself. As he passed her a plate, he looked again at his watch, wondering aloud how long Vomberg would be.

Easy took four of the small smoked salmon sandwiches, and Bond helped himself to an equal number. "The chicken had better be our main course. Heaven knows when we'll eat again. Cheers." He raised his glass and Easy leaned over with a smile, touching her glass to his. There was something decidedly sensual about the way she did it, Bond thought. Then he reached for the first sandwich.

He was lifting the little brown triangle to his mouth when his eye caught something odd. For a second he imagined he was suffering from some kind of illusion. He held the sandwich a couple of feet away from his mouth and looked at it again. It was no illusion. The bread moved slightly, and, as he peered closer, he saw two tiny feelers reach out from the middle of the smoked salmon. A second later, the whole small body appeared.

He turned to see that Easy was about to bite into her sandwich. "No! Easy, don't!" His hand came up chopping lightly at her wrist. The triangle of food barely touched her teeth as it fell from her hand.

"James! What the . . . ?"

"I don't know." He was on his feet, slamming the cover back onto the dish, and, taking a fork, slowly prizing the two halves of his sandwich apart. Layered within the smoked salmon were what looked like tiny white pellets. Among the pellets, small eight-legged creatures had already begun to emerge. Though they were only newly hatched, Bond recognized them immediately. The poisonous Fiddleback spider is instantly identified by its unique shape. Even baby spiders have that violin outline which marks them for life, and these did not live long. Bond dropped the sandwich onto the carpet, slipped out of his right shoe and beat the bread, butter and salmon into the carpet. Then he did the same with the sandwich Easy had dropped.

She stood, cringing back, her face grim with horror, asking, "James! What? What are . . . ? Oh, my God!"

This last as Bond lifted the cover from the dish again, to reveal the swarm of tiny Fiddleback spiders which had begun to hatch emerging from the food, and in their midst two bloated creeping adult females, forcing their way upward through the bread, meat and fish, pushing the crumbs to one side as though hungry for some other delicacy. He slapped the cover back on and began to collect the two splatted messes from the floor.

"Someone mistimed," he said, revulsion sounding in his voice as Easy choked and gagged on her handkerchief. "Some bright and enterprising fellow filled our food with the eggs of a Fiddleback spider. God knows what would have happened if we'd eaten them. Chances are some would have hatched in our . . ." He stopped, the thought of the insects, with their nasty poisonous bite, was too much even for him. People rarely die from the bite of one Fiddleback, but the small bites of several, internally, or semi-internally. . . . "Don't think about it, Easy. The point is that we're blown like a couple of grenades. Whoever wants Cabal wiped out clearly requires us to be wiped out as well, and they're not above laying exotic traps. That's really death through the mouth, with a vengeance."

The telephone began to ring.

5

||||||||||||||||||||||||||||||||||||||||||||||||||||||||||||||||||||||||||||||||||||||||||||||||||||||||||||||||||||||||||||||||||||||

Death of a Queen

Easy St. John was retching in the bathroom, and Bond had to admit that the bizarre and terrible method of death, which they had just escaped, had turned his stomach.

He picked up the telephone and gave a gruff *"Ja?"* into the handset.

"Have I reached the room for Mr. Joseph Cranbourne, visiting from England?" inquired a male voice at the distant end. The accent was undeniably German, though not as thick as Vomberg's. The words were also *Tester's* telephone sequence code.

"Mr. Cranbourne's here. Who shall I say is calling?"

"Heini Wachtel of Inferscope BV. We met a couple of years ago. I'm very much hoping he has time to see me now."

"Where are you?"

"In the hotel. In Kempinski. Downstairs."

"I'll see if Mr. Cranbourne's available." He covered the mouthpiece and told Easy to start packing.

"But we've only just . . ."

"Arrived, I know. But I think we might have to leave. This place could be infested."

"Oh, Christ."

"Precisely." He turned back to the telephone. "Herr Wachtel, I'm sorry but Mr. Cranbourne isn't available to come to the phone. He can meet you downstairs in fifteen minutes, if you can spare the time."

"Sure. I'll wait. It's pretty urgent we talk. Big business opportunities."

"Will Mr. Cranbourne recognize you?"

"I'll be sitting at one of the tables in the main lounge. I'll stub my cigarette out when I spot Mr. Cranbourne. I will also stop reading my copy of today's *Die Welt.* But, really I think Mr. Cranbourne will have no difficulty in recognizing me."

Bond had no difficulty at all. The man who stubbed out his cigarette and folded up a copy of *Die Welt* had a leather coat slung over the back of the chair. He was the man who had been slapping his thigh with a newspaper while looking irritated, pacing outside the arrivals terminal at Tegel. He rose as Bond approached.

"So, Herr Wachtel, we meet again." He thrust out a hand, pulling the young German close enough for him to whisper, "Give me your IFF."

Harry Spraker smiled, sat down again and quietly quoted:

> *"Of modern methods of communication;*
> *New roads, new rails, new contacts, as we know*
> *From documentaries by the GPO.*

"Is out of date that last bit, eh? Now you have British Telecom and the Post Office. Not GPO any more."

Bond nodded. Certainly the description of the man was right—the small crescent scar showed livid to the right of a generous smiling mouth; while the eyes were a startling black: unusual, like dark, still pools. Bond thought he had never seen eyes quite that sinister, though he could imagine how they might soften and do a great deal of damage to the composure of ladies.

He gave the answerback, unsmiling and flat:

DEATH IS FOREVER

"May, with its light behaving
Stirs vessel, eye and limb
The singular and sad."

"Painless," Harry Spraker, aka Herr Wachtel, and *Tester*, smiled. "Singular and sad. That's how you have come across Cabal, sir. We are all singular and sad. It's good to meet you, and even better to know there is someone on our side."

"I was expecting you to come with a friend." Bond could not see Vomberg anywhere in sight. "How's his hand? Was he detained at the hospital?"

Spraker shrugged, looking away. "Bad news. Yes, he has been detained at the hospital—permanently. There was an accident. On the U-Bahn an accident. I'm sorry. I could do nothing for him, and these people who seem to surround us like ghosts are very fond of accidents."

"You want to explain that?"

Spraker gave a sad smile. "Our friend showed amazing courage trying to tackle you, Mr. . . . ?"

"Just call me James for the moment."

"Okay, James. It's not Vomberg's style—was not his style at all, I should say. He's more of a thinker. His work was scientific, as you know, and he was not a natural spy. He must have screwed up great bravery to even approach you. His sexual preferences did not help him. Me, I couldn't care less what people do in privacy, or in public: as they say, as long as they don't frighten the horses. But Oscar was a rare sport. *Mab*. He used to laugh when we called him Queen Mab."

"So what happened?"

"So he made contact with me before going to the hospital. I met him there. You certainly know how to hurt people, James. The hand was broken in four places. They gave him painkiller shots, set the bones, put it in a cast. Then we left to come here. We were on the street only three minutes when we knew they had us boxed in. Old Oscar was expert at spotting surveillance.

He was a natural at that, and we were both afraid of leading them here . . ."

"I think they're already here."

"I had noticed. Don't look too quick, but there's a tall, middle-aged man, sitting alone drinking coffee, near the doors. He's one of them, I've seen him before. Definitely one of them."

"Whoever *them* might be." Bond had one of those strange twitches of intuition which come to experienced field men. It could be nothing, but he found Harry Spraker difficult to trust. Maybe, he thought, he had contracted a deep paranoia. It would not be the first time.

"I have a shrewd guess as to who they are, but Praxi knows for sure." Harry gave him a quick little look, the eyes lifting and then sliding to one side. "Anyway, we split up—Oscar and I—led them a little dance. By accident we both ended up on the same platform of the Charlottenburg U-Bahn station. It was crowded, we were well separated, and the thing was done with great precision. They are very precise, these people. Oscar went under a train." He gave a little shudder. "I heard him scream, James. It was most unpleasant. The line is closed for the next hour or so."

"I'm sorry." Bond felt a tiny worm of accountability stir in his mind. "My fault, I think . . ."

"No, sir. Not your fault. It is the fault of those who told us to close down and scatter . . ."

"*Nacht und Nebel?*"

Spraker gave a little nod. "It was a disaster. They've been picking us off, one at a time ever since. I believe Praxi, the one called *Ariel,* and myself are the only three left. We're like a decimated army. If *you* gave that order, yes, I hold you responsible, for that was the beginning of Cabal's end."

"Would it surprise you to hear that the order was never given?"

"Nothing would surprise me now. Nothing."

61

"You say you suspect who the mysterious *they* are?"

"Praxi knows for sure."

"Give me a hint."

"I imagine the Poison Dwarf and his lady friend are in it somehow. Mischa Wolf has come back, but not . . ." He allowed it to trail off, the eyes giving Bond a look suggesting that he should fill in the details.

"You're talking about Wolfgang Weisen and Monika Haardt, I presume?"

"I would say so, but only Praxi knows for sure. She has information. She would also like to see you."

Bond leaned forward, eyes glittering with anger. There was no way he would trust Harry Spraker, or, for that matter, Praxi Simeon. "Don't mess me about, Harry." He sounded cold and very serious. "You saw what I did to poor old Oscar. If you play games with me, I'll personally bite off your nose and make you eat it. Got me?"

"I wouldn't play games with you, James. To be honest, I'm bloody frightened. Look, I'm running to you for help. None of us are safe on the street anymore. Believe me."

"We'll see. But I mean what I say; and should I disappear into the *Nacht und Nebel* myself, I guarantee that six more, much worse than me, will come looking for you. I say this because, anxious as I am to meet Praxi Simeon, I have worries that she isn't as white and pure as she pretends to be."

"Are any of us clean, James?" Harry Spraker leaned back in his chair. A waiter was hovering as if to say they should order something or get out of the lounge. A pianist had started up. He played all the new standards with a lot of flourishes and runs: his medley from *Cats* sounded as though the creatures were having a night on the tiles, while his variations on *Phantom of the Opera* would have made Puccini and Verdi spin in their graves. His embellishments made it quite clear where he thought the melodies had originated.

Bond ordered a martini, giving precise instructions regarding its composition. The waiter bowed and said it sounded like a symphony, but that was water off a duck's back as far as 007 was concerned. Harry Spraker asked for a beer, and the same waiter looked down his nose and left as silently as he had appeared.

"Why, James, do you think I would play games?"

"Because you have a line to Praxi."

"So? She is most trusted."

"That's right. She received the *Nacht und Nebel* order. I don't know about the other deaths, but she gave instructions to my predecessor, *Vanya*, via Oscar. *Vanya* obeyed her and died. Also she fixed up a sit down with the original *Eagle*, who also came to a sticky end pretty soon after. You, Harry, knew them well, because they ran Cabal for a long time—*Vanya* and *Eagle*. I am *Vanya Mark II*. Upstairs, *Eagle Mark II*, is waiting to meet us. Our originals are, as we speak, probably going through a debriefing with that great Director of Intelligence in the sky. I am anxious that we—my partner and myself—are not sitting in on the same meeting in a matter of days or hours."

The waiter came with the drinks. He spilled some of Harry's, but placed the martini in front of Bond as though it contained a booby trap.

Harry looked both worried and shocked. "But Praxi is . . ." he began.

"She'd better be." He sipped the martini, found it wanting and put it down, pushing the glass away as though proximity to it was an affront to his senses. "She really had better be, Harry, because if she isn't, and we all end up in a German meat wagon; the others, of whom I spoke, will come after her, and they won't just stop at doing things with her nose. How far away is she, Harry?"

"She's in Paris."

"A French meat wagon, then. How does she plan to meet us?"

"I've taken the liberty of booking two sleeping compartments on the Ost-West Express. One for, what do I call her, *Eagle* . . . ?"

"It'll suffice."

"Okay, one for *Eagle*, and a double for us. It leaves the Zoo station at twenty-three minutes past midnight. I thought it better to book us from there rather than from the starting point—the Hauptbahnhof. More secure, particularly if we have to throw off company. You can be ready, yes?"

"We *are* ready, Harry. All I have to do is pay the bill." Bond had already repacked his small case, and the briefcase, before coming down. "You sit here where I can see you. If you move a leg, even to go to what the French so coyly call the *cabinet*, I'll stop you in your tracks. Forget about Oscar's hand; forget about the tail sitting near the door. Just think of more sensitive portions of your anatomy. London tells me you like the ladies. You'll be no good to them if you don't behave."

"James, why so aggressive? I've done nothing . . ."

"I know; it's simply to discourage you, Harry. There's an old military saying which goes, 'Never share a foxhole with anyone braver than yourself.' Harry, you just made that mistake. Now, stay. Right?"

"Right, James."

Bond went over to the house phone and called suite 202, telling Easy to come down and bring her coat. "I'll send them up for the luggage."

"But, James."

"I have friend *Tester* down here, and he's longing to meet you. So, come down."

"Yes, James."

The under manager, on duty at Reception, could have been an extra in World War II movies. He was tall, blond, immaculate and without a smile. There was even a scar of some kind on his right cheek, though it looked more like a motor accident than a duel. Bond asked for the accounts for 207 and 202.

"Mr. Boldman, is there something wrong? We have you booked in for a week. You reserved these rooms? You do not like these rooms?"

"It's not the rooms. You have a problem in your kitchen, I think."

"Sir, I . . . No, a problem in our kitchen is unthinkable."

"There were insects in the lady's sandwiches."

"Mr. Boldman, if there's anything. . . ."

"Fire the waiter, or the chef."

The tall under manager leaned forward confidentially. "It is against hotel policy for us to have a problem in the kitchen, Mr. Boldman."

"One of the room-service waiters, then."

Still without a smile the under manager inclined his head. "It is sometimes difficult these days to get correct employees. Very difficult." Then, again very confidentially, "There has been trouble with one of the floor waiters, but I did not tell you this."

"Dead or just dead drunk?"

"A little of both."

"I see, like being slightly pregnant. Let me have the accounts and send someone sober up for the luggage. Both suites. We would also like a car at eleven forty-five."

"Certainly, Mr. Boldman. Where do you wish to go?"

"I'll tell the driver when the car arrives."

The under manager bowed his stiff bow and proceeded to present a printout of the two accounts, which Bond paid with a credit card. The under manager did not click his heels; he did, however, report the whole incident to the night general manager, who nodded sagely: after all, night general managers are only one step down from God.

It was, of course, unthinkable that anything could be amiss at a hotel as punctilious as the Kempi. Only later, looking at police records for that night, did Berlin Station note two seemingly unassociated incidents. First, a unit with an ambulance had been called, very discreetly, to the hotel. A floor waiter had been discovered, badly beaten, tied up and without his uniform, in a closet on the second floor.

Earlier there had been a report of a break-in at a shop

specializing in macabre pets—insects, snakes, lizards and the like. They mainly supplied schools and universities, and the place was down in the Friedrichstrasse area, close to what used to be Checkpoint Charlie. When the police arrived, the owner, a migrant Turk, showed them what was missing: a special glass box, complete with temperature control, housing several Fiddleback spiders and a multitude of eggs. "It was nursery," the owner explained. Everyone was at a loss as to who would lift a case of Fiddlebacks. Hospitals were warned, though the shop owner was convinced that the eggs would never hatch, and that the creatures would die quickly in a Berlin autumn. He appeared to be quite upset about it. Nothing more was heard of the Fiddlebacks, except in a report coming from the British Secret Intelligence Service's files, and that was classified until the year 2500. Such is the enforced secrecy of the British island nation.

Easy St. John came down from her suite, dressed in a belted trench coat with a fur collar. Under the skirt of the coat a pair of highly polished calf-length black boots were visible, causing looks of sheer lechery as she walked over to the table where Bond was sitting with Harry Spraker.

"Ah, the eagle has landed," Bond muttered. "Meet Harry. Harry, this is your other case officer."

"And I couldn't be more delighted that she's on my case." He stood, took her hand, bowed and kissed it. Predictably his eyes moved up from the hand, holding a long, and undisguised, look of lasciviousness.

Watching, Bond could not help thinking that, so far, Harry Spraker was a cipher. He looked impressive, and had a gleam in those black eyes which were, by turns, amusing and sinister. He stood, walked and talked, but gave away nothing of his real persona. He could have been a well-programmed android for all Bond could tell. He had known agents like this before, and handling them became almost hallucinatory.

"James?" For the first time, Harry looked uncomfortable. "I need to use the men's room. I can go, yes?"

"Not without me. Excuse us, Easy."

She gave him a small, uncertain smile. "What's going on?"

"We're off to see the Wizard." Bond smiled. "Off to see *Sulphur,* who just happens to be in Paris."

"We're flying to Paris?"

"James?" Harry said with urgency.

"No. We're going by train, won't that be fun? Night train to Paris. Sounds like a 1930s movie title."

"James?" Harry again.

"See you in a moment." Bond gave Easy a dazzling smile, took Harry's elbow and guided him rapidly to the nearest facilities.

"Why can't I even go to the bathroom alone, James?"

"Because, my dear Harry, I trust nobody until we're safely in Paris and sitting, alive and well, with the lovely Praxi."

"She's certainly that."

"Lovely?"

"Indescribably."

"Good, perhaps she'll take your mind off *Eagle.*"

When they returned to the table, Easy had ordered a vodka and tonic. She had also put a small piece of folded paper next to Bond's lonely martini.

He opened it and read:

James, she had written. *On no account are you to leave me alone with that man. I don't like his eyes.*

"Too close together, are they?" Bond turned to her, smiling.

"They belong to the 'All-the-better-to-see-you-with-my-dear' variety." She did not even twinkle.

"Harry, we have a small problem." Bond beamed at the German.

"So what's new?"

"The accommodation you've so helpfully booked on the Ost-West Express. I fear you'll be in the compartment for one. My colleague and I need to confer."

"For the whole night?"

67

"These conferences do sometimes go on. Perhaps we'll have dinner with you, how about that?"

"Whatever you say."

Bond gave Easy a sideways look. "Friend Harry says the middle-aged gent by the door is a surveillance spook," he said without moving his lips.

"You learn that in prison," Harry said brightly. "I know a lot of guys learn it in prison, speaking without moving lips."

"No, Harry. I learned it from people who've been in prison. Experts." His lips still did not move. "If you're right, I don't want our eyeballing friend to read my lips. Now, Harry my lad, are you one hundred percent, gold-plated certain that this chap's spooking us?"

"Two hundred percent. He was once with Stasi. Name of Korngold. Klaus Korngold. They must be short of people, because he should know that I can finger him . . ."

"Which might just be why he has hidden himself behind a copy of *Stern* ever since you marked him for me."

"You know, there was a time when I thought *Stern* was an SM magazine," Easy said brightly, and Bond did not know whether to take her seriously.

"Did our bags come down?" he asked.

"There's a nice uniformed bellboy standing over them. He's watching them as though they're going to grow legs and run away."

"Good. Your baggage, Harry?"

Spraker tapped the large briefcase by his chair. "He travels fastest who goes light, or whatever the saying is, James. I got the briefcase, one handy large-size blackjack—is that right, blackjack?"

"If you mean as in rendering someone unconscious, yes. No other things, Harry? No artillery?"

"Just one little pistol. Only .22. Wouldn't hurt fly."

"Right." Turning to Easy, whose name he did not want to say aloud in front of Harry, "I suggest that you deal with the bags. Have them brought around to the front entrance. Harry and I will do our best to make Klaus see the error of his ways. I should imagine they have a team outside—or at least one bright lad in a car." He leaned forward and in a whisper told Harry what he intended to do.

"Herr Korngold?" Bond and Harry stood at the spook's table. Easy had gone to deal with the luggage and check to see if their car had arrived.

"You speaking to me?" Korngold looked like a thug who had gone to seed. His suit had once been fashionable and, some years ago, had carried a sizeable price tag. The face was marked by stress, with those deep crow's-feet shooting out of the corner of his eyes, like the gold decoration on a sunburst clock. The shoes, Bond noted, were down at heel, something he was always twitting the MI5 Watcher Service about. Watchers are the same the whole world over: they all wear the most comfortable shoes, which often means the oldest they possess. It is no fun to do an eight-hour shift on city streets in uncomfortable footwear. Korngold's eyes were rheumy and contained a tired, almost sleepy alertness, the paradox look of a man whose life had been spent surveying other people's problems and movements. Deep in the eyes, Bond also saw the signal that he was right. The man might well have an alias, but his name was certainly Korngold.

"Yes, Herr Korngold," Bond said in German. "I asked if you were Herr Klaus Korngold."

"Go away," Korngold snapped. Harry moved around to the back of his chair.

"I suggest you stand up, don't make a fuss, and just come along with us, Herr Korngold," Bond smiled as he said it, and shifted his balance, just like any good policeman trying to make a point.

"*Himmel*, you mean it." Korngold looked surprised.

"In trumps, Herr Korngold." Bond continued to smile. "Just a short ride and a few questions. You recall how that's done, I think—and don't try to deny it. We have your photograph on file."

"You're not cops. Go away!" Korngold said again.

"Try us!" Harry put some pressure on the man's neck. Korngold's mouth opened in a silent scream of pain and he rose, as though being levitated by a magician.

"Surprising what a little pain will do." Bond nodded thanks to Harry. "Now, mein Herr, I think we should just walk gently to the front of the hotel."

The commissionaire opened the door for them, telling Bond that his car was ready. Easy stood by a gleaming black Mercedes, and was supervising the loading of the luggage into the trunk.

"I think you should call an ambulance," Bond said, looking serious. "Herr Korngold, here, is not at all well."

"Of course." The commissionaire hurried into the hotel, leaving half a dozen people waiting for taxis.

"What're you talking about?" Korngold began to speak loudly. "What d'you mean. I feel perfectly . . ."

"You don't, you know." Even Bond did not see Harry's arm move, it was so nicely executed, the sap catching the former Stasi man on exactly the right point: the base of his skull.

They both caught him, looking anxious and trying to support the man's sagging body.

"Hope you haven't killed him," Bond remarked while looking around for the commissionaire.

"No way, James. I've been doing it for years. He'll be okay as long as he hasn't got an eggshell skull, and I know he hasn't. This one's been given a rubber anesthetic before. I know. I saw it happen."

The commissionaire had reappeared, accompanied by two of the porters.

"I'm afraid he's had a heart attack." Bond helped to stretch Korngold onto the cold pavement and began calling loudly in German for a doctor. In the distance the wail of an ambulance siren began to slice through the Berlin night, getting louder each second.

"Can we leave him in your good hands?" He crammed a wad

of deutsche marks into the commissionaire's hand. "We have a plane to catch."

In the Mercedes, he gave the driver exact instructions, which would take them around some of the nearby back streets before heading in the direction of the Zoo station.

"You guys spies?" the driver asked, with a big laugh. "You're telling me to do things like spies do it on the TV."

They all had a big laugh, and then Bond made his day by saying they were, in fact, running away from Easy's husband. "He's a big fellow with a lot of push. She wants a divorce. We're private eyes. Helping the lady out."

"This I always wanted to do," the driver said in a voice which suggested he was Bond's man for life. "Always like those private dicks."

They did the scenic route with nobody on to them, and got to the Zoo station with a good seven minutes to spare. Bond overtipped the driver with much winking and stroking of fingers along the sides of noses.

"They can pull out my fingernails and I won't tell them," the driver maintained. "Trust me, I can get real lockjaw when I put my mind to it."

"Good, become deaf also."

Minutes later they were aboard the Ost-West Express, and Bond's spirits rose. He was still not altogether certain of Harry Spraker, but he had not traveled on a continental railway train for years, and the noises, sights and smells came back like a once-loved song, reminding him of earlier, probably more dangerous, days when he had crisscrossed Europe on the great network of express trains while on operations at the height of the Cold War. It also reminded him of childhood. Peaceful times when the railroads of the continent were more exciting than sitting cooped up in a metal shell, thirty-five thousand feet above the earth.

The double sleeper was comfortable and had everything they needed. Harry had gone straight to the single, without a protest, and they had made arrangements to meet for dinner.

Bond rubbed his hands as the train began to pick up speed. He thought of the route they would take through the night. Through the old checkpoint at Magdeburg and on through Hannover and Hagen. They would breakfast just outside Cologne, and would be at the Gare du Nord, Paris, by twenty past one the following afternoon.

"Which do you want?" he asked Easy, indicating the bunks. "You want to be on top, or below?"

"Oh, I think we should just let nature take its course." She smiled, and he saw her eyes light up and start to burn.

"This could be an interesting journey."

"I was just thinking the same thing." She moved towards him, swaying with the train. Then came the knocking at the door.

"Harry will never let it rest," she said, and before Bond could stop her, she had slid the bolt and opened up.

The driver of the Mercedes stood in the corridor. Behind, and towering above him, were two very large men. Neither of the men smiled as they pushed their way into the compartment.

The driver shrugged. "Sorry," he said. "I lied."

6

|||||||||||||||||||||||||||||||||||||||||||||||||||||||||||||||||||||||||||||||||||||||||||||||||||||||||||||||||||||||||||||||||||||||||||||||||||||||

Death and a Pair of Aces

The compartment suddenly became very crowded, and Bond saw that one of the two men was, in reality, slightly taller than the other—by around half an inch. Mentally he immediately christened them Big Hans and Very Big Hans.

Very Big Hans opened the batting. *"Polizei!"* he said, in the same way a man might snap out, "Rubbish!"

"I think he's saying they are from the police." Bond turned to Easy, using a suitably bewildered shrug.

Big Hans, not to be outdone, also said, *"Polizei!"* pulling out a wallet and flashing it open and shut to reveal, for a second, a badge and laminated card. The whole thing was done with the dexterity of a conjurer adept at close-up magic.

"Yes, they're definitely police," Bond said.

"That one had a badge," Easy joined in. "How can we help you?"

"Sprechen Sie deutsch?" Big Hans asked.

"I know what that means. Er . . . *Nein* . . . no . . . no, we don't *Sprechen deutsch."* Bond waved his hands indicating he was at a loss for words. "You," he pressed Very Big Hans in the chest with the index finger of his right hand, "You *Sprechen* English?" Poking policemen with an index finger is not a recommended form of strategy.

73

"Just a little, I think." Very Big Hans wrapped a large paw around Bond's hand and removed it from his chest. "We must questions ask. Also we will alight from the train at Potsdamer train station, which is in a very few minutes we get there."

"No, you *do* only speak a little English," Bond said loudly. "We're going to Paris."

"Yes," Easy spoke clearly and very distinctly. "Paris. We—go—to—Paris."

"*Ja*, Paris. I see. But we must ask questions."

"Ask away. Anything we can do to help." Bond smiled and opened his hands in body language which said he had nothing to hide.

"We might ask you to also alight from the train at Potsdamer Station. . . ."

"No, we're going to Paris," Easy said firmly. "What is it you want?"

Very Big Hans jerked his thumb in the direction of the Mercedes's driver who lingered in the corridor. "Helmut, here is what in English I think you call a snatch."

"No," Bond shook his head. " 'Snatch' means something else entirely. You mean a 'snitch,' but that would only be in America. In England we call it a 'grass'—an informer."

"Please?"

"Never mind. What did Helmut—an in-for-mer, yes?—tell you?"

"Helmut says you acted very strangely in his car. He is of the opinion the lady here is being abducted. Is right, abducted?"

"The word is right, sir. But the answer is no."

"No?"

"No." Easy pushed herself between Bond and Very Big Hans. "No, your in-for-mer, Helmut, has it wrong. We were being stupid. Behaving badly. Cuckoo, you understand?"

"So, I think we should all go to headquarters until this is made plain. The cuckoo."

"You mean you want to take us off the train?" Bond's tone

changed. "Officer, there is nothing wrong. We were just acting silly. Playing the fool. In the car we were being stupid. Making jokes. Nobody—you understand? Nobody—has been abducted. . . . "

"I think, perhaps . . ."

"And if you even attempt to take us off this train, I shall insist on calling the British ambassador immediately. He is a close friend, and there will be much trouble. If you do not allow me my rights to telephone from the Potsdamer Station, I shall make a lot of noise. Many people will see."

"And I shall scream that it is police brutality." Easy smiled pleasantly. "If you think I am being abducted, I will prove, loudly, that I am not. Except, possibly, by you."

"There was another man. Perhaps he . . ."

"He's in compartment C7, just along the corridor."

"Then we talk with him." Very Big Hans looked perplexed.

"Do that." Bond stepped towards him again. "But we shall make a great deal of noise, and we shall follow you if you attempt to take our friend from the train. We've not broken any laws. Your informer is an idiot."

"Possibly," Very Big Hans said the word clearly, almost as though he spoke English well.

"No, definitely. An idiot. A cretin."

Very Big Hans nodded slowly, then gave Bond a beatific smile. "If he has given us the wild-duck chase, I shall chastise him. *Ja?*"

"Good."

The large cops gave stiff little bows and left the compartment, closing the door behind them.

"What was that all about?" Easy looked nervous.

Bond held a finger to his lips and opened the door again, peering into the corridor. "Get ready to make good any threats. If they try to take Harry off, we've got to stop them."

"They gave up a tad easily."

"Of course. They're not cops."

"No?"

"When did you last see cops wearing thousand-dollar suits and Gucci shoes?"

"I would never have thought of that. They could be corrupt cops."

"I don't think so. As you said, they gave up very easily. There'll be real cops on the Potsdamer Station—any station, in fact. We could attract a lot of attention."

"Yes, and I can scream very loudly when roused." Easy's compact little frame seemed to radiate anger.

"I shall have to remember that."

"Oh, I won't scream at you, James. Maybe I will, but in the nicest kind of way, if you follow me?"

"Really?" Bond raised his eyebrows, pushing open the compartment door so that they could step out. "You go right, and I'll head for the door at the other end." The train was rocking its way into Potsdamer Station. "Watch out for the bogus cops, and take your cue from me if they try to remove Harry."

The Ost-West Express is divided into two portions: Paris and Ostend from whence travelers can go on to London. It originates in Moscow and is, therefore, one of the most romantic trains still running in Europe—the overpriced Orient Express apart.

Both sections of the train can just get into the Berlin Potsdamer Station, so when it came to a standstill, Bond was able to hang from the carriage door and view almost the entire length of the train. He signaled to Easy, who hung out of the door at the other end of the carriage, indicating that she should watch her right.

There was the usual bustle and smell of a continental train station. He thought it odd that, although the trains now run on either electricity or diesel, he still seemed to detect coal smoke among the little galaxy of odors which assaulted his sense of smell. Perhaps the smoke was a ghost from the past: from childhood.

All the other smells were very real—humanity, continental

tobacco, bread, wine and that strange, indefinable smell which changes from city to city. On Swiss train stations it is cleanliness; on French a mixture of wine, coffee and newsprint; in England there are still traces of smoke, but the overlying whiff is envy. Here, in Berlin, it was dust and, when it rained, woodsmoke. Odd that the scent from the continual bombing of over fifty years before still crept up from under the new buildings on rainy days.

Mostly people were getting onto the train. Very few left it, and—for the entire seven minutes in the station—Bond saw nothing of the two German ersatz cops, or Harry. As the various officials blew their whistles and waved flags, Bond stepped back into the carriage and closed the door, though he still leaned from the window, in spite of the stern warning telling him it was *Verboten.*

It always amazed him that it seemed to take half a dozen officials to set a train in motion from a German station. They trooped along the platform doing their particular pieces of mime: waving flags, slamming doors and letting out shrill blasts on their whistles, answered by the engine drivers at the front and rear of the great snake of carriages.

They were a mile out of the station before Bond gave up and returned to the compartment where Easy was already waiting. "Nothing?"

She shook her head.

"Okay, let's check on Harry." They made their way along the swaying corridor to C7, where Harry, quite unconcerned, was stretched full length on his bunk reading a book by an overpraised English thriller writer.

"You ever notice how this guy never describes people?" He looked up at them.

Bond peered forward to see the author's name. "Can't say I've ever read him."

"Well, what he does is he tells you that this or that character looks like a movie star. Gets away with it every time. He's got one here who 'could've been Rex Harrison's double', and another has the 'rugged good looks of Sean Connery.' This is cop out, yes?"

Bond sat on the edge of the bunk. "Someone once said I looked like Hoagy Carmichael with a cruel mouth."

"Who's Hoagy Carmichael?" Easy asked.

"He was . . ." Bond began. "Oh, Easy, if you don't know, I'm not going to explain."

"I think you have got a cruel mouth," she said, "though I wouldn't put it in a book."

"How did you get on with the pair of synthetic sleuths?" Bond asked of Harry.

"What is synthetic sleuths?"

"Charlatan cops. Impersonators."

"Never heard of them."

Bond look up sharply at Easy. "You didn't see them leave the train?"

She shook her head vigorously. "I watched the station exit, it was only twenty yards up the platform. They didn't get off."

"Then we still have the pleasure of their company."

"Would you tell me what you're talking about?" Harry asked, putting down the paperback.

Bond gave a fast account of the visit by the two expensively dressed men who had claimed to be police.

"Still on board, then. We'll hear more from them."

"Shouldn't be at all surprised." Bond stood up. "It's almost time for dinner. You going to change, Easy?"

"I thought I'd slip into something a shade more formal."

"I'll escort you back. I didn't bring much but a change of shirts myself."

"Like I said," Harry was reaching for his book again, "he who travels lightest, and all that."

"I'll come back and talk while Easy's changing."

"There's no need for you to go and sit with Harry." Easy gave him an arch little smile as they reached the door of the compartment. "I'm not shy or anything."

"It's the 'or anything' that interests me." Bond put a hand on her shoulder and she came closer to him. "When I met you, I thought you were just another of those power ladies with starch in their veins." he smiled. "I wouldn't have even told you that you had nice hair in case you screamed sexual harassment."

"Oh, I can do that, James. Have done it. But we power ladies can make our own choices now, which is one of the great charms of living in the last decade of the century. You want to stay?"

"I think I'll go and have another word with Harry. After all, we do have a whole night on this train."

She stood on tiptoe and gave him a small kiss on the cheek. "Rock and roll," she whispered.

"Just keep this door closed and don't open it to anyone except me. Got it?"

"Wouldn't want it any other way."

Back in Harry Spraker's compartment, Bond described the two men who had tried to lure them from the train. "Sound like anyone you know?"

Harry frowned. "Sounds like too many people I know. If this business *is* all down to Wolfgang and Monika, they'll have almost an army to call on. They both had followers, people who did not want to see the regime change. The kind of men and women who became embroiled in the Moscow coup. You know what it was like when the Stasi fell apart, James. It seemed complete. They even sold off the filing cabinets, shredders and office furniture in the old Normanenstrasse headquarters. Now the place offers *Sauna for Everyone*. As for the inmates, some ran like chickens without heads; others just called it a day and went home; but the majority simply faded into the woodwork.

"It was the same with the HVA. Mischa Wolf was already retired, but he vanished into the night. Now Wolfie Weisen and Monika Haardt were two people who wouldn't just sit down and weep. They had too large an investment—like others. People who've enfolded themselves in an ideology do not wish to walk naked."

"That's a sharp observation, Harry. I'll remember it."

Spraker threw back his head and gave a little laugh. "Wait till you meet Praxi. She has all the truly sharp observations."

"Yes. Yes, I'm looking forward to the tryst with Praxi." Bond's face clouded over. "Providing we all get to Paris safely. Harry, for god's sake, watch yourself. If those two overpriced thugs are really out to get us, I suspect they'll fight hard. Take care."

Harry Spraker gave him a solemn look. "I intend to. But, just in case anything goes very wrong, I give you a telephone number. You should call as soon as you get to Paris. Ask for Peggy Jean—in English, just like that. You'll get Praxi." He rattled off the number which Bond added to the great store of telephone numbers he kept in a locked compartment of his memory. Like many in his line of business, he used a simple system of color-coding, an *aide memoire* which he had learned many years ago in training.

They both went back to the double compartment to pick up Easy, who had changed into a neat little white dress that showed off her figure, revealing a hidden territory not even suggested before this.

"You really *have* changed," he said, abnormally elated. When they had set out on this venture, he really had not imagined Easy would match up to her name.

They ate in the dining car, where the food was passable, if not great in choice. The smoked salmon was exceptional, but James Bond had never really cared for escalopes holstein. "Why ruin a perfectly good piece of veal by putting capers and a fried egg on top," he observed. The wine was only just drinkable. A couple of hours later Bond and Easy said goodnight to Harry and went back to their compartment.

Almost as soon as they were inside, Easy slid the bolt, then closed in on Bond, wrapping her small body around him, kissing him as though she would explode. Bond thought that a man could effortlessly drown in those large pearl-grey eyes. The kissing did not stop.

"The bottom bunk, I think," she whispered.

"Whatever you say."

"And James, it must be safe."

"Always," he whispered. "Nowadays nobody takes chances."

Presently she said, "No, James, there's a little hook and eye here. Let me put your hand on it . . . Not, not there. There. Now the zipper."

In less than a minute they fumbled their way to the bunk. "Oh, yes, James," she panted, "I've always had a fantasy about playing trains on a train. Wow. Hello there."

"Hallo, yourself."

"I think you can really just lie there and let the train do the work, darling. . . ."

So, in the swaying, bumping train, they rattled through the night, dozing occasionally then waking to the comfort of each other's arms. "This is definitely the way to pass the time on a long journey," Easy whispered as the train sped through the German countryside.

When they woke in the morning, it was to see they had arrived at Wuppertal Elberfeld, in the heart of the Ruhr Valley. The views were less than romantic: factories and power plants flanked the track. Within the hour they would be in Cologne.

They dressed quickly. "You're the first woman I've met in a long time who can actually wash, dress and put on a new face in minutes as opposed to hours," Bond said as Easy finished putting on her makeup. He was wiping traces of shave cream from his face, and she came over and kissed him, some of the cream transferring itself to her nose. Her eyes flashed with humor and happiness.

"Jaunty," Bond said.

"Jaunty?"

"Yes. I've been trying to find one word that sums you up. Jaunty would be about right." Dressed now, and checking the ASP automatic which he slid into his waistband, hard behind his right hip, Bond led Easy along the corridor.

81

Harry was not in his compartment, neither was he in the dining car, where they had to wait for fifteen minutes before getting a table for breakfast.

The train pulled into Cologne Station as Bond was finishing his second cup of coffee. Spraker's absence from both the compartment and the dining car had brought a small cloud of worry into his head. He leaned across the table to speak quietly to Easy, "Our German friends don't seem to have shown themselves, unless they left the train overnight. I just hope they didn't leave with Harry."

She nodded, a shadow of concern crossing her face. "You think we should take a look? Go through the train and see . . ."

"We'll have to be quick about it." The train was now gliding out of the station. "We've got around an hour and a half before we're due in Aachen, which is the last stop before crossing into Belgium, and there the train splits up. We go on to Paris, the front portion heads for Ostend."

"Then what're we waiting for?"

Bond paid the bill and they checked Harry Spraker's compartment again on their way back to their own sleeping car. Easy wanted to get a sweater, for in spite of the heating she felt chilly. Outside the industrial and urban sprawl was giving way to flat countryside, and the signs of late autumn were well advanced: trees had shed almost all their leaves, the fields and roads looked wet, and most were tilled. The harvest was over and the world seemed poised, waiting for the onslaught of winter.

Bond put his key into the lock, and started to turn it when the door swung open and he almost staggered inside. A hand stretched out to pull him across the little room, throwing him against the big window which still had the shade down.

The same hand caught Easy by the arm, flinging her against Bond. She gave a little squeal of fear and pain as her back hit the glass, and Bond had to reach out to prevent her from falling.

"Good morning, I trust you slept well," said Very Big Hans. He now had his back against the door, and his large hand clutched a Browning 9mm equipped with a long noise-reduction unit. He held it near the hip, against his body, and his hand was steady as a proverbial rock.

Bond took a deep breath. "You've come alone. Your friend not joining us today?"

Very Big Hans treated them to a broad smile. "My friend is looking after your friend. We are all going to be very cosy here until we get to Aachen. I promise you if you try anything, I will kill you both. I don't want to do this, because someone else is anxious to talk with you. But I am, as they say, licensed to kill. You understand?"

"Perfectly." Bond had quickly regained his composure. Breathing deeply, summing up the chances. "Your English has improved during the night."

"Oh, yes," a chuckle which rose from the belly. "These Berlitz courses are wonderful. I passed the time with earphones glued to my head."

"Thought you had to get off at Potsdamer Station."

Very Big Hans shrugged. "That was the original plan, but I think you would really have caused us much discomfort. You see, all things are arranged in Aachen. In about half an hour my colleague, Felix, will join us. By then he will have given Herr Spraker a small injection to put him to sleep. Herr Spraker will be wreathed in bandages. His face obliterated with gauze dressings. You will also be in a similar state very soon. There will be ambulances, and people at Aachen, to take the three of you from the train."

"Don't tell me, let me guess." Bond sounded exceptionally relaxed. "We've all been in an accident. How's that happened?"

"We haven't been specific." The smile spread over Very Big Hans's face. "We simply telephoned ahead to friends. Nobody's going to ask questions. People have been paid a great deal of money not to make a fuss. Now, I think it is necessary to begin work. Mr. Boldman, you will sit on the edge of the lower bunk while the lady comes quietly towards me."

Nobody moved. "Come along, my dear. It's okay, you'll just have a nice sleep for a few hours—about three to be precise. Just come towards me, and when I tell you to stop, you must turn around and face your friend Mr. Boldman—or whatever his real name is. Come."

Slowly Bond sat, and Easy began to move towards Very Big Hans. "Not too fast," he counseled. "Just slowly. Any quick move and I promise there'll be bits of you spread all over the place."

She had reached a point about a foot in front of him when he told her to stop and turn around.

"Now. Roll up your left sleeve and extend your arm. Good."

Easy was trembling, but Very Big Hans still held the pistol in his right hand, the weapon unwavering. From where he sat, Bond knew the evil eye of the muzzle was trained right on his face. He did not stand a chance. Any move, even a feint to the right and a spring forward, meant suicide. The man was demonstrably good: well-trained and quite prepared to kill. All Bond could do was watch as their captor's left hand slid into the pocket of his jacket and emerged with a small hypo, in a plastic case.

For the first time, Bond noticed that he wore a gold Rolex Oyster on his left wrist. Cops did not wear those kinds of timepieces, unless they were on the take.

"Just hold out your arm. Straight out. I promise you'll feel nothing." His eyes flicked for a second—no more—towards Easy's arm. The rest he did by feel: deftly ridding the hypo of its little plastic container, moving it in his hand so that the needle protruded from between his index and second fingers, and his thumb pressed against the plunger. He shook the hypo and sent a small squirt of liquid from the needle to make certain there were no bubbles of air. Then:

"Just relax, my dear. Relax."

Easy gave a little jerk and expelled air from her mouth as he

84

plunged the needle into her upper arm. Less than two seconds later he dropped the hypo and Easy began to weave, taking one difficult step forward.

"Sit on the bunk," Very Big Hans commanded, and she sat, then dropped backwards, her eyeballs rolling up, the lids closing as her body surrendered to the drug.

He smiled at Bond. "You see. This is very good, very fast, stuff. Your turn next, Mr. Boldman, then I shall be able to get Felix in to help me bandage you. He's only a couple of compartments down, and I should imagine your friend, Harry . . . is that correct . . . ?"

Bond nodded and began to get to his feet.

"I should imagine Harry is in dreamland by now, and will be trussed like a turkey by the time you're ready. The coat, Mr. Boldman. Just take it off and put it on the bunk. Gently, don't be stupid."

"You can be certain I'm not a fool. And only a fool would be stupid enough to try anything in these circumstances."

For the first time, Bond saw that the big man had been set a trifle off guard. His eyes flicked between Bond and the sleeping Easy, and, while he still had a firm grip on the pistol, the aim was not directly on Bond.

Slowly he took off his jacket, and, as he turned to fold it, he saw Very Big Hans already preempting matters by reaching for the second hypo in his left pocket.

He transferred the jacket to his left hand, holding it by the collar. When he threw it towards Hans's right hand, it was almost a lazy movement, but it caught the big man off balance, just as he was removing the hypo from its plastic case. The barrel of his pistol drooped in his hand, and his eyes were off Bond for a crucial moment.

The train was picking up speed, and had started to roll slightly as it took the long wide bends. The jacket fell right across the gun hand, and, in the fraction of time it took Hans to react, Bond had the ASP out of his waistband.

The two shots made a lot of noise, but the train was also

rattling and creaking. Bond stepped to his right. Big Hans dropped his pistol and the hypo, clutching towards his head in a reflex. Most of his face had ceased to exist, and there was a great deal of blood on the door and wall. The man's body crashed backwards, then down. He was dead long before his pistol even hit the ground.

Bond replaced his weapon, snatched his jacket from the floor, and folded it neatly. There was cleaning up to do before he could deal with Felix.

He lifted Easy's unconscious body from the lower berth and hefted her up out of the way onto the top bunk, covering her with a blanket, and placing a pillow under her head. Her color was good, and she breathed to a deep rhythm. If Very Big Hans had been telling the truth, she would come to naturally enough in three hours. Around eleven o'clock, he thought. Plenty of time, for they were not due in at the Gare du Nord until twenty past one.

He took a sheet and wound it around the bleeding pulp that had been Very Big Hans's head, hauling the body onto the bottom berth before starting to use another sheet to wipe down the door and walls. Then, using water from the little washbasin, he started on the floor. Traces would remain, but, with some luck he would have time to do a more thorough job after they had disposed of the body. He thought for a moment, and decided the most efficient way would be to take Very Big Hans's colleague by surprise.

He picked up the Browning and checked the action, testing the noise-reduction unit to be certain it was fully in place. A couple of compartments down, Very Big Hans had said. He would just have to risk getting to the right door.

The corridor was empty. Not even a guard or ticket collector. Bond went down two doors and rapped hard, softly calling, "Felix?" his ear pressed against the door.

Felix himself opened up, and Bond, seeing the right hand slightly behind his thigh, hidden from view, knew there was only one thing to do. He had no conscience, no compunction about the work. He shot Felix twice, straight through the left side of the chest and then in the throat. The pistol made a little popping sound, less noise than a child's cork-firing wooden gun.

As he fell backwards, Felix simply looked surprised. He made no sound. Only the weapon—a twin to the Browning that had killed him—clunked onto the floor. It had been in the hand hidden behind his thigh, as Bond had suspected.

This was how it happened, Bond thought. You can go from life to death in the twinkling of an eye, at the snap of fingers. He had seen it dozens of times, and was still not completely used to it, but his approach was that of a realist. The very large man, and this one, Felix, would have killed all three of them without even feeling compassion. This was the law of the jungle of secret Europe where they still fought for survival.

He caught Felix by the lapels of his jacket before his body hit the floor, kicking backwards with his right foot to slam the door closed.

Harry Spraker slept peacefully on the lower berth, and there was a large pile of gauze, dressings and bandages lying on the long seat which had been let down along the other wall of the little cabin.

Bond snatched a sheet from the upper berth and wrapped it around Felix's throat: the wound that produced the most blood. This done, he lowered the body to the floor and lifted Harry onto the top bunk, as he had done with Easy.

Only then did he start the really difficult job of bandaging the body. First he removed Felix's clothes, stanching the blood from both wounds, using handfuls of gauze and bandages.

He saw, among the pile of medical supplies on the seat, there were three hospital gowns, so he heaved and hauled at the body, pushing and pulling until he managed to get the gown onto the man, tying it tightly at the neck, then bandaging the face, leaving only a slit for his mouth.

It took a considerable time, and he knew the other body would have to be dealt with at speed. He wrapped the dead

Felix's clothes in one of the pillowcases, opened the large window and dropped the bundle straight down onto the track. A chill blast of air cut into the compartment and, as he turned for a moment, Bond had the illusion that Felix was moving on the bunk. It was only the wind, whistling and snagging at the gown.

He grabbed an armful of bandages and gauze, together with another gown, and, locking the door behind him, all but ran back to his own compartment, where he went through the same ritual with the man he had thought of as Very Big Hans.

When it was done, he went through the clothes, took out an ID wallet, and a billfold containing credit cards and deutsche marks, sticking them in his hip pocket. Then he stuffed the clothes into a pillowcase and repeated what he had done with the effects of dead Felix.

Glancing at his watch, he realized that he had less than fifteen minutes to do the most important business. He was on mental autopilot by now, going through the motions, making decisions quickly. This compartment was in the worse state of the two. Very Big Hans had lost much blood, and not a little brain matter. It would not be easy, but, if things were to go smoothly, it would be necessary to move the big fellow's body down to join his friend. First, Harry would have to be brought back here, to join Easy.

The corridor remained empty, and he quickly went down to get Harry, hoisting him from the top bunk, and getting him in a fireman's lift so that he could transport him down the rolling and shuddering train. Harry was heavy, but not as heavy as Very Big Hans. He gently laid Spraker down next to Easy.

Then, calling upon all his strength, he lifted the German's body from the lower bunk. He was a dead weight and felt like a sack of pig iron. Taking the strain, Bond peered out into the corridor again, and began a slow, desperate walk to where Felix lay. His legs protested against the burden, and his back seemed to creak like old wood subjected to strain.

When he was finally able to lay the body on the top bunk, every muscle in his body screamed with pain, and he was breathing heavily. But the job was done—only just in time, for already they were slowing, running into the outskirts of Aachen.

He locked the door and returned to Easy and Harry, lifting the latter down from the top bunk. Once he had bluffed the two bodies from the train, there would be more for him to do. A thorough cleaning of the compartment.

He saw the ambulance men standing on the platform as the train came to a halt, and, from the carriage door, he signaled to them.

"How many did they say?" he asked the uniformed officer in charge, speaking in immaculate German, and praying that nobody knew the faces of the two supposed policemen.

"Three."

"There're only a pair." He smiled. "One of them decided to walk."

The ambulance man gave a curt nod, grinned and waved his men in, carrying their stretchers. "I don't think they're going to last long," Bond said as they got to the door. "Just get them away as quickly as possible."

"Don't worry," the head ambulance man replied. "We know what to do. If they don't recover, it's too bad."

Two of the railway personnel had arrived by this time. One of them, in the uniform of a *Chef de Train,* nodded. He spoke German with a French accent so, no doubt, was an SNCF employee. "Your friends had a bad accident, we heard. I am sorry. You will be going with them?"

Bond shook his head. "I *must* be in Paris today. For now I'd like to be left alone." He gave the number of his compartment. "Perhaps a large jug of coffee when we get going again."

Both of the officials nodded with understanding.

"Who informed you? The people here?"

"Oh yes, the police. By radio. They said to leave you alone. That you and your friend were doctors. That you would contact us if you needed assistance."

Certainly, whoever had given the orders had a great deal of

pull with the police and the transport system, Bond thought as he stepped to one side to let the ambulance people carry the stretchers out of the carriage.

It all seemed somehow too simple, he considered, but it had been the two fake policemen who had arranged matters. It had been easy for them. How many palms had been well greased in the hope of removing himself, Easy and Harry from the train? How many people had been persuaded to become blind, deaf and dumb? He recalled Harry's words, "If this business *is* all down to Wolfgang and Monika, they'll have almost an army to call on. . . . Wolfie Weisen and Monika Haardt were two people who wouldn't just sit down and weep. They had too large an investment—like others. People who've enfolded themselves in an ideology do not wish to walk naked." So, the defunct HVA and the Stasi might have an underground army of hundreds. If that was so, they would be a criminal and terrorist force to reckon with in Europe.

A waiter came with coffee, which Bond took from him at the door, overtipping the man outrageously. He drank two cups straight off, easing his muscles to take the ache out of the joints. He spent half an hour going through a series of mental and physical exercises which he had long discovered were a great help to him—relaxing and resettling his body; freeing his mind. Then he set to work, doing a more thorough cleanup of the compartment. Not, he considered, that it would matter much. Whoever they were, the people he had killed belonged to some larger group who knew how to roll unpleasantness out of sight.

Shortly before eleven o'clock, Harry Spraker began to moan and grumble in his sleep. Then he stirred, starting to move his arms and head.

"Harry. It's me. James. You're okay."

Spraker came out of it slowly. He was a man surfacing from a deep and troubled dream. At first, when he opened his eyes, it was obvious he could not focus on Bond's face, but, after a few minutes, his eyes cleared and he seemed to be searching his mind. How had he gotten wherever he was going? Where was he?

"You're still on the train, Harry. We're going to Paris. The two fake German cops tried to get you off."

"Oh, my God . . . Hell . . . Felix Utterman and Hexie Weiss . . ."

"Who were they, Harry?"

"Thirsty," was all he could say.

Bond went out into the corridor and along towards the dining car. Halfway there he saw the waiter who had brought the coffee earlier.

"Certainly, sir. I bring a mega-size coffee and three cups. Right away." Which went to prove, Bond thought, that sometimes overtipping pays off.

As Harry started to sip scalding coffee, Easy began to groan.

"Harry, you said two names . . ."

"Sure . . ." His voice was still thick and slurred with the drug. "Sure. Felix Utterman and Hexie Weiss."

"Who were they?"

"Felix and Hexie? Originally Stasi, but later they worked for HVA under Wolfie Weisen. They were first-class thugs. Everything: extortion, persuasion, hard interrogation, killing even. Weisen called them his two Aces. It was his joke."

"Well, they're two aces in two holes now." Bond smiled grimly and began to turn his attention to Easy who was shaking her head wildly in a fear that gripped her as she came out of her personal nightmare.

In a couple of hours, Bond thought, they would be in Paris, and he would be able to ask Praxi Simeon a few awkward questions about Utterman and Weiss, the pair of aces he had just trumped.

7

|||||||||||||||||||||||||||||||||||||||||||||||||||||||||||||||||||||||||||||||||||||||||||||||||||||||||||||||||||||||||||||||||||||||||

Death Threat

Easy St. John wept for a good twenty minutes after recovering consciousness. Bond put it down to the drug, and the extreme fear she had experienced in the minutes before Hexie Weiss—Very Big Hans—injected her. She shook with terror, and her eyes were wide with fright as Bond poured several cups of coffee into her. He even thought, briefly, of having her relieved of the job once they arrived in Paris, but rejected the idea. He would allow things to progress for at least another twenty-four hours before making a final decision. In the meantime, he spoke to her calmly, soothing away her stark memories.

When things had returned to normal he decided to drop the bombshell he had been keeping in reserve.

"Harry," he began, "you know your way around. You're streetwise and smart, so I'm going to ask you something once, and once only. I want you to give me an honest reply. If you decide you're not up to what I suggest, then we'll have to think again."

They were less than an hour out of the Gare du Nord, and Harry looked at him with interest. There were no traces of either alarm or concern in the dark, good-looking lothario's eyes. "Shoot, James. What's the score?"

Bond told him. When they arrived in Paris, he said, they would have to leave the train separately. "I'm not going to take any chances. The two thugs were experts. You've described them as old hands, friends of people like Wolfgang Weisen and Monika Haardt. They were out either to take us somewhere safe—for themselves, that is—or kill us here. My reading of the situation is that, in the long run, we were to be disposed of anyway: just as the bulk of Cabal has been wiped out."

He watched as both Harry and Easy nodded in agreement before continuing. "My main problem is who can we trust? I have to be honest with you, Harry. I cannot, as yet, rule out Praxi Simeon as dubious. In turn, this means I can't really trust you either . . ."

"They were after me as well, James. Surely . . . ?"

"They appeared to be after you, yes. I am going to suggest some very simple safeguards. When we arrive in Paris, I'm going straight to an address where I know I can be safe. It'll be a question of hiding in plain sight. It's not a safe house or anything like that, but I *know* that I shall be okay. I also imagine that I can get rooms for you and Easy, but I'm not going to do that immediately . . ."

"We're supposed to contact *Sulphur*—Praxi—as soon as we arrive," Harry quickly reminded him.

"Yes, that's what you told me Praxi wanted. In turn, I said I needed to talk to her as soon as possible. But, Harry, I honestly don't know if I can trust her—or you, for that matter."

"James, this is . . ."

"This is precautionary, Harry. No more and no less. What I am going to propose is a simple damage control. A test of loyalty."

The silence which followed hung in the air for around a full minute, until Harry asked what Bond intended to do.

"I want you, Easy, to get a cab and go straight to the Sofitel Hotel at Charles de Gaulle airport. They deal mainly with overnight travelers, so you should have no difficulty getting a room. Check in and wait. I'll call you there and give further instructions. In a few minutes I think we should all head for different carriages, with our baggage, so that we do not all leave the train from the same point. Easy, you'll go from here: you have the most luggage. I'll leave from the middle, while Harry'll be the last to go, and from the furthest point possible from the gate. None of us will show any recognition if we happen to see each other in the taxi queues, and *you* have a very special job, Harry. You will watch my back. If you don't feel happy with that . . . "

"What about *my* back?" Easy asked, with a tinge of petulance.

"You're trained. You speak French . . ."

"Like a native—a native of Uruguay."

"It'll do. Just run the back doubles. Get the cabdriver on your side. Paris cabdrivers know their way around, but they are not the most helpful folk in the world. The French really don't like any of us, but it's nothing personal. They just can't stand foreigners—except when you give them a world-class tip. If you do that, they laugh at you behind your back, but they will cooperate. Got me?"

Easy nodded, but did not look completely happy.

"What about me?" Harry asked. "What do you really expect me to do?"

"I've told you—the most difficult job. The test of a lifetime, Harry. You're simply going to watch my back. Follow me. See if anyone else is on my tail. If you happen to lose me, or if there's trouble, I want you to go straight to the Ritz. Try to look respectable, and wait for someone to page you. You'll be paged in the name of Maurice Charpentier, okay? How good are you at surveillance, incidentally?"

"Sixty percent good, ten percent luck, and thirty percent incompetent."

"Big word, incompetent."

"Just telling the truth."

"But you'll take a shot at it?"

Harry shrugged, "Praxi's not going to like it."

"Praxi has no option in the matter. She'll just have to sit and wait until I decide to see her."

Both Harry and Easy looked unsettled by the news, but Bond let it pass, and a few minutes later told Harry to move. "Get yourself back to the far end of the train and watch me as though I'm carrying a million dollars of your money."

Spraker left, subdued and carrying his little case.

"You're playing games." Easy gave him a knowing grin.

"Yes and no." He reached up and kissed her. "What idents do you have on you?"

"I've got a Gail Merchant, editor for a New York publisher—medical books; and a Martha Grazti, company secretary to Shelley, Byrd and Stretcher, law firm in D.C. They exist. Agency legal, and very respectable."

"They are? Don't people know they're Agency?"

"Very few."

"Okay. Get your luggage together. I presume you can manage it?"

"I'll get a porter."

"Yes, why not? Draw attention to yourself." He looked up at her three cases. "There's one change in plan."

"What?"

"You don't go to the Sofitel at Charles de Gaulle. Go to the one at Orly. You'll still get a room. No problem. Tell the driver Charles de Gaulle, then as you pull away, get him to do the runaround. Give him big money. Don't be mysterious. Just tell him you're trying to throw off a persistent lover. They like that, Paris cabbies—that and the money . . ."

"What if he's like the Berlin driver?"

"No chance. You'll be taking a lucky dip at the Gare du Nord. It's first come, first served, so there's no way anyone can force you into a particular cab. Take your time. Really make him do a runaround, then head out to Orly. I'll call you as Martha Grazti as soon as things become clear."

"What's the real game, James?"

He paused, lifted an eyebrow, then gave her a quick, parting kiss. "I thought we deserved at least one more night in a decent bed. Lord knows where we'll be sleeping once we've made contact with Praxi."

Easy looked extremely happy.

Of all the train stations in Europe, Bond liked the Gare du Nord best. The place held special memories for him. It was also within walking distance of one of his favorite restaurants in Paris—Terminus Nord.

Bistros and restaurants hovering in the shadow of any great railway terminus should normally be avoided. Inevitably, their clientele consists of birds of passage, people leaving and arriving at the station. So it follows that the service is perfunctory, at best; at worst, slapdash; while the food is only passable. Happily Terminus Nord, directly opposite the Gare du Nord, is a prestigious exception. Its service is impeccable, while the food attracts gourmets who are not merely passing through the French capital or using the train station.

Bond, therefore, did not join the queue at the cab rank. Instead, he crossed the suicidal road from the station, pleased that the Parisian weather was mild, with an autumn sun giving more than usual warmth for this time of year.

He loved Paris, had spent much time there, and knew the city as well as he knew London. Avoiding it in the summer when it was crammed with tourists, he preferred either early spring or this very time of year. Autumn in Paris, he always thought, should have been the name of a popular song. He certainly preferred it to April.

Terminus Nord was full, but a table on the sidewalk had just been vacated, and a lithe, white-aproned waiter, who slid through the crush of people with the agility of a fencing master, showed Bond to the table, held back the empty chair for him, placed a menu on the table and asked what he would like to drink, all in fluid movements and in a voice which hinted that his customer was safe with him.

Bond ordered a martini, giving none of his usual directions.

The Terminus Nord could be trusted to provide a reasonable facsimile of what he regarded as the perfect martini—an idiosyncrasy not shared by many of the great experts in the art of cocktail making.

At his curbside table, Bond had an excellent view of the station facade, and while he examined the menu he also kept an eye out for signs that Harry Spraker was doing his job. If he had read the man correctly, he was an expert, but it was still possible that Bond could turn the tables on him. Indeed, the whole object of this exercise was to outmaneuver Spraker, who was too much of a cipher to be anything other than a first-class operator in the trade of espionage and terrorism, two activities which have a great deal in common.

This was not the only reason Bond had left the station confines so quickly and headed to a place where he could both eat and observe. Though Spraker had been charged with watching his back, James Bond wanted to watch his own back. His mistrust of everyone connected with the shattered Cabal network had trebled since he had boarded the Ost-West Express, and his years of training and intuition told him he could trust only one person—himself.

He ate a plate of escargots doused in garlic and butter, followed by a medium rare filet de boeuf with Lyonnaise potatoes and a mixed salad. He drank a small carafe of the house red. There was no point in ordering anything more expensive than the house red at Terminus Nord for the wine was as excellent as anything else on their list, unless you were going for a real gastronomic experience, or were out to impress a client or a young woman. Finishing the food, he now sipped his coffee as he sat back, enjoying the farce that was being played out across the street.

At first, Harry had been completely thrown. At the very moment Bond was shown to his table, Harry had come out and joined a swelling taxi queue. Easy, with a porter in attendance, arrived soon after, but Harry, realizing that Bond was not there, obviously imagined that he had either already left, or was loitering on the main concourse.

He dodged out of the queue, showing the same kind of irritation he had done outside the arrivals terminal at Berlin's Tegel. He waited to see Easy get away in her cab, and stayed in sight long enough to assure himself that nobody appeared to follow her. No car stirred from the parking spaces behind the taxis, and the people who had been behind her in the line, a pair of elderly ladies, went off in the other direction.

In the end, Harry disappeared into the station again, and, while he was there, Bond watched the taxi line, and the people who were hanging around in the vicinity. Also, he made sure the bill was presented long before the meal was completed, in case he had cause to leave quickly. Sure enough, he soon spotted at least two watchers. One sat in a small blue van parked just behind the taxis, while another detached himself from the queue, as though suddenly changing his mind about traveling in a taxi.

He was a short man who walked and dressed like a second-rate jockey: tweedy trousers and jacket over a dull beige rollneck sweater. There was a small-checked cap on his head, and, even in this clothing, he appeared to have the ability to blend into a crowd. It was an art beloved of watchers: a man who would be immediately apparent and easily picked out by those who knew him, yet the kind of person who others would not look at twice; a man who could disappear into a crowd and merge completely into the background.

Fifteen minutes after he had left the queue, the jockey, as Bond now thought of him, reappeared, seconds behind Harry who came out of the station looking bewildered. This time, the jockey carried a small cheap suitcase, and placed himself directly behind Harry in the taxi line.

So, Bond decided, Harry would almost certainly be heading for the Ritz to await the message for Maurice Charpentier, and behind him, the jockey would be playing tag—his shadow.

He left exact change, plus a tip for the waiter, poured himself a second cup of coffee and was ready to move at a minute's notice.

Over in front of the station, the long queue slowly wound down, and when Harry was only three places from the front, Bond moved, catching his waiter's attention and pointing to the table.

There were plenty of empty taxis passing on his side of the road, and he managed to flag one down before Harry reached the top of the queue.

"Keep your engine running, but pretend to have trouble pulling out." He spoke French with a Parisian accent, and passed a large denomination note to the driver. "Police," he added. "Undercover, not from the local shop."

The cabbie did not appear to be impressed. "What am I to do? A uniform'll come up any minute and move me on or worse." It was plain that the cabbie regarded Bond as a possible crook rather than a flic—a cop.

"Let me deal with any uniforms coming this way, just do as I say. This is something of national importance."

"Naturally." The cabdriver stared straight ahead. There was no way he was going to even look at his fare.

Harry was climbing into his cab now, and the jockey again slipped quietly from the queue and trotted back to where the little blue van waited. The van pulled out two cars behind the taxi.

"You see the blue van?" Bond spoke quickly. "Follow him. Don't get close, but don't lose him. If you foul up, you won't have a licence to drive by tomorrow morning."

"Sure, I'd bet on it." The driver imagined this was heavy sarcasm.

"Just do it!"

The cabbie nodded and mouthed a quiet curse against all cops and lawbreakers. The Parisian cabbie hates the police almost as much as he hates foreigners. Lawbreakers he can take or leave.

They were now in the dense traffic which flows in a never-ending stream through the main streets of Paris, and there was no doubt that Harry was heading for the Ritz. There was also no doubt that the blue van was keeping tabs on him.

So, Bond reasoned, Harry Spraker was already either well known to the opposition—whoever they were—or the men shadowing him were free-lancers hired by the remnants of Cabal. At this point he would not like to have put money on it either way.

He did not even have to follow the route closely, for it soon became obvious that Harry, with the van at a safe distance behind, was making straight for the famous, and fabulous, Place Vendôme. They were on the Faubourg St. Honoré now, crossing the Rue Royale, which links the great Place de la Concorde with the Madeleine, that incredible Christian church which looks like a Roman temple. Then, quite unexpectedly, the taxi was braking and the driver agitatedly asked what he should do now. Ahead, Bond saw the blue van had pulled over for a few seconds: just enough time to allow the jockey to exit onto the pavement.

"Let it go. Then drop me another hundred yards up." The van was still ahead of them, back in the mainstream of traffic again. Peering from the rear windshield, he saw the jockey walking, unconcerned, to a street crossing.

"Pull over and let me out." He pushed a bundle of notes into the driver's hand and left without even looking back.

The jockey was on the other side of the road, walking jauntily and quite unaware that anybody else had any interest in him. What was happening became quite clear. The jockey knew exactly where Harry was headed, for the Place Vendôme lay only a hundred yards or so to their left. All he had to do was turn into the narrow Rue St. Hyacinthe and, a minute or so later, he would emerge into the splendid, possibly most prosperous square in the whole of Paris.

Sure enough, as he glanced back, the jockey turned left.

It took several minutes to cross the wide street. There was plenty of pedestrian traffic on the pavements, and Bond wove

100

his way through the crowds, hurrying into the Rue St. Hyacinthe. The jockey had disappeared, and he quickened his pace, breaking out into the lovely square with its great arcade at ground level, and the Corinthian columns rising to two stories above; Napoleon's statue in the center, and the expensive shops glittering, their stylish windows beckoning to those who had enough money to shop in this most extravagant area. The Place Vendôme really boasts nothing but banks, high-priced shops, the Ministry of Justice and the luxurious Ritz Hotel.

Then he saw the jockey again, as his head turned towards the entrance to the, arguably, most famous hotel in the world.

There, on the pavement he was greeting Harry Spraker like a long lost friend. The pair embraced in full view of passersby and the smiling doormen. He could almost read their lips. Harry was speaking in German, "Good to see you again, old friend," he seemed to be saying. "Let's get a drink."

The pair, looking almost comically tall and short, turned and disappeared into the gilded extravagance of the Ritz.

It was time, Bond thought, for him to make his call to Monsieur Charpentier, and within minutes he was standing in one of the little line of telephone booths, which, in the Place Vendôme, seem to take only Visa, MasterCard or American Express.

Quickly he tapped out the six digits—60–38–30—dredging it from his memory bank of telephone numbers.

The operator passed him to the front office who, in the person of a young woman with a starched voice, said certainly, they would page M. Charpentier. Within two minutes Harry was on the line.

"James, where are you?"

"Never mind where I am. I want you to move, and move damned fast."

"Why? What's . . . ?"

"Don't talk, just listen." Bond was suddenly aware that the man in the next booth was speaking softly into the telephone and doing the impossible, for the fingers of his right hand pushed down on the receiver rest. Somewhere along the road, he had collected a Shadow of his own.

"You there? James . . . ?" Harry sounded agitated.

"Yes. Leave immediately. You're not safe. Neither am I."

"Where do I go?"

"Get a cab. Drive around a little, then go to the Crillon. I'll call you there in about half an hour." It would take around twenty minutes to walk to the Crillon Hotel, nearby in the Place de la Concorde. Almost superstitiously, Bond crossed his fingers for good luck, then he left the booth and walked quickly back towards the Rue St. Hyacinthe. This time it was his turn to try and lose a tail.

He paused for a moment to look at the diamonds displayed in a jeweler's window. Added together, their cost would probably go a long way towards wiping out the American budget deficit. The Shadow passed him, and must have known that he had been made. In the window reflection, Bond saw him glance quickly in his direction: a tall man, middle-aged, in a tailored grey double-breasted topcoat and an old-fashioned, but smart, grey homburg.

He followed, as the Shadow strolled quite lazily up the Rue St. Hyacinthe, then turned into the St. Honoré. Bond quickened his pace and, rounding the corner, cannoned into his Shadow.

As he began to apologize, he felt the hard prod of a pistol barrel in his ribs. The Shadow smiled, touching his homburg with his free hand. "I'm so sorry." He spoke immaculate English. "Captain Bond, I fear I have to detain you. It's a formality only, but I'm sure you'll understand."

"If it's a formality, why the hell're you sticking a gun in my ribs?"

"Ah, well, that's not a formality. That's genuine. Really a kind of death threat, I'd say." The Shadow had a slim grey moustache, and looked very military as he prodded Bond towards the edge of the pavement, raising his hand to signal.

102

The car was a black, well-polished Honda, which only went to show that the Japanese get everywhere.

"Mind your head," said a voice from the rear as the Shadow opened the door. "Do get in, Captain Bond. I've been waiting to meet you."

He glimpsed a mane of dark hair and an oval face. The Shadow gave him another little jab with the pistol and said, "Please hurry, we're holding up the traffic."

Bond's nose twitched at the hint of a very expensive scent and he found himself sitting next to the girl, who looked at him and smiled. "How do you do? My name's Praxi Simeon."

The Shadow pushed against him, making him the middle of an interesting human sandwich.

8

||||||||||||||||||||||||||||||||||||||||||||||||||||||||||||||||||||||||||||||||||||||||||||||||||||||||||||||||||||||

Death in Proximity

The car pulled out into the traffic. It was one of those expertly timed moves: fast, smooth and confident. The driver certainly knew his stuff. Obviously he did this for a living. From Bond's viewpoint, the driver seemed to be sharp-faced with a short pudding-basin haircut. Military, he guessed. Or, given the facts of life, a man who wanted to look military.

"I'm sorry, what did you say your name was?" If this woman was Praxi Simeon, Bond considered, then he, Bond, must be the result of a liaison between King Kong and Fay Wray.

"Come on, Captain Bond, you're visiting Paris in order to see me—Praxi Simeon."

"Never heard of her."

"May I call you James?"

"I'm a firm believer in formality, Ms. . . . what was it? Simon?"

"Simeon," she enunciated. "Praxi Simeon?" A query phonated with slow care, as though she spoke to a retarded child.

Some people would call her a "big girl." Not unattractive, but heavily built, with a plump face which probably took around ninety minutes to put on. The hair was very dark: a lot of it. Long curly locks kept falling in front of her face. She was constantly pushing them away with splayed fingers heavy with rings. A wig, possibly. This was the kind of woman who, in a clinch, might well suffocate a man with the pneumatic beauty of her breasts. Squeezed between her and the Shadow, he could feel what he thought of as voluptuous curves against his flesh. While her fingers carried a lot of rings, she also wore a silver bracelet on her right wrist: a pattern of twisted shapes; animals entwined.

Quietly, he murmured:

> *"A bracelet invisible*
> *For your busy wrist,*
> *Twisted from silver."*

"I beg your pardon?" Her voice was pure affected English. Jolly hockey sticks, outmoded schoolgirl Home Counties, larded with elongated vowels.

"Nothing. I was admiring the bracelet." He had quoted Robert Graves: the three-line answerback to Praxi Simeon's IFF code. Better to be safe than dead.

"Well, now we're together, let's talk."

"I wouldn't know what to talk about, unless it's your first name. Praxi doesn't sound either English or French."

"Bulgarian originally. My people go back a couple of generations to pure Bulgarian."

"Lucky Bulgars."

"You're still saying you don't know me?"

"I'm sorry. The name just doesn't ring a bell, and, by the way, if you're Ms. Simeon, could you introduce me to Dandy Jim here?" He nodded towards the Shadow.

"He is a friend of ours. Quite safe."

"No friend of mine. Friends don't stick pistols in your ribs."

"My dear Bond, I had to get your attention." Close up, the Shadow seemed a grey man, though this could have been his clothes. "Dangerous times. Had to get you into the car and next to Praxi as quickly as possible. There was only one sure way I could do that. You want an apology?" He also spoke in that kind of over-perfect, almost Yuppie, English which is a travesty

105

of the language. Old school military with no trace of any original accent—French, German, Italian or even Hindi. He would certainly say "gels" instead of "girls," "ra-there" instead of "rather" and "ja" in place of "yes."

"No apology necessary, Mr. . . . ?"

"Call me Sprat."

"As in Jack who could eat no fat?"

"Very droll, Captain Bond."

"There's no need to be cagey." The girl edged nearer, and Bond felt the hard button of a garter against his thigh. The button was surrounded by a large amount of flesh. Under different circumstances it could have been quite sexy.

"I really don't know what you're talking about." The driver, he noticed, was taking them nowhere fast. He was either driving a random pattern or doing a counter-surveillance routine. "Where're we going, by the way?"

"Nowhere in particular." She leaned even closer. "It's just safer to talk in the car."

"Really. You have the vehicle wired?"

She gave a disgusted little sound. "You're the giddy limit, Captain Bond. Truly the giddy limit." It was an expression that even well-brought-up girls, from high-class English backgrounds, would not use these days. Maybe, Bond considered, these two were old KGB. A pair of Moscow squirrels. He thought about it, then rejected the notion. Ks would only talk in the open, even if they did have the car wired: especially in these days of change, when they would not want to incur wrath from their new boss. The new chairman of the KGB had most recently cleaned out their colleagues in the MVD—Internal Affairs cops.

"You would prefer to get out in the open?" Sprat asked.

"I'd simply prefer to get out. As far as I can see, we have nothing in common."

In the short silence which followed, a spark seemed to leap across the car: a small lightning bolt, arcing between the girl and Sprat.

"You came in on the Ost-West Express from Berlin. You don't deny that?"

"Of course not, though I could've joined the train in Moscow."

"No, it was Berlin. The Zoo."

"Okay."

"And two dead people were removed from that train at Aachen?"

"I wouldn't know."

"You're saying you have no knowledge of two murdered men taken by local ambulances from Aachen station?"

"Not a clue."

"Really? You traveled with a woman, yes?"

"No, I traveled alone. There were women on the train, but I did not actually travel with one. Chance, as they say, would be a fine thing."

"You still traveled with a woman. Who was she, Captain Bond?"

"I really don't know what you're talking about."

"You came to Paris," snapped Sprat, or whatever his name was, "to meet Praxi. You flew from England to Berlin. Then by train to Paris. The object was to meet with Praxi."

"You're way out, Jack. Don't know a Praxi. You got the bit about London-Berlin-Paris right."

"Okay, if you didn't come to Paris to meet Praxi . . ." She realized, too late, that she had sprung a leak in her cover. "To meet me. Why *did* you come to Paris?"

"Truth or dare?"

"Truth."

"Okay. I went to Berlin to see a couple of old friends. I've come to Paris strictly for the fun."

"Really?"

"Yes, really. Look, I don't particularly care for this inquisition. I don't even know what it's about."

Sprat gave an unpleasant little laugh. "You don't have any option. Why *did* you come to Paris?"

"Look, I have a few days' leave. I planned to do the rounds. I've got friends here, also I thought I'd go to the Louvre and, possibly, the Lido. Just for old times' sake."

"Nothing else?"

"Maybe lunch at Fouquet's. Possibly a trip to Maxim's."

"You're saying that you're not here on business?"

"What business could I possibly have in Paris?"

"You deny that you're a British intelligence officer?" The girl took over. They were a quick-fire team of interrogators.

"I don't know what it's got to do with you, Ms. Simon . . ."

". . . Simeon."

". . . but I'm a Royal Navy officer, on detachment to the Foreign Office. You want to see my credentials?"

"We know who you are, Captain Bond." This from Sprat.

He had them now, almost for certain, and they were not really very good. DGSE. The French Foreign Intelligence Service. In fact, he realized why Sprat was familiar. The man had worked out of the French Embassy in London for a season. The French are notoriously touchy about any other country's intelligence service operating on their turf. So, given the recent history, they were either working on direct orders from French Intelligence, or—just possibly—from Wolfgang Weisen. The man was supposed to have contacts everywhere, so why not in French Intelligence?

"Look . . ." the girl began.

"No," Bond turned to her with a smile. Then he glanced at Sprat, sharing a small amount of the smile with him. "No, *you* look. I don't know what you think. Or even why you think it. I am here, in Paris, to enjoy myself. Plain and simple. If you really have problems with that, why don't we all go straight to la Piscine and play with the grown-ups—the people I usually gamble with when I'm here on business."

There was a slight jolt as the driver hit the brakes a little too hard. The Piscine was the name everyone gave to the cheerless ten-story headquarters of the DGSE at 128 Boulevard Mortier in north-east Paris. It was situated next door to the large mu-

nicipal swimming pool on the Rue des Tourelles. Hence la
Piscine.

After a count of around ten, the girl spoke again. This time
the friendliness had gone from her voice. "There's no need.
We'll put you off wherever you want to go. However, I'm serving
notice on you, Captain Bond. You have twenty-four hours. One
day. If you're not out of Paris—out of France—by this time
tomorrow, you will be picked up, put on a plane and sent back
to London with a flea in your ear. Also a formal note of protest
to your government."

"I would prefer to stay on for a couple of days."

"We would rather you didn't stay in the country any longer.
I would prefer you to be out by tonight, but I have an unfortunate tendency to be soft-hearted." She did not even look at
him.

"Particularly with *Misanthrope* coming. . . ." Sprat bit off the
sentence.

"Enough! Twenty-four hours," the girl intervened crossly, as
though Sprat had somehow overstepped a hidden boundary.

The car pulled up to the roadside, a symphony of angry
motor horns in its wake. They were on the Quai des Tuileries
in a no stopping area.

"There's still time for you to take in the Louvre," said Sprat
maliciously. "Only ten minutes walk, if that. Please take us
seriously, Captain Bond."

He took them seriously. He always took the French seriously.
Hotel guests still had to fill in a little card, with details and
passport number, when they checked in. The local cops picked
up the cards during the night and ran them through a central
computer. They knew where every visitor was staying in France,
and it was information which had led to many an arrest. In spite
of the European Community, which was not truly off the
ground yet, the French were even more suspicious about visitors than the Brits. In the United Kingdom hard-liners were
forever suggesting the government should use the French
method, which kept tabs on everyone. French citizens were

forced to carry identity cards which, in Bond's book, was no bad thing given the criminal and terrorist rate.

"Thanks for the ride," he said as the door slammed shut and the car drew away.

Out of the corner of his eye, he realized another car had also stopped and was just rejoining the traffic. Its license plate was familiar. During the ride with the French Intelligence people—if that was what they were—part of Bond's mind had been taking in the surroundings. In particular he had noted car license plates as they passed, or drew alongside. It was a trade-craft reflex. If the plate appeared more than once, then someone was probably accompanying them. Such was the car now heading after Sprat and the girl.

He glanced behind him, as though getting his bearings. Several people were in view, on the edge of the Tuileries Gardens, and he had one of them marked immediately. A woman wearing a raincoat, which was probably reversible. She also had a Hermès scarf on her head, and did not carry a handbag, or even a shoulder bag, which is unusual in women; yet usual in watchers, who carry accessories in their pockets. Handbags, large purses and shoulder bags—like shoes—are difficult to change.

He set off to cross the Tuileries Gardens, seemingly oblivious to little Ms. Hermès, who gave the impression that she was not going in his direction. How many more pairs of eyes would be watching? He had no idea, and they would be difficult to flush out in an open space like the Tuileries. If he walked with some purpose, he could be back on the Rue de Rivoli—into the métro station—in a matter of minutes. Though he needed speed, Bond did not want to hurry. It would be out of keeping, even in late afternoon with the light just starting to fade.

The Tuileries Gardens was one of his favorite places in Paris, with its wonderful formal layout, and the beauty of its trees, pools and statuary. The gardens were a place to linger, though the ghosts of historic violence remained in this otherwise peaceful place. Massacre, riot, romantic escape had all happened here, in this spot, where Queen Catherine de' Medici had built the now vanished Tuileries Palace.

The palace had once stood between the two great projecting western pavilions of the Louvre, visible to his right. Only the Arc de Triomphe du Carrousel remained. Strangely, he always felt a merge of past and present here, as though phantoms from another life were able to dodge seamlessly through the mirror of time to mingle with the present. Queen Catherine had never lived in the palace, because of a warning from her astrologer, who, it seemed, had been correct. The history was a long tale of death and destruction, ending with the sacking and burning of the palace in the 1870s.

Now the gardens appeared peaceful on the surface: a place for strolling lovers and nannies with their charges. Bond had known other, more sinister, times when the past seemed very close.

As he glanced at the archway to his right, his memory was assaulted by other incidents, other dangers. He recalled several meetings here, among the flowers and serene statues. That was one summer, years before, and the meetings were with an agent they were running out of the Russian Embassy. There was an even worse day, at the height of the Cold War, when the tourists, lovers and pram-pushing nannies turned out to be a team from his old adversary, SMERSH. On that occasion they were out for his life.

The past almost became the present for him now. He quickened his pace, and felt the danger, his throat dry with the knowledge of death stalking close behind him; the old sense of urgency, and the thought that he might be outgunned and outnumbered. The fear returned, and with it the instinct that his life could be forfeit this time. On that former occasion, he had headed through the arch and across to the Louvre, where he ran them a melancholy dance through the many floors and galleries. He had even killed two of the SMERSH death squad: right there among the Egyptian Antiquities on the ground floor. He smelled the blood again, and saw the bodies—one of

111

them a Russian woman who looked as though she was an ordinary wife and mother. He had killed her, silently with a knife, and dispatched her partner by breaking his neck from behind. With the woman there had been a lot of blood and he had never quite forgotten it. The vivid mental picture brought bile into his mouth.

Now, he did not have time to do the same diversion into the Louvre. He did not even know how many pairs of eyes were on him. But he did sense the proximity of death; the whiff of a violent end in the autumn evening.

He made straight towards the Rue de Rivoli, and the Tuileries métro station. By the time he reached the entrance he was certain he had thrown the girl with the Hermès scarf, but he had no way of knowing how many others were nearby. Everyone was a potential enemy, and he scanned his fellow travelers, looking for the telltale signs of danger. Everything around him seemed magnified and even malignant—from the clatter of echoing footfalls, the buzz of conversation, the shouts of the raucous, the sweet and sour smell of humanity trapped underground, the sudden blasts of wind bellowing from the tunnels, to the clamor of the trains themselves.

At the Opéra station he changed trains, plunging into the crowds, heading towards one platform, then going back in the opposite direction, convinced that he had marked two people on his tail: a man and a woman he had spotted before. They rode in the same compartment with him as far as the Gare du Nord, where they both did a quick change somehow: reversible coats, eyeglasses, a carrier bag heavy in the man's hand. But the woman still carried a bulky shoulder bag, and he could almost see the weapon inside it.

Eventually he threw them on the station concourse, ducking from one platform to another: onto a train about to leave, then off again.

In all it took an hour—riding the métro, changing trains, using every trick of surveillance throwing—before he was one hundred percent sure he was clean. Nobody had shown up twice, and the couple who had been the most successful appeared to have vanished completely. By this time he had reached the Trocadero station, only a ten-minute walk to his goal, a small hotel which lay off the Avenue Kléber, a stone's throw from the Arc de Triomphe.

The Hotel Amber had been owned and run by the same family since the end of World War II. Three generations of Ambers had actively operated this comfortable, pleasant, if small, hotel in a quiet backwater. Indeed, the current manager, Antoine Amber, was the grandson of the founder—a man who had been with Section F, the French Section, of SOE: the Special Operations Executive which had run resistance, intelligence and sabotage groups in Nazi-occupied France.

Antoine's parents and grandparents had left Paris for a warmer retirement in the shadow of the Alpes Maritimes, but Antoine, and his wife, Dulcie, had known James Bond for years, and under a dozen different names. In a simple sense they were, like their ancestors, working assets of the British Secret Intelligence Service: assets who had never been either discovered or suspected by the omnipresent French counter-intelligence organization: the murky DST. The Ambers were living proof that allies mistrust each other, and run the secret gauntlet even in the heart of mutual friendship. Suspicion within the European Community is as strong as the mistrust between long-standing enemies. It is one of the facts which assures that the game of espionage will go on until the end of time.

Rarely did the Ambers refuse a member of the SIS, and when Bond arrived on this evening, he was greeted with delight, shrouded in that reserve which was necessary to secrecy. He registered as James Bates, a computer-software salesman: an identity he had never used in France until now. Then, in a pleasant second-story room, he briefed Antoine about the other guests who would eventually arrive, and the young man assured him that they would all be safe.

Alone, Bond went into the bathroom and looked into the mirror. He hardly recognized the reflection staring back at him. His hair was tousled, and his eyes showed the strain of the past twenty-four hours: They looked bleak and tired with dark smudges below them. He needed a shave and shower. He needed sleep, but there was little time. Even if Sprat and the girl were dogs set on him by Weisen, it was necessary to take them seriously. The team he had thrown off was dangerous. He had felt the hot breath of their killer instinct on the back of his neck and, if he was not careful, they might find him again. Next time luck could run out.

He was also certain that, if the pair in the car were honest-to-goodness French Intelligence, or even the more malign Security Service, he had to make some show of leaving the country. A day. Less now.

Bond splashed cold water over his face, then went into the bedroom, sat down and dialed the Sofitel Hotel at Orly airport, asking for Martha Grazti. Easy St. John was on the line seconds later.

"James, what happened? I've been . . ."

He cut her off quickly. "No time for talk. Things've got tricky. How tired are you?"

"I'm okay."

"There's a lot to do. You'll have to keep your eyes open. Now, listen carefully." He gave the instructions clearly, telling her to take a cab to the Montparnasse station. "Get a porter. Take all your luggage." She was then to board the next train to Chartres. "They run about every hour. Just ride and watch your own back. Get off at Chartres and wait for the next train back to Paris. It's less than an hour's run. Don't return on the train that takes you out. Wait and watch, then ride back. You have to be certain nobody's with you. If it's clear, you get a cab at the Gare Montparnasse and come straight here." He gave her the address of the Hotel Amber.

"What if . . . ?"

"If they *are* on to you, call me on this number. Ask for Bates." He rattled off the digits. "Then head for the hills—which means go to the Sofitel at Charles de Gaulle airport. They

114

might have a team there, but we'll have to take a chance on it. If the worst comes to the worst, I'll join you there, and we'll get the hell out on the first flight back to London."

"What about Harry?"

"Don't concern yourself with Harry."

When he was satisfied she understood everything, he called the Crillon and asked a helpful girl to page Maurice Charpentier. There was a long wait. Then a male voice came on the line.

"You are waiting for a M. Charpentier?" The voice was one of authority.

"Yes."

"I am the duty manager. You are a friend to M. Charpentier?"

"Yes, I'm supposed to meet him. I'm running late."

"Then I have some unpleasant news. There has been an accident, Monsieur. Outside the hotel. M. Charpentier was not a guest with us . . ."

"I know. He was with a friend. I was coming over to see them."

"I'm sorry, Monsieur. M. Charpentier is all right. His friend, a M. Rivière, was killed. It is most . . ."

"How?" He heard the shock in his own voice.

"Unfortunate, Monsieur. It is not the kind of thing that happens near our hotel. It is unpleasant. M. Rivière was stabbed. He died just outside our main entrance. The police seem uncertain of how it happened. Possibly a mugger, but here it is unusual. There were problems.."

"And my friend? M. Charpentier?"

"He is still with the police. There were some plainclothes men, who were a little rough with him."

A voice in his head told Bond to get off the line now.

"I heard one of them say something about taking him to the Rue des Saussaies . . ."

Bond heard no more for he quickly replaced the receiver. The headquarters of the Direction de la Surveillance du Territoire—the DST—was at number 11 Rue des Saussaies, and

115

the DST had one of the most efficient telephone-tapping organizations in the world. They ran their telephone surveillance
out of a large office close to the great military museum at Les
Invalides. He had been on the telephone to the Crillon for a
good two minutes. It was possible that they had traced his
number. He was not going to hang around and find out.

Grabbing his briefcase, Bond went downstairs and out into
the night.

Harry was with the DST. Harry's friend, the jockey, whom he
did not know from Adam, was dead. Harry had given him a
telephone number which he was to call and ask for Peggy Jean,
in English. This, Harry had claimed, would put him in direct
contact with Praxi Simeon, but he wanted to take her by surprise for there were too many unknowns about Praxi Simeon,
Sulphur of the Cabal network.

Out on the street, he headed straight for the Avenue Kléber,
and headed towards the Place Charles de Gaulle and the Arc de
Triomphe, crossing the wide road and walking quickly. The
temperature was dropping and the usual evening rush hour
was in full swing, the streets clogged with traffic. He paused at
cafés and shopfronts two or three times, crossed the road, and
recrossed at two points, still checking that he was alone.

Finally he turned right into the Rue Copernic, then left into
La Perouse, praying that the post office had not yet closed. It
had not, and he changed notes into a pile of change, then
waited for one of the telephone booths to become vacant.

Inside he dialed the direct number of the Secret Intelligence
Service's resident at the Paris Embassy. The line, he knew, was
secure, even from the snooping operation at Les Invalides.

"Bruton et Hicks." A female secretary answered.

"Predator." Bond gave his international work code.

"Un moment, Monsieur."

There was a click on the line, then: "Ecstasy."

"Predator."

"How's the weather?"

"There's a storm coming up. South cones have been hoisted."

"Can I help?"

"I want a reverse directory address on this number." He slowly recited the digits Harry Spraker had given him.

It took less than a minute. The address was an apartment building, off the Champs Elysées near the Lutheran church. "Apartment Fifteen," he was told. Less than quarter of an hour's walk. He spun it out to a full half hour, going through the routines like a man whose life depended on it: which it probably did. Every sense was strained to detect the unusual. The events of the afternoon had unnerved him. He could not remember when he had felt so vulnerable.

The apartment building was in the *de luxe* class, with a doorman who looked like a former heavyweight champion, and a reception desk from behind which two security guards eyed him with open suspicion.

He took no notice, going straight for the internal phone which sat in a small alcove just inside the door.

One of the security men called out, asking if he needed help, and Bond just shook his head, dialing 1–5. There was no way he was going to use Harry's "Peggy Jean" code. He would stick to the one given to them in London.

The voice that answered sent a tiny frisson up the back of his neck, as though a piece of ice had been run against the grain of the short hairs. It was the kind of female voice which he loved best and came across rarely. A voice that sounded like a magnificent instrument, the deeper notes of a cello, perhaps.

"Hallo?" One word, two syllables that dipped musically.

"Can I speak to Carlotta?"

"Who wants her?" No hint of suspicion, just the music, now covering three notes rising and falling.

"My name's Joe Bain. I met her at a conference last year . . ."

117

"That would be in Boston, yes?" The merest hint of an accent, hardly a touch.

"Yes, Boston. We shared a car from the airport and I promised I would look her up whenever I was in Paris. I work for Dombey and Company."

"Of course. Come up. It'll be nice to see you again."

"I think you'll need to tell the Guardians down here, before they'll allow me to even get into the elevator."

"I'll call straight down. Wait until their phone rings, then walk to the reception desk. It'll be fine."

The line was disconnected, and he put down the receiver very slowly, and very deliberately picked up his briefcase.

The telephone at the reception console rang and one of the security men answered, giving Bond the fish-eye.

"You may go up, Monsieur. Fifteen's on the second floor."

He nodded and walked to the elevator. The doors opened as silently as he had ever heard elevator doors. The carpet under his feet seemed ankle deep, and the car moved up without a sound.

He saw the light wink on for the first floor, but did not even feel the car stop. When the doors opened, his hand was nowhere near the ASP automatic, rammed against the small of his back.

The man who came in was tall, even distinguished-looking, well-dressed in a tailored grey suit. He wore the striped tie of a regiment that Bond could not identify. The pistol in his hand was easier: a Browning Compact, the one with the very short butt that was still capable of firing full-power 9mm Parabellum cartridges. One shot would make a large hole, leaving a high portion of Bond splattered over the glass.

"You understand that we have to take precautions." He spoke English with a distinct American accent.

"Of course." He sounded edgy, and why not. Once in twenty-four hours could be plain bad luck. Twice was inefficiency.

When the doors next glided open, the view had improved dramatically.

118

She wore a white silk shirt and beautifully cut white slacks. A broad snakeskin belt, with an ornate buckle helped show off the narrow waist, and her eyes seemed huge: brown with long lashes that were a gift from God, not a purchase from Estée Lauder.

"Vanya?" she asked, her cello soaring over the one word.

Bond nodded, glancing down at the shoes, which matched the belt and did not come from a chain store.

> *"Yet, having always drifted on the raft*
> *Each night, always without provision,*
> *Loathing each night."*

It was the way any poem should be spoken. She would have made a good actress. Perhaps, indeed, that was what she was.

Bond replied with the IFF answerback. The same one he had tested on the girl in the car:

> *"A bracelet invisible*
> *For your busy wrist,*
> *Twisted from silver."*

"Oh, it's good to meet you, *Vanya,"* she said, and Bond had to force himself to remember that, if this was, at last, Praxi Simeon, she would have a large number of questions to answer. At her apartment door, he asked the first one.

"Praxi, a small question. Would you introduce me to your friend the gunman?"

She laughed and invisible silver seemed to shimmer around her. "Of course, but you must know already. This is *Tester,* Heini Spraker, though he prefers to be called Harry."

This might just be the end of a promising friendship, Bond thought.

9

Death on Wheels

James Bond did his best to suppress the anxiety which en-
veloped his mind and turned his stomach over in unpleasant,
lazy, drooping circles. There were so many question marks
against Praxi Simeon already, and now he was faced with this
new, unbelievable, claim that the man with her was *Tester*—
"Harry" Spraker.

He had been with Harry right up to the time they had arrived
in Paris. The man he knew as Harry had provided the correct
IFF code—something so individually secret it was unlikely to
have been given to anyone else. The Harry he knew fitted the
description, and had assisted before, and during, the journey
from Berlin. He had also given Bond the telephone number of
this apartment—Praxi Simeon's apartment—and now, it
seemed, *that* Harry was in the hands of the DST.

It felt longer, but, in less than three seconds, Bond's mind
flashed through a series of pictures and conversations. Harry
Spraker, *Tester*, and their first meeting at the Kempi. The ex-
change of codes; *Tester*'s version of the way he and Vomberg
had traced Bond and Easy from Tegel to the hotel; the story of
the death of *Mab*, Oscar Vomberg; his version of the events
which had led to the deaths of the original *Vanya* and *Eagle;* the
identification and sapping of the former Stasi man, Korngold,

directly outside the Kempinski; the fingering of the strange pair of thugs, Felix Utterman and Hexie Weiss, on the train; his lack of emotion on learning that Bond had killed them: two ex-Stasi enforcers who had once worked for the HVA under Wolfgang Weisen. All this, plus the physical description committed to memory in London. He heard Easy's voice as she had parroted that delineation:

"Exactly six feet; well-built; muscular; full dark hair; complexion dark; eyes black; very piercing look. Small scar, in the shape of a bracket, just to the right of his mouth."

With a smile he turned towards the man who now claimed to be *Tester*, to see he was quietly sliding the magazine from the butt of the Browning Compact, clearing the breech and putting the weapon on a side table near the door, the magazine protruding from the butt: safe and unloaded.

Bond looked him up and down, lingering on his face. It was all there: height, curly dark hair, the black eyes, striking and twinkling. As he looked at Bond, the new claimant to *Tester*'s name appeared to duplicate the piercing look that had been described in London—a look he had first detected in the Kempi with the man he had known, until now, as Harry Spraker. There was also the scar, the curved bracket to the right of his mouth, though on this man's face the mark was more pronounced, telling of a deeper wound.

"Give me your IFF," Bond said, hearing a somewhat overstated calm in his own voice.

"Again?"

"What d'you mean, again?"

"We established bona fides in Berlin, when you called me. Poor old Vomberg gave you the number."

Bond sighed. "I've never spoken to you in my life, *Tester*. Now you say that I called you in Berlin?"

"Just after Vomberg telephoned, telling me to meet him."

"Where were you to meet him?"

"Charlottenburg U-Bahn station. I arrived too late. Oscar did his swan dive in front of the train just as I spotted him."

121

"And you didn't call me back?"

"I got hold of Praxi. Here in Paris. . . ."

"And I told him to get the hell out." Praxi was beginning to look edgy, her eyes flicking around the room: from Bond to the door, then towards the table where the little Browning Compact lay, and back to Bond again. "He was in obvious danger, and I felt it might be linked to you. I even flashed London, asking them for another, definite, identification. It was the first time I'd spoken with London since Cabal scattered. I broke the rules to check you out."

"They reply?"

"Yes. They said you had an emergency password, should there be any doubts about your identity, or the new *Eagle*. London knew we needed extra safeguards. They told me to trust you. We're all pretty paranoid."

That was true enough. Almost at the last minute, M had given both of them a single password and ID. "It'll be used in an emergency only," the Old Man had told them. Then he had banished Bond from his office while he went through the final safeguard with Easy. She was removed while he gave the words to Bond.

"And?" he now asked.

"Vainglorious," Praxi said firmly. The word could only have come directly from M. Nobody else was privy to it.

"Systematic arch." These were the words given to him alone.

"Correct. You *should* be *Vanya.*"

"I am *Vanya.*" But he could still read doubt in her eyes, possibly reflected from his own.

He turned to *Tester*, or whoever he was, and asked him to give his IFF, "Even though you think you already spoke with me."

The man shrugged, then recited:

> *"Of modern methods of communication;*
> *New roads, new rails, new contacts, as we know*
> *From documentaries by the GPO."*

Bond nodded and, for the sake of things, repeated the answerback, just as he had done at the Kempi with the other Harry Spraker.

"May, with its light behaving
Stirs vessel, eye and limb
The singular and sad."

"Correct," the possible pretender nodded. "Now we all know who we are."

"Maybe not." The ASP was out and in his hand, moving in a manner that could not be mistaken. The pistol ordered this *Tester* to go and stand next to Praxi Simeon. "Now sit down, both of you. On the couch."

"Shit," Praxi's eyes flared. "I knew it was all wrong. This damned . . . You're straight from little Wolfie, I suppose."

"Just sit. And, no. No, I'm not from Weisen."

In spite of the apartment being in a *de luxe* building, it was strangely utilitarian. There were no pictures on the walls, only those dull squares and oblongs, outlined with dust showing where pictures had once hung. The furniture was also on the light side—two tables: the small one by the door, on which the Browning Compact now lay; and another low, glass-topped, standing as a kind of centerpiece in front of a black leather couch. Two chairs, in similar black leather, made up the furnishings. On the table there was one white telephone and a big glass ashtray. Underfoot, an off-white deep pile carpet. Matching curtains hung at the three long windows which ran across one wall. The center one was a sliding glass door which led to some kind of balcony. The city's lights spread out behind it, twinkling and deceptively peaceful. There were also three doors leading off this main room. A pair of bedrooms and a kitchen, he thought.

"So where do we go from here?" Praxi's musical voice now contained a note of bitterness. "You people have all of us but one—unless you've already wasted *Ariel*?"

"If he's a little fellow, looks like a jockey, he's gone, but it wasn't done by friends of mine."

"Oh, Jesus!" Praxi was praying, not indulging in blasphemy. From the back of his mind Bond again heard the original Harry Spraker say, "I believe Praxi, the one called *Ariel*, and myself are the only three left."

"The jockey was *Ariel?*" Bond asked, though he knew this could not be. The files he had read in London described *Ariel* as a big bruiser of a man: formerly on the bodyguard detail at Karlshorst, tending to visiting Soviet bigwigs or baby-sitting high-ranking KGB or HVA officers. *Ariel* was what the old secret jargon of the Cold War called a Lion Tamer.

Praxi shook her head, confirming Bond's thoughts. "No, *Ariel*'s very large. He was the real muscle employed by Cabal. It's one of the reasons you haven't got him yet." She gave a short laugh. You could almost taste the sharp wormwood and gall on the air behind the sound. "A man who looks like a jockey?" She turned to the man who claimed to be *Tester*.

"Could be Dmitri. You know him. Axel's friend. I told you Axel was hanging around Tegel when we fingered this one and the woman coming in from London."

"And who is Axel?" There was a new tension in the air. It was as though a further dimension of uncertainty had been added to a situation already faced by both Praxi and the man.

It was Praxi who answered. "Axel Ritter. One of the Poison Dwarf's top operators."

"By the Poison Dwarf, you presumably mean Wolfgang Weisen . . . ?"

She nodded, and her companion spoke. "He worked very closely with both Weisen and the Haardt woman. You *do* realize that Cabal's been well and truly penetrated by those two?"

"It had crossed my mind, but I honestly have to tell the pair of you that there is an entire encyclopedia of questions you're going to answer. You're both prime suspects . . ."

"You're joking . . ." from Praxi.

"This is crazy!" The new *Tester* looked bewildered. "*Us?* With

Ariel we're about the only ones who can be trusted. Apart from the others who've already died."

"The problem is that you're the ones left alive. If Cabal was penetrated—and we all know it was—the persons responsible wouldn't be dead. As far as any mole's concerned, death would take some well-earned leave. A vacation . . ."

He was cut short by the sound of a telephone ringing from behind one of the other doors. It rang three times and then stopped.

"That the emergency number? The 800?" Bond asked.

Praxi nodded; she had gone as white as the silk shirt she wore, and looked thoroughly shaken. "London provided it, through *Vanya*—that is the original *Vanya.* It has an interface box which means I can plug it into any modular jack, anywhere in the world, and it will be live, secure, scrambled and have its own number. That's what he said, anyway."

Bond knew what she was talking about. Major Boothroyd and his assistant, in Q Branch, had demonstrated the package of electronics a couple of years ago. Everyone had been very pleased, for it now meant anyone in the field could have a constant unique number: anywhere, even in a hotel bedroom. It would be a boon of great proportions to those members of the intelligence community who actively fought terrorism.

"We've been without it for quite a while." Praxi seemed to be explaining something important, and it now struck Bond that they were outstaying their welcome in this apartment. If the man he had known as Harry Spraker had talked, down on the Rue des Saussaies, they could be having visitors any time now. London station did not have the monopoly on reverse telephone directories.

He backed towards the door, lifted the Browning Compact from the table, slammed the magazine home, and slipped it into the pocket of his slacks. After all, that was what it had been designed for: a pocket pistol. "I have to make a telephone call," he said. "I also think we should see what's come in on the 800 number. Before we do any of that, I should warn you of two

125

things. First, any little tricks and I'll kill you: whether you're real or fake. I can't take chances. If you happen to be the real thing, then *I've* been blown out of the water because I've spent the past twenty-four hours or so with another Harry Spraker . . ."

The sound of a sharp intake of breath came from Praxi Simeon, while the other *Tester* cursed.

"Second," Bond continued, "if you do happen to be the genuine article, I don't think it'll be long before we have visitors. The man I knew as Harry Spraker gave me this telephone number, and he's now probably handed it on to others who are less scrupulous than myself. I'm talking DST, and they can be vicious. When they throw you into their interrogation rooms down at 11 Rue des Saussaies, they rarely inform your embassy."

He told Praxi to go and get the 800 telephone. He knew the thing came as one complete and portable unit which would fit into a briefcase, leaving room to spare. Her companion should go with her, he said, and they would both move very slowly, keeping well apart and with their hands firmly on top of their heads, fingers laced. "Except, that is, for the time Praxi needs to unhook the machine. And please don't do anything stupid, because I'm not joking. I *will* shoot first and ask questions later. If you're survivors, you'll do as I ask."

They did exactly as they were told. Neither of them seemed inclined to take any actions that might nudge Bond into violence. Praxi unplugged the slim black console and carried it, as though it were a live bomb, into the main room where Bond told her to plug the electrics into a wall socket, so that the recorder would have the necessary power.

After she had rewound the tape, she pressed the "play" button, and the usual subdued background crackle came through the built-in speaker. Then the beep, followed by:

"Phantom, this is Ghoul . . ." in German.

"Ariel," Praxi whispered as the voice continued:

". . . There are problems with *Vanya* and *Eagle*. They came off the Berlin train separately, and with an old friend shepherd-

126

ing them. Axel Ritter was on the same train, and I don't know if they were aware or not. Axel had made some major changes to his appearance which'll interest *Tester*. He's never had sight of me, so I got close enough to see he wore contact lenses to change his eye color, and he had a little fake scar just where *Tester* has one. If you see *Tester*, tell him that it looked like a pinprick compared to his. He hung around the station for a while, and *Vanya* went across the road for lunch at the Terminus Nord. But Axel had another old friend in tow: Dmitri. I don't know his proper name. Little fellow. Looks like a jockey: worked the streets for Weisen before the Wall came down.

"They did a kind of brush pass, exchanging a few words, then Axel went out of the station again. I followed *Vanya*. Not close enough, but he was picked up by a couple of other people in the Faubourg St. Honoré. I think he had been in the Place Vendôme. A tall guy jumped him in the St. Honoré. The guy was well-dressed. Grey topcoat and a homburg. A bit of a macaroni. I think he had a gun on *Vanya*, but I couldn't be certain. All I know is that they both got into a car. There was a woman in the back, and they drove away pretty fast. I didn't get close enough for a proper identity, but the car was one of those Hondas the DST use. There's more . . ." He paused, as though collecting his thoughts. German was obviously his first language, and he spoke intelligently, occasionally sounding amused by what he was saying.

"I would've called sooner, only I've been monitoring the police frequency. There was a stabbing outside the Crillon, and from the stuff I heard, it sounded as though Axel and Dmitri were involved so I went over there to take a look.

"Dmitri's dead, and the cops've taken Axel downtown, only they don't sound like ordinary cops. I did my usual interested-crime-reporter-on-vacation act with the doorman there. He's got a runaway mouth, and told me the cops sounded like DST—you know them, equivalent of the old Stasi, leaning towards MI5, but not very much. They snoop. Very strong on wiretaps so I would be careful. I've no idea where *Vanya* or

Eagle have gone. For all I know *Vanya*'s down at the Rue des Saussaies with Axel, or even out at la Piscine. The people in the car could just as well have been DGSE. I'll be in my usual place at midnight if you want to make contact. Good luck."

The tape went dead.

"Where's his usual place?" Bond asked.

"A bistro in Montmartre." Praxi was blinking back tears. "He's known there, but it looks like we're all in trouble."

"And some." Bond picked up his briefcase. "I'm sorry, but I'm going to have to search both of you. I don't want you going off like loose cannons. Now, you'll both have to assume the position—as they say in the U.S. of A.—against the wall."

They knew what he meant, and, leaning against the wall, palms flat and legs spread, they submitted to Bond's careful frisking. He apologized again, particularly to Praxi. They were clean.

"Now, is this the only safe house you have in Paris?"

Tester said, "Yes," and Praxi nodded. "I have a case packed for emergencies," she added.

"Let's get it, then. What about you?" to *Tester*.

"Just what I'm standing up in. I've got a case with spare clothes in a locker at the Gare de Lyon. It can wait."

"It'll have to wait." Bond indicated they should both follow Praxi as she got her case, which turned out to be a small airline carryon. She also brought out a briefcase into which she put the 800 telephone. Then, after shrugging herself into a heavy, military-style street coat, in burgundy suede, they all headed out of the door.

"Your phone call?" she queried as they waited at the elevator.

"Downstairs, or even further away. If your friend Axel has been performing arias to the DST, their people at Les Invalides could've been activated, which means the telephone up here might now have ears." He felt the anxiety rise again, almost out of control. Experience jabbed at his mind. Maybe they were already too late. The feeling was very strong, and he told the others to make straight for the door. "Tip the security people as well, you have money?"

"Some." *Tester* dug into his pockets.

"Give it to Praxi. Pass out very large helpings. You might also suggest to them that if people come looking for us, they should all suffer sudden amnesia."

Down in the foyer nothing stirred, except for the security guards and the pugilistic doorman. Praxi spread largesse around as though she had just won the lottery. She also had muttered conversations with both of the guards and the doorman. As they left everyone was very polite, in that manner which suggests that money does not only talk, but can also buy silence.

It was much colder outside now, and Bond hunched against the brisk east wind which had started to slice through the streets.

They walked quickly, taking side roads rather than staying on the major arteries. He did not tell them where they were going, but he was heading in the general direction of the Hotel Amber, taking the scenic route, and looking for public telephones on the way. Finally, having accepted Praxi and *Tester* as at best genuine, at worst too frightened to try anything, he made them duck into the Victor Hugo métro station, where there is a large bank of public telephones.

He told them to stand where they were visible to him, and let them know he was still in earnest about shooting first. With one hand on the Browning in his pocket, he used the other to lodge the receiver under his chin, insert coins and dial the Hotel Amber.

Antoine picked up on the fourth ring.

"It's one of your guests, Jim Bates," Bond told him in French. "Any messages for me?"

"Your package has arrived." Antoine meant that Easy had checked in.

"Nothing else?"

"Nothing I can see."

"Would you like to take a look? In the street. Perhaps other people are waiting for me. They might even have a car parked illegally, or be on foot."

"Just give me a moment, sir."

He waited for a good ninety seconds.

"Nobody. *Rien.* All clear."

"I'll be bringing a couple of friends, and we'd like dinner in my room."

"It can be arranged. Don't worry."

Bond led them down Rue Copernic, past the Liberal Synagogue, and onto the Avenue Kléber once more.

"You are starting to trust us a little, I think." Praxi's voice had become more normal: the cello notes as pleasing to Bond as when he first heard them on the telephone.

"Don't jump to conclusions. I need an awful lot of answers. It's going to be a long night."

"You'll get all your answers."

They rounded the corner, with the Hotel Amber's entrance in sight. None of them even heard the van until it passed them, pulling sharply in, over the curb, blocking their progress. It was a maroon Toyota Previa: the one with the streamlined nose, large enough to carry two families, a dog and a couple of spare geishas.

The driver's and front passenger's doors opened, and the panel behind the driver's seat slid back. A familiar voice shouted in sharp, commanding English. "Stand still! Police! Stay where you are!"

Bond turned to see Jack Sprat, Dandy Jim, the Shadow, whatever, coming around the back of the van. He had discarded the homburg, but still wore the smart long grey overcoat. Two burly men followed in his wake, and a short little tough had climbed out of the driver's seat.

Looking past the nose of the Toyota, he saw Easy being led from the Amber's entrance, a thuggish stocky man almost dragging her, with one hand clamped tightly on her upper left arm.

"Just stand still!" Sprat barked. He then repeated the command in French and German.

"He's Weisen's man. Owned and paid for," Praxi whispered as the posse descended on them.

Bond turned to face the man who was dragging Easy. He looked at Praxi. "You haven't met," he said calmly, flapping a hand between the two women. "My dear, this is my old friend Souxi Banshee."

As his hand flapped towards Easy, he turned on the balls of his feet, making a fist, his arm whipping through the air, the fist colliding heavily with Sprat's jaw, lifting him from the pavement.

Sprat went backwards at an angle, the long coat flapping as his head hit the Toyota with a crunch.

One of the two men behind him sprang forward, but Bond swung his briefcase hard, with all his weight behind it. The case caught the tough straight in the conjunction of his thighs. He doubled up, curling into a ball and rolling on the pavement, moaning and shrieking in an agony known only to men. Bond kicked him hard in the face and the screaming stopped.

Sprat was out for the count—maybe forever—his pallor would have worried any passing doctor. Bond realized that the man might not make it. "What a waste of good clothes," he muttered.

He was aware of other things going on around him. Praxi had dropped her case and briefcase, springing at the second of Sprat's men, going for his face, her fingers clawing at his eyes as he desperately tried to reach for a weapon under his jacket.

Tester had gone in the opposite direction, heading around the van and making for the driver's door. The squat driver, who sported a shaved bull head, had reached the front of the van when he saw where *Tester* was heading. He turned in mid stride, heading back for the driver's seat, and was ducking to climb into the van when *Tester* came at him from behind. The driver began to turn, as *Tester* reached over his shoulder, throwing out an arm for the door, which he flipped back with intense force. The door connected with the driver's face, which had half completed the turn. It slammed into him, head on, so that the wretched man reeled back, doubling up, blood streaming from a broken nose, and his hands covering his eyes. *Tester* finished him off with a knee to the face and a couple of heavy blows to the back of the neck.

"Driven to it, I suppose," Bond smiled. Then glanced around. Easy had taken the initiative with the tough who had been hauling her by the arm. He did not see the moves but they were obviously well coordinated, for the man's arm now hung at a strange angle as she spun him around and flipped him onto his back: the whole move timed so that his head smashed against the pavement with the sound of dry sticks being broken.

Praxi had also finished off her assailant: Her hands linked behind his neck, went with his backward movement then pulled him forward, bringing her knee up to his face, then a similar action to the groin, which gave them the second screamer of the night. As he went down, she followed through with two quick chops to the back of the neck. The blows were well placed for he dropped like an animal in a slaughterhouse, and remained silent.

"Very humane, Praxi," Bond applauded.

Tester was already in the driver's seat, with the engine turning over, yelling for them to get in. As people began to spill out of the hotel and a couple of nearby cafés, the Toyota moved off. Everyone, and the luggage, on board, the vehicle picking up speed, eventually turning into the Avenue Victor Hugo and mixing with the deadly stream of traffic. No sirens sounded in their wake.

In Paris, drivers seem to be a law unto themselves, and *Tester* was no exception. "Where the hell do we go now?" he shouted, brushing dangerously near to a Citroën driven by an elderly lady who looked like death on wheels, then sashaying into the far lane, picking up more speed to overtake a bus, heading towards the race track that was the Place Charles de Gaulle, with the Arc de Triomphe at its center.

"There'll be the French equivalent of an APB out on us by now." Bond was surprised to hear himself speaking calmly. The fight around the Toyota had taken less than two minutes, and they all looked reasonably pleased with themselves. He reflected that, as a team, they *had* been impressive.

"I wouldn't be too sure about that." Praxi was breathing hard, winded, and occasionally closing her eyes as her colleague did things with the van that would not be found in any driving manual.

"The one in the grey coat is part French, part English," she said. "Ex-DGSE. Now one of Weisen's lackeys. He got bumped from DGSE for irregularities during interrogation which put him on the Poison Dwarf's wish-list straightaway."

"He was the one that caught up with me in the Faubourg St. Honoré. But it doesn't mean the cops aren't looking for us." Bond glanced back through the rear window. "Too many bystanders."

"Nobody tried to step in, though," from *Tester*. "You want to try and make the airport?"

"We'll never get anything out at this time of night, and I don't think I can raise one of my people's safe houses. Now we've crossed swords with these buggers, my Service'll deny me a dozen times over. Any other ideas?"

"Dump this thing," Easy said softly. "I have access to a place in Paris. Sleep all of us at a pinch."

They rounded the Place Charles de Gaulle for the second time. "Beat that bastard in the Lamborghini," muttered *Tester*.

"Really, I think we should dump it," Easy repeated. "I can get us a place to sleep. Safe as well as sound."

"There won't be much sleeping done tonight," Bond said grimly as *Tester* finally pulled the van into the Avenue Foch. He recalled that it was here, on this street, during the German occupation in World War II, that the gestapo had their headquarters. It was where they performed most of their diabolical interrogations. Well, he had a lot of interrogating to do before the morning.

10

Appointments with Death

Safe houses usually reek of transience. Normally they are small, ill-furnished, and exude an aura of sadness. These are places used for brief meetings by men and women with much to fear, and they contain only the appurtenances of clandestine activity. The safe house provided by Easy St. John was altogether different. For one thing it was palatial.

Dumping the van made sense, yet Bond was uncertain about the provision of a safe house—presumably supplied by Easy's masters at Langley, Virginia.

They finally abandoned the Toyota Previa in a parking lot off the Boulevard St. Michel on the Left Bank, after which they waited for fifteen minutes while Easy made a telephone call.

"An hour and a half," she said on returning. "They need an hour and a half to have the place ready." She then gave them the address, at which Bond's eyebrows shot up. *"Les Apparte-ments Atlantique?"* he queried.

"Uh-huh."

"That plush building near the Elysée Palace?"

"Apartment Twenty-six. One of the corner ones."

"With a view?"

"With a great view."

"Easy? You're sure?"

"'Course I'm sure."

"We're talking billionaire class."

"That's right." She smiled sweetly. "Did you think it was an agency property?"

"Well, yes. Naturally."

"Wrong, it belongs to Daddy's company. We always use it in Paris. Daddy does a lot of business in France."

"He does? What's he in? Private gold and diamond mines, or dodgy arms deals?"

"Something like that."

They split up, Easy with Praxi, and Bond with the man who he had become almost certain was the true Harry Spraker. He was sure nobody had them in their sights, and the four of them met up an hour later at the open-all-hours huge Pub St.-Germain-des-Prés, where they took a taxi across Paris to the luxurious Appartements Atlantique. There the doorman and reception staff greeted Easy like not only a long-lost friend, but also a kind of queen. The apartment had been fully cleaned and made ready, they assured her. The girls had been brought in especially, at this time of night, and the refrigerators—Bond noted the plural—had been stocked as Mr. St. John had suggested.

"Your father fixed it all?" Bond said to her quietly, as the elevator hurried them up to a huge and truly beautiful apartment.

"I just called Daddy and he said, 'Okay, leave it to me.' He's usually very good about these things. Lucky his people didn't have anyone staying here."

There were incredible views from the balcony windows, magnificent furnishings, marble floors, a massive kitchen with everything they required, and more.

"It should be safe to use the telephones here," Easy said, but Bond did not reply at once. He was taking a long look at the original Jackson Pollock which hung over a fourteenth-century stone mantel, imported from Lord knew what chateau.

Having already seen two Chagalls and a Picasso, he was very

impressed. Also he counted the photographs of four United States presidents who had stayed in this very flat. He considered that might just be a minus as far as security was concerned.

Easy repeated that she thought it safe to use the ordinary telephone.

"Depends what your father's really into."

"I doubt if the DST listeners would be interested."

"Who knows?" Bond decided immediately that they should not take the risk, and instructed Praxi to connect the 800 machine and call in *Ariel*.

While they were waiting for this last member of the party to arrive, Easy and Praxi prepared omelettes and a large salad. Not that it was woman's work. Easy tipped off Bond that she was trying to get closer to Praxi, a tactic which was doomed to failure. It had very quickly become obvious that the women had taken to each other as an arachnophobe would take to a tarantula. They were physically and mentally two very different people and, while they kept up a pretence of harmony, the mutual unease showed through as clear as the sun at high noon, and could be felt like a freezing dawn.

Finally, around one in the morning, *Ariel* arrived, all six foot three of him: a very visible spy with a pug-ugly face, knuckle-dragging arms and the smile of a saint. Within minutes it was obvious that he was particularly protective of Praxi and not a man to be roused. "Call me Bruin," he growled. "Like the bear, yes? I answer to Bruin from everyone. Okay?"

Of course it was okay. Bruin was not a person with whom you picked a fight, even though Bond had an inkling as to why he preferred to be called Bruin. His real name was slightly ridiculous—Karl Kuckuck. In English, Charlie Cuckoo. In London someone mentioned he was touchy on the subject.

They ate, and afterwards, when Praxi started to talk about being tired, Bond began the unpleasant part of the night's work.

"There won't be sleep," he announced. "At least not for some time. There are a heap of unanswered questions about

Cabal, and what's been going on. Our job is to make sense of the situation, and then see what has to be done."

They sat and lounged around the long, high-ceilinged, main living room, and he told them that he had to approach the whole business like a detective. "You'll have to bear with me," he said calmly. "This is essential. I'm no Sherlock Holmes, but it's going to sound as if I am. *Eagle* here'll be my Doctor Watson."

He wanted to start straight in on the deaths of the original *Vanya* and *Eagle* but felt he should not get there by the direct route.

"Praxi, I want to ask you about the *Nacht und Nebel* order. What were the protocols for this signal?" he began.

She went into a lot of detail. The *Nacht und Nebel* signal had been devised in the mid '80s. "Things got very tense at one point," she said. "So London and Washington gave us the safest method they could think of. If we received the signal, everyone was to disappear and there was to be no contact with either London or Washington. This was stressed, absolutely no attempt was to be made to get in touch with our controls. It was for our benefit, in case the controllers had been blown. I actually passed on the instructions to every agent in the Cabal network separately. I know everyone understood. Basically we were to set up bolt-holes. Places which we could run to. Places which had to remain private to each member of Cabal. I warned everyone not to say where they would go."

"And you think they all complied?"

"I'm pretty sure of it, judging by what happened after the signal arrived."

"Cabal would scatter, I realize that, but was there any stipulation about where individuals would go?"

"I don't follow."

"I mean could they stay in the East?—after all, this was set up long before the Wall came down. Or were there specific instructions to get into the West? I presume most of you *did* go into the West regularly."

"Well, I wouldn't say regularly. I suppose all of us went over a few times. *Vanya* and *Eagle* did not, as a rule, come into the East. If it was necessary, individuals went out to them, though in certain cases this was not possible. I know *Vanya* came in to debrief at least two people in the past three years. *Eagle* made occasional visits. But normally information was supplied on the spot: the usual games, dead-drops, the odd brush pass. *Vanya* and *Eagle* had drones they would use. As did Cabal. We had quite a lot of specialists who were not strictly within the Cabal network. I'm still using some of them."

Bond nodded, "And you think everyone did as they were told? They scattered as soon as the storm warning came in?"

Praxi gave a sad little smile. "In the first four months after the instruction came, we lost no less than eleven people right there in the East: four in Berlin, two had gone into Poland, three in Czecho, and a couple who had holed up in Yugoslavia."

"So, even though by that time Germany was unified again, and the other barriers had come down, it wasn't safe to stay on old Eastern Bloc turf?"

"Obviously not."

"So, Praxi, how *did* the instruction arrive? Did you get it on the 800 number or some other way?"

"You know what I did?" She chose not to pause for an answer. "I worked at the KGB facility in Karlshorst barracks. We all had Soviet military cover, so we were still there, even at the moment of reunification. I acted as liaison between KGB and the old Bulgarian Service: the Dajnava Sigurnost. During the run up to reunification the Soviets were bending backwards to show they were helping. We were all doing jobs which made it look reasonable for us to stay on—for a while at least. Everyone knew it was only a matter of time before the unit would be closed down, and I thought, maybe, London and Washington would want Cabal to stay in place while things were sorted out. *That* made sense. What happened did not make sense. I received the *Nacht und Nebel* call on my extension at Karlshorst. Highly insecure, but it was obviously a flash."

"The caller? You recognize the voice?"

"It was familiar, but I couldn't put a name to it . . ."

"Neither *Vanya* nor *Eagle?*"

"Definitely not."

"So, how did you cross-check that the order was genuine?"

"There were three built-in safeguards. All of them checkable very quickly. You must understand that if Cabal was to break and scatter, the instruction had to get to everyone very fast. In years past it was crucial. I suppose when it *did* come things were not quite so dangerous, but . . ."

"The three safeguards, Praxi?" Easy spoke for the first time.

Praxi, who back at that time had been *Sulphur*—the uncrowned leader of Cabal—frowned. "They were all there, just as both London and Washington had stipulated. One was a telephone number that would give out a disconnected tone when dialed; then a physical signal. This one was a chalk mark. A peace sign scrawled in green chalk on a wall near the Alexanderplatz. I did the telephone number as soon as I had put down the receiver after getting the original call. The chalk mark was out in the right place. I made a small detour on my way home. It was there."

"And the final one?"

"From my home I called a number we had never used before. If the *Nacht und Nebel* signal was genuine, someone at the number would recite a particular line. Shakespeare—in German, of course. The code was changed every month."

"And that turned up trumps?"

"As you would say, on the button. I still remember it. 'Words without thoughts never to heaven go.' It is from *Hamlet.*"

"I know, I saw the movie." Bond added with a hint of sarcasm, "I thought Mel Gibson was outstanding. Tell me, Praxi Simeon, how many Cabal members could have received the *Nacht und Nebel* order, and knew what to do? How to check the safeguards?"

"Four. No, five including me."

"Any of them still around, apart from you?"

She nodded towards Harry Spraker. "He knew them. The others are all gone. Two of them definitely. One we're not quite certain about."

"Who?"

"Orphan."

"Who is, or was?"

"A cop. A member of the old Vopos. A captain, by the name of August Wimper. He was also on liaison work, but between the Vopos and the Soviet military. He often reported to Karlshorst and, to tell you the truth, he went missing *before* we received any orders to break up Cabal and run. His name was always a bit of a joke."

Bond gave a tight smile. *Wimper* in German means "eyelash."

Vopo was a contraction of Volkspolizei, the so-called "People's Police" of the former East German state: the DDR. As well as performing normal police duties, the Vopos were heavily deployed along the former East/West border, particularly along the Berlin Wall.

"The other two? They're definitely dead?"

Praxi gave a quick nod and bit her lip. "I saw one of the bodies myself. The other, there is no doubt . . ."

"But you're not sure about *Orphan?*" He remembered old Oscar Vomberg telling him that *Orphan* had been dragged out of the Grand Canal in Venice only a couple of days before his first, and last, meeting with the scientist in the Kempi. He also recalled that Vomberg claimed *Sulphur*—Praxi Simeon—had passed on the information, but he was not going to tell her about *that* conversation.

"No," she answered without elaborating.

"No, why?"

There was a long silence, as if Praxi was wrestling with her conscience. At last:

"What do I call you? *Vanya?* Or something else?" She began to sound angry, her voice rising and a flush crossing her cheeks.

"I mean we all knew the real *Vanya*. We knew his proper name as well, but . . . well, he was like a father figure to us. We don't know *you* as *Vanya*. You aren't *our Vanya*, anymore than the lady here is *our Eagle*. D'you know what I mean? Or have you just come over to patch things up?"

"I know exactly what you mean." Bond sounded genuinely sympathetic, for he had experienced situations like this before. Long-term agents often formed extraordinary relationships with their controllers, or case officers. Sometimes it was like a marriage without the sex. The ties were not easily broken by death. Always there was resentment.

"You have to understand a number of things," he went on as calmly as possible. "First, you all have to realize that the so-called *Nacht und Nebel* instruction never went out. That is, it was never activated from either London or Washington. Imagine how everyone felt. Suddenly, a network—which had done incredible work during the Cold War—went dead. No explanation. Cabal just closed down. Then, old members of that network really went dead. Former agents were involved in accidents; or were overtly murdered. There was more than a natural interest. In many ways there was a kind of panic.

"Your own beloved *Vanya* and *Eagle* came out into the field again. Late on, yes. Time had passed. There were no fresh trails. Everything seemed to have gone cold. Then both *Vanya* and *Eagle* were killed within a week of each other, and you—yes, *you* Praxi—were involved on the periphery of both their deaths. You can call us what you like. Call me James, and call *Eagle* Elizabeth or Easy. Which d'you prefer?" He cut his eyes towards Easy St. John who said she really preferred being called Easy.

For the first time since Bond had begun, *Ariel,* the ham-fisted amiable giant Bruin, spoke. "You are making out that Praxi, or one of us, is traitor?" In Bruin's mouth these words came out as a threat, and Bond was conscious of the slight shift in the way Bruin moved in his chair, as though preparing to knock the hell out of somebody.

"No, Bruin. No, I'm not suggesting that any of you are, or have been, traitors. But you have to understand there are a lot of unanswered questions; a very large number of things that must be explained completely to me."

"Nobody should even think Praxi's a traitor." Bruin's smile had gone now and he looked positively evil. A little like one of the gargoyles on Notre Dame Cathedral.

"Nobody does," Easy's voice took on a soothing tone. "Just let's hear it all out, Bruin. Nobody's accusing anybody."

"Well, it's better they don't."

Bond seized the conversation again. "*Orphan,* Praxi? Kapitan August Wimper of the Volkspolizei?"

"He was one of the five who could monitor important signals. He could have as easily received the *Nacht und Nebel* signal as I. And followed up the checks. I didn't even get to tell him the order had been received."

"Any clues as to why?"

"None, except that he had a lady friend, an Italian girl he used to see regularly. Sometimes he took a weekend leave specially to meet her. He used to travel a long way just to visit her. He could get a pass with no trouble."

"You knew her?"

"No, I knew her name. Lena. She lived in Italy, near Pisa. He never told me her family name. But I have other things to say about Lena before we're through."

"You saw photographs of her?"

"No, but he would talk of her. *Orphan* was very proud of his sexual prowess. A little boastful."

"And she was the only one? He didn't run a string of girls?"

Praxi blushed. "I don't think so." A long pause, "He did try it on with me several times."

Bruin exploded. "*Schweinhund!* Praxi, you should've told me. I'd have taken care of his sex life for ever."

Bond stepped in again. "You say he wasn't around when the *Nacht und Nebel* arrived?"

"He usually let one of us know when he would be out of Berlin. This time he told nobody, and he left without leave. AWOL you call it. He never resurfaced. At least, not till three or four days ago. I had a report that a body had been pulled out of the Grand Canal in Venice. It had been in the water for some time. Days. A floater, you call that, yes?"

"A floater, yes. Bloated: been in the water for some time?"

"Yes. My contact said the remains were unidentifiable. Half the face was gone. No teeth, so dental records wouldn't help. Yet I was told that the Berlin authorities were informed it was the missing August Wimper."

"You tell anyone else?"

"Yes. Oscar Vomberg knew, also Harry here."

"And where did your information come from?"

"From Venice."

"You have a contact in Venice?"

"Several."

"Something special about Venice? Something we should know about?"

Harry Spraker laughed. "Tell him, Praxi. Tell him just how special Venice is."

"Since the scatter command, James, as you well know, Cabal has been decimated. Death by every means. Now, you see the remnants of a great network. It's like in the army when you lose a whole regiment. The few who are left swear vengeance. Well, we have sworn vengeance . . ."

"Retribution," Harry Spraker all but spat.

"Revenge!" Big Bruin's voice rose almost to a shout. It all seemed very melodramatic.

"Then you're one hundred percent certain of who's been cutting Cabal to pieces?"

"Of course we're sure. You must be sure by now, James. Wolfgang Weisen and his whore, Monika Haardt."

"How do you know this?"

"Because he swore that he would do it. Some of us knew him

well, James. I knew him, Harry also. Wolfie Weisen is a special kind of person . . .''

"The kind that needs roasting, then drawing and quartering," Harry Spraker whispered.

"Look, both of you—James and Easy. If Mischa Wolf was the cunning, the brains within the HVA, so Weisen was a power behind the throne. The man is evil, and very clever. Towards the end—when the regime was collapsing and reunification of Germany became certain, he would say constantly that, as long as he was around, every person who ever worked *against* the Communist Party, and the old state organs of the DDR, would die. At Karlshorst they knew the name Cabal. They knew it was a network. They knew we had penetrated them, and Weisen was furious.

"He's a fanatic; a devoted Communist, hard and dedicated. James, this man was a child at Joseph Stalin's court. He learned evil from the man who twisted Communism. Stalin was his hero. You should also know that he's far from alone. Yes, Weisen's gone to earth. But he has a vast army at his disposal. Do London and Washington not realize that there are men and women in Europe—especially in the old Eastern Bloc—who've given their lives to the religion? To the ideology of Communism? Do they not understand that these people are organized and ready to fight back? Or do they think the only dangerous ones are those few drunks in Moscow who completely failed to carry out a coup? Those idiots are only the tip of the iceberg. Weisen has hundreds of people, all organized in Europe, and he's not foolish enough to show his hand until he's ready . . ."

"And when he does show it," Harry took over, "it won't be just a half-cocked coup. He'll go for some major destabilization of Europe. I wouldn't put it past him to have lines out to the worst terrorist organizations, people who still want to see the Western alliance fall apart. Weisen and his people are drunk with ideals, which means in their own light they're stone-cold

145

sober, and very well organized. They also have a lot of hardware: weapons, transport, aircraft, helicopters. Weisen squirreled things away in case he needed them."

"What's all this got to do with *Orphan*—August Wimper—and Venice?"

Praxi answered. "Wolfie Weisen is holed up in Venice, James. He's sitting there pulling secret strings all over Europe."

"You know this for a fact?"

Harry Spraker's face was hard. "Certain. I've seen him there."

"So have I." Praxi's eyes glittered with anger, not at Bond or Easy, but because of the facts. "He's killed over twenty, nearly thirty, members of Cabal. He's going to kill us all if we're not careful. He nearly had you tied up. Only Weisen could've been behind Axel Ritter managing to convince you that he was Harry Spraker."

"And you think the body they pulled out of the Grand Canal might not be that of your former colleague?"

"I'd bet my life on it."

"You just might have to."

"Meaning?"

"Meaning that I think we've got to have a face-to-face with Wolfie Weisen and Monika Haardt. They're both still on the wanted list, you know."

"We should tear them apart." Like the others, Bruin sounded angry. "Just screw their heads off. Weisen would be easy. After all, he's only a munchkin."

"A man of limited stature," Bond smiled.

"*Ja,* a dwarf." Bruin pronounced it "dvave."

"Let's just take a look at Axel Ritter for a moment." Bond was anxious to get onto the deaths of the original *Vanya* and *Eagle.*

"He took you for a fool." Harry Spraker looked very serious.

"Then did he also take your friend Vomberg for a fool?"

"Meaning?"

"Oscar Vomberg was quite clear that he was working closely with you—*Tester*. He was going to bring you to me at the Kempi. Actually I saw the man you claim is Axel Ritter, while I waited for a cab at Tegel. That's what convinced me he was *Tester* when he turned up and told me Vomberg was dead. That, and the fact he fingered a former Stasi man, and disposed of him, at the Kempi." Bond continued, telling them the entire story—the two thugs on the train, Axel Ritter being drugged and showing no alarm when Bond admitted to killing Felix Utterman and Hexie Weiss.

"Axel is a hard man," Praxi said.

"He would stay in character," the real Harry Spraker added. "And we all knew Felix and Hexie. Ruthless. Weisen's enforcers. They were probably behind a large number of the killings: the deaths of former Cabal agents. You did us all a favor in killing them—if they are indeed dead."

"Oh, they're dead all right."

Praxi gave a wan little smile. "I don't believe anyone connected to Weisen is dead unless I see the body."

"I can assure you." Bond felt a cold bitterness. His pride had been bruised by the manner in which he had so easily been gulled by Axel Ritter. "Tell me, Harry. Was it really *you* working with old Vomberg? Following us at Tegel Airport when we came in?"

"Of course. Yes, I was slightly alarmed. I saw Ritter there, at Tegel. I knew there was danger."

"But *you* worked with Vomberg?"

"I told you, yes. We knew the flight numbers from the warnings posted by London. We knew you were going to be very visible, that you were booked in to the Kempi, but we were being very careful. To some extent the required silence with London had been broken. We were cautious. After all, a lot of people had died—including *Vanya* and *Eagle*. We knew Weisen was tracking us down one at a time. I was concerned that Axel was there, at Tegel. He didn't see me, though. Vomberg was watching the Kempi, and I was in telephone contact with him all the time. We were to meet later."

It was the story Vomberg had told him, at the Kempinski, before he had left to get his hand fixed; before he had left to keep his appointment with death. Bond said as much, adding that he felt responsible. "If I had taken more care, Oscar might still be alive."

Quietly, Harry Spraker said, "We all have our personal appointments with death. Perhaps it is as well that we have no foreknowledge of time and place."

"Certainly your friends *Vanya* and *Eagle* had no foreknowledge." At last, Bond was getting to the murders of Puxley and Liz Cearns. "I want to talk about that."

Praxi shifted uncomfortably. "You want to know, what?" she asked in a small voice.

Bond started with Puxley, saying they knew he had been alerted by a telephone call from *Mab*—Oscar Vomberg. "That call set up a meeting, at a club right there in Frankfurt. Der Mönch, and the face-to-face was to be with you, Praxi. With *Sulphur*."

"Yes. I don't deny that. Both *Vanya* and *Eagle* were obviously trying to make contact. London, and Washington, of course, were not sending any messages through newspapers—as they did when you came over: though we were even suspicious about that, as you know. They seemed to be standing back, just letting our former controllers search." She looked towards Harry Spraker, as though to get his confirmation. He nodded.

"So," Praxi continued. "I tried to make contact myself. I had retrieved the 800 phone by then . . ."

"You didn't leave Berlin with it?" Easy asked.

"I said we did not have the thing for quite some time. When I worked at Karlshorst, it was run around to different locations. I would have it for a while; then Harry would take over; or one of the others . . ."

"August Wimper?" Bond queried.

"Why do you ask about him?" Behind her eyes, suspicion lurked like a waiting mugger.

"He seems an interesting possibility. Did he ever control the 800 machine?"

"No. No, because he was with the Vopos, and had people in and out all the time, he was not happy to use it."

"But he did know about it?"

"Oh, yes. I don't think he ever realized that it couldn't be tapped, but he certainly knew it was in use."

"And why didn't you take it out of Berlin?"

Praxi sighed. "When the instruction came, I was in a panic. It was a serious thing, so I got out very quickly indeed . . ."

"Where did you go?"

"Freiburg . . ."

"In Switzerland?"

"Yes. I have friends there. It seemed to be the safest place for me. To start with anyway. I stayed a couple of months, then began to move around."

"But you didn't take the 800 machine with you, Praxi? That seems strange."

She shook her head. Very positive: a number of little movements to emphasize the point. "It was not in my apartment. You must understand that, within days, Weisen's people were actively seeking out members of Cabal, as if they had known all the time, and now wanted to settle the score. When I left Berlin, Weisen's men and women were watching airports and railway stations. I put the 800 into a security box at Tegel. I flew back for it. Just for the 800 unit."

"To take it where?"

"Back to Freiburg. Almost as soon as I connected it, the thing started to ring. I was aware there had been deaths, but . . ."

"How were you aware?"

"I told you, Cabal employed many extra people. Specialists. Criminals even. I had two informers who thought I was KGB.

I also had one woman, a cleaner, who regularly serviced a dead drop. She had been instructed to send things on—to a *poste restante* in Munich. From there they got to me."

"Via another of your drones?"

"Yes."

"So the circle of knowledge was wide."

"A little too wide, yes. But nobody talked. They didn't trace me. After the 800 was up and running again, I established contact with a lot of people. Genuine Cabal people. Later, when *Vanya* and *Eagle* came looking, I used Vomberg as a go-between."

"Why Vomberg?"

"Because he was the least likely person. You met him. You saw him. He was elderly, beginning to—how would you say it?—to look seedy?"

"That would describe him."

"I tracked *Vanya* to Frankfurt, and had Vomberg nearby. Yes, James. Yes, I set up the meeting at Der Mönch, but Weisen's people got to him first. All I can guess is that they already had him boxed in. The next time he went from that hotel, they would have had him. My call was incidental. If you feel responsible for Oscar Vomberg's death, how do you think I feel about poor *Vanya*?"

Bond bought around ninety percent of the story. He still felt there was something else hidden under the surface. "You think you were being manipulated?"

Praxi shook her head again. Vigorously, as before. "No. Every call in and out of the 800 instrument was safe."

"So what about *Eagle*?" This time it was Easy who did the asking, which was natural. She had been a friend of Liz Cearns, and knew some hazy details, like the love affair the original *Eagle* was having in Germany.

"*Eagle* was not so straightforward." Praxi was flagging. It was getting very late and they were all tired, but Bond could not let it stop now.

"After the Frankfurt debacle? After *Vanya*'s death? Where did you go?"

"Berlin. I wanted to contact *Eagle*. We were close."

"I was also a dear friend. You should know that, Praxi."

She did not reply.

"Why Berlin?"

"We had an understanding. *Eagle* and I had a joke. To make any physical contact we said we would show ourselves only in the best places. I stayed two nights at the Kempinski. On the second morning, I saw *Eagle* and checked her room number. I was still being very cautious, so I left the hotel and called her, using our usual codes."

"We've heard the tape," Easy said, sharply as though she still remained suspicious. "You set up a meeting at the Hotel Braun for the next day."

"I went to that meeting. I went to see her. But already she was dead."

"Describe what you saw."

Praxi told them, and it matched up with the file evidence. "I must have arrived only minutes after she was killed."

"You had no doubt it was murder?"

"I was sure of it, I didn't know how. But I did find out something. In fact, I removed a memento." Her hand went to the briefcase, which she unlocked. From among the papers she pulled out a thick Filofax-type book. "This belonged to *Eagle*. I took it from her room at the Braun, and I've read it completely and believe I probably disturbed the murderer, because his orders would almost certainly be to remove it from the scene—if someone knew she had it with her."

"We'll go through it, of course." Bond took the book. "What's so special about it?"

"*Eagle*—Liz—was breaking the rules."

Easy and Bond exchanged a quick glance: both thinking of the unidentified lover.

"She was breaking all the rules. Not only was she having an

affair, it was with a member of Cabal, and, worst of all, she kept a record of it in that diary thing. Coded, of course, but a child could break the cipher."

"When in love . . ." Bond began.

"I know. When in love you take chances. You run great risks. Liz Cearns—*Eagle*—was taking absurd gambles. She was probably the real traitor. Unwitting, of course, but a source used unscrupulously by Weisen."

"How?"

"*Eagle* was Lena. Liz Cearns was Kapitan August Wimper's 'Italian' lover. It's all there."

In the aftershock, the 800 telephone began to ring.

11

Death Comes Expensive

James Bond stood on the balcony watching the dawn come up over Paris. It was a spectacular view, even with the light mist which wrapped itself around the Tuileries Gardens, and snaked just above the water of the Seine. Far away, he could see the Ile de la Cité: the tall grey towers of Notre Dame rising as if out of a cloud. Everywhere the stunning autumnal colors—red, gold, yellow-brown—were just visible, as though seen through opaque glass, and the dampness of the misty morning had about it one of Bond's favorite smells: wood smoke, the very scent of the fall.

Everyone else either dozed or slept, for the long session of question and answer had not stopped with Praxi's revelation and the call that had screeched in on the 800 line.

The voice at the distant end had identified himself as *Moonshine*—the base in Oxfordshire which had monitored everything from the original *Vanya* and *Eagle*. They were asking, in soft desperation, for the new *Vanya*. It did not take Bond long to realize that London was pulling his chain.

There had been no reports, no traffic on the frequencies which swept the air to pick up conversations, messages, and telephone calls via the credit card–sized transceivers. The simple answer was that neither Bond nor Easy had even bothered

153

to activate the slim pieces of gee-whiz electronics. In Easy's case it had been first-night nerves—her baptism in the field. She had forgotten. But Bond had deliberately left his card deactivated from the start. He had no desire to see his words and actions boiled down to transcripts on M's desk.

Moonshine sounded almost panic-stricken, though there was little doubt that the contact was being made on M's orders. The Old Man wanted to keep track, and the message was clear. Everything should be heard. There was even a sour line about not switching off if Bond was up to no good: M's way of telling him to watch the sexual escapades which, with the advent of AIDS, Bond had more than watched with extreme caution.

He apologized, after a fashion, then, because the 800 line was one hundred percent clean, asked a couple of favors. Could *Moonshine* run some kind of check on the French police and DST wavelengths? In particular he wanted information about a stabbing earlier that evening outside the Crillon Hotel, and a brawl in one of the side streets off the Avenue Kléber.

They promised to try, and would call back on the 800 line in an hour. Information would be forthcoming. The Service had human lines into the Paris gendarmes and, no doubt, the DST also.

While they waited, Bond asked more questions, talking first about Axel Ritter, and then the smartly turned-out grey man who had forced him into the Honda at gunpoint, to meet the chubby lady passing herself off as Praxi. After the fight outside the Hotel Amber, Bond would not be surprised if his tall grey chum was dead.

They began with Ritter.

"Those of us with a way into information at Karlshorst knew Ritter as one of Weisen's agents," Praxi told them. "Axel was forever in and out of the Poison Dwarf's office. He often used to eat in the canteen with Monika Haardt as well. Eventually, we realized that Weisen was attempting to use him as a penetration agent, and the target was Cabal. He didn't make it, of course. Weisen suspected several people, and was right ninety-five percent of the time, but we were able to keep Axel out. The man is very dangerous, as you've already discovered. He also knows a great deal about Weisen's contacts, his secret army. If we had been given enough warning that Axel was in Paris, he would be a prime target for us. I should imagine there are ways we could have made him talk."

Bruin gave a seraphic smile. "I would know ways."

"Now if the French DST have him, maybe they'll get him to squawk," Easy grumbled.

"If he talks to them, it'll not be the truth." Bond looked at Praxi as though wanting her to confirm a theory. "Friend Axel's more likely to blow all of us out of the water than give away his own people."

Praxi agreed, and they turned to the second subject.

"When he came barreling out of the van shouting 'Police!,' was he telling the truth?" Bond asked.

Harry Spraker shook his head, but it was Praxi who answered. "We know for a fact that he's a Weisen man, and has been since 'eighty-eight when they threw him out of the DGSE. A cipher clerk died while he was being interrogated by Cold Claude." It sounded better in translation; she actually said "Claude de Froid."

"His full name?"

"Claude Gaspard. He works for a security firm here in Paris, but that's a front for Weisen's people."

Bond described the dark-haired girl whom Claude had introduced as Praxi, and Harry Spraker laughed. "Michelle, ma belle." He sang the old Beatles' number. "She's also known as Fat Michelle, and Michelle Roundheels. Her real name's Michelle Gris, as in Grey. Camp follower, occasional operator, but mainly the light relief for Weisen's Paris people. No, that's not fair. She's really very bright and rumor has it that she's Monika Haardt's protégée. I wouldn't be surprised. She also works out of the security firm. It's called Sécurité de la Bastille. They have a smart little shop near the Pont Neuf. Windows full of briefcases with tape machines in them, and microphone pens. They advertise security systems but I don't think they do much work in that direction."

Something jabbed at Bond's memory. It had to do with this Michelle and their conversation in the car. He worried at it for a minute or so, then let it rest. It would pop back to his mind through the maze of information he was now stacking away.

They had just begun to discuss the jockey, Dmitri, and his place in the pecking order (he was, it appeared, a gofer for Weisen's Paris operation) when the 800 line screeched again.

This time, the conversation went on for around ten minutes, and when he had finished, Bond turned back to the remnants of Cabal, his face hard and serious.

Axel Ritter, he told them, was still at the DST headquarters and, it seemed, was providing the French with a catalogue of crimes and information—mainly concerning the remaining Cabal people, plus Easy and himself.

"They're advising us to get out before half the cops and DST people start clamping down on the harbors and airports. We should get out very fast, and in any way we can, so you'd better grab a little sleep while I try to find the best routes. You've got an hour at the most."

"The fight?" Praxi asked. "Our mêlée outside the Amber?"

"Two still unconscious; three kept in for observation. The cops are guarding their wards, and Cold Claude is one of the pair still in a coma. They've got a plainclothes man at his bedside."

"And Dmitri?" from Harry.

"Dead," Bond sighed. "Seems like one of those things. Genuine. Some little thief, they suspect it was a junkie, went for Axel's pocket right outside the Crillon. Daring, therefore unexpected. Axel tried to fend him off, but the guy ran away. Not before using a shiv on Dmitri though. My folks say they get the impression the DST have been trying to lure Axel inside for quite a while. This was a good excuse, but bad for us."

They began to drift away. Bruin curled up on a couch, the others found beds. Easy gave Bond a little look which said she was ready even if he was not. He told her to rest. "I've a lot to do," he called out across the room. "Oh, and switch on." Though he had not yet activated his transceiver, he would do so before morning.

Just as he was about to use the 800 machine, Praxi came over.

"Can I be of help?" She stood over him, tall and slim-waisted, looking cool in the tailored white trousers and snake-skin belt. Her pleasant face showed signs of strain, dark smudges under the eyes, her rather thick lips braced in the semblance of a smile that looked as though it was not felt by any other part of her.

He wanted identities—names, passports, documents—for her, Harry Spraker and Bruin. Preferably ones they had not used before. In London they had said the major Cabal people were well-supplied with that kind of paper.

At one point, Cabal itself had run an experienced forger who worked in a basement near the old Berliner Ensemble Theater, on the Friedrichstrasse—the theater which had been home to the late great Bert Brecht and Kurt Weill, and was still haunted by songs like *Mack the Knife* and *Moon of Alabama*. The forger had been a legend. Almost ninety years old when he died after a lifetime of creating replicas for people escaping Hitler, and then for other men and women working secretly against the Communist regime.

Praxi had all the answers in her head, ready for him. She would travel as managing director of a company specializing in fabric design; Harry had an unused passport which gave his occupation as an assistant movie director for Phobius Films. They even had a real office in Potsdam: a room, desk, chair and answering machine tended once a week by one of Praxi's casuals—or drones, as she preferred to call them. Bruin was easy. He traveled everywhere as a small-time prize fight promoter, under half a dozen different aliases.

Bond noted the names they would be using. Praxi lingered. "Something else?" he asked.

157

"Yes, James. The business with August Wimper."

"What about it?"

"I wanted to make certain that you understood the seriousness."

"If he's still alive, it's serious, yes."

"He *is* still alive. I have no doubt, just as I'm now certain he was Weisen's man within Cabal. There had to be someone with all the details. Weisen's tracked down all but three of us, and most of those who died were killed very soon after we got the phony *Nacht und Nebel* order."

He gave her a hard look. "How're you so sure he's not the floater they fished out of the Grand Canal? I see how it might be dubious, but what if Weisen had finished with him? Let him go, so to speak?"

"The report I had came from a very good source. Right there in Venice. The body they took from the water had been immersed for the best part of three weeks . . ."

"So?"

Her eyes held his and then cut away. "There was something I didn't tell you. I'm ninety-nine percent sure I saw August. In Berlin. The day before *Eagle* was killed. If forensics in Venice are correct, he couldn't have been in Berlin."

"Not unless he wanted to frighten people and drip all over their carpets."

"James, don't be frivolous. August knows everything, and he was Liz Cearns's lover. Read the book." She gestured to the Filofax on the floor beside the telephone. "Whatever else, if August Wimper knew, then Weisen knew." Her hands washed each other constantly, the fingers tying and untying imaginary knots.

"I'll bear it in mind, Praxi, but I really believe we have to try and surprise the little dwarf in Venice. You say you know where he is . . ."

"Near enough. I can find out."

"Okay, one more question for you. He will presumably have people watching the airport and railway. Where would he not expect his enemies to go? I mean just that. Where would he *not* look for enemies in Venice?"

She thought for a moment. "Wolfgang has a blind spot. As a convinced Communist, a Stalinist, he cannot believe that people opposing him would stay in luxury. That's why *Eagle*— Liz—and I always showed ourselves in the best places. The Poison Dwarf just doesn't expect men and women in our line of business to stay in *de luxe* hotels, or even visit really high-class shops. He thinks that we would prefer to fight him on his own terms: among society's lower-paid workers."

"What you're really saying is that he's a cheapskate?"

Praxi actually laughed as she nodded, "You've got it."

Alone, Bond began to make telephone calls. Cabal's original scattering was to be repeated, but this time the remnants, plus Easy and himself, would end up in the same place. Venice.

Now, at dawn, alone on the balcony, he reviewed what had happened since M had called him into his office, less than three days ago. In the field he rarely stopped to think deeply of the dangers. Life was too short. But looking out at the beauty of Paris, unveiling herself to another day, he went cold with the knowledge that death had been stalking him from the moment of his arrival in Berlin.

There had been the macabre incident with the Fiddleback spiders; the attempt to take Easy St. John and himself from the Ost-West Express. He did not doubt that the final outcome of that botched effort was meant to be the separation of his mortal body from his immortal soul. Then there was the equally fumbled try to pull Easy, Praxi, Harry and himself off the street.

Lastly, he pondered the most mystifying puzzle of the lot. Cold Claude, as he now knew the man, had unmistakably shadowed him from the Gare du Nord to the Place Vendôme. The man was manifestly a surveillance professional of great expertise, for he had not even felt Claude's breath on his neck. Claude and the girl, Michelle, had him cold: in a car and with no easy method of escape. Yet they had let him walk away. That did not make sense.

What was it Harry Spraker had said? ". . . I wouldn't put it past him to have lines out to the worst terrorist organizations, people who still want to see the Western alliance fall apart."

Also Praxi. ". . . Wolfie Weisen is a special kind of person . . . holed up in Venice, James. He's sitting there pulling secret strings all over Europe."

Was that it? Did the former East German spymaster have some plan already in motion? And did he require the remains of Cabal to pull it off? Perhaps.

The only way they would find out would be by confronting the man: but was that just what he wanted them to do? Possibly.

Behind him someone was moving about in the apartment. As he came back into the main room, he could smell freshly brewing coffee.

Within an hour they were preparing to leave. Bond had given them instructions, and they would all meet, later in the day, at the most luxurious hotel Venice had to offer—the famous Cipriani on the island of Giudecca, five minutes by motor launch from the fabled Piazza San Marco, and the only Venetian hotel to boast a swimming pool. If Praxi was right, this was certainly not the kind of place from which Wolfgang Weisen would expect an assault.

Bruin was the first to go. From Paris he would fly to Rome, then on to Venice. Praxi and Harry were to leave together, then split up at Charles de Gaulle Airport. Praxi to Venice via Madrid, Harry to the same destination via Lisbon.

Bond and Easy would leave last. Easy to take an Alitalia flight to Pisa, and from there a commuter aircraft to Venice. Bond would fly Air France into London, Heathrow, where after a short meeting he would take a British Airways flight out to Marco Polo Airport, Venice.

The Air France A-310 was on time into Heathrow's Terminal Two. He had two hours to kill, and took his time deplaning, lingering and walking slowly down the endless ramps, people-movers and corridors that take you into the immigration, customs or transit areas.

Long before he reached any of the authorized zones, a figure appeared in a doorway marked PRIVATE. Minutes later, James Bond was sitting down in a comfortable office. Across the table was his old friend and ally, the leggy, tall and elegant young woman who was Assistant to the Armorer, that is, second in command of Q Branch—Ann Reilly, known to everyone in the Service as Q'ute.

"Well, fancy meeting you here." Bond gave her a quick appraisal with his eyes, smiling with the pleasure which he could never conceal, for Ms. Reilly had always been a faithful friend as well as a very useful adviser over the past decade. "D'you come here often?" he asked, the good humor lighting his eyes.

"Only when I'm off to romantic places, James—which means rarely. I bring you gifts."

"And I have a couple for you." He unlocked his briefcase, touched the button springing the specially lined compartment which made small handguns invisible to airport X-ray machines, and took out the Browning Compact stowed next to his own ASP. It was the weapon he had taken, less than twenty-four hours earlier, from Harry Spraker, the real *Tester.* "I want you to go over that with everything you've got. My fingerprints are all over it, so I think you should concentrate on the ballistics. Check them particularly against any of the stuff on file concerning dead Cabal agents."

"Even if they were strangled?"

"I think you should confine it to those who bought it with a bullet, but use your discretion."

"Fine." She slipped the pistol into a plastic evidence bag.

"As for this," he slapped Liz Cearns's Filofax onto the desk. "It is either an outrageous forgery, or something that could blow all of us out of the water. I talked to the Chief of Staff about it last night. Well, in the early hours of this morning actually."

"I know." She took the black-bound book. "He's going around like a man in a dream this morning. Bill needs his

161

beauty sleep, James. You shouldn't wake him in the middle of the night."

"If I have to be up, I don't see why he shouldn't be up," he chuckled.

Ms. Reilly slid the Filofax into another evidence bag. "Now, I suggest you take anything else you need from that old brief-case, because I've brought you a brand new Cardin, complete with detachable side for spare clothing. Major Boothroyd himself provided the shirts, ties, socks and underwear: and I must say I didn't take you for a man who wore silk next to his skin."

"Always, in the mating season." He raised his right eyebrow.

Ann Reilly did not even blush. "This is the business side of the case." It took half an hour for her to explain all the extra refinements which had been added into the special piece of equipment.

"You don't let the grass grow, do you?" He was impressed with the new, and very sophisticated, additions to the case, which was slightly larger than the one he had handed over. Carefully he stowed away the ASP and spare magazines in the compartment similar to the one he had been using for several years; transported a few necessary papers, and his sleek shaving kit, into their correct places and snapped his new acquisition shut.

"Very nice. All the tricks of the trade."

"And a couple of other things we've dreamed up. Just in case." She demonstrated the use of two pens—one gold, the other silver.

"Just what I wanted. Santa's little elves've been working over-time." He accepted the pens and clipped them to the inside pocket of his blazer.

"Use them well, James."

"I'll do my best. No last words for the condemned man?"

"Yes, M sends his regards and says would you please keep the transceiver on at all times."

"Tell him his boon is granted."

As he reached the door, Ann Reilly stopped him. "And, James . . ."

"Yes?"

"Take care."

"Oh, I shall."

"I mean, take care of the briefcase. It's very expensive. It's also a prototype."

"So am I." He winked. "They smashed the tools and burned the plans when they completed me." Hefting the briefcase, he added, "Death comes expensive these days."

There was a car waiting to transport him to Terminal One, from where the British Airways Airbus would leave for Venice. On the way over he almost captured the elusive piece of conversation he had tried to remember. Words said when he had been in the Honda with Cold Claude and Big Michelle. The thing was there for a second, then gone.

Half an hour later he boarded, and was shown to a window seat in Executive Class. Dumping the case in the overhead bin, he fastened his seat belt, accepted a copy of *The Standard* from the flight attendant, and became engrossed in an article on the season's new plays.

He did not even glance up when his traveling companion settled next to him. Only as they began the push-back from the gate did he recognize the voice.

"How nice to see you, James. A pleasant surprise."

Bond slowly raised his head. Axel Ritter sat in the next seat, his mouth hard and his eyes mocking.

12

Keeps Death His Court

Bond slowly folded his newspaper and tucked it into the seat pocket in front of him.

"Well, what a pleasant surprise." He smiled warmly at Axel Ritter's stone face. "I thought this was going to be the usual boring flight: sitting looking at clouds and listening to the captain telling us about the problems he's having with Air Traffic Control."

"I wouldn't be too happy if I were you, Mr. Bond. You've caused enough trouble already." He spoke softly, leaning in towards Bond's ear.

"Oh, they say it's better to travel hopefully than to arrive."

Ritter nodded. "So I've heard, but the arrival will be more interesting than usual."

"I dare say."

They were taxiing out, and the flight attendants were going through their dance of death, arms and hands moving to the accompaniment of a tape—pointing out the exits in case of an unlikely emergency, and telling passengers what would happen should they suffer a severe decompression: They stressed that this was most unlikely. This routine rarely varied, and gave Bond little comfort. He knew what would almost certainly happen if they suffered one of those "unlikely" severe decompressions. You would probably not have need of dangling oxygen masks if the worst happened.

"I hear some mugger offed your little jockey friend." He retained the friendly smile. "Dmitri, wasn't it?"

A storm cloud crossed Ritter's face. "It was no mugger," he all but snarled, then the captain blotted him out, coming through on the communications system to say they were seventh in line for takeoff.

"Oh, I was told some crackhead with a knife . . ."

"Then you were told wrong, and I suspect you know exactly who pulled that stunt."

For a few seconds Bond was thrown. He glanced away, looking out of the window. An El Al 747 was piling on the thrust and rumbling away on takeoff. He felt their aircraft shake from the reverberation. London had told him that the stabbing of Dmitri had been a genuine, common or garden mugging, nothing to do with Cabal, or what was going on with those members who still lived. Presumably London had got its information directly from the police in Paris. Somewhere along the line either the tale had been garbled, or something was wrong with the story to begin with.

"No, I'm afraid I don't know anything about it. Nor do I regard death as a stunt."

"You didn't appear to have any problems with it on the Ost-West Express."

"I thought I was saving *our* lives then, Axel, remember? That was when I used to call you Harry, and you should know that I'm not proud of the incident. Killing people is an unpleasant occupation."

"But someone has to do it, eh?"

"It appears to be constantly inevitable. That doesn't change the basic immorality. There's enough death and destruction in the world as it is."

Ritter laughed. A shade too loud. "You're getting scruples, then, James Bond?"

"Not really. When I have to do my country's dirty work I

regard it as pest control." He turned away from Ritter and stared out of the window again.

The captain ordered all doors to automatic, and asked the flight attendants to take their seats. A warning bell clanged twice, to let the cabin crew know the aircraft was about to get under way. Bond reflected that the orders given from the flight deck nowadays appeared to have been filched from science fiction. The Airbus trembled, turning onto the threshold, then the engines wound up to full thrust and they were bowling off, bumping down the runway.

Seconds later, Bond was looking at the model buildings and toy cars that were the outskirts of London far below. He thought the one thing about which any passenger could be certain was that, after takeoff, the aircraft would eventually return to earth. He remained with his head turned away from Axel Ritter. The man posed a problem that he could do without. The question was, had Ritter boarded the aircraft knowing that he—Bond—would be there, or was this just an unhappy accident?

Certainly Ann Reilly had been at Heathrow to meet him, so logic told him that members of his Service would have automatically checked out the passenger list, or at least monitored people going on board. Yet he had not seen Ritter in the departure lounge, which pointed to a last-minute decision: or, at worst, a decision that looked like an unfortunate coincidence.

He wished he could turn on the credit-card transceiver, but it had been stressed that the things had to be deactivated when flying on a commercial aircraft: something to do with interfering with communications and navigational equipment. The current situation was one of the few he would prefer to be monitored by *Moonshine* at the base in Oxfordshire.

In the end, after they had climbed through heavy rain-bearing cloud, he decided that this was no accident. Axel Ritter somehow knew Bond would be on board, and had managed to organize matters so that he was seated next to him. In turn, this meant those who controlled Ritter would also be expecting Bond to arrive at Marco Polo Airport. So, if Praxi and the others were correct, Ritter would be delivering him into the arms of his superiors—Weisen and Haardt.

He accepted a complimentary glass of champagne from the flight attendant, as did Ritter. How, he wondered, could he give Weisen's agent the slip? Ritter was the sheepdog, sent to drive Bond into the pen, where the Poison Dwarf of the former East German Intelligence Service would be waiting.

Bond thought of the pair of pens given to him by Ann Reilly at Heathrow. The gold one was lethal, but the silver would do the job without adding another death to his conscience. There were two problems. How could he possibly use either of them in the restricted space of an aircraft without giving himself away? Certainly Ritter would be watching every move he made. Secondly, did Axel Ritter deserve to live or die?

If Praxi and Harry had got it right, comrade Ritter was an accomplished killer under the now defunct regime: But that was in another life, and another time. He decided that doing something to the man in the close confinement of the aircraft would be more likely to cause problems than dealing with him once they had landed.

Even with Ritter sitting next to him, the flight turned out to be just as dull as any other. The food was usual airline: plastic and all but inedible. Ritter did not try either to talk, or even threaten him—except to block his way when he stood in an attempt to head for the lavatory.

"Oh, no, James. You stay just where you are."

"What d'you think I'm going to do, jump out?"

"My instructions call for me to stay with you: not to let you out of my sight."

"Well, you'll have to trust me, Axel."

A few seconds' pause, after which Ritter reluctantly let him go. Alone, Bond made his decision. He would act once they reached Venice, and before going through immigration. Provided the opportunity presented itself, he might even be able to evade any of Weisen's people who would certainly be waiting for them on the other side of the customs hall.

An hour later, the Airbus began its descent through dense cloud. Bond's eyes strained to catch a glimpse of the unique city of Venice from the air, but all he saw were the approach lighting system and runway threshold pass beneath the aircraft before it touched down gently, the engines howling into reverse thrust. The magic of navigation and electronic approach systems had brought them into Venice, which was now shrouded in a late afternoon mist. While the weather conditions would slow any transfer from Marco Polo to Venice itself, it might just be ideal for Bond's purposes.

Ritter was out of his seat belt and on his feet as soon as the aircraft came to a halt at the gate. He opened the overhead bin and grabbed at Bond's briefcase. "Let me carry this for you." He looked down, unsmiling. "I'm traveling even lighter than you, Mr. Bond. I have everything I need here in Venice. There should be a launch ready to meet us. So if you would go first, please."

He had no option but to move in front of the German, though a couple of passengers did get out between them. It gave him just enough time to make for the nearest restroom, knowing Ritter would follow. Possibly this was the only way he might alter the odds. Now he prayed that no other deplaning passenger required the facilities. As he entered the restroom, he moved his hand over the transceiver in his pocket, reactivating it. At least from now on the monitors in Oxfordshire would be receiving conversation and noises.

There were two men already standing at the urinals when Bond entered, and three more, including Ritter, came in after him. Bond whistled quietly as he stood in front of the urinal, hoping that nobody else from the incoming flight would enter the restroom. The two men who had been there on his arrival had washed their hands and left. Ritter, his eyes constantly flicking towards Bond, occupied a position three porcelain receptacles to his left. Nobody else came in, and eventually, one, then both, of the passengers who had entered with Ritter, finished and left.

Ritter stepped back. "Come on, Mr. Bond, you're just wasting time." He still clutched the briefcase.

Bond made a great show of adjusting his fly and going to wash his hands. Ritter stayed with him, not more than a foot away, his hand clamping on Bond's arm as he reached inside his blazer. "Axel, just relax. I'm not going anywhere without you. D'you think I've got a gun in here?" Bond withdrew his comb, gave Ritter a quizzical look, and slowly ran it through his hair. "If we're going to meet your boss, I'd prefer to look my best." Replacing the comb, he turned, his hand removing the silver pen from his inside pocket.

"If you want to write with it, just twist the two halves," Ann Reilly had told him. "Pressing the plunger does the other thing, so don't make any mistakes. Pressing when you mean to write could cause grave embarrassment."

His hand came up, and he pressed the pen's plunger as it came level with Ritter's face. A thick cloud of a Mace-like substance filled the air around Ritter's head. The irritant, inherent in Mace, was beefed up with a small quantity of CS gas, and the result was immediate. Ritter dropped the briefcase, hands flying to his face as he staggered back, making little grunting noises. He did not have the time to shout, for Bond stepped in and stiff-armed him on the side of the jaw, hearing the click as either a bone broke or the jaw was dislocated.

Ritter staggered backwards, half turning to bump against the door of one of the toilets. Bond moved in close now, for the cloud of unpleasant chemical had quickly dissolved in the air, the bulk of it clinging to the German's head.

With his hands outstretched and flat, thumbs bent backwards to strengthen the cutting edge of each, Bond chopped Ritter on both sides of the neck, following up with a vicious one-hand cut to the bridge of the nose.

The German sprawled backwards, arms and legs flying as though he had lost all control. He spun once, then collapsed

169

hard onto the lavatory seat, his head lolling, his face covered in blood. Ritter would stay silent for some time, Bond thought, closing the door on him, snatching up his briefcase and retiring to one of the other stalls to retrieve his automatic from the case. Less than two minutes later he strolled out of the restroom and walked unhurriedly to one of the little passport-control booths. The officer merely glanced at the British passport in the name of John E. Bunyan—a small jest perpetrated by The Scrivener, Brian Cogger, who dealt with all extra identity documents. The passport-control officer looked bored, and waved him through towards the baggage claim and customs area.

The baggage area at Marco Polo resembles a very large Victorian waiting room: a lot of wood and big old-fashioned windows, the whole leading off towards the dock area where launches from hotels and for private hire wait, together with a group of optimistic porters and hotel representatives.

Usually the trip, by launch, to the Cipriani, took half an hour, but, as he came into the baggage claim, Bond realized that today's weather would mean considerable delay. The mist was thickening across the water, and with the amount of traffic which plied to and fro over the lagoon, the going would be necessarily cautious.

He walked straight through the crush of passengers claiming their luggage, using his own techniques—giving the impression that he looked into the far distance, yet taking in everything, and everyone, within his peripheral vision. During the couple of hundred yards he saw at least six people whom normally he would have marked for closer scrutiny. As he emerged onto the wooden jetty where the launches were tied, there were two men who gave off vibrations which said either cop or hoodlum. They both wore grey suits and unneeded Ray-Ban sunglasses.

October often provides pleasant, balmy weather in Venice. The holiday season is over, and the one-week package deals have almost ceased. Autumn brings music aficionados, for it is the time for the opera and concert hall, just as late winter brings a special kind of visitor for the carnival. This year the weather was not cooperating. Once out in the open, Bond felt the damp chill which is associated more with winter than the autumn.

He tried to look unhurried, sauntering towards the launches until he saw a dark-suited, small man wearing a cap with CIP-RIANI embroidered above the bill.

"Bunyan," he introduced himself. "I have a reservation."

"Mistair Bunyan, yes. Of course. Yes, we were awaiting you." The English was very good. "You have no other luggage?"

Bond shook his head, lifting the briefcase as though it were enough.

The Cipriani representative shrugged, the porters looked dejected, then brightened as he said something about one more passenger, and showed Bond to a sleek launch tied up nearby. He climbed down into the stern well, ducked his head, entering the enclosed area, open at both ends. There was a man at the wheel for'ard, wearing a heavy black slicker over his white uniform. He nodded and smiled, welcoming his passenger in English.

They waited for ten minutes, Bond expecting to hear shouts and the activity of police any moment. It would not be long before someone discovered the comatose Ritter. Then, with a sudden flurry of activity, the Cipriani rep appeared again, on the jetty aft. "He is here," he smiled at Bond, while a porter who had got lucky, heaved a big suitcase into the baggage compartment.

A few seconds later, an actorish-looking man arrived with the hotel guide. The newcomer looked as if he was doing everyone a favor by being there at all, and stood for a moment as though waiting for his photograph to be taken. He was a little under six feet tall—somewhere around five-nine—wearing highly glossed Gucci loafers: the first part of him that Bond could see. When he descended into the aft well, there was a better view: an immaculate Armani silk suit; a cream silk shirt and a Sulka tie.

171

He had a waisted camel-hair topcoat slung across his shoulders, suggesting the casual ensemble men were wearing this autumn.

His iron-grey hair was thick and swept back above an undoubtedly good-looking, weathered and tanned face which reminded Bond of somebody. He recalled Axel Ritter on the Ost-West Express. It was when he had been doubling as Harry, and reading a thriller, complaining about writers who did not bother to describe characters, but simply depicted them as looking like a household personality, usually from the movies. The newcomer had the distinct appearance of Anthony Quinn. Zorba the Greek came readily to mind, though the man was a shade younger than Mr. Quinn, not quite as tall, and almost certainly did not have the charisma of the actor. As he ducked into the cabin, the Quinn look-alike flashed a smile, as though he knew Bond very well. Indeed, there was more than just a passing resemblance to the actor that struck Bond as familiar. Something else began to emerge as he searched his memory.

The motor roared, the screw churning the water into foam, and the launch began to move away from the jetty. The Cipriani representative jumped into the for'ard section and began a conversation with the pilot, their words almost drowned by the clamor of the engine.

The newcomer, gathering the camel-hair topcoat around him, gently sat down next to Bond and loudly said, "How are you? Have a good flight from London?"

"How d'you know I was on the London flight?" He continued to rack his brain. He knew the face and the description, but . . .

"I was on it also, actually. You had that imbecile Axel Ritter with you. Drop him off somewhere?"

"He was unavoidably delayed." Alarm bells clanged in Bond's head.

"Mmmm." Anthony Quinn the Second nodded and gave him a smile which showed perfect teeth. "I fear he's not going to make it at all now, actually."

"Really?"

He shook his head sadly, giving Bond another view of the perfect teeth. "You didn't quite finish the job. So I did it for you. Let some air into his head. He didn't look any worse for it, and it's a distinct improvement for the world as a whole."

"Have we met?" Bond's brow creased and he felt there was a name, just out of reach, in his mind. He had a picture of his hand straining towards a card index and not quite making it.

"No, we haven't, actually. But we've met now. How are you?" The proffered hand had a large signet ring on the middle finger. "You're so highly spoken of that I thought you'd know me immediately. How about:

> *"All murdered: for within the hollow crown*
> *That rounds the mortal temples of a king*
> *Keeps Death his court, and there the antic sits . . ."*

"Jesus!" In spite of himself, Bond breathed the blasphemy as the shock hit him like a bucketful of the cold water that sprayed around them. The launch continued to plough slowly over the lagoon. The quote was Shakespeare, from *Richard II*, and automatically he supplied the answerback to the man's IFF code:

> *"This royal throne of kings, this scepter'd isle,*
> *This earth of majesty, this seat of Mars,*
> *This other Eden, demi-paradise."*

"Thank you, *Vanya*. I'm very glad I was following you. I really believe you're going to run into big problems when we get to the hotel, actually."

"I imagine I've already run into problems just meeting you, Kapitan Wimper." He was still slightly alarmed to discover that the smooth, beautifully dressed and immaculate man sitting next to him was August Wimper, *Orphan* of Cabal. The ex-Volkspolizei officer whom both Praxi and Harry had fingered as Weisen's agent. The man who had both penetrated Cabal and been the original *Eagle*'s lover and murderer.

173

Casually Bond reached behind him and slowly drew the ASP from where he had stuck it, in his waistband, hard against the small of his back. He turned, so that neither the launch's helmsman nor the hotel rep could see the gun.

"Please don't try anything stupid, *Orphan*. If all I hear is true, then you've a great deal on your conscience already. You can almost certainly answer some questions that've been worrying everybody connected with Cabal. Just sit quietly until we get to the Cipriani. After that, who knows? We might even get you to tell us where your boss, Wolfie's, hanging out with his lady friend . . ."

"Please put that thing away." Wimper looked at the automatic with a touch of scorn etched around his eyes and mouth. "I've had a lifetime's experience with guns and they've taught me one thing, James—I may call you James, yes?"

"If you must. What have guns taught you, Wimper?"

"That the gun, in itself, incites violence. The gun alone can't harm you. But the man who carries one is bloody dangerous."

"You speak exceptional English for a German."

Wimper gave a little smiling bob of the head which was his way of saying "thank you."

"Is that why you got on so well with Liz Cearns, *Eagle*, the girl you murdered in Berlin? Your former lover?"

Wimper gave a long sigh. "So," he said quietly. "So, that's what you've been told."

"Told and deduced for myself. Liz kept a diary in some keckhanded code that could be cracked by a ten-year-old."

"Yes, I know about that. I warned her, actually."

"She took no notice of you. She kept the thing. It was left in her room. You didn't even remove the evidence."

"I didn't, did I? Well, let me tell you something, James. If it was found, then someone put the damned diary there. Because she did as I told her. She got rid of the thing. She didn't have it with her when she went from the Kempi to the Hotel Braun. She left it with me. I was going to destroy it. Then some bright spark stole it. Right from under my nose."

"From the Kempi, I presume?"

"Right. From the Kempi."

"You were seen there—by Praxi."

He gave another sigh. "Yes. Yes, I thought she'd seen me, actually. Was Spraker around at the time?"

"I'm not sure. I don't think so."

"I would suspect he was. Just as I'd suspect, *he* saw me as well."

"You're not trying to tell me you're on the side of the angels after all, August?"

"Please. Please call me Gus. That's what my friends always call me, and put away that damned gun, James. You *do* have the wrong man. You've had the right one for some time, actually, but we'll go into that when we get to the hotel. As I've told you, I think we'll find there's one hell of a problem when we get there."

They both had to speak very loudly because the launch was bucking under them and the helmsman kept increasing, then decreasing, the power. They were gliding into a canal now, walls rising on either side of them, passing under a bridge, the mist patchy, giving their surroundings a sinister look, like something out of a thriller movie. You could almost hear a soundtrack score by the late Bernard Herrmann, who wrote the music for many Hitchcock movies.

"So, you're telling me that you're a Boy Scout? That you didn't sell Cabal down the river to Weisen?"

"I can do more than tell you. I can prove it to you."

"You can? I suppose you've got the answer to why you went missing *before* Cabal got the order to scatter? Before the *Nacht und Nebel* signal."

"That was actually a coincidence. A lucky one for me, as it's turned out."

"I'm sure."

"Don't pull the trigger of that thing if I reach into my pocket, James. I'm getting the proof for you." He slid a hand into the inside of his silk suit and pulled out a cream envelope.

"I think you'll find part of the answer here. Complete, actually." He proffered the envelope with one hand.

"No, you open it." Bond commanded. *"Actually,"* he mimicked.

August Wimper nodded and slit it open with the index finger of his right hand. "Want me to read it to you as well? I don't think it would convince you unless you take a look yourself. It was handed to me only an hour and a half before I got on the flight. I'd have given it to you on the aircraft if I hadn't seen friend Ritter was around. The last thing I needed was to be spotted by him."

"Read it, then I'll make up my mind."

"Let me turn it around so that you can, at least, see the paper, which I think you'll recognize."

Slowly he reversed the letter so that Bond could see, not only the paper with its embossed heading, but also the writing, which was immediately recognizable. The heading was M's name and private address. He had seen that notepaper on many occasions—Sir Miles Messervy, *Quarterdeck,* and then the address, on the edge of Windsor Forest.

In his usual green ink, in the familiar hand, M had written:

> *Predator,* the bearer of this letter is *Orphan,* formerly a member of Cabal. You may, by this time, have reason not to trust him, but I can assure you that *Orphan* has my whole unequivocal backing and trust. Call me by telephone if you still doubt. In the meantime, perhaps proof is best given to you with the word *Byline.*

It was signed M, and the one word, *Byline,* was an adequate testimonial. Years ago, M had devised a warning code, known only to himself and Bond. He almost certainly did the same thing with other agents, though Bond liked to think this was a unique understanding between him and the head of the British Secret Intelligence Service. They changed the words annually.

If August Wimper had coerced the Chief, he would have used *Crossroad.* Instead he had written the safe signal: *Byline.*

"Actually, he sent his best wishes." Wimper gave a deprecating smile, as though he was now a member of a small and trusted circle: which, in a way, he was.

Bond nodded and returned the pistol to his waistband. "And you know where Comrade Weisen can be found?"

"If I don't, then we're in more trouble than I think we are already. If you're expecting to meet friends of yours here, I should forget about it. Wolfie would never allow that, which means he might have relaxed his guard in time for us to do something about matters in hand." Wimper adjusted the camel-hair coat around his shoulders as they slowly came abreast of the Cipriani's landing stage.

13

||||||||||||||||||||||||||||||||||||||||||||||||||||||||||||||||||||||||||||||||||||||||||||||||||||||||||||||||||||||||||||||||||||||||||

Talk of Death & Disaster

The Hotel Cipriani can only be reached by water. Some Venetian hotels have entrances accessible from the narrow streets and small piazzas, but the Cipriani, located on a separate island, needs a water-borne trip every time.

The launch glided in towards a series of gold-topped black-and-white striped poles, reaching up from the water, like large fireworks, all set for the Fourth of July. These poles are seen all over the Venetian waterways, gaily decorated, and there for securing gondolas. Not that many gondolas come out to Giudecca and the Cipriani, for the hotel itself is served mainly by its own fleet of launches, which run between the hotel steps and the Piazza San Marco as often as residents require, and at no extra charge.

The launch tied up at a set of stone steps, above which there were wrought-iron gates, hovering bellboys, and a couple of guests waiting to be taken to the Piazza San Marco. Bond and Wimper were assisted from the boat, shepherded by the dark-suited representative, who, discarding his cap, was transformed into an obvious under manager. They followed him through the gate into an enchanting garden, walking under trellised archways, with bushes, ferns and flowers on either side. To their left a small fountain splashed into the misty cold early evening.

Another under manager greeted them both by name, as though he possessed some sixth sense which told him exactly who was who. "Mr. Bunyan, Herr Kray. Welcome. All is ready for you."

"You didn't tell me your name was Kray." Bond gave Wimper a sidelong look.

"Your wife, who is registered in her maiden name, has left a message for you, Mr. Bunyan." The manager handed over a thick envelope. "Your friends have gone out to dine, I understand."

Bond nodded, feeling the alarm rise slowly as he took the envelope. In spite of an acute desire to rip it open on the spot, he quietly filled in the registration form, then offered an American Express Platinum Card, which the manager waved away. "We don't require to check any guests' credit here." He sounded a whisper away from condescension, just keeping to the right side of social convention. What he really meant, Bond thought, was if you cannot afford to stay here we would already know and you would not get a room.

As Wimper completed his registration, Bond slit open the envelope and read the short message in Easy St. John's round, almost schoolgirl, American hand.

Darling—she had written—*we've all decided to go across for a look at the sights, and have an early dinner at La Caravella. If you get in at a reasonable time, come over and join in the festivities. I'm sure you'll find us. If not, I'll see you in bed. We're all as hungry as wolves. Love ever, E.*

The last sentence jerked at Bond's stomach, while he immediately noted the penultimate line and the hint in the word "wolves." "See you in bed" really meant something else.

The immaculate manager came around to their side of the reception desk, preparing to show them to their rooms.

"Your wife and friends have gone out?" Wimper gave him an "I told you so" look. "Shall we dine here together, Mr. Bunyan?

179

I could do with the company, and I dare say you'd welcome it also. It's unpleasant out there and I certainly have no intention of wandering around Venice in this mist."

"You're right, sir. It can be unpleasant in this kind of weather." The manager was eager to please. "I think they must be right about the ozone layer and the ecology. We seem to be close on winter already. I've never known it like this in October."

Bond nodded, as if to say the manager was right. Then, turning to Wimper: "Of course. Join you down here in, say, an hour?"

"An hour would be admirable. I look forward to it."

A bellboy had appeared with Wimper's suitcase, and another of the dark-suited managers arrived to show the German to his room.

Bond's guide led him along passages and up short flights of steps to a large suite, "One of our junior suites, sir." He opened the door, and began to enumerate the amenities. Easy's clothes were in the closets, and there were other signs of her recent occupation of the room. He had not really thought about sharing a room with her, but Ms. St. John had obviously made the decision for him.

It was a large room, with a king-sized bed, comfortable chairs, a couch, table and desk. French doors opened onto a small path which led cunningly between the rooftops to a private sun deck. "I fear you'll not be using that if the present weather continues." The manager appeared to be taking the entire blame for the inclement weather.

To the right of the bed, a large curved screen, fashioned in a thick opaque dark brown unbreakable glass, reached up to the ceiling, and marked the bathroom area. He followed the manager back to the entrance vestibule and was shown the bathroom design, of which the man was obviously very proud. The curved screen had been added to make room for a small swimming pool–sized Jacuzzi. It was a clever use of space, and, had this journey been one of pleasure, he would have enjoyed living in the comfortable surroundings provided by the hotel.

The pièce de résistance was saved until last. With a great flourish, the manager pointed to a glass-topped table which stood at the foot of the bed. When a button was pressed by the bed, a television rose with an almost silent hum from the center of the table. It was all very 1960s kitsch, but Bond managed to keep a straight face.

As soon as the manager departed, Bond made for the bed. Easy's note pointed him in that direction, and, after stripping all the linen back, he found what he was looking for: a piece of paper, crumpled into a small ball which he took over to the desk.

Unfolding and smoothing out the paper, he read the note which covered the page in tiny script:

> I am concerned. Things are just not right. Praxi and Harry insist that we should go into Venice, but something stinks. Praxi has put the 800 machine under lock and key at reception and I have already seen a pair of well-dressed thugs hanging around. They attached themselves to me at the airport and are registered as Dominic Jellineck and Dorian Crone. The names seem to fit as they are both English with the kind of accent that renders "round" as "rind" and "house" as "hice," but, if they are merely a pair of Yuppies, they are very muscular Yuppies. Neither Praxi nor Harry see anything wrong. Have we backed the wrong horses? I will try and leave you a note at reception that will lead you to this. Urgently suggest that you use one of your magic telephone numbers to get instructions. It all feels wrong, as though we are about to be thrown to Wolfie and his crew. I shall feel better when I see you again.
>
> E

Certainly, Easy had taken a chance leaving this *en clair* letter, which Bond burned in one of the ashtrays before putting the bed back together again.

Have we backed the wrong horses? Possibly, he thought, but he would have been the first to admit that his own mind was in a state of confusion. Wimper's story, with the backup letter from M, certainly had weight, but, while he had already suffered second thoughts about Harry Spraker, he trusted Praxi completely. Since the whole Cabal business began nobody, it appeared, was who they seemed.

Bond sat, looking at the gathering gloom outside the French doors, turning matters over in his mind. Without the 800 machine there was no completely safe way he could make contact with London, except one particular line which they kept as well screened as possible.

He dialed the Italian get-out and UK access codes, followed by the number. A quiet voice answered. "Prodigal Hotline."

"Can you get hold of the Chairman?" Bond asked.

"I think so. Who's calling?"

"Just tell him it's an old friend from the European office."

M was on the line in seconds with a curt "Yes?"

"Surprise," said Bond. "I'm in Venice and thought I should ask you about an orphan I've just heard from."

"One hundred percent credit rating. Highest possible line." M was not going to remain on the telephone for a long, and possibly unsafe, talk.

"What about the man we used as a tester?"

"Unsure. Until we know more, I would not grant him any credit at all."

"And the one who smells like sulphur?"

"Again, ninety-nine percent rating. Not quite as good as the fellow you've just met. We're still checking for a more convincing rating."

"Thank you, sir."

"You can always use the 800 number if you want more details."

"I'm afraid that's out of the question now, sir. Some of the baggage has gone missing."

"Sorry to hear that. Nasty accident earlier this afternoon, I see."

"It became worse, sir. Completely finalized."

"That all?"

"Thank you, sir. Yes."

"Kindly don't use this number again until you're back in the UK. Good day." M closed the line abruptly. That was it, Bond thought. As he suspected, he was deniable, which meant there was no official sanction for any operations in France or Italy. M had cut him loose. The Chief was never a man for taking chances with communications. He had once confided to Bond that, early in his career as head of British Intelligence, he had lost two agents because of a terrible foul-up concerning a series of conversations on an insecure line. Since that time M had been paranoid about using telephones for sensitive matters. Neither did he like the irritable and time-consuming business of getting formal permission for his agents to work in other European countries.

Bond gave a sigh of exasperation, and turned to the business in hand.

The new briefcase was a two-sided piece of luggage: a normal briefcase with an extra, double-sized section attached to it by hinges and a combination lock. He snapped the tumblers to the correct set of four numbers, and removed the larger leather box which contained neatly packed clothes and his toilet set. Then he opened the briefcase section, took the silver pen which had been the undoing of Axel Ritter out of his pocket, un-screwed the two sections and took a refill from one of the many compartments built into what he thought of as the business side of the case. If he needed the non-lethal weapon again, it would be ready.

He stripped, went through into the bathroom, showered and shaved for the second time that day. Half an hour later he was in reception waiting for Wimper, who arrived looking like an ad in a male fashion magazine, having changed into a dark suit which would have left little change from two thousand dollars. Bond was amused to see that the German was improperly wearing an old Etonian tie. He probably liked the colors.

They went through to the dining room, which had about it the air of a cathedral dedicated to food. In fact, this sense of a religious aura was heightened by the waiters, who moved among the tables like acolytes, speaking in hushed voices and rarely smiling. Food at the Cipriani is a very serious business.

There were only two other couples dining in the room: a bored, fragile-looking Italian girl with black hair and dark languid eyes, accompanied by a man old enough to be her grandfather. From the way in which he constantly reached across the table to fondle her hand, he was unlikely to be any permanent relation. The other pair were elderly Americans who hardly exchanged a word. It was either a case of long-term monotony, or companionable silence.

Wimper and Bond chose a table far away from the two other couples, ordering lobster followed by *boeuf en croûte*, drinking an '85 Cortese di Gavi with the lobster, and a splendidly elegant Gattinara—the '83—with the meat. The lobster was a spectacular gift from Neptune, and you could cut the succulent beef with a fork. The food was, Bond thought, in line with the atmosphere, worthy of beatification.

They left business until coffee, which followed a splendidly light chocolate mousse, laced with brandy.

"My chairman bears out his letter," Bond began. Before leaving his room he had decided that, if he had to trust someone, Wimper was now his best bet. "In fact, he tells me that your credit rating is stratospheric."

Wimper looked a little hurt. "You doubted me?"

"I doubt everyone now. You already know the others have gone out. They're supposed to be having dinner at La Caravella, on San Marco."

Wimper gave a little nod. "I know it well. Place is done up like a caravel: a little over the top. They have menus on parchment, but the food is good, particularly if you like service with a lot of bowing and scraping. I'm told Americans're usually impressed by it." He paused, pursing his lips into a little, rather prissy, smile. "You don't really believe they've gone there?"

"I have my doubts now."

"So where do you think they've gone?"

"I hoped you'd have the answer to that, but I need another answer first."

"The question?"

"How did you manage to become the prime suspect as Cabal's main traitor?"

The prissy smile turned into one of more broad pleasure. "Liz knew—*Eagle*, that is. I played at being a double. Liz kept it very close to her chest. Under her bra, actually. We worked very closely . . ."

"So I believe."

"Oh, yes. That also. We broke the rules and she paid for it." His eyes flared with anger. "Every day I curse myself that I wasn't able to save her."

"You were running on both sides of the street?"

"That was the impression we wished to achieve. I became very close to Weisen, but it didn't quite work. I rather think Comrade Wolfgang, and that dark warped woman who ruts with him, are wise to me now. The object of my personal operation was to flush out the real penetration, if there was one. We certainly did that, and it cost Liz her life."

"You want to talk about it?"

He gave a small shrug. "I fancy you've already guessed. In the end, little Wolfie was too clever for me. He did have someone else in Cabal. Or, I should say, he finally suborned someone else."

"*Tester?* Harry Spraker?"

"It would seem so."

"What about Praxi?"

"Spraker has a lot of influence with her, but I'd say she's safe. He could, of course, be using her as an unwitting agent. The old guard at Karlshorst were very good at that."

"But Harry definitely."

Wimper nodded. "Yes, though I don't know how long he's been on the team."

"Can you guess?"

"I'd say it was reasonably recent. By which I mean just before the Poison Dwarf sent out the infamous *Nacht und Nebel* signal. He was a very good clandestine communications expert when he was at Karlshorst—*Tester,* I mean. He really did know all the KGB tricks, and most of the East German Service's gambits."

"So, he could've activated the *Nacht und Nebel,* you mean?"

He paused for a moment, his eyes sliding away. "You might not like me that much when you hear all of it."

"Liz Cearns liked you, and she was running you as a double. You've said as much."

He nodded, silent for thirty seconds. "You know how it goes, James? Being a double?"

"I've worked for my firm for a very long time. I know exactly how it works."

"Then do you know how to get rid of the guilt?" For the first time there was a harsh anguish in his face and eyes.

"To gain entrance to Weisen's club you couldn't go empty-handed. I presume you gave a little truth here and there."

"*Ja,* yes. Yes, I gave them the *Nacht und Nebel* signal for one. It seemed safe enough. We didn't think it would ever be used. Also, I passed a few real names. Three, if you're counting. They were the first to die."

"It happens." Bond did not want Wimper getting maudlin on him. In any war there are casualties, and in war some of the KIAs die by friendly fire. It was also true in his own world, and it had been a cross borne by all intelligence services during the Cold War, of which Weisen was simply an extension.

"What's he really after? Wolfie, I mean. Not simply vengeance surely. Not just the genocide of Cabal?"

"Oh, no. How much did they give you on Wolfie?"

"Enough."

"Then you know about his childhood?"

"Brought up with Joe Stalin . . ."

"Brought up!" Wimper's voice rose to an unacceptable level in the cloistered temple to the goddess of food. A waiter froze in the act of serving the Americans, and the dark Italian girl shifted in her chair, turning lazy eyes on Wimper in a look of contempt she had so far reserved only for the man with whom she was dining.

"Brought up," he repeated, lowering the voice to almost a whisper. "He actually called Stalin 'Uncle.' Uncle Joe. He *called* him that. He thinks of him as a father. Still. He imagines that he's the one true and holy receptacle of that monster's political faith, and he'll wage war by all the means at his disposal. Wolfgang Weisen hated everyone who came after Stalin, because he regarded them as a bunch of Judases who sold out on the old man. He's pledged to return not just Communism, but Stalinism to Europe."

"A leftist fruitcake."

"Maybe, my friend. Maybe. But please don't underestimate the man. He has a small army at his disposal, actually. If he can crack his way into a disrupted Europe, then there is a chance— slim, I admit—that he might just bring back the ice age. He believes the time will come when the true believers'll rise up again in the old Soviet Empire. Things are so shaky there that, should Europe begin to tilt, Weisen might get his toe in the door."

"You're serious?"

Wimper gave him a little smile meant to denigrate. "You haven't met him. He has all the good characteristics of a dictator. He can be charming, make you believe black is white. He's a magician in many ways, and he seems absolutely open and dedicated to his people. He regards the Russians as his people. Behind a colorful, enchanting facade, the man's a walking nightmare."

"And you think he's on to you?"

"I'd put money on it. I've been, supposedly, doing a couple of things for him in Europe. Passing incomprehensible instructions to some of his agents . . ."

"What kind of instructions?"

"Oh, World War Two stuff. You know the kind of thing. I call a number and say, 'Anastasia is not dead.' Or 'The grey goose will be at the windmill.' "

"So, something's up?"

"Meaning Weisen has some kind of an operation running? My dear fellow, Wolfie always has some kind of an operation running. Come to think of it, though, the messages this time seemed more urgent. Yes, he just might have something going down, and if that's the case it might be very big."

For a second, Bond's mind slid back to Paris. He was in the car with Cold Claude and Big Michelle. Once more his mental fingers almost touched something: a word, a phrase? Then it was gone. Put it away. It will return soon enough. He looked at Wimper. "And he's called you back here?"

"I'm supposed to arrive tomorrow afternoon, so I thought I'd slip in a day early. I didn't expect a reception committee at Marco Polo today."

"There was one?"

"For you, I suspect. That was why I kept you hanging around in the launch. It's okay. His hired guns didn't see me. I'm pretty sure he doesn't know I'm here yet."

"But he *does* know about me."

"Oh, yes. Probably knows everything about you. Even when you go to the bathroom, actually. Especially if the others've walked into his ambush. Harry Spraker, I suspect, was the drover. Got them all penned down nicely. Someone'll probably turn up for you later, that's why I suggest we get in first."

Bond raised a hand, "Hang on a minute . . ." A waiter approached to serve more coffee and ask, in the tones of a celebrant, if everything was satisfactory. They told him more than satisfactory, but he did not go away looking happy. It was too serious a matter.

"You've already got some kind of plan up your sleeve," Bond continued, "but I've a couple more questions to ask you."

Wimper leaned back in his chair, placing the tips of his fingers on the edge of the table, as if to say, "Go ahead. Shoot."

"You know any Weisen men called Dominic Jellineck and Dorian Crone?"

Wimper chuckled. "They here?"

"Yes. You know them?"

"Did Fred Astaire dance? Of course I know Dominic and Dorian. A pair of, how do you say it in English? Likely lads?"

"Possibly."

"I shouldn't laugh, actually. They're unpleasant, and that's complimenting them. They're what you might call Champagne Stalinists. They work with money, and they also have a penchant for hurting people. The kind of Stalinists who think it's okay as long as you're well in with the boss. They've made money for Weisen, and for themselves. If his uncle had been Hitler, they would have been Nazis, I think, actually."

"They make money and pain?"

"In equal proportions. I hope Wolfie hasn't set them on our friends because the bastards're sadists. I believe they have delusions of grandeur. They imagine he's going to appoint them as joint heads of his secret police on the day of his second coming: a day of wrath and doom if it arrives. A day of death and destruction also."

"You've worked Weisen's side of the street for how long now?"

" 'Eighty-seven . . . 'eighty-eight."

"And how do you get orders, report to him, all that kind of thing?"

"The usual complex arcane ways. Dead drops, telephone codes. The occasional face-to-face. The stuff of spy novels, but it is *the* stuff, actually. As well you know."

"The last time you saw him was . . . ?"

"Paris, nine weeks ago. Wolfie has a tendency to appear, in a puff of smoke, when you least expect him. Before Paris, I saw him in London during the summer. I *have* spoken to him a number of times since then. Silly little telephone codes. You know."

He knew all right. "And he's called you in?"

Wimper gave a small sinister laugh. "I suspect it's like his Uncle Stalin all over again. Old Joe used to call people back to Moscow to give them the bullet, actually, but you know that. Yes, Wolfie's ordered me to meet him here, yes."

"Here? Where exactly?"

"In his small, private palazzo, actually."

"You've been here before?"

"You mean to the Palazzo Weisen? Of course. That's why I thought we'd pay him a private visit tonight, actually. Maybe catch him off guard. Maybe not."

"The two of us?"

"Well, I wasn't thinking of calling in the Carabinieri. We don't know who he might have on the payroll."

"And you have a way in? A way to get around his security at this Palazzo Weisen?"

"Oh, my dear fellow, it's not really the Palazzo Weisen, actually. That was a joke. But it is a small palazzo. Fronts onto the Grand Canal just below the Rialto—*Rialto di lá*, actually."

"Di lá?"

"How well do you know Venice, James?"

"On the surface. I've been in and out several times. Seen the sights: Doges' Palace, St. Mark's Square—Piazza San Marco as you'd say. Done the Bridge of Sighs and the Rialto. . . ."

"Let me explain, then, the Rialto . . ."

"I know, was once the great center of commerce."

"Yes, and the Ponte di Rialto is a somewhat ugly, clumsy bridge, with a lot of shops built into it, and a market running riot. The whole area is the Rialto. The San Marco side of the Grand Canal, as it runs through the Rialto, is always known as *Rialto di quà*. The far side is *Rialto di lá*. 'This side' and 'that side.' Weisen's little palazzo is on 'that side.' "

"Is this going to help us?"

190

"In a way, yes. I don't advise that we try and tackle it from the Canal, actually. That would be like assaulting a fortress, I think. But, if we cross the Rialto Bridge, take a left through the labyrinth of streets, we come to the Campo San Silvestro. A small piazza, in front of St. Silvestro—since the success of Mr. Stallone, I suppose St. Silvestro is the patron saint of boxers." He thought that was no end of a joke, but Bond did not even smile.

"And how does this help us, Gus? You're giving me a geography lesson."

"That church, San Silvestro, contains a beautiful Tintoretto. Very dramatic, actually."

"For crying out loud, does it help us?"

"Very much so. The rear wall of Wolfie's Venetian lair forms part of one side of the square. How are you on climbing buildings?"

"With the right equipment I can hold my own."

"I'm rather good at it. If we leave here around one in the morning, we should make the roof of Wolfie's mini-palazzo by about three. It'll be all downhill from there. I know the interior well."

"And how exactly do we get over there?"

"We steal one of this hotel's nice launches. I also know a man from whom we can get ropes and the like. He owes me a favor. What weapons have you got, actually, James?"

Bond told him.

"I can lay my hands on an Uzi, so we should be well set up."

"And if we're not?"

"Oh, I think there'll be death and destruction, actually. Not just here, but through Europe as a whole, now I've had time to reflect on the messages I've been passing out. Yes, very much death and destruction."

In spite of Wimper's grave and serious face, Bond smiled. He had remembered two lines of poetry:

This is the way the world ends
Not with a bang but a whimper.

191

14

Signing a Death Warrant

Bond waited, silent in the darkness.

They had lingered over their coffee and brandy for a good half an hour as Wimper gave a floor-by-floor description of Weisen's house on the Grand Canal. Again he stressed the difficult climb they would have to make from the Campo San Silvestro, and Bond recalled that in Venice all the squares but one are called *campi*—literally translated, *fields*. The only square in Venice is the Piazza San Marco.

"Let me draw you a diagram," Wimper said, then realized, grabbing a napkin, that here in the Cipriani, the napkins are the real thing. "Second thoughts, I just sketch it in words." He looked sheepishly at the linen and put away his pen.

"The roof's flat, and there's a large skylight right over the top-story landing," he said, copying the soft tones the waiters used to talk of food.

"The hired help have their quarters up there, so we have to get the thing open quietly and drop down, silent like ghosts. Weisen seldom has less than six heavies in residence, sometimes more. We can count on four at the top of the house, and a couple roaming around the place. The Dwarf likes someone awake at all times. Oh, and they have one bathroom up there.

When Dominic and Dorian are around, they're always fighting over the damned bathroom."

The second story was used as Weisen's personal quarters: a large bedroom usually shared with Monika Haardt; a room they used for relaxation; a conference room; two small bathrooms and another spare bedroom—"He uses it when he gets fed up with Monika. Me? I'd use it all the time if I lived with that bitch."

At ground and water level there were two reception rooms: "They're like a slum," Wimper declared—a big kitchen and the front hall. "The furnishings look as if they were stolen from a city dump."

"I suspect he'll be holding everyone in the cellar. The place used to belong to a bishop, several centuries ago, and for a man of the cloth he had a big wine cellar. Also he had some kind of lock-up down there. I think this bishop did a little torture and bondage on the side—no pun intended, James. It's like a big cell with one wall made up entirely of bars, and a padlocked gate. There're no windows and it's as damp as a jogging Yuppie: way below the water level. But that's where we'll head for. If we can make it with luck and a following wind, we take them back the same way as we get in. Okay?"

Bond said it was okay by him, but secretly wondered if they could get through the house and back again with three prisoners, without waking anyone. He did not like the thought of a firefight. Long experience had taught him that weapons used within the confines of a relatively small building are even more dangerous than when you use them out in the open. Luck and low cunning would be their only allies tonight.

They had two more brandies, then Wimper came back to the junior suite. "You got some pull with this hotel?" he asked with a grin.

"Why?"

"You got a better room than I, actually."

He stayed while Bond changed into a black cotton rollneck and a light zippered nylon windbreaker, both of which had been packed in the larger section of the briefcase. While in the bathroom, he also raided the business end of the case, distributing various articles in the pockets of the windbreaker which would hide the butt of the ASP, in its usual place, hard against the small of his back.

They were just leaving to go to Wimper's room when the telephone buzzed: even the phones in the hotel emitted a soft noise, as though apologizing for the intrusion. Bond answered with an equally placid "Yes?"

"Mr. Bunyan, this is the front desk. We tried to get you earlier, but didn't wish to bother you during dinner. Your wife telephoned. She's staying with your other friends in Venice tonight and says they'll all be back first thing in the morning."

"She leave a number where I can get her?"

"I'm afraid not, sir."

He returned the handset to its rest. "I imagine that means they're all with Weisen."

Wimper nodded. "Not good, James. They'll be here for *you* before the night's over, so let's hope we're long gone before they arrive. Until I've got hold of the stuff we need, I suggest you stay very alert." He looked Bond up and down, like a tailor showing disgust at the suit worn by a prospective client. "Your shoe size?" he asked. "I think we both require black trainers."

They agreed on that, and went through the list of items that Wimper would have to assemble if the assault on Weisen's palazzo stood any chance of success. When they concurred, Wimper led Bond to his room, a much smaller single without such necessary items as a levitating television set.

"I should be back in an hour—two hours max," the former Vopo said softly. "I should keep the lights off if I were you. Double lock the door. I'll tap out a Morse code W, but check me through the fish-eye, just in case. I've seen Weisen doing fast interrogations. He's rabid and very enthusiastic, so I might not be able to hold out if he gets his hands on me, so keep your fingers crossed."

"I'll keep everything crossed." He punched Wimper lightly on the shoulder. "You sure you can get all this equipment?"

"I told you. I have people here who owe me a lot of favors. Trust me. By the time I get back, I should know how we're fixed for a boat."

He explained that while, technically, the Cipriani's launches ran all night, they usually only had one of the pilots on duty once all guests were accounted for. "The guy sleeps on the ground floor, they wake him up if anyone wants to go over in the wee small hours, and they moor the launches down from the landing stage, near the pool—so sleeping guests won't be disturbed. We'll simply walk through the gardens, cast off, and start the motor when we're offshore. Just don't get yourself taken while I'm away."

"The same applies. I wouldn't want to come searching for you by myself."

"Look, if I disappear you should call in reinforcements. Don't try the Dwarf's place on your own."

"I'll bear it in mind." He followed Wimper to the door, double locking it as soon as he left.

Then Bond pulled a chair into a corner of the room from where he had an unobstructed view of the door and window, and waited, silent, in the darkness.

His eyes quickly adjusted, and he concentrated on staying alert, mentally going through the weapons and specialist accessories already available to him.

Apart from the ASP and four extra speed loaders, he carried his favorite fighting knife—a finely honed updated version of the old Sykes-Fairburn commando dagger—which had been concealed in a sliding compartment at the base of the briefcase. The scabbard was strapped to his right calf, while on his left was a Buck Master survival knife which would obviate the need for an anchor once they had reached the top of Weisen's building and were ready to go down the skylight.

The Buck Master is *the* survival knife for special forces. The handle is hollow and the blade razor sharp, slightly curved on one side, while the upper half of the other side is wickedly serrated. Inside the handle are detachable anchor pins, used for grappling hooks, and the skeleton handle, under its outer haft, is fashioned into a knuckle-duster.

He also carried the two pens, with two refills for each, nestling within a shock-proof case inside the windbreaker, while in other pockets there were two Haley & Waller Dartcord rapid-opening systems: explosive charges in strip form, with a primer and detonator for each. With its chevron cross-section, the Dartcord will blow precision holes through doors, steel and brickwork with minimum effort.

In small leather pouches attached to his belt there were further instruments, including three so-called "flash-bang" stun grenades—in the handy cartridge size, which Ann Reilly had assured him were "super-effective," with a new type of explosive and a higher grade of flash powder. Also, within easy reach, he carried a steel Leatherman. A tool measuring only two and a half inches by less than an inch, the Leatherman converts into a pair of heavy-duty pliers, knife, screwdriver, file and other implements. In all, he found it easier and more sturdy to use than the omnipresent Swiss Army knife.

Weisen's men arrived about seventy minutes after Wimper left. They came intent on a frontal attack, knocking at the door—just as they had doubtless already knocked at Bond's door.

Silently he moved from the chair to stand, back flat against the wall, directly to one side of the door. His automatic pistol was out, safety off, the weapon held high, close to his left shoulder.

Waiting. Listening to the scratching sounds. The room had already been made up for the night, so he was under no illusion that this was maid service. Chambermaids usually carry master keys, and would not, therefore, try the locks with picks. He stood, still as a tree on an airless morning, hearing only the sounds of the picklocks and his heart thudding in his ears.

Whoever was there worked for ten minutes, but the two double locks defeated them. He heard the soft footsteps move away from the door. It would take them only a short time to climb across the roof, and check out his own room, via the window, before reaching the French doors of Wimper's room. That was the next natural move, so there was time to prepare a small surprise for them.

Softly he opened the French doors, which could be forced by a five-year-old with a toothpick. These were not five-year-olds, and he was certain they were armed with much more deadly weapons than toothpicks.

The French doors out of Wimper's room led to a narrow path, culminating in a private sun deck, similar to the one outside Bond's room. These small circular plots, complete with table, sun-umbrellas and smart wooden loungers, had slatted wooden floors and were hedged about with bushes and ferns which gave them complete privacy.

Wimper's deck, like his own, he figured, would have a view of the hotel pool below, for the ferns and bushes camouflaged a brick wall which dropped sheer to make up part of the pool's surrounding sun trap. Silently he moved forward. Already he could hear the sound of at least one of the intruders testing the strength of the vines growing against the wall about thirty feet below.

Kneeling, Bond took out the Leatherman and opened up the pliers. From one of his windbreaker's zipped pockets he drew out a length of thin wire, measured off several feet, then cut it with the wire-stripping recess of the pliers.

The vine was shaking gently as one of the men began to climb. He heard a whispered conversation from below.

"It'll take you also. It's strong enough."

"You're sure?"

"Certain. Come on, we can both be in at the kill."

All this in German.

Working quickly, he secured one end of the wire around the solid metal stem of the table, which was set in a heavy stone base. He ran the wire at an angle, just above the slats of the floor so that anybody trying to reach the path to Wimper's room would certainly either trip or tread on it.

Taking out one of the cartridge-sized "flash-bangs," he rammed the base hard between two of the slats at the very edge of the deck, and winding the end of the wire through the little ring, he loosened the pin. The wire was taut across the floor. One hard knock and the stun grenade would explode.

He retreated, closing the French doors but remaining on the outside. Sinking to his knees, he removed the long padded box from inside the windbreaker, and lifted out the gold pen. This one he handled very carefully, reminding himself that you could write only death warrants with it, and it gave you but two chances.

The weapon was a pen gun—a refined, more sophisticated, version of the En-Pen used by the clandestine services of World War II. The old En-Pen was a single shot device, with a kick that bruised your hand and made the business of killing highly problematic. This new weapon, which Q Branch had unofficially named the Mont Non-Blanc, carried a pair of modified .22 rounds. The bullets were hollow point and filled with a small charge of explosive which was detonated on impact. One of these .22 bullets, grazing a man in the shoulder would, most likely, take the target's arm off—unless you were lucky and only lost most of the bone in the resulting explosion.

The safety catch was incorporated into the pen's clip. Pushing back on the clip activated the safety, pushing forward, took the safety off. You then held the weapon firmly between the first and second fingers, making sure that the end was cushioned against the palm. Aim was instinctive, and slight pressure on the clip fired the first round, the gases of which automatically loaded the second ready for the next shot.

Bond waited, feeling the cold chill of the night air for the first time, and realizing that the mist still hung around the building in patches. Once more he could hear the beat of his heart, and he took in steady, slow, deep breaths. At moments like this he never allowed himself to think of the brutality of killing, but kept his mind apart from the reality, concentrating only on the technique of his work. He saw the leaves at the top of the wall start to shake, and a male figure came silently onto the deck, reaching back to assist a second man across.

Bond slid the pen's clip forward and brought his hand up, steadying it by wrapping the fingers of his left hand around the right wrist. As the two figures moved forward, he closed his eyes against the flash that would come as soon as the wire was tripped.

Stun grenades cannot kill or wound, unless you are foolish enough to hang on to one after the pin has been pulled. They do however produce one—sometimes two—explosions, described in official literature as "distracting." In fact, the noise level can be like that of a light artillery shell landing nearby, and the accompanying violent flash will temporarily blind anyone in the vicinity.

The flash came before the explosion. Bond felt it through his eyelids, and a fraction later the blast was strong enough to shatter the windows behind him.

He opened his eyes, looking straight at the smoke pluming out and swirling around the sun deck. The pair of trespassers were reeling around the area, very close to the wall. He lifted the pen and fired, twice and in quick succession.

One of the men had time to scream as he went backwards out of sight, a thud coming from below, just as the hotel alarm system started to shriek. The second man was luckier. Unharmed by the bullets, he vaulted unsteadily over the wall, scrabbling with his hands for the vine before his disorientation and semi-daze caused him to clutch air. He made a squeaking noise as he disappeared, and the crunch that followed contained the noise of breaking bones.

Back through the broken windows, Bond could hear the sounds of panic in the corridor outside Wimper's room. This was no time to hang around and answer questions, he decided, but as he approached the door, he heard an urgent knocking, tap-bump-bump, tap-bump-bump. The letter W in Morse code.

He did not even bother to check out the fish-eye, but opened up to find August Wimper, leaning against the door jamb, the familiar camel-hair coat around his shoulders, and one hand holding a tote bag.

"Was it something I said?" he asked, deadpan.

"No," Bond was halfway out of the door. "No, Gus. I forgot that I'd left the gas on. Silly of me."

Guests and staff seemed to be milling around in a kind of panic. The reception foyer was full of people in various forms of dress and undress. The majority of the women wore toweling robes and hair curlers. Some looked decidedly embarrassed. As they passed through the crowd, Bond saw the languid, dark Italian girl, from dinner, trying to pretend she was not with the elderly man who did not look as suave without teeth.

Wimper stopped one of the dark-suited managers. "Was it a terrorist bomb? This is disgraceful. I doubt if I'll ever stay here again."

The man tried to calm him, but Gus stuck his head into the air and marched back in the direction from which they had come, Bond following, his face registering the annoyance which had sounded in Wimper's voice.

"Where in hell're we going, Gus?" he inquired.

"The gardens are out of the doors on the other side. We're going to rescue the ladies, aren't we? What they say in the old cowboy movies? We're the Fifth Cavalry riding to save *Eagle* and Praxi."

"Don't forget Bruin."

"*Ja*, yes, we can do with that old bear's strength."

Outside, from across the water, came the sound of sirens as fire, ambulance and police launches slid through the mist towards the Cipriani.

Bond stayed in the light from the hotel for a moment in order to reload the pen gun, Wimper nagging at him to move.

"Can't think of a better time to rip off one of their boats,"

200

Wimper said. You could hear the smile rather than see it. "You've obviously had a very exciting evening. You get them?"

"One for certain. The other could well have damaged himself on the way down. There'll be a lot of people asking for explanations."

They were in the garden now, and there, hovering near the moored boats, were two Cipriani employees, wearing the caps of the hotel's launch pilots. "Bluff it out." Wimper increased his stride. "I can never go back anyway, and I had some very good clothes in that room. I hope you've left nothing important."

Bond felt his pockets. As well as the weapons and equipment, he had three passports, several small envelopes containing credit cards matching the different identities, the equivalent of £2,000. in sterling travellers cheques, and a wad of deutsche marks. He would, reluctantly, have to forget about the briefcase, though he could afford to lose the blazer, spare shirts, socks and underwear. Never leave home without it, he thought of his AmEx Platinum card. He could go shopping tomorrow—if he was still alive.

"You there." Wimper spoke Italian with a thick German accent. "We need to get over to San Marco now. I'll return in the morning, but we're certainly not staying in this hotel for another minute." He flashed his Cipriani guest card and the two men conferred for a few seconds while he kept up a flow of Italian invective about how useless the hotel was, how he would sue them if any of his property was damaged, and how this kind of thing would never happen in a good German hotel. At last one of them beckoned. "We'll take you over." He headed towards the moored launches. "I'm on duty anyway, and Franco here has to get home. It was a big bang there. What happened?"

"It could've been one of the waiters self-destructing," Wimper muttered. Then, louder, "It must've been terrorists. We could all have died in our beds."

The Italian nodded sagely and said something about the

world getting more dangerous every day, and times being out of joint. It would have sounded almost Shakespearean if he had not used a large number of Italian curses.

One of the police launches hailed them as they pulled away, and there was some good-humored banter between the cops and the two Cipriani men.

Franco, the one getting a ride home, came through the long cabin to examine something in the stern. The man at the helm did not even glance back.

"You get everything?" Bond asked in almost a whisper.

"The lot. You feel up to the climb?"

"I feel up to getting the others away from Venice."

"I think we'll have to take care of Weisen and Haardt before we finally wave farewell."

The mist was patchy, sometimes almost clear, with a swirl like thin smoke hanging close to the water, then they would hit what seemed to be almost solid cloud.

It was not until they came out into a stretch completely devoid of mist and fog that Bond realized they had turned away from the landing stages at the Piazza San Marco and were heading into the Grand Canal itself.

"We need San Marco!" he called to the helmsman.

"Yes, but I'm afraid we need the Grand Canal and you with us." Franco stood in the stern, an automatic pistol in his hand.

The helmsman glanced over his shoulder with a smile. "We brought two guys over to get you," he said in perfect English. "I think we'll get a bonus for bringing you back alive."

Wimper pulled his coat more tightly around his shoulders, and smiled straight into the helmsman's face. "Oh, I'm sure you will, Antonio. I'm sure you will." He turned his head towards Franco. "Herr Weisen will be very pleased with you," his voice soft and pleasant as honey.

15

Death on the Grand Canal

Gus Wimper sighed, a touch loudly—a long melancholy sound which seemed to come from a dark place within his very soul. Then he squared his shoulders, allowing the topcoat to drop onto the padded bench behind him. He began to rise from the seat, hands open, arms held away from his body to show he was unarmed.

"Watch it, Kraut." Franco, the one in the stern toting a gun, took half a step further into the cabin.

"Oh, don't be stupid . . . What's your name? Franco? I'm not about to hurt anyone; and I should be careful with the racist remarks, your boss wouldn't like it." He followed through, standing up and turning towards the helmsman. As he did so, Bond felt a slight pressure as Wimper's leg touched his knee. The signal was meant to tell him something, and he could only translate it in terms of Wimper trying to distract the two men.

"Antonio," Wimper moved a fraction to his left, facing the helmsman's back. "I didn't recognize you with a beard—but, then, the light wasn't very good . . ."

"It's going to get even worse when the chief sees you, Gus. He didn't buy the stunt you pulled with the body they fished out of the canal, but it was a good try."

"Yes, I thought so." He moved again, and this time the coat, bunched precariously on the padded bench, slid to the deck.

Bond stooped forward to retrieve it.

"Don't do anything silly," from Franco who was waving his gun around as though directing traffic.

"I never argue with people holding guns." Bond turned his head so that he could look Franco straight in the eyes as he fumbled for the coat with both hands. Often the best method of diversion is to make sure your adversary's eyes are occupied with your own face. Slowly he lifted the coat with his left hand, and for a second it shielded his legs. His right hand slid under the bottom of his trouser leg, and the Sykes-Fairburn dagger came out of its scabbard without a sound.

He threw the coat straight at the gunman, and almost at the same moment the dagger flicked through the air, its razor point cutting into the man's throat with a force that drove the blade through the side of the neck.

Franco looked as though he did not believe what had happened. The gun dropped from his fingers and his hands re-flexed, tugging at the dagger, trying to pull it from his throat.

Behind him, Bond heard a yell, followed by a series of grunts, but he was occupied with the death of the gunman, who had now crumpled to the deck, making unpleasant rattling noises. Bond reached down and pulled hard on the dagger, one foot on the man's chest. He must have died at the moment the knife came out, because the rattling stopped.

Glancing behind him, he saw that Wimper had taken care of the helmsman, and was standing back, detaching a wire garrote from around the man's neck. "Silent killing's much better than all those bangs," he murmured.

Their eyes met and Bond winked as he caught hold of Franco's ankles and pulled him back into the stern, heaving him over the side, while Wimper did something similar with the one who in life had been called Antonio. The launch wallowed, alarmingly out of control.

"I do apologize, James." Wimper had taken the wheel and

was turning the craft back out of the Grand Canal. "Unforgivable of me. I should have recognized friend Antonio. He never was a subtle man: one of Weisen's gofers. Oh, lord, he's bled all over the deck."

Bond was leaning across the side, his right hand holding the Sykes-Fairburn in the water, washing off the blood. He dried off the blade with a piece of rag lying in the stern well, then returned it to the scabbard. "Couldn't we just pull over to the starboard side and tie up?" he asked. "We're almost opposite San Silvestro."

"We *could*," Gus called back, "but we're not going to. I want to get as far away from those floaters as I can. Anyway, engine noise carries on a night like this. No way am I going to risk any of the Dwarf's people being alerted. They'd think in terms of a frontal assault, so we go back and make the journey on foot. Okay?"

"Whatever you say, Gus."

They ploughed into a thick mist, then out again. The houses on either side of the wide Canal looked eerily shrouded, and some were almost invisible in more dense fog. Their lights, refracted through the damp clouds, gave an impression of absurd unreality.

Venice could do that to you even on a hot cloudless summer's day, as you walked through its narrow streets or floated along its maze of canals in gondolas, *traghetti*—the public gondola ferries—or *vaporetti,* the water buses.

Of all the cities in Europe, Venice is perhaps the only one in which you experience constant changes of perspective: A well-known street, bridge or *campo* can appear deceptively different in late afternoon from the way it did when you were last there in the morning. Bond recalled that, years before, he spent two hours trying to find a store he had seen on the previous day. The place, which sold handmade paper, appeared to have vanished overnight, and when he finally discovered it again, the entire locale looked dissimilar to his memory of it.

A friend had once jokingly said that he was certain Venice

was built like a puzzle of movable squares, with one vacant space. Venetians, he maintained, came out at night and pushed the pieces into a different pattern to confuse visitors.

Now, as they slid through the water, it was as though he had never seen the Grand Canal before: its aspect had been so changed by the mist and fog.

"Gus?" he asked. "Your body was supposed to have been pulled out of this water—what happened?"

Wimper steadied the launch as they rounded the wide exit from the Grand Canal and headed towards the jetties near St. Mark's Square. "I told you, I have people here who owe me favors. I came to Venice often with Liz. We discovered, almost by accident, that Wolfie Weisen had a hideaway here. Over the years I got to know quite a lot of Venetians, including the police. It became very necessary for me to disappear when the Dwarf began to suspect something. I simply did a deal."

"A deal as in money changing hands?"

"The Dwarf's people are never short of money. I think he has his own presses. No, that's not it. Wolfie's been skimming money off the top for years. Transferring it out of the old Germany; stashing it away in banks all over Europe, and even in the States, I think."

"And the deal was?"

In the murk, Gus turned and smiled. "First unidentifiable body they netted was to be identified as me. Also the word would be passed along. They have a great whispering grapevine here in Venice."

"Wouldn't surprise me at all." Bond reflected that in the sixteenth century the Venetian Republic had what was probably the most advanced intelligence and security service in the world—the infamous Council of Ten which, in spite of its name, consisted of around thirty people. The powerful Council had employed an international network of spies, agents, informers and assassins. In the history of the secret world, the Council of Ten was arguably the most efficient intelligence organization of all time. But who knew? he wondered. The myth that the old Venetian Republic had the greatest political constitution the world has ever known, certainly influenced the founding fathers of America when their constitution was drawn up.

"You've handled one of these before." Bond was impressed by the way Wimper skilfully brought the launch inshore, past the Palazzo Contarini, with its extraordinary exterior hanging staircase, then alongside the deserted little jetties which run out from the strip of waterfront adjacent to the fortress-like Zecca, the ancient treasury and mint.

They tied up at an empty berth, and Gus Wimper unzipped the tote he had been carrying, tossing out a pair of black Nike trainers for Bond, slipping out of his own elegant shoes, replacing them with trainers similar to the ones Bond was lacing up. Then, he took off the jacket of his tailored suit and began to wrap a length of thin, nylon climbing rope around his body, covering it with a bulky black pullover which had been chosen to hide many things. He cleaned out the pockets of his suit, transferring his few belongings—a wallet, the garrote, and a small 6.35mm, so-called "Baby Beretta"—to his trouser pockets and waistband.

"You carry a peashooter, Gus?" Bond gave the weapon a look of disdain. The "Baby Beretta" required exceptional marksmanship at close quarters to be effective, and was certainly not a "stopping" pistol.

Gus grinned. "I don't like them big, and I usually work up close. One between the eyes at three feet does it every time. Anyhow, bangs frighten me." He tossed a length of the nylon climbing rope to Bond, who took off the zippered jacket, circled the rope crosswise, from right shoulder to left hip, then covered it with the jacket again.

"You have all the other things we discussed?"

Bond nodded as the German added one further item to his waistband: a bulky Hilton pyrotechnic pistol.

"What happens if the gendarmes stop us?" he asked.

Wimper gave him the old grin which was now getting infectious. "It's the Carabinieri, actually, James."

"I know that, *actually*, Gus. What if they do stop us? Seriously?"

"Tell them we locked ourselves out of the house?"

The mist was rolling in off the water now, thickening considerably, almost obscuring the ornate multi-bracketed lamps which were supposed to illuminate both the Piazza di San Marco and the Piazzetta di San Marco, that open area which extends, past the Doges' Palace—once called "the central building of the world"—to the waterfront.

They left the launch and, hugging the wall opposite the Palace—for seven centuries, the seat of government and ducal residence of the Venetian Republic—turned left into that unique square, with the great Campanile of St. Mark's Cathedral, the tallest tower in Venice, almost invisible through the fog. The cathedral was enmeshed in metal scaffolding, Bond saw just before they turned to enter the long stone arcade running around three sides of the square which is so often a backdrop to history, and normally surrounds the most unusual entertainment in the world: though not now, on this chill, foggy, doleful night.

Bond recalled the piazza as he had last seen it, during a summer day three or four years before, tourist infested, with the arcade shops full of slightly tawdry goods, and the orchestra at the Florian sawing out gems from Andrew Lloyd Webber.

It was the ever-changing light and the almost theatrical background which somehow made the entire experience different. Put the same people in Trafalgar, or even Times Square, and they would become simply a rather tacky crowd. Yet here, in this incredible and magic place, even a wandering file of sightseers, led by a lady holding up a glove on a stick, seemed quaint and diverting. The Piazza di San Marco is the greatest people-watching site in the world.

Not, however, at almost two o'clock in the deserted desolate morning, when you could not even see the cloistered archways on the far side. Already, as he glanced back, Bond saw that the massive needle of the Campanile, topped by its stone spire and gilded angel, had disappeared from view. The mist was pulling itself in across the entire city, blanketing the alleys and narrow streets, rolling up the canals, and distorting the appearance of every step, bridge, archway and tower.

It was a night, he thought, made especially for such an exploit as this attempt to rescue Easy, Praxi and Bruin. The serious, clandestine nature of their task became wrapped in a kind of romance of near gothic proportions. Even when swathed in fog, the strong necromancy of Venice had the last word.

By now they had plunged into the maze of streets through which Gus Wimper seemed to navigate blind. The mist lifted and then billowed around them again, as they moved fast and almost silently over bridges, out into small squares, down cobbled steps. In the whole world, it was as though they were the only people awake and about on this night.

It took almost half an hour to reach the Rialto Bridge, the sight of which always surprised Bond, no matter how often he visited the place. It was a clumsy design, somewhat out of proportion, with its covered stone shops rising from each side, flattening off along the center and looking strangely as though it were defying the laws of gravity. On seeing it now, looming from what looked like heavy smoke, his first thoughts were not of its long history but of its oddity. Yet, for all its ugliness, he remembered days when he had stood on the outside walkways and marveled at the spectacular views of the Grand Canal.

Now, in the early hours of a new day, the silence around the Rialto felt somehow wrong. He was used to coming here to look at the market stalls, the open-fronted stone shops, and to brush shoulders with the ever-moving crowd which crushed and flowed in both directions. Now, as they climbed the steps of the first section, all was silence, except for the barking of a dog far away, and the sound of gondolas bumping softly in the swell of the water below.

By the time they reached the far side, they were both soaked with sweat, combined with the fine droplets of mist. Gus paused for a second to indicate they had not far to go, then he struck out to the left, inland. Five minutes later he came to a halt, at the edge of a small square, back against the wall, turning to Bond, motioning him to wait. The mist was thinning, and it was as if faraway voices whispered out of sight in the dark—the sound of water from the Grand Canal, which was now in front of them, behind the buildings they faced.

Wimper reached under the baggy pullover, gently unwinding the climbing rope, and quietly telling Bond that the wall, which was the rear of Weisen's house, was directly in front of them, some forty yards away, across the little square.

"I think you go up first," he said. "You can prepare the way down through the skylight and start working on the latch."

Bond nodded, feeling for one of the pouches on his belt, to take out a small flashlight no larger than his index finger. He switched on the light as Wimper produced the large-barreled Hilton Pyrotechnic pistol. The Hilton has many uses, from firing CS gas charges and smoke bombs to sending grappling irons up rock faces or, as in this case, to the top of a building. There was a whole series of detachable barrels, making the instrument a highly flexible asset to the armory of police and anti-terrorist units. Its portability was a plus, though both men wished they could have carried a larger dedicated mortar, for the only Hilton Gus could lay his hands on was an old model.

From the barrel of the pistol, Wimper eased out the shining steel end of the grapple which lay spring-loaded inside. It worked like an umbrella, folded within the barrel, about eight inches in length. When fired from the clumsy blunderbuss of a weapon, the steel arms would pop out and, theoretically, anchor themselves to the nearest obstacle. The protruding steel rod of the grapple ended in an oval ring which Wimper held out as Bond located the end of the rope to which was fixed a spring clip. The clip snapped into the ring and Wimper pushed the grapple back inside the Hilton's barrel, then broke the pistol like a shotgun. From another pocket he pulled out a long thick cardboard cartridge. The cartridge was pushed home and the breech closed. With Gus Wimper carrying the pistol and Bond holding the length of rope, they moved across the square until they came to within about fifteen feet of the wall.

Wimper nodded, and Bond indicated that the rope was clear, on the ground, and could not be fouled around either of their legs. The ex-Vopo raised the gun, his arm stretched up at an angle of forty-five degrees. He turned his head away and pulled the trigger. The pop from the cartridge sounded alarmingly loud, magnified by the enclosed space. They saw the streak and flash of metal as the grapple soared upwards, the rope following, snaking out like a white con trail disappearing into the darkness.

Wimper pulled gently on the end of the rope. From above they heard a scraping as the metal was drawn across the roof, the noise intensified by the silence of the night. Then the grating noise stopped, and Wimper felt pressure on the rope.

When they planned the rescue, over dinner, Gus Wimper said this was the only way. "It's the clumsy method, I know. But, actually, I can only get hold of old equipment, and a full-sized grapple mortar would attract a lot of notice in the streets of Venice."

"They attract a lot of attention anywhere. You sure this pyrotechnic cartridge'll work?"

"James, of course it'll work. If it doesn't, I'll end up with my hand blown off."

They moved in close to the wall, and Bond tested his weight on the rope. The grapple seemed to be holding firmly. Without looking back, he hauled himself upwards, swinging out until his body was parallel to the ground. Then, slowly, but firmly, he began to walk up the wall, his hands moving, one above the other in time to his feet, as he prayed the grapple would not break against whatever was holding it in place. As he walked upwards, he heard, in his head, an old Naval song which, long ago, was used by sailors working the heavy capstan. Its rhythm helped in the climb as he repeated the words under his breath:

"We're off to Samoa
By way of Genoa,
Roll on Shenandoah
And up with the line and away.
We're towing to Malta
The rock of Gibraltar
With only a halter
And Davy Jones lying below."

His shoulders ached, and his hands felt like fire by the time he reached the roof. It was flat, as Wimper had said, with a stone coping surrounding the top. The grapple had two of its anchors firmly against the coping which looked solid enough, with no cracks visible. He shook the rope lightly to signal that all was well.

The view, as he stood, after tiptoeing across the roof, was breathtaking. The mist, so dense only a few minutes before, was starting to lift. To the left he saw the grey bulk of the Rialto Bridge, the water below as smooth as black ice. In the other direction he could see the whole of the Grand Canal as it ran down towards the lagoon. Lights twinkled through the last remnants of the mist, and the buildings on either side of the Canal appeared to be slowly coming into focus—silhouetted against the other city illuminations which were starting to brighten as the mist lifted. The illusion was as though some invisible force was turning up a huge dimmer switch.

He found the skylight easily, for a bulb burned below it on the top story landing. It was secured by a heavy-duty padlock which had rusted, almost fusing with the D-ring which held it in place. As he found the screwdriver on the Leatherman tool, he felt something was wrong. In a house like this they would use the roof from time to time. The view was too exceptional to miss.

He shone the torch all the way around the skylight until he found what he was looking for. The rusted padlock was a dummy. The oblong, wooden, outer frame was only there for show. The opaque glass skylight was set into a metal frame, and the whole was secured by bolts below, and inside the house. The three hinges on one of the longer sides were in good condition and well oiled. They would be the only way in, so he began to work on the screws, and had one hinge free by the time Wimper was on the roof, beside him. The screws came out easily once they were loosened, and together they tested the framework when all the hinges were free. The heavy skylight moved in their hands. They got it up to almost a forty-five-degree angle, and Bond reached inside and shot the bolts.

They were now certain the skylight could be lifted off, so Bond began to remove the hilt of the Buck Master knife. When it came off, a pair of curved and pointed anchor arms were revealed along each side of the flat skeletal handle, lined with finger holes to double as a knuckle-duster. The two anchors moved easily, and Bond pressed down on them, feeling the welcome click as they locked into place, splaying out on either side of the handle.

Unzipping the nylon jacket, he removed his section of climbing rope—thinner than the one they had used to get onto the roof—and clipped it on to what would have been the thumb hold in the knuckle-duster skeleton framework. He looked up, raising his eyes questioningly to Wimper, who nodded. "Yes," he was saying. "Let's go. Let's go down and get them out."

Together they began to lift the skylight. The framework squealed in protest, and at the first noise they both froze, waiting for any movement below. Silence. Nothing. Again they lifted and the skylight came off easily.

Bond dropped the rope through the open well, securing the Buck Master knife against the surround so that the pair of splayed arms bit into the wood. He took the Sykes-Fairburn dagger in his left hand, swung himself into the well and went arm over arm to the floor below, followed a second later by Wimper. As soon as he hit the floor, Bond drew the ASP and took the safety off. The next minutes were crucial; their aim was silence, but, should they be detected, he was ready to use the gun to get out in one piece.

The landing and stairs beyond were covered with a thin, utilitarian carpet which helped silence their footsteps. Nobody stirred; no movement or noise came from below. They reached the second floor, where Weisen had his quarters. The house still slept, but, as they reached the top of the stairs leading down to the ground floor, Bond saw a figure in the large, marble-flagged hall, his back to them as he sat dozing in a chair about six paces from the bottom of the stairs.

Wimper nodded, slipped past him, and began to make his way stealthily down. The man in the chair was big, broad shoul-dered, and dressed in jeans and a sweater. From where he stood, covering the rear, Bond could see a pump-action shot-gun lying on the floor beside the chair.

He waited, palms damp with sweat, as Wimper inched down-wards, the garrote dangling from his right hand. Two paces from the chair, the German took the taped ends of the wire in each hand, then crossed his wrists so that the garrote flexed, forming a loop. One more step and the noose went over the man's head.

Bond thought he had never seen it done so well. The guard was well-built, and had obviously been half asleep in the chair. As the wire bit into his neck he arched his back, arms flailing as he struggled to get out of the seat. Wimper simply went on applying pressure. The first pull on the noose had been enough to crush the victim's windpipe. He did not even have a chance to cry out or gasp. It took less than thirty seconds for the body to sag, lifeless, back into the chair.

Wimper gently kicked the shotgun away, signaling Bond to come down. Mouthing that there would be another guard somewhere, he indicated a passage which ran alongside the stairs, leading to the kitchens and, presumably, down to the cellars.

They were halfway along the passage when they saw the other guard. The kitchen door stood open, and the man sat on the edge of a scrubbed wooden table, eating some kind of sandwich with his right hand, and holding a mug of coffee in his left.

Once more, Wimper tapped Bond's shoulder and brushed past him. This time the "Baby Beretta" was out and in his right hand. He reached the kitchen door, then increased speed, coming up behind the figure who was munching on his night snack. The guard sensed Wimper's presence a fraction of a second before the former cop jammed the little pistol into his right ear and said, "Good morning, Giorgio. Please don't do anything silly, because I hate violence and don't want to kill you." He used his Germanic Italian, but it appeared to serve the purpose.

The man stiffened, dropping the cheese roll and lowering the mug of coffee almost to the table. "Hand off that mug, Giorgio," Wimper commanded. You could tell by the tensed muscles of his back that he was seriously thinking of doing something about his predicament, so Bond moved into the kitchen, went around Wimper and stuck the ASP into Giorgio's mouth.

"Nod if you understand," Bond hissed. "Take us down to the prisoners and you'll be fine. Nothing's going to happen to you. But, if you're stupid, your brains'll be all over the wall. Okay?"

Giorgio nodded convincingly. His face came from a nightmare: strange high cheekbones, a broken nose, bulging eyes, one of which was set lower than the other, and a mouth which needed the work of a good orthodontist. He also seemed to have no neck, and all the hair was shaved from his head.

"Whisper when you answer," Wimper said. "Are there keys we need?"

"*Sì!*" The voice was throatily reminiscent of Marlon Brando's portrayal in *The Godfather*.

"Where are the keys?"

"Left pocket. My jeans."

Wimper leaned over and removed a key ring the size of a beer coaster. There were six large deadlock keys, old and solid, hanging from the ring.

"Now, just walk very slowly and show us how to get to our friends. Understand?"

Giorgio nodded, then paused. "You got past Carlo?" he grunted.

"If we didn't get past Carlo, we wouldn't be here, dummy."

"Carlo okay?"

"Sorry, Giorgio." Wimper shook his head. "Come on, stop wasting my time."

The kitchen had a second door, set in the wall some six feet from the entrance they had used. Giorgio indicated they should go in that direction, so they shuffled him across the room and Wimper tried the handle. The door opened to reveal a heavy second door. It looked as though it was made of steel and should really be in a bank vault. There was a spoked wheel in the center, a combination lock and a keyhole.

"Just tell us how." Bond whispered.

"Combination's 6963. Then you turn the key. Then the wheel."

"Tell you what, you do it for us, except for the key. Set off an alarm and you've pulled the legs off your last fly, okay?"

Giorgio nodded slowly, as though he had to use considerable concentration, but everything worked. Behind the door they could just make out a long flight of wooden stairs. "Lights." He nodded towards an old switch set in what looked like a small brass jelly mould.

Bond thought he had not seen a switch like this for a long time. He remembered them from his childhood, and for a moment a host of memories floated into his head. A naked bulb flashed on just above the stairs showing the flight going down to a stone floor.

"After you, Giorgio." Bond gave a mock bow, and they began the descent.

Another switch at the bottom of the stairs illuminated a cold damp chamber which looked like a set straight out of a Verdi opera. To the right a huge stone archway was completely barred off: great thick iron rails, with heavy crosspieces and a gate section with a big, flat, metal lock.

Behind the bars something stirred. Then Bruin's voice. "It's the middle of the night. What the hell's . . . ? You brought Harry back?"

Another figure moved from the shadows of the cell. "James! Oh, thank heaven. James!" Easy St. John clung to the bars, her clothes tattered, hair matted and her face dirty and stained.

"James and *Orphan*. You were supposed to be dead." Praxi had rolled into view from a pile of old blankets. "You're alive?"

"I'm not a ghost, Praxi. Neither am I what you've been thinking."

"Prove it."

"Unlock the damned thing." Bond rammed his gun into Giorgio's head. "Which key'll get them out of there?" Then, to Praxi, "Gus is okay. Trust us." It was more of an order than a statement.

Giorgio indicated the key they should use, and the gate swung back, the mechanism well-oiled.

"I don't believe it." Praxi was still openmouthed, looking at Wimper.

"Takes more than water to get rid of me. I presume you now know about your friend Spraker."

"They took him away earlier tonight. Has that bastard Weisen killed him?"

"Harry's probably on his way to killing you," Bond said softly. "We'll tell you all about it later, we really have to get a move on." He stood back as they came out of the cell, and Gus Wimper began to instruct them on what they would have to do. "This has got to be quick and very quiet."

217

Bond pushed Giorgio through the gateway, and the ASP caught him on the back of the neck, sending him to his knees. A second blow had him flat on his face.

"You should kill him," Wimper snarled.

"Too noisy."

"You've got a damned dagger."

"Leave it." He closed the gate and turned the key. "Do they know what's expected of them?"

Wimper nodded, and Bond threw the keys into the far corner of the chamber, well away from the cell.

Gus led the way, with Bond at the rear to cover their retreat. As they reached the top of the stairs to the kitchen, Praxi began to protest again, saying she needed to know what had happened to Harry Spraker, and did Bond not realize that Wimper was almost certainly a traitor?

"Spheroids, Praxi." Bond smiled. "Just do as you're told, we haven't much time. Trust me."

The house remained still and quiet. By the time they reached the top floor Bond could hardly believe their luck. Now they were within an ace of pulling off the rescue.

They sent Bruin up first, then Praxi and Easy. Wimper followed, and Bond, putting the dagger back in its scabbard, but still holding on to the ASP, swarmed up the rope into the chill of the night.

They removed the Buck Master, and put the skylight back in place. The trio of prisoners were stretching their limbs, paying little attention to the cold night as they savored freedom.

"James, I was so worried . . ." Easy began.

"You were also a shameless hussy. Booking a suite for yourself and your husband."

"Well . . ." She grinned in the darkness.

Bond had just replaced the Buck Master and was leading them across to the rope which would get them from the roof, when he became suddenly aware of engine noise from the direction of the Grand Canal.

At first he thought it was some heavy watercraft starting up, but as they reached the grapple, he glanced to the left.

From behind the Rialto Bridge the squat black shape of a helicopter rose, hovering like some terrible, dangerous insect. A searchlight slashed the night. Then bullets began to hail down onto the roof around them.

16

Death in Venice

There was no cover. It was a case of being out on the roof with the metal beast chopping away above them, the bullets sharding the stonework. They had nowhere to run and no place to hide. All five of them instinctively threw themselves to the ground, and it took Bond a few seconds to realize that whoever was firing at them from the helicopter was not shooting to kill or wound.

"Get down the rope!" he yelled. "They're trying to frighten not kill. Get down the bloody rope. Give yourselves up to the police. They're bound to be here soon."

He saw Easy make it to the grapple and go over the side. The helicopter continued to move only a hundred feet or so above them, its searchlight picking them out one by one. Now, only an occasional burst of fire came from the chopper's doorway, and there was not much noise apart from the engine and rotor blades. Bond guessed they were using something like an Uzi with a silencer, or even a Swiss SIG which lent itself more easily to a noise-reduction system.

He saw Praxi go over the coping, with Bruin hunched, kneeling and waiting to follow her down. Strangely he did not even return the fire. A lucky shot might easily take out the gunner or pilot at this range, yet his instinct told him to hold back. If he, or Gus Wimper, began shooting, the gunner might well start aiming to kill. As it was, he had just put a couple of short bursts quite near to where Bruin had climbed over, following Praxi: little splinters of stone flew away as the bullets chipped at the coping.

"Get over, Gus. Leave me to follow!"

Wimper was not going to argue; he disappeared before the final words were out of Bond's mouth.

The helicopter seemed to be moving closer, its searchlight holding Bond in a pool of dazzling white light as he ran, crouching, towards the rope. He could just about see the grapple and the top of the rope, which he grabbed, pulling to be certain Gus was already down. He tried to peer into the Campo San Silvestro, but the brightness of the light had played havoc with his night vision. The rope was free of strain so he slid down for ten feet or so then abseiled the rest of the way.

Still blinded by the light, Bond reached the ground. For a moment he was baffled. The helicopter was turning away, its engine noise receding. Why in hell, he thought, were they all just standing there looking at him? Easy, Praxi, Bruin and Gus, together, in a half circle.

Then a hand caught him by the shoulder.

"Stand quite still, James." Harry Spraker's voice was not a welcome sound. Other hands began to frisk him expertly and, one by one, his weapons were removed.

"That's enough," Spraker ordered. "Do the rest inside. Go." He found himself being hustled, with the others, through a small door near the church.

"We have a direct way in and out on this side of the house," Spraker chuckled. "It would've saved you a great deal of time and energy if you'd known about it." Then, with a sharpness in his voice, "Dorian, the police'll be here any minute. Go out and say some damned helicopter was letting off fireworks. Complain in your best bad Italian, and tell them the Man is very angry. They know this address, and shouldn't cause any problems. The Man gives regularly to the police charities. Well known for it."

"Anything you say, Harry." Dorian was very definitely English. You could cut the affected accent with a blunt letter opener.

They were huddled together in some kind of reception room on the ground floor, and the furnishings, as Gus Wimper had already maintained, could well have been collected by a posse of bag ladies. An old settee, ragged at the arms and with a spring trying to force its way out of the seat, was pushed against one corner; there was another chair nearby, with a small table. Both had long passed the stage when they could have reasonably been called antiques—or even usable items. Paper peeled from the walls, and a rusty music stand was propped up, incongruously, near the window, which was covered by old and mould-mottled velvet drapes.

They could hear a commotion going on in the little square, and the sound of a police siren coming from the Grand Canal.

"Stay quite still, and don't make any noise," Spraker ordered. He carried an Uzi, as did the other young man with him. This one, Bond considered, must be Dominic Jellineck: a strapping figure in a smooth grey suit, his blond hair silky and just a shade long to be fashionable. He had the face of an innocent and the eyes of a dangerous sadist. His smile was so evil that the hairs on the back of Bond's neck stiffened, hard as porcupine quills.

As they waited there was an opportunity to study the others properly. Already, as he had helped them from the cellar, he had felt a little shocked at their disheveled appearance; now in the bright light, they looked even worse. The girls had been wearing dresses for the dinner party with Spraker. Once upon a time—last night—Praxi's had been a white number with a little jacket. Now the dress was stained and torn at the hem. Easy was wearing what had been a blue-and-white bodice and matching full skirt, in a silky material, with a white belt studded with brass diamond shapes and a large elaborate buckle. It too was torn and dirty. There were oil stains and a big discolored patch as though someone had thrown a glass of red wine at her. Bruin, never a contestant for the best-dressed man of the year award, had gone to the party in a suit which by now would be rejected by the Salvation Army.

Worse was the appearance of their faces. All of them looked tired and strained. There were dark smudges under Easy's eyes; Bruin had obviously been roughed up, and Praxi sported a black eye, a swollen jaw and a long cut down the side of her cheek. The blood was dry and crusted, indicating she had not even been given rudimentary first aid.

"These bastards do that to you, Praxi?" he asked, and Spraker immediately rapped out:

"Keep quiet, I won't have you talking to one another."

"What're you going to do, Harry? Kill me?"

"Possibly."

"Well, good for you. Who did it, Praxi?"

"That pair of strong-arm thugs, Dominic and Dorian. And the Dwarf, of course. He called it an interrogation. . . ."

Bruin muttered something untranslatable in German which had a great deal to do with the sexual preferences of Dominic's and Dorian's parents.

"I should be careful what you say about me." Dorian was back, standing in the doorway. "I get uncontrollable rages, as you well know, Herr Bruin."

Turning his head, Bond saw that he was almost a twin to Dominic: an inch shorter possibly, with features a shade more patrician, but he had the same weak chin and silky blond hair. There was also an evil smile: unnerving and spine-chilling.

"You take care of those idiot cops?" Harry asked.

"Slice of gateau, Harry. As soon as I mentioned their benefactor, they started to bow and scrape like courtiers."

The conversation went on for the best part of a minute, and it was time, Bond knew, to try to salvage something from his

223

store of assets. They would possibly resort to a more detailed search at any minute and, while he did have one or two small surprises—which, in all probability, would be missed in close examination—he required other things if they were ever going to even attempt an escape.

Casually he turned towards Bruin, shielding the right side of his body from his captors, and slipping one of the cartridge-sized "flash-bangs" from their container on his belt. Withdrawing his hand, he palmed the small stun grenade, neatly holding it between the soft base of his thumb and the middle knuckles of his first three fingers.

Years ago, he had taken instruction from an eminent stage magician and learned the rudiments of sleight of hand. Provided they did not ask him to turn his hands over for inspection, he should be able to keep the four-inch tube out of sight, yet still appear to use his hands normally.

Harry Spraker abruptly concluded his conversation, and moved, looking at each of his prisoners in disgust before he ordered Dominic to take them back to the cellar. "Oh, no, James Bond, you stay here; and you, Wimper." Then, to Dominic again, "Make sure that walking carrot, Giorgio, has fully recovered. We're a man short, and I'm damned if I'll see all the plans go up in smoke because some English spook has been meddling."

"British spook please, Harry."

"Shut up." Spraker sideswiped Bond's face with the back of his hand.

"What a witty retort, Harry. You really ought to do a cross-talk act with Giorgio. You could call yourselves 'The Two Sophisticates.' "

Spraker pushed his face close to Bond. "I've just about had enough from you. If Herr Weisen was not set on having a long talk with you, I'd flush you down the tubes myself."

"Harry, we'll have plenty of time to make him suffer." Dorian shifted his feet, the Uzi at the ready. He looked at Bond. "You haven't seen anything until you've taken a look at Herr Weisen's interrogation methods." He grinned, and a dark shadow of malevolence crossed his face.

Bond shrugged. "I have nothing to tell Herr Weisen. I wouldn't know what he'd want to interrogate me for."

"He'll think of something." Spraker took a step back. "But first we'd like you two gentlemen to strip. I'm certainly not going to risk having you in this house without personally searching every inch of you, and your clothing."

They found just about everything during the next fifteen minutes, making a little pile of the odds and ends on the junk settee—the two Haley & Waller Dartcord systems, the other stun grenade, the bits and pieces in their leather holsters attached to his belt. Finally Spraker told them to get dressed again. "Interesting pocket litter, Bond." He threw the various passports and credit cards into the pile. "These might come in useful. Ingenious."

"Could I possibly trouble you for my belt, Harry?" Bond asked. "If I'm to suffer indignities, I'd rather suffer with something to hold up my trousers."

Spraker examined the broad leather belt with its large solid buckle, then handed it to Bond. They had removed all the pouches and leather holders, but getting the belt back was a small consolation, for it still contained a couple of things that had proved impossible to detect. As he dressed, he slipped the small grenade back into his trousers' pocket. Now, if he and Gus survived and were given even a little time with the others in the cellar, there was a tiny chance of escape.

Dominic had returned.

"You tell them to say their prayers?" Harry said bleakly.

"I told them to concentrate their minds." Dominic had a grim laugh, which reminded Bond of the kind of cackle you heard in the haunted mansion at Disney World.

"Come along, then, gentlemen." Spraker prodded at Wimper with a pistol. "You're about to have the singular honor of meeting the man who's destined to be the greatest power in Europe."

"That'll be the day." Wimper received a heavy clout with the butt of Spraker's pistol.

"Yes, it will," muttered Dorian.

"Sooner than you imagine." The gallows laugh again from Dominic.

They were led into the hall where the unfortunate Carlo had died, then up the stairs to the landing of the floor where, according to Wimper, Wolfgang Weisen had his suite of rooms.

Spraker tapped on one of the three doors which led off the landing, and a soft voice from within called, "Come."

Harry opened the door and they were pushed into the presence of the man who had systematically wiped out the entire Cabal network and, it appeared, had pretensions to greatness.

Bond had never seen a photograph of the Poison Dwarf—once a high officer in the former East German Intelligence Service—but he had already formed an image in his mind. In the darkest moments of the past few days he had seen Weisen as a midget, deformed, his face peppered with warts: a kind of cartoon horror.

Weisen was *not* a dwarf. Certainly the man was not tall, around five-one, but you could not classify him as dwarf-like. He sat in a large leather-padded, high-backed wooden chair—the armrests carved with gargoyles, mouths open showing sharp fangs, while the intricate work at the top of the tall back represented a boar, entwined with brambles. The studded leather padding was polished to a high gloss which seemed to complement the sheen of the man himself.

He wore a burgundy velvet smoking jacket, which looked almost Victorian, dark trousers and a silk shirt, with a white cravat neatly tied at the throat. Everything about him was smooth, for he appeared to have no hair on either his head or face, which was moon-like, pink with rosy cheeks. Weisen could easily be the model for some Dickensian character, and the comfortable, even pleasant, benign look of the man belied everything Bond had heard about him. The evil, ruthless, un-compromising dwarf who had been brought up at Stalin's knee seemed to have shrunk from diabolical malevolence to chubby, cherubic benevolence.

"Come in, gentlemen. Come in." The voice was soft, almost soothing, containing nothing of the repellent depravity suggested by his reputation.

"You'll want us to stay?" Spraker asked.

"Oh, no, Harry. Just wait outside for a short time. I'll call if I need you."

As Spraker left the room, in the company of Dominic and Dorian, Weisen beamed. "Gus," he continued, friendly and welcoming. "It's so good to see you again, though I have to admit I'm a little cross with you. I ordered you back to Venice today, not yesterday. Did you misinterpret my instructions? Or were you simply trying to aggravate me?" For Bond's benefit, he spoke English, perfectly and with no trace of an accent.

Wimper gave a nervous laugh. "I knew why you had summoned me. You think I'm a fool, Wolfie?"

"No," the smooth ball of a head shook slightly. "No, I would never take you for a fool, Gus. Treacherous? Yes. Foolish? . . . Well, perhaps foolhardy, but never foolish." His gaze shifted to Bond, the eyes a strange, almost violet color. They twinkled as merrily as some delightful character in a cheerful Christmas tale—joy to the world, with all the trappings of unctuous righteousness. "And Commander Bond, also. It's a . . ."

"*Captain* Bond, if we're using ranks."

"Really? I hadn't heard you had been promoted. My congratulations, sir. But welcome. Welcome to my humble home, *Captain* Bond." He turned back to Gus Wimper. "Gus, why did you disobey me? And why, in heaven's name, did you see fit to tamper with things that you must know are inevitable?"

"Because I was certain what you'd do. Your damned Uncle Joe used the same techniques."

Weisen nodded, still with his cheery smile. "Yes. Yes, he did, didn't he? I can remember sitting with him as we watched movies. He was very fond of Charlie Chaplin, and, particularly, he liked the Tarzan films. He would tell me exactly what was going on. 'Look,' he would say. 'Wolfie, look, he's calling to the animals. I think I must call to a pair of animals myself.' Then he would say a couple of names. 'Wolfie, I'm certain those two are plotting behind my back.' He would summon them to Kuntsevo—the villa he used there. The message would be friendly. Come to dinner. Come for drinks. Something like that. But he would touch his nose and tell me he was certain they were traitors. He was always right, Uncle Joe. Always, the people he called to him finally confessed their infidelity. His rule was, always be understanding. Give them the benefit of the doubt—until you knew for certain. He would welcome them in, but, once they confessed . . . Ah, that was a different story."

"And mine would've been a different story, as well. I presume you would have simply given me over to your hired thugs, Dominic and Dorian?"

"No, Gus. It would've been Carlo and Giorgio. You see, you've only just caught me. I leave later today. You must know how I hate violence. I just didn't want to be around when they . . . Well, you know what they would do." He gave a sad little smile. "Too bad one of you did away with Carlo. Those two were not the brightest of men, but they were thorough. Also faithful to the cause. To the Party. Unlike some I could mention, eh Gus?"

Wimper did not answer. "Gus, Gus, Gus," Weisen tutted. "You had so much to gain. When I discovered that you were playing a double game—that foolish business of pretending you had drowned, for instance—I was very sad. Yes, Gus, you saddened me. For some time I really believed you were made of the right stuff."

"What *is* the right stuff?" Bond asked. Weisen's soft voice and innocent appearance had suddenly begun to chill him. This was a devil in cherub's skin, and being in the presence of the man turned his spine to ice.

"Well, it's certainly not the stuff those buffoons Gorbachev and Yeltsin are made of. They are also traitors, and will suffer before we're through. All that great work done in the name of mankind's progress has crumbled to dust in the hands of cretins. To gainsay the Party, and the vision of men like Lenin, my Uncle Joe, and dear Lavrenti Beria . . . It's unforgivable." He started to murmur to himself, and it was at this moment Bond knew—as he must have known from the start—that the smooth, comfortable man was a raving lunatic.

He glanced around the room to see it was decorated in a spartan but more clean and pleasant manner than the desolate dump of a place downstairs. There were crimson drapes at the windows, and the furnishings—tables, chairs, a sideboard along one wall—all looked Victorian. Heavy, but utilitarian and with few frills, except for the magnificent carving on the chair in which Weisen sat. As well as the door behind them, Bond saw a second door, in the center of the wall to his left. Weisen's sleeping quarters? he wondered. Again the chill went through him as he saw, beside the door, a large, icon-like painting of Joseph Stalin.

"No, Gus," Weisen stopped muttering. "Gus, you betrayed me, so you will, like the others, suffer the penalty. Don't feel too badly, for you are not alone. Many hundreds of traitors will pay the same price in the next weeks and months." There was no malice in the way he spoke, and he hardly raised his voice to call Harry Spraker.

"Take Gus down and put him with the others, Harry. Goodbye, Gus. I trust you will at least die like a man, with dignity."

He waited for Wimper to leave, Spraker pushing him towards Dominic and Dorian. When the door closed, he turned to Bond. "Please, sit down, my dear sir. We must talk, though there is much I have to do before tonight when I leave." As he spoke, the door on the left opened.

"Ah, my darling. You've come to say farewell. Good, you can meet Captain Bond before you leave."

"Captain Bond, it's a pleasure." She was much younger than he had expected. Tall, slim with a fall of blond hair which bounced on her shoulders as she walked.

"My companion, Captain Bond. My companion and my inspiration, Monika Haardt." A small, plump pink hand lifted from the chair arm for a second.

She was not beautiful in any accepted sense: the mouth, slashed with bright lipstick, seemed too wide, and the nose too small. It was a face which seemed to have been fashioned out of proportion, but the slender body looked just about perfect as it moved under the black slacks and gold-faced cossack jacket. She extended a hand, the fingernails scarlet, matching the lipstick. Automatically Bond shook the hand and felt an unpleasant dryness. It was like touching a snake, he thought.

"I'm sorry we won't have time to talk." She flashed him a neon smile, on and off like a colored sign. Bond had a sudden vivid picture in his head: Norman Bates's motel in Hitchcock's *Psycho.*

"You see," she continued, "I must go ahead and see all things are ready for dear Wolfie. The days ahead will be hard, but we have virtually won. What a pity you won't be here to see the glory."

There was a movement near the door through which Monika had come, and Bond turned his head. Standing just inside the room was the dark-haired, plump Michelle, whom he had last seen in Paris.

"You know Michelle, I believe," Monika gestured.

"Yes, I took a car ride with her."

"Indeed you did, Mr. Bond." Michelle did not sound as temptingly seductive as she had when imitating Praxi Simeon in the car, with old Cold Claude Gaspard, in Paris. "You also inflicted great suffering on a particular friend of mine. M. Gaspard."

"Cold Claude, eh, Michelle? He simply got what he was asking for."

Michelle mouthed an oath at him, and Weisen made a little

hushing noise. "My dear Michelle. Claude will recover. Mr. Bond here will not. It couldn't be more fair. But I must not detain either of you. Tomorrow we'll all be together again, eh?"

Monika bent over and kissed Weisen, on his mouth, then his cheeks. "Tomorrow," she whispered.

The smooth bald head nodded, and Weisen gave his cherubic beam. It made him look like some happy choirboy who had just won an award for the best solo. Then he gave a delighted little chuckle. "Just remember, dear Monika, that, like Mary Tudor, you shall find Calais lying in my heart."

Monika gave an unexpectedly musical laugh, and Big Michelle giggled.

"Very good, Wolfie. Tomorrow."

As the door closed behind them Bond once more had the strange feeling that he had missed something. He was back in the car, on the Faubourg St. Honoré in Paris with Claude Gaspard and Michelle, grasping at what had passed between them. A word, a sentence, flashed through his head, then eluded him again, dancing and thumbing its nose at him from the darkness on the edge of his memory.

"Now, Mr. Bond, we must talk. You'll understand that my time is limited. There is much to do before I leave tonight."

"So, what do we talk about, Herr Weisen?"

"Oh, please call me Wolfgang; and I must call you James, I think."

"As you will, but what do we talk about?"

Weisen seemed to sparkle, as though his face and head had been immersed in glitter dust. "Well, I must tease certain things from you, such as how much your excellent Secret Intelligence Service knows of me. Also, I am certain you will want to ask questions of me. A great deal has happened in the last days—*your* last days—and I am really not such a monster. I would hate you to go to your grave without me filling in some of the blank spaces. The Fiddleback spiders, for instance—Oh, I want to know about that. Did you actually *consume* any?" The word "consume" came out with the accent on the second syllable—"con-sooom"—his eyes wide open with a childish look of intense interest.

"No."

"Ah, pity."

"When we finish talking about the gaps we both wish to fill in, Wolfie, what do we talk about then?"

"I suppose we have a few words about death. I'll give you plenty of time to compose yourself. If you believe in such things, you might even like to lead your friends in prayer, or hymns, for a while. Or simply meditate on the irony of things. Yes, we can talk about death. Your death, and the deaths of others. Death in Venice, perhaps. What a wonderful book that is, and what an irony it is that you will face your destiny here, in Venice of all places. Come, ask away. You go first. I want to hear your questions."

17

Death Squad

"Well, yes, I suppose there are one or two things I don't under-stand." Half of Bond's mind was on how to slip Weisen's noose, and get all of them out of the house and away, before this lunatic fanatic could do any real harm. True, there were some unanswered questions, but his main concern was staying alive, followed closely by neutralizing Weisen. Heaven only knew what horror the man was planning.

"Go on then. Ask." Weisen pulled himself back in the chair so that his feet only just touched the floor. He began drum-ming his heels on the carpet, like a well-fed child being know-ingly annoying.

"Why Cabal, Wolfgang? Why go to the considerable trouble of writing off a network that would have been broken up any-way?"

"Ah! Good question, James. Very good question. You see, when things began to change for us, I knew that only one group of people could cause me a great deal of trouble. I suppose there was an element of revenge, but Cabal was a successful network. So successful that they were still able to cause me embarrassment even though I knew most of their operational technicalities—and most of their names. After all, I had Harry Spraker, and, for a time, thought I had Gus Wimper as well."

"And, of course, you couldn't just accept the fact that, in the end, Communism has failed?"

"Why should I? Those who talk of failure are heretics."

"What about your former colleague, Mischa Wolf?"

For the first time, a small cloud of anger crossed his face. "He was never my colleague. We worked on different sides of the street. I hardly knew him."

"But, even though you had penetrated Cabal, you still feared them?"

"Look, James. I couldn't afford to let any of them pass information to either you Brits or the Americans. Some of those people knew exactly where my bolt-holes were—Venice was only one of them. In any case, they didn't deserve to live."

"So it *was* vengeance?"

Weisen gave a sneaky, sly little smile. "Now that you mention it, I suppose it was." Then, as though realizing the implications, he quickly added, "But I still thought they could damage me. They all certainly knew I wouldn't give in easily. They knew I would not—I will not—accept the demise of the greatest political ideology ever known to man. I should imagine they told you that I would rather die than give up my beliefs, and that I shall continue to fight—and win—to see the restoration of International Communism. It's been my life, and the lives of many others. Members of Cabal knew this."

Bond nodded, "So you began to kill them off?"

"Mmmmm." A gleeful grin, the feet drumming on the carpet in pleasure.

"And when the American and British services became concerned, you took out the controllers?"

"Of course. Your Ford Puxley and the American, Liz Cearns, were getting dangerously close."

"Who *did* kill them?"

"Harry, of course." He looked surprised, as though it was a foregone conclusion, then he gave a little laugh. "A clever man, Heini Spraker. He said to me, 'Wolfie, if we're going to take them out, let's do it in a way that'll leave a message: in a manner which stamps Cold War all over them.' I agreed, naturally. So, Puxley went by a flyswat, and that nice Liz Cearns died from a cyanide pistol." His eyes became dreamy. "You know, the Cearns business was an historic event. The pistol Harry used was the last of its kind. I picked it up at Moscow Center some years ago as a museum piece. KGB haven't made things like that recently. It's probably worth thousands to a collector of Cold War memorabilia."

"And what about Easy St. John and myself?"

"Ah." His head rocked to one side, the pink face assuming a mask of apology. "We had no quarrel with you or the girl. I never intended that you should be killed."

"But you tried."

"Not really. The spiders were a kind of warning. We thought you'd get the message. That was an off-the-cuff thing. A bit of macabre humor."

"Yes, very droll."

"Oh come, James. It was fun for us. We really did think you'd take it as a caution."

"We didn't."

"No. No, of course you didn't. I should have known better. Anyway, I had you under control very quickly."

"Putting Axel Ritter in to pose as *Tester*—Heini Spraker?"

"It worked . . ."

"For a while, yes."

"James. Oh, James." He shook his head sadly. "If only you had not been so violent. Axel made sure you would be on the train to Paris, and we had a nice little operation going. I used two of my very best boys . . ."

"Felix Utterman and Hexie Weiss?"

Weisen's tubby chest expanded and contracted in a heavy sigh. "Felix and Hexie, yes. They were so good, and, truly, James, we still didn't intend to hurt you. Neither you nor the girl. You were to have been taken from the train and hidden away until my current business was completed." The pink billiard ball of a head shook very slowly. "If only you hadn't been so impetuous. I began to get very cross with you after Felix and Hexie were—well, killed. You shouldn't have done that, James. No, it was very wrong, particularly as we meant you no harm."

I bet, Bond thought. He also contemplated the truth. He did not believe for a moment that someone like Wolfgang Weisen would not have disposed of Easy and himself.

"Yes, very cross. Yet I still didn't intend to have you killed. You must know that. After all, Claude Gaspard and Michelle let you go. They allowed you to walk away in Paris."

He recalled having been surprised, on reflection, that Cold Claude and Big Michelle had just let him go. "But old Claude came looking for us again, pretty quickly."

"I was somewhat discomposed with Claude over that." He sounded like an affected parson giving the text for his sermon.

"Because he came after us again?"

"No. James, you can be very dense." His voice was petulant. "I was angry with Claude because he did a botched job. He should've taken you inside the hotel. Never, never try and take people illegally in the street: too many bystanders, too much room. I thought Claude knew better."

"By then you *had* decided to do away with us?"

"Not altogether, no. But you were with Praxi. I wanted her. Oh dear, yes. I wanted *her* very badly. And I think my dear Monika was also keen to assist in debriefing her. James, it's a pity you didn't have time to get to know Monika. She's changed my life. The things that woman can do for a man." His eyes rolled up towards the ceiling, then he switched, abruptly changing the subject. "Praxi really was good. Very good. She evaded everyone. Clever. Clever as a monkey. But I have her now, so that's all right." The beam again. He could have been practicing to play Santa at a Christmas party.

"What of Axel Ritter and the little fellow? The one we called the jockey? Dmitri?"

"Dmitri Druvitch, yes. Pity about him. Dmitri was quite efficient. I used him a great deal. Family settled in Paris. Originally

Ukrainians. Oh, it would have been Dmitri's grandfather who left Russia and went to France a long while ago. Poor little Dmitri, he didn't even speak any Russian, but he was a true member of the Party. Worked hard."

"His death, Wolfie? Axel seemed to think Cabal was responsible. Do you know what happened? What really happened?"

Weisen raised his head, and Bond could have sworn there were tears in his eyes. "Such good men, and you were the cause of their deaths. Felix, Hexie, Axel Ritter, the two men I sent to winkle you out of the Cipriani—yes, they both died. I have friends with the emergency services here. Both are dead. Then there was Carlo, and little Dmitri. Good men, and because of you, James, and Gus Wimper, they're dead."

"You, Wolfie, did away with a lot of good men and women."

Weisen's face showed a mask of surprise, as though Bond was falsely accusing him. "That was very different, James, and you know it."

. "Who killed Dmitri, Wolfgang?"

"Axel didn't know what to do when he got to Paris. He expected to arrive on his own, and little Dmitri was at the station to meet him. Of course, you and the American girl were still around. I think it was all very confusing for both of them. But there was another small problem. Axel and Dmitri were very close. Almost too close, if you follow me."

"So?"

"So, I really couldn't tell the truth to Axel. It would have upset him. Possibly turned him against me."

"And the truth?"

There was a long pause. Somewhere, far off it seemed, a bell tolled. "You're right, I have to be honest with you. Dmitri's death had absolutely nothing to do with you, or Ms. St. John, or Cabal. It was a necessary internal discipline. You see, Dmitri was a thief. He stole from both Harry and myself. Money mostly. A great deal of money. Operational funds that I've built up over many years."

237

Yes, Bond thought to himself, you built up your so-called operational funds as a comfortable fallback, a hedge against hard times.

Weisen was still speaking. "You say he looked like a jockey, well, he liked horses—the old story: slow horses and fast women. We had known for a month. In fact, he had been a dead man for a month, only we were worried about Axel's reaction. I couldn't afford to lose him as well—though I did lose him in the end, didn't I?"

"So, you had Dmitri killed."

"It was the only way. He knew—as all my people know—that I am a strong disciplinarian. I believe he knew that death was near for him. Claude set it up. A feint at Axel, then the stabbing of Dmitri. As his man, who was very expert, ran off, he shouted, 'That's from Bruin.' It certainly hardened Axel's heart towards Cabal. From that point of view, it was a success. It stiffened Axel Ritter's resolve. Next question."

"Your plans? What are you planning now?"

"James." Admonishing. "James, James, James. Even though you are a condemned man, I can't possibly talk about that. This is a technical matter. We just don't discuss operational moves. If the tables were turned, you'd be the same. We cannot talk about . . . There, I nearly said a name. But I just can't talk about it. Not even with a dead man like yourself."

One more try, he thought. The devil in cherub's clothing obviously wanted desperately to show off, explain how clever he was, or even tell more. "Wolfie, if I'm a dead man, then it won't hurt. Just give me a hint."

"One tiny hint, then. By tomorrow night, Europe will be rocked on its heels. The stock markets of the European Community—and heaven knows they're in difficulties as a community already—will cry havoc. Destabilization will sweep across Europe like the Black Death. There, that's all. Now, I think, it's my turn to ask the questions."

He sounded very firm. The only thing to be done was effect

some kind of escape, then drive Weisen to reveal what he was up to. Bond nodded in agreement.

"Good." The beam broadened across Weisen's face, and he jiggled up and down like an excited child, drumming his feet again. "This *is* fun. Now, I don't require much. All I really need to know is, are either your Service, or the Americans, aware of this place? Do they know I'm in Venice?"

"Probably. They've almost certainly put two and two together by now. I can't give you details, but I'd say the answer was yes. Yes, they know you're in Venice."

"How will they react to that?"

"I really have no idea."

"Will they send in a backup team when they find you and the lady are missing?"

"Not immediately. In a day or two, possibly."

He leaned forward, barely able to contain his excitement. "Not immediately. Oh, wonderful. You're telling me the truth? Not immediately."

"I'm telling the truth."

"And have either your Service or the Americans suggested they have intelligence on any operation I might—just might, mind you—be planning in Europe?"

"No." Firm and unequivocal.

"Good. You're a great agent, James. The British will be losing an experienced, fine and loyal man. I hope they appreciate this. If all goes well for me, I shall personally see to it that you are honored in some small way. Unlike the present regime in Germany, I do not intend to hound those who have done sterling service for my one-time enemies. Now, if you'll excuse me, I have much to do before I leave tonight. It's been a pleasure talking with you and, I hope, putting your mind at rest."

Bond rose with a shrug. "How long have we got?"

"Oh, I don't know. An hour. Maybe a little longer. I don't leave until tonight, but, unfortunately, I think all my people here will have to come with me. I had not planned it that way. So I shall go out for a turn through the streets, when the time comes. When Dominic and Dorian . . . you know?"

"I'm sure we can all compose ourselves in an hour."

"I'm glad to hear it." He raised his voice a fraction, calling for Harry Spraker, who was through the door with the pair of fair-haired heavies before Bond even turned to meet them.

Weisen stuck out a chubby hand, with its small fat fingers. "A pleasure to have met you, *Captain* Bond."

He turned away, not giving Weisen a nod, let alone a handshake.

"Oh, well, if you're going to be like that. Go, and good riddance to you." Wolfgang issued some rapid orders. Dominic and Dorian could not wait to get their hands on him, hustling him from the room, down the stairs, then into the kitchen, through the door and into the cellar.

They unlocked the gate to the cell and Dominic threw him in, Dorian standing back threatening—or more likely inciting—the others with his Uzi.

Easy, Praxi, Gus and Bruin stood against the far wall of the cell.

"See you soon." Dominic turned the key and the deadlock went home with a clunk.

"See you very soon," Dorian parroted. Then: "See you for the last time."

They left, switching off the main light, then the bulb in the stairwell, leaving only a small night-light bulb burning high above their heads, behind the bars of the cell.

The place felt damp and depressing. The anxiety came off the others in a great wave, and, in its wake a sense of desolation. This, he thought, was what it would have been like for many in the Lubyanka waiting for death; or further back, in the cells housing those earmarked for the guillotine during the French Revolution.

Easy was the most upset. She threw her arms around him and buried her head in his shoulder, sobbing. He made soothing noises and gradually she pulled back. "I didn't expect to fall in love with you so quickly, James, my dear. Sorry about the floodgates. It's just all so unfair. I've found you, now I'm going to lose you."

"We're all going to lose everything," Praxi said softly. "Unless . . . ?" Her eyes were bright with what was probably the last remnant of hope as she looked at Bond, who turned to Gus, making signals with his hands, asking, in effect, if he thought the cell was bugged.

Gus shook his head. "No way, James. They're all too busy anyhow."

"You got a plan?" Bruin asked eagerly.

"Maybe not a plan." He spoke very low, the others craning in to hear him. "But I do have the means if they give us enough time, and if luck's with us." He bent and kissed Easy lightly on the neck, whispering, "You know, I didn't expect to fall in love, either." He felt his own emotions well up as he realized he meant it, knowing that this was the woman for him. "But I did fall in love with you, Easy—funny little toughie that you are. It's only really happened once or twice in my life." This was crazy. He had hardly talked with her about anything but the job they were doing; he did not know if she liked hard rock, jazz or Wagner; they had spent one night together on a train; he knew nothing of her background, and all the other things one should know. Yet, there he was: looking at her and loving her.

"Truly?" She looked at him, eyes shining. "Then we *must* get out."

"Yes, my thoughts exactly." He looked at each one of them in turn, holding their eyes in his for a few seconds, willing himself to pass hope into their hearts and minds. Gus, who had proved to be such a staunch ally; big Bruin, with his daft face and huge muscles; Praxi, who had been through so much already, and Easy, who, almost in a second, had come to mean something very dear to him. "Now, this is what I'm going to try and do," he began. "It's only going to work if they give us the time, and if I manage to pull it off, you'll all have parts to play.

241

If it works, we have to act in harmony, and we'll only get the one chance." He spoke, fast and decisively, going through the part each would have to play. Then he began to work on the first moves that could just give them the edge on Weisen's death squad.

The small bulb, high above them, gave the most light towards the back of the cell. He found the ideal spot and slipped off his belt.

The buckle was an unusual design: a silver square D-ring with two tines, instead of the usual one. The strong metal tines unscrewed easily, and once out they proved to be just as Ann Reilly of Q Branch had described. Made of hard steel, both were telescopic so that, fully extended, they each formed a metal probe, a little under four inches long.

He went to the other end of the belt, found the dividing line in the stitching, and pulled the two overlapping pieces of leather apart. The stitches broke easily, and on the inside, cushioned by soft material, was a series of other small metal objects, so skilfully hidden that even a detailed examination of the belt had not revealed them.

Choosing two of these thin hard-tempered steel tips, Bond screwed them onto the extended tines, then lifted the objects, smiling with relief. They were instantly recognizable. One was a typical lock pick, with a slightly curved end; the other, a tension wrench, curved at a ninety-degree angle, with an almost flat end.

The pair of tools could be the first way to escape, for they were the only instruments required to pull back the bolt on the gate lock.

It took almost ten minutes of probing within the keyhole. The tools were small, but strong, and Bond finally managed to hold the picklock and tension wrench in the exact position to simulate the key. For a second, as he was moving the picks to draw back the bolt, he thought they might break under the strain, but slowly the bolt came back and at last slipped free with a heavy thump.

"Now, the rest is going to be really tricky. Bruin." He opened the gate.

The tall, strong Bruin smiled, nodded and walked softly into the main cellar. Within thirty seconds he was back, having reached up and unscrewed the light bulb which was the main illumination outside the cell. The switch was at the bottom of the stairs, and on both occasions he had been in the cellar, Bond noted that they tripped the switch at the top of the stairs first, then the last man down would flip the second switch, lighting the cellar.

He took the bulb gently, whispering that should he make a mess of what he was attempting, they would have to resort to a more simple, and definitely more dangerous method. He held the metal screw portion in one hand and the glass bulb in the other, gently turning and twisting, trying to loosen glass from metal. It can be done, and he had practiced it many times in a recent training refresher course on booby traps. He did not tell the others that only about one attempt in four had been successful. With care, you can separate the glass at the neck of the bulb from the metal. The vacuum within the glass also goes, but the filaments remain on the stem, and the stem keeps contact with the metal base. A bulb, thus tampered with, will spark and fuse when switched on, but that spark is enough to ignite a charge. After a few minutes the glass began to crunch away at the neck. He was able to turn the rest of the bulb and draw it down so that a gap showed between the neck and the metal. The filaments were still intact.

In this case, the charge would come from the flash powder and explosive in the small cartridge-like stun grenade he had palmed before the search. Taking the pick which he had used on the lock, he eased away the thick waxed cardboard ring at the base of the grenade, then pressed the cylinder to form a pouring lip. Slowly the sand-like substances were transferred from the grenade to the inside of the light bulb.

It took almost twenty minutes. He did not want to lose a grain of the mixture, for he had devised this method because it would be the most simple way of shocking and distracting Dominic and Dorian as they came into the cell.

If they had been forced into using the cartridge-like grenade by itself, it would have meant throwing it through the bars, thus alerting the pair long before he, and the others, could expect to overpower them. Now, the pouring finished, he jammed the glass neck back into the metal stem, and, whispering a word of caution to Bruin, handed the doctored bulb back to the big man.

They could not see Bruin rescrewing the bulb into place, though the soft scraping sounds made them collectively hold their breath. Bond realized that his palms were now soaked with sweat as he waited. The final test would come when the bulb was in place, and the glass had not fallen to shatter their chances on the stone-flagged floor.

Bruin returned, and Bond left the cell, placing himself to the right of the stairs, just out of the sightline of any person coming into the cellar. The gate had been closed. Each member of the team knew what was expected of them.

They waited.

A good fifteen minutes passed, then from the top of the stairs came the sound of the lock being taken off, and the voices of Dominic and Dorian floated down. By the sound of it, they relished the job they were about to do.

Bond kept flat against the wall, glancing towards the cell to see that Bruin and Gus were ready to make the leap from the gate. Praxi and Easy would form the second wave. Praxi had insisted that they draw lots for the various jobs. She and Easy could do just as good a job as the two men, she said. So, in the end, fate, not gender, had ruled.

Above, the stair light came on, and the sound of two pairs of feet seemed like drumbeats.

"Hope you've said your prayers," Dorian called from halfway down.

"You can say one for us while you're at it," chimed Dominic as he entered the cellar, an Uzi tucked under his arm. "I'm going to enjoy this."

Weisen's death squad was almost in the cellar.

Bond closed his eyes, turning his head away as Dorian flicked the switch at the entrance to the cellar, and a great bolt of light shot from the bulb, with a thunderclap of noise that left ears ringing for a good minute after.

He leaped, caught Dorian on the side of his head with a punch which had all his strength behind it. The younger man reeled away, yelling and dropping his weapon. Then Bond was on him, hammering him with blow after blow.

Gus and Bruin were through the gate long before Dominic even knew what had happened. He dropped the Uzi as the explosion ripped out above them, then as he fought to see through the dazzle of blindness, he grabbed at his back, tearing out a handgun. He even managed to fire two rounds which ricocheted, whining in the close precincts of the cellar. By then, Gus and Bruin were on him, both pounding at his head and face.

Bond only stopped striking Dorian when he heard Praxi shouting—"James, quickly! Easy! She's hurt!"

The two English thugs lay, sprawled and bleeding on the flagstones, but Easy St. John's body had about it that bent and terrible look of stillness. Even before he touched her, Bond knew she was dead. One of Dominic's bullets had smashed into her chest, entering near the heart. The exit wound was huge, and as he turned her over, Bond saw that the front of her silk dress was a welling mass of blood, while her face was twisted in shock, her teeth bared in horror. He felt the pulse on her neck and there was none. Then he closed her eyes and gently laid her back on the cell floor.

Turning, and with a terrible rage, he grabbed at one of the Uzis. "Kill those two bastards!" he commanded. "I'm going after their master, and God help him."

His eyes were stinging with tears as he raced up the stairs, crashed into the kitchen and came face to face with Harry Spraker.

18

A Matter of Life or Death

Spraker must have heard the explosion of the "flash-bang," and the shots which followed. Now he was heading full tilt through the kitchen, straight for the cellar door, an automatic pistol in his right hand.

Bond took no notice of the pistol, bringing his arm up and smashing Spraker in the face with his elbow, following through with a vicious kick to the groin. Weisen's lieutenant dropped the gun, doubling up, one hand to his face, the other clamped around the junction of his thighs. Bond kneed him in the face, and felt the man's teeth dig into his own kneecap.

Spraker went down, striking his head on the table, moaning and whimpering with pain. "You're a clumsy devil, Harry," Bond said, then kicked him in the face. "You should really watch where you're going." Harry Spraker and consciousness parted company.

When Bond looked up, he found himself staring into the nightmare features of Giorgio. The Italian gave a menacing growl, making him sound like an enraged Rottweiler. His lips parted, curling back to show sharp, uneven teeth. It seemed to be his version of a smile, and he had plenty to smile about, for Bond was looking into the dark circle which was the muzzle of a .44 Magnum Smith & Wesson revolver.

Giorgio gave a little giggle. As his finger tightened on the trigger, he spoke in Italian. "Go on, punk. Make my day." He thought that was terribly funny and the pistol trembled slightly in his hand.

"No, punk. Make *my* day," Gus said from the top of the stairs, the other Uzi up and ready to remove Giorgio's head.

The Italian thug thought about it for a few seconds which, to Bond, seemed like minutes. Finally, Giorgio lowered his revolver.

"On the table," Gus ordered, and Bond stepped forward to take the gun, then scooped up Harry Spraker's automatic from the floor.

"Just ease up, James." Gus touched his arm. "Let's not go crazy. I know you want Weisen's hide, but he *has* got something going on, and we should keep him in one piece: for a while at least. He's a dangerous brute—we all know that—and, from what you've said, he's been behaving as though he's already king of the hill."

While working on the lock and booby trap, Bond had given them a brief version of his conversation with Weisen.

He gave Gus a quick nod, then took a deep breath. Suddenly he felt drained, and saw that his hands were shaking. He had killed, in the line of duty, many times, but during the last few days death seemed to have been as much a part of his life as eating and sleeping. He was sickened by the thought, and the reality of Easy's death sent a bolt of almost physical pain through him.

"What do we do now, Gus?" His voice trembled, as if he was on the verge of collapse.

"We finish the job. Bruin and Praxi are taking Easy's body out of the cell. We'll see that she has a proper burial later. Let's get these jokers down there and, more important, find where Weisen's got to."

"He went out for a walk." Giorgio, faced with a pair of Uzis, was trying to be helpful—as well he might.

"When're you expecting him back?"

"About an hour. He did not wish to be in the house while Dominic and Dorian executed you." He gave a little grin to show that the very idea of the two Englishmen being able to execute anybody was ludicrous.

"I'll take him down." Gus used the Uzi to prompt Giorgio, indicating that he should go through the door and into the cellar.

The ungainly, ugly man muttered *"Scusi, Dottore,"* giving Bond a little bow as he did as he was told.

On the floor, Harry Spraker groaned and moved.

"I'll be back for him in a minute." Gus disappeared down the stairs, goading Giorgio with the Uzi.

Spraker groaned again, and spat out some blood, together with a tooth, as he tried to prop himself on one elbow. His nose had been broken; if they allowed him to live, he faced many hours of painful dental surgery.

"Ot oo dud oo batard?" he tried to ask, but even speaking seemed to cause grave discomfort.

"Just what you deserved, Harry." Bond felt warm with delight. Apart from the unctuous Weisen, he disliked Harry more than any of the others.

"Oo'll 'ay fo' 'is, Bon'. 'eisen 'an't 'ossiby 'ail. Oo'll 'ay. Ah 'omiss oo'll 'ay."

Bond translated this as a threat—"You'll pay. I promise, you'll pay."

"You want some more, Harry?" He kicked him lightly in the ribs. "There's plenty more where that came from, and when we've cleaned up Weisen's little nest of vipers, I think you'll find yourself locked away for a very long time. Maybe you'd like me to put you out of your misery now."

Spraker tried to say something that was anatomically impossible, then relaxed, putting his head back onto the floor, indicating it was more comfortable for him to lie down.

Gus returned with Bruin, who picked up Spraker as though he were a sackful of feathers and carried him away.

"Praxi's coming up in a minute. It seems you killed Dorian. Dominic's still in the land of the living, but he's going to have one hell of a headache. Bruin's locked them in, and friend Giorgio's swearing devotion to us for life."

"He'd swear allegiance to a snake if he thought it'd do any good."

"True. You want me to go back and finish off Dominic?"

Bond shook his head. "It doesn't really matter now."

Praxi came up through the door and went straight to Bond, putting her arms around him, squeezing in a long hug. "What can I say, James? She's the second *Eagle* I've lost. I'm so sorry."

Bond held on to her for a moment, then disengaged himself and gave her what passed for a smile. "The only thing we can do is sweat Weisen."

A look of troubled concern crossed her face. "James, he's not alone. Weisen has a very large number of allies out there. We still have to be very, very careful. I know this little man: He looks like a jolly Pickwickian, but he's one of the vilest people I've ever met. Cunning as a bagful of monkeys, deadly as a green mamba. He's got the conscience of a great white, and has total belief in the final vindication of Stalinism."

"You really believe he . . . ?"

"Yes, very dangerous. The man's a walking bomb, and I imagine a lot of equal extremists follow him. Weisen's the kind of leader they flock to. I've heard him briefing agents. He was amazing. They'd go out willing to die for him, if not for their beliefs. You probably see him as a freak. Don't be deceived, James. Wolfgang Weisen's the oddball kind of leader people see as a divine savior."

As though on cue, a door slammed somewhere in the house, and Weisen's voice called out, "Harry? Dominic? Dorian?"

Bond nodded, cocking his head towards the door. He tucked Harry's pistol into his waistband, passed the Smith & Wesson to Praxi and walked calmly in the direction of Weisen's voice. Weisen was still calling to his men as he went up the stairs.

Bond stood in the hall, Gus and Praxi at his side, watching the strange figure waddle up to the top before he raised the Uzi. "Wolfie!" he called softly.

Weisen spun around on the landing, saw the group at the foot of the stairs, deliberated about whether he should make a dive for his room, then hesitated.

"Don't even think about it," Gus called. "My friend here would just as soon blow you away now. I've persuaded him to wait for a while."

"Oh, dear." Weisen said, like a host who has just accidentally spilled wine on a guest's expensive suit. "Oh, dear," he repeated.

"Stay where you are until we come to you." Bond had never heard himself sound as threatening and unpleasant. "I'd advise you to remain quite still, because if you even fart I'll send you to the Grim Reaper before you know it."

"Oh, dear." Weisen still used the same tone of voice, like a needle stuck in the groove of an old-fashioned gramophone record. "That would be singularly unpleasant, James." He seemed neither afraid, nor surprised. "How're my people?"

"Dorian's dead, Dominic's half dead, Harry isn't feeling at all well, and Giorgio's thinking about joining the witness protection program." He reached the landing. "Just turn around, spread your legs and put your palms against that wall, Weisen. I'm not about to take any chances with you."

Praxi and Gus came up the stairs, and the three of them searched the chubby little man who, inexplicably, made an attempt to joke about it. "Please, I'm very ticklish," he squeaked at one point, then stopped joking when Gus suggested that he might inflict pain by doing something obscenely disgusting with the barrel of one of the Uzis. Gus sounded as though he meant every word. After that Weisen seemed to forget about the jokes.

"We're going into that nice room of yours, Wolfie. We're going to sit down and have a long talk about life, liberty and the pursuit of happiness." Bond caught hold of the fat shoulder and dragged him off the wall.

"That should be interesting." Weisen did not sound as though he thought it might be fun. "I have my own particular ideas about those subjects, as you know."

Bruin plodded up the stairs. "You want me to beat the shit out of him, Gus?"

"Maybe. But later. After we've talked."

"Good." Bruin sounded happy at the thought.

"Oh, dear," Weisen remarked, as though it really did not matter either way.

They sat him in the chair with the gargoyles and the boar carved on the back, and he immediately started drumming his feet on the floor. Gus told him to sit still, put his hands on the chair arms, listen and only speak when they asked him a question.

"Might I just say one thing before you start?" His little eyes opened wide and the cheeks seemed to swell, growing more pink by the minute.

"You have to?" Bruin slapped the palm of his left hand with the fist of his right. The noise would have made a heavyweight boxer uneasy.

"Yes. Yes, I think I do. It'll save time in the long run." Now that he was settled in the chair, Weisen appeared to have conquered any initial shock. He looked unperturbed, and even a little smug.

"Go on." Bond thought he might never smile again.

"Well, I'm supposed to leave in about two hours," Weisen began.

"You're not going anywhere," from Praxi.

"Let him finish," Gus said with quiet reason.

"As I was saying," Weisen looked at Praxi as though she had committed some terrible breach of social etiquette, "I'm supposed to leave here in two hours, and I would suggest, for your own sakes, that you simply allow me to go. Losing some of my

251

good people to you is unpleasant, I admit. But, as far as the Party, and the future, is concerned, the situation here cannot stop the train of events." He gave a small, nervous giggle. "The train of events cannot be changed. Keep me here by all means, but the final outcome will be the same. In the end, you cannot win."

"That all?" Bond asked.

"It is enough. It means I have warned you."

"About what?"

A slow, sly smile formed like a slit across Weisen's hairless face. "That's for me to know, and you to find out." He sounded positively amused, so Bruin repeated his earlier offer.

"I didn't mean to be facetious," Weisen added quickly. "The point is that you can do nothing."

"We could kill you, Wolfie." Bruin gave him a look that almost cut the man's heart out on the spot.

"Well, of course, you could do that. Though I still think it wouldn't have the effect you desire. Monika would simply take my place." His voice rose half an octave. "The fools in Moscow, in London and Washington tell you Communism's dead. I promise you it only sleeps, just as Stalinism, the most rarefied version of Communism, has only slept for years. It has lain dormant, in hibernation, and is about to waken. Its rekindling will occur whether I'm there or not."

"You want to tell us what you've got up your sleeve?" Bond asked.

"I think not. It'll happen, and I'm not about to let anyone know the details. Do what you like."

"I'll tell you exactly what we're going to do. After this chat, we're going to take you to the airport and ferry you to London, where people will decide where you should be tried."

"For what?"

"Murder. Treason. A whole lot of things."

"So, you're going to take me to Marco Polo Airport?"

"That's the general idea."

"Put me on a plane?"

252

"Why not?"

"How?"

"How what?"

"How do you propose to do all this? The airport, a flight to London?"

"In the usual way."

"I think not. You see, James, I am far from being alone. You may have put my close bodyguards out of action, but there are at least ten armed men at Marco Polo Airport. I really don't think you'd stand a chance."

"We'll take you out of Venice by train, then." Gus shifted the Uzi in his hands, like a man who would get great pleasure out of using it.

"Same problem." Weisen sounded matter-of-fact, as though he was invulnerable, fireproof from any action they might take.

"Then we'll find another way, Wolfie."

"It still makes no difference. There is no possible scheme you can devise. No plot. No plan. No diversion. You're all trapped within something bigger than any of you can comprehend. When my people come to take me over to Marco Polo, there'll be a little action no doubt. But if you delay them, others will come looking, and others after them. Even if you hold out for a day, it will make not a jot of difference. What is to be will be. Tomorrow, the whole structure of Europe will be changed. Altered out of all recognition."

"Who's coming to pick you up, Wolfie?" Gus gave Bond a glance, suggesting that they might be in a difficult situation after all. "The helicopter? Is that the way you're going?"

Slowly, Weisen shook his head. "I fear, after this morning, my helicopter has been put in mothballs. No, I am to go by the more normal method. In about one hour forty-five minutes." The beautiful slim gold Patek Philippe watch looked ludicrous adorning the puffy little wrist.

"Then we'd better get you out of here very soon." Bond turned to Praxi. "Why don't you go and see if Monika's left any clothes you can use. It might be a good idea to take a water taxi

253

over to the Cipriani, pay the bill, and get your things together."

Weisen made a tutting sound. "Wrong." He smiled like a child asking riddles. "Oh, very wrong." The feet began the irritating drumming again. "The bill was taken care of this morning, and your things have been removed. That interesting telephone's at the bottom of the Grand Canal. I wondered if I could use it in some way, but decided against it."

"Wolfgang, I don't believe you." In his head, Bond doubted his own sincerity. The former spymaster was a very tricksy gentleman, and he could well be telling the truth.

"Call them, then." The pouting choirboy look. "Call them on my telephone." He nodded towards the instrument which sat, silent, on a solid table between the windows. "Go on, you want me to give you the number? It's 5207744."

"Do it," Bond snapped at Praxi. "Bruin, go and take a look at our guests in the cellar. Make sure they're happy. Then start to search this place. We're looking for the passports, IDs, and weapons. But first, find his plane tickets. He must have tickets."

Bruin gave Weisen one of his killing looks, and quickly left the room.

Praxi talked into the telephone, listened, then thanked whoever was at the distant end, and replaced the receiver. "Yes, he's telling the truth." She looked as disturbed as Bond felt. "The bills were paid this morning. All our baggage has gone."

"All right, Wolfie. Perhaps you'd like to tell us where you're supposed to be going tonight."

"Find out for yourself. Why should I tell you anything?"

Gus moved forward, and it was Bond's turn to stop *him* this time. "Don't get rattled, Gus; and don't use violence. We might need him in one piece before the night's over."

"Quite right. Well done, Captain Bond: You're a man of sound common sense." Glee sprang almost tangibly from Weisen's face.

"Don't bank on it." He touched Gus on the shoulder and indicated the door. "Praxi, stay with him, would you, and just kill the little rat if he even moves a finger."

"With pleasure, James."

As they went out, Bruin came up the stairs. "I'll tear the place apart," he muttered, bunching his shoulders as he went past them.

On the landing, Bond asked Gus Wimper what options he thought they had. "I mean how can we get him away? I've no doubt he's telling the truth about having people at the airport and railway station."

"We could hire a boat, but he could be a handful. We'd have to get someone to take us to an unauthorized landing point. I agree, he's probably got a whole army out there; and if he doesn't show up at the airport I think they *will* come looking for him."

"I want to find out where he's supposed to be headed. Perhaps, if we can get him there by another route . . ."

"We might find out what he's up to, or what his people—as he calls them—are up to. I don't think he's bragging. There really is something heavy about to go down. The man's crazy, certainly, but he's too sure of himself. I really . . ." Gus stopped as though suddenly remembering something. "James, look. He's being picked up. Probably a couple of his men with a launch. There's always Quinto di Treviso."

"What's at Quinto di Treviso?" Bond began. Then, "Of course, the airport at Treviso. Forty miles or so inland, right?"

"Absolutely. We could hire an aircraft there, I'm pretty certain. They must have charter firms. Executive jets. We could phone ahead."

"But how do we get him to bloody Quinto di Treviso?"

"We could always hire a car."

"Hire a car? Here? In Venice?"

"You can hire cars at those damned great multi-story parks in the Piazzale Roma. Out towards the railway station." His face lit up at the thought. "It's before you even get to the station. I'd guarantee he hasn't got any thugs hanging around there."

"How do we do it? A couple of doctors, a chauffeur and a nurse? A patient covered in bandages? Mercy dash?"

"It's about the only way."

Bruin came onto the landing. "Our stuff's in there. He hadn't even bothered to hide it: weapons, papers, everything; and look what I've found." He brandished a handful of papers.

"Airline tickets." Bond grabbed them, flicking open the first folder. "Paris!" For the first time since Easy had died he sounded elated. "Charles de Gaulle . . ."

"And this," Bruin passed over another paper.

"A private charter. He's going on to Calais. Tonight." Memories flooded back into his mind. He heard Weisen speaking to Monika Haardt as she was leaving. "Just remember, dear Monika, that, like Mary Tudor, you will find Calais lying in my heart."

Weisen and Monika had thought that line was no end of a joke.

Again, just out of reach, on the cusp of memory, he thought of Claude and Michelle in the car in Paris. Once more he half heard something, then it was gone. This time, though, he knew who had said it, this elusive sentence. Claude. Cold Claude Gaspard had said something that alerted him, but he still could not grasp at the words and hold them.

"How long do you reckon we've got?"

"An hour. Maybe less." Gus looked at his watch.

"Right, let's go and do some telephoning. A car, or a van would be preferable; and then a charter direct to Calais from Quinto di Treviso Airport." He touched Gus's arm. "This must be a real matter of life or death."

19

Death on the Road

They came fifty minutes later. A sleek, expensive-looking launch, with a pilot and two big lads in rollnecks, leather bomber jackets, and jeans. The big lads looked as though they would kill their grandmothers for a couple of dollars, and inform on their grandfathers for even less.

The time, from the plan's conception to the arrival of the launch, had been full and active. They took turns at guarding Weisen, who sat, unperturbed, carrying on a one-sided conversation with whoever was looking after him. It was as though he regarded the entire business as an opportunity to hold court. None of them were happy about it. The man's behavior was too confident and relaxed. "It's like he already won," Bruin said in his slightly fractured English. "Like he's in somehow command of us."

"He might be, actually," Gus agreed, his brow deeply furrowed.

Praxi came back from the bedroom with a light-blue dress which looked suspiciously like a high-class nanny's uniform. It was a deliciously tight fit, and she could easily pass herself off as a nurse. When Bond commented on the "nanny" look Praxi raised her eyebrows. "I think that's what it is. You should see the collection of stuff they have in there. Leather, whips, chains, the whole strict discipline armory."

"We like a bit of the old slap rather than the tickle, do we, Wolfie?" He looked at Weisen, who did not actually blush, but would not meet his eyes.

Bond went through the bathroom cabinets on all floors, bringing a cache of pill bottles to Gus, who had found a stock of gauze and a lot of bandages in a large first-aid kit.

"Know anything about these?" He pushed one of the bottles under Gus's nose.

"*Tranxene. Take one at night.*" Gus read the Italian pharmacist's label. "Yes. If I remember correctly, these are Valium-based. Fifteen milligrams. I suspect if we feed him three he'll go out like a light—unless he's been taking them regularly. You can get hooked on these things. Build up an immunity."

"Better give him four, then. Just to be safe."

Bond went down to the kitchen, very much aware that Easy's body lay below, in the cellar. As he waited for the kettle to boil he hesitated for a moment, then descended the stairs.

They had found a pair of trestles and a board. Easy lay, covered by a sheet, well away from the cell. Behind the bars, Giorgio called out, saying he would help them if they needed an extra pair of hands. "I'm not that desperate," Bond told him. Harry Spraker still groaned a lot, but there were no sounds from the others.

Giorgio started again, and Bond ordered him to be silent, walking over to the makeshift bier and uncovering Easy's face. Praxi had manipulated the features, so that she now seemed composed and peaceful in death. He stood for a few minutes in silent respect, looking at her face for the last time; making a solemn vow that Weisen would pay dearly for what had happened. Slowly he left the cellar.

In the kitchen he found milk and a box full of commercial packets of sugar. The little paper sacks had the Marriott Hotel chain logo stamped on them. Then he made the coffee, wrinkling his nose in disgust as he used a jar of instant granules.

He filled a mug with the black liquid, pulled four of the Tranxene capsules apart—dropping the white powder into the mixture. Then, for good measure, he took a fifth and added that, hoping Weisen used sugar.

Putting the mug, sugar and milk on a small tray he went back up to Weisen, who had been moved into the bedroom while Praxi made telephone calls to the car hire companies in the Piazzale Roma, and to the most likely of the three air-charter companies listed in the commercial directory, under the Quinto di Treviso Airport.

Gus had made Weisen lie on the bed. He sat nearby, with the Smith & Wesson, make-my-day .44 Magnum, held across his left thigh.

Weisen was prattling. ". . . and as for Beria—head of Uncle Joe's NKVD, that was what they called KGB in those days. Well, of course, Beria, I called him Uncle Lavrenti, had bizarre sexual proclivities—young girls, you know. His agents from Dzerzhinsky Square used to get them for him. He was very fond of third-year students from the ballet school, I remember. Used to say they were wonderfully supple. Apart from that he was always very kind to me. I recall one Christmas he gave me a beautiful gift. Really my favorite that year. I think one of his people must've brought it in from France. A little toy guillotine. There was even an executioner, and a tumbrel with aristos. And it worked. The heads of the aristos were fixed on special stalks. You laid them in the block, pulled a string, and the blade came down. Whoosh. Clunk. The heads rolled into a basket—no blood though. You stuck the heads back on again. You could use the little aristos over and over. Then, another year he got one of his men to make me a toy gallows. Now that was fun. Had a trap, the lever, everything. . . ."

"I've brought you some coffee, Wolfgang." Bond cut off the litany of grisly childhood memories.

"Oh, my. How kind."

"We were having some," he lied. "So I thought of you. You take milk and sugar?"

"No milk, lots of sugar though. Black and sweet, that's how I like it. You know, Uncle Joe had servants who tasted everything before he ate or drank. He had a phobia about being poisoned."

"Well, we need you alive, so I promise not to poison you." He poured several packets of sugar into the coffee and stirred it in. "You drink that up, Wolfie. I don't know when we're going to eat, but you'll get food when we do."

"You're too kind, James."

"Yes, I am, aren't I?"

He left the bedroom. Praxi had just put down the telephone. "All done." She sounded happy. "We've got one of those Previa vans. They said it would be best if we were bringing a patient."

Bond remembered the maroon Toyota Previa in Paris. The one Claude and his gang had leaped from in the attempt to take them in the street outside the Hotel Amber, off the Avenue Kléber. In his head he saw Claude Gaspard again, and heard his voice when Michelle had stopped him talking in the car after the snatch in the Faubourg St. Honoré.

This was another step forward. Michelle had cut off his words, and the spoken sentence lay, decapitated, in the corner of his mind. He tried to drag it into the light, but whatever Claude had said remained hidden. At the time Bond had felt a twitch of recognition. There one minute and gone the next. Maddeningly it remained in the shadows, and he still could not pull it fully into the open.

"James? James, are you listening?" Praxi shook his shoulder. "You didn't hear any of that, did you?"

"Sorry, I was miles away."

"The air-charter firm—Aereo Tassì—have got something called a *Gulfstream I,* so I've booked it. They're filing a flight plan now. I said I wasn't certain when we'd arrive: It depended on the patient. Costs four arms and legs, James, but I suppose a jet . . ."

"The *Gulfstream I* isn't a jet. It's small and noisy, even though it's got a couple of Rolls-Royce Dart engines, but it'll do the job, Praxi."

"Oh, well, it cost six arms and legs then. Incidentally, they say the airfield at Calais is quite small, but they can get in easily. What's that mean, James?"

She batted her eyelids and, for a second, he thought she was either flirting with him, or trying to take his mind off Easy. Whichever, he was grateful. "It means, my dear Praxi, that it's safe to land there. That they can 'get in'—land. Presumably by day and night."

He asked Bruin to keep a lookout along the Grand Canal side of the house, and Praxi to watch the back. "I don't want any surprises. You've said he's a slippery devil, and we can't afford things to go wrong now."

It was ten minutes to five in the evening. Already going dark and chilly, but with no mist.

Gus came out of the bedroom. "He's snoring his head off. Time to get the bandages on, I think, actually."

"I think, actually as well, Gus."

Wolfgang Weisen was out and, even though they shook and pummeled him, he showed no signs of waking. "Doped to the eyeballs," Bond said as they got to work with bandages. Gus stuck a wide piece of plaster across Weisen's mouth and taped his eyes with gauze pads. They tied his ankles together with more tape, and secured his hands, at the front, with handcuffs Bond had found, together with the other exotic, weird and erotic gear in the large bedroom closet. Then they wound him tightly in bandages, so that after ten minutes he looked like a small round mummy. "King Tut-Tut-Oh-Dear." Bond stood back and looked at the parcel.

"He looks better wrapped, actually." Gus grinned, and at that moment Bruin came panting up the stairs to say the launch was pulling up in front of the house.

They had arranged that Gus would be the one-man reception committee: he was to go out and instruct any arriving bodyguards that Weisen wanted them inside before they left. It was a slight risk, but Weisen, Gus said, was tight-lipped about all operations, particularly when he suspected anybody. "I've seen these fellows around. They know me." He peered out of the half-open door. "They might even have been told to look for me at the airport, but I doubt if they know I'm in purdah, actually. Good old Wolfie learned a great deal from his Uncle Stalin. Like speaking softly and carrying a bloody great gun." He checked the Smith & Wesson, now regarded as his personal weapon, rammed it into his waistband against the small of his back, and went out the front door.

From where they stood, inside against the wall, Bond and Bruin were able to hear the conversation clearly.

"Hi, Gus," one of the lads called out. "We were told to look for you at the airport today. You give us the slip? The chief wanted you brought over here like a crate of eggs." He spoke German.

"Yes, sure. I know he had you out there. I came in by train early this morning."

Another voice said, "He's got the whole place boxed in tight. Our people're at the airport waiting for him, and he's got a team over at the railway station as well. What's going on?"

"Don't ask me." Gus sounded almost conspiratorial. "I'm only the hired help like you guys, but something's up, that's for sure. You know what he's like."

"*Ja*, Big Mama and Big Michelle left this morning."

Gus made a crude remark about Big Michelle, and they all laughed.

"You're right," one of the lads chuckled. "Like riot helmets."

Then Gus told the launch pilot to stay where he was. "He wants you guys inside for a minute. He's nearly ready to go, but he has last-minute instructions for you. Maybe we're all going to find out what he's up to."

Gus came into the house behind them, drawing the Smith &

Wesson just as Bond stuck the ASP into the back of one neck, and Bruin jabbed the other man with an Uzi.

"Don't become heroes," Gus said. "You'll only end up dead heroes."

The two hoodlums were lightly armed, for people in their kind of work. Gus did the searches, and only removed two Browning automatics, a knife and a set of knuckle-dusters from the now cursing men.

They were marched away by Bruin and Gus, while Bond went through the front door and called for the launch pilot to come up for a minute. "Leave the engine running. He wants to see you as well."

The pilot was not armed at all, but he was angry, and became vocally obscene as he was marched to the kitchen, and down the stairs to the cellar, the ASP against his ribs.

"We'll send the police to get you out. In a couple of days, actually." Gus waved cheerily to the assorted bunch of prisoners now herded behind the bars of the cell from where they shouted curses and profanities. "Sounds like a soccer crowd." Bond went back up the stairs.

"And don't make too many noise!" Bruin ordered.

In spite of the stream of abuse, they could hardly hear a thing once the heavy vault door was closed in the kitchen.

Bond did not like the idea of Easy's body being down there with Weisen's trapped hoodlums, but he consoled himself that it would not be for long. When he turned the key and spun the wheel on the door he also wondered if it had all been just a little too simple. None of them had even tried to put up a fight. He said as much to Gus as they climbed the stairs to get the drugged Weisen.

"You'd try to fight?" Gus shrugged. "Uzis and pistols everywhere? You think that scum has courage? I tell you, I wouldn't have fought, actually."

Bond decided he was probably right.

They had improvised a stretcher from a mattress and heavy

brass curtain rods. When Weisen was laid out and covered with blankets, it looked quite professional, and they found it was surprisingly easy to carry, even down the steep stairs and out to the launch.

They hid one of the Uzis under the blankets on the makeshift stretcher, and all of them carried handguns. Bond still had his ASP; Gus, the make-my-day gun; Bruin took the Browning dropped by Harry Spraker; and Praxi, showing no embarrassment, lifted her skirt to reveal lacy blue underwear, including a garter belt. "It was Monika's." She gave them a smug look as she tucked Gus's "Baby Beretta" into a stocking top. "Truly, it was Monika's. Take a good look, all of you. You think I'd wear tarty stuff like this?"

"You'd miss an awful lot if you didn't," Bond drawled, and she blushed, hastily dropping her skirt. Then, once more she gave him a lingering look which seemed to say she could show him a thing or two if he had the time and inclination.

Gus took the wheel and set the launch on a course up the Grand Canal, gently handling the craft as he turned to port, into one of the many narrow waterways that eventually led to the wider Rio Nuovo which, in turn, took them to the Piazzale Roma on the fringe of the city.

Bruin and Praxi went to sign the papers and take possession of the Previa. So, about an hour after they had left Weisen's Venetian hideout, they were driving across the bridge which links both road and rail services to the mainland. Gus drove, and soon they were heading north, following the signs, taking side roads off the 245 which led to Scorzè, then onto the 515 to the airport at Quinto di Treviso. They had agreed that it would probably be easier to use these relatively rural roads than the arterial A27, where the traffic could be heavy.

It was not until they turned onto a narrow secondary road a few miles south of Scorzè that Gus told them, "I think we have company, actually."

Weisen was on his stretcher, towards the rear of the van, and they had only folded down one of the backseats which Bond had agreed to take. The road from which they had turned off had not been busy, but he had watched several cars overtake them, leaving one which kept pace with them, lagging behind. Twice other car headlights had lit up what he thought was a dark-colored Ferrari. Now, as Gus spoke, he saw that the Ferrari had turned off, following them onto the secondary road.

Inside the Previa, tension sparked for the first time since they had left. The air seemed to have suddenly become charged with static. There was a sharp metallic double click, as Bruin cocked the Uzi. Bond drew the ASP, aware of Praxi, up front, sliding her hand up a thigh to get at the Beretta.

"What am I to do, James?" Gus asked. Since leaving Weisen's house they had all deferred to him as their natural leader.

He peered, narrowing his eyes, squinting to see that the Ferrari was just holding back from them by around thirty yards. Ahead there were no signs of life or cars, just the occasional turning onto even narrower roads—tracks almost—with signposts to villages you would only find on the most detailed maps.

"When you get to the next right-hand turnoff, just go," he said quietly. "Don't signal. Just turn. Put on some speed, then stop—in the middle of the road, no matter if it's only a track." The land seemed flat and there were bushes and trees, stark and black in the lights of the Previa. "As soon as Gus stops, I want everyone out. Jump for it, dive for the roadside and keep down. If the car follows, do nothing unless they either see you or try to get at Weisen. Use your common sense."

"I'll try to give you a warning." Gus tightened his hands on the wheel, then asked if the car following them was close. "Their headlights are damned bright and I can't judge the distance." His voice hit the upper register, another indication of the anxiety that filled the van.

Bond turned, squinting his eyes against the lights. "I think they've dropped back a little. Maybe thirty-five—forty—yards."

"Okay, here we go!" Gus shouted. The Previa van slewed to the right, leaped forward into a road only about half its width, and came to a halt with a screech of burning rubber.

The doors slid and clicked open. Bond threw himself from the back, hurling himself into a clump of bushes to his left—the right of the van. He was aware of the others—mostly in shapes and sounds—scurrying for cover. Nobody was in sight when the van and road were lit up like day by the Ferrari's powerful headlights. The car stopped, with only inches to spare, behind the Previa. Then the doors opened, and death vaulted into the night.

There were four of them. Big men whose silhouetted shapes gave them an even more menacing and sinister look. Two walked forward towards the back of the Previa while the other pair, one on either side of the Ferrari, leaned against the car and began to spray short bursts of automatic fire along the side of the road.

Bond felt the bullets chopping into the earth beside him, and wriggled back, down a slight incline. There was a short lull, during which he smelled the cordite, and felt the fact of death close to his shoulders. Then came the click of new magazines going into the machine pistols, followed all too soon by a renewed, terrible, clatter.

They were firing systematically, little bursts of six or seven rounds, the machine pistols moving from left to right, then back again: mowing down anything in their path. Bullets whined off the road paving, thumped into the earth, or ripped through the bushes. A burst hit the road directly in front of Bond, then, as the shooter moved his feet, another tore into foliage on his right.

Then, with no warning the shooting stopped. He felt the earth cold on his cheek, tensing for the shooting to begin again.

The car doors slammed shut and the engine noise rose, as the car reversed at speed. Bond cautiously peered over the incline. The Ferrari had almost reached the turn. He raised his pistol and fired four rounds in quick succession. All must have gone wide. The car stopped for a second as it slewed broadside on. There was a flicker of fire from a rear window, and a hail of bullets splattered the road ahead of him. Then, the car was gone with a roar and clash of gears, its engine note fading on the night air, leaving a terrible silence behind.

Bond went to the back of the van. Even before he reached the doors he knew what he would find. Weisen had gone, the blankets thrown off the stretcher, which hung halfway out of the open door.

"They got him," he shouted. "The bastards've rescued him."

"James! James, quickly!" Praxi's shout almost touched the barrier of hysteria. She was calling from the left of the van, right by the roadside. She continued to shriek until he found her, kneeling over Bruin whose head was almost completely blown away by the three or four bullets that had smashed into it. In the light from the Previa he could see that her dress was soaked with Bruin's blood.

He took her gently by the shoulders, held her tightly, lifting her, half carrying her back to the van, cradling her head as she sobbed with shock, disgust and horror at the way death could come so quickly by an Italian roadside.

"Just stay here, in the van," he whispered.

Then James Bond went in search of Gus, knowing already what he was likely to find, for there had been no other sound near at hand, apart from Praxi's screams.

20

Curse of Death

The roar of the twin Rolls-Royce Dart engines had settled into a soporific hum. Bond looked out, across the Swiss Alps far below, marveling at the beauty of the sunrise. At this height, the great crags and peaks were backed by a soft pink glow, which slowly changed to an explosion of crimson, fading against a pearl sky that would soon be blue and cloudless.

Beside him, Praxi Simeon dozed. She had hardly slept in the past twelve hours, and her features bore the marks of anguish and horror which still lingered from the events by the roadside on the previous evening.

As he had feared, Gus lay in a clump of grass, some ten feet from the spot where Bruin had died. Gus was not as terribly disfigured as Bruin. For a moment Bond had even thought he was still alive, until he turned him over and saw, in the lights of the Previa, the black spreading pattern of blood from the chest wound that had killed him.

"You bought the farm, actually, Gus," he muttered. Then went about the business of concealing the two bodies, covering them with leaves, fallen branches and whatever he could find. He hoped they would not be discovered until Praxi and himself were far away. The Italian Intelligence and Security Services were as touchy as the French when it came to other countries operating on their turf. If they caught up with him it would be a storm in a teacup, but a great deal of time would be wasted: even in these days of struggle towards a new understanding between members of the European Community. Whatever lip service the governments of the twelve countries gave to open frontiers and the ideal of free trade, each had, in reality, clung on to their individual sovereignty.

He went back to the van, closed the doors and climbed into the driver's side. Praxi sat in the front passenger seat, shaking her head, unable to stop the flow of tears down cheeks which were smudged with dust and dirt from the roadside. Gently, he told her that it was all over. "They've got Weisen, and Gus has bought it." There was no simple way to break the news, and she began sobbing again.

He took a deep breath. "I feel the same, Praxi, but we have to go on."

"Why?" She looked at him in the light of the van—he had yet to close the driver's side door—and her eyes spoke bleakly of shock, dismay, grief and incomprehension. "Why, James?" she repeated, as though about to argue with him.

"Because, the Poison Dwarf's got something going for him. Because so far he's won, and if we don't keep after him, he'll win again."

"So?" A tiny voice which broke between the sobs.

"I don't know what he's planning." He took her hand in his, feeling Bruin's sticky blood on her fingers. "I have no idea what Weisen's up to, but going by his past form it's something unpleasant."

"He said it would happen whether he was there or not. Wherever *there* is. What can we do? We don't know anything, and the man has allies all over Europe. Truly, he has an army of men and women." The sobbing stopped, now anger set in. "There really are *hundreds* of them." Her grip tightened on his. "People who've spent their entire lives believing and being faithful to an ideal, and a goal. Now they've been told their hearts have been in the wrong place; their countries have let go of the order they hold very dear. How do you expect these people to react? In the end they're not going to try and stage half-baked drunken coups, like the Moscow Putsch last year. Eventually, because there are enough of them, they'll rise up and strike. Wolfgang had a huge following in Berlin, and his tentacles stretched out across the whole of Europe. Whatever he's planning, there's not much we can do now."

"We can try."

"How, James?"

"We know he was heading for Calais. We go there and see if we can pick up a clue. If we don't find anything, we're close enough to England to get back to London. They might know something by now, but I'm certainly going to be careful about contacting them before we have any facts."

They drove into the outskirts of Scorzè where Bond found a telephone kiosk. Praxi had to stay in the van. If he allowed her to be seen she could be arrested on sight, covered as she was with blood, and in a dangerous state of near hysteria.

He called Aereo Tassì at Quinto di Treviso Airport—introducing himself as the doctor whose assistant had booked a charter flight to Calais—and told them that, unhappily, their patient had died. They would not require the *Gulfstream* that night, but he would like to book the same aircraft, to the landing strip at Calais, leaving at dawn. He would telephone again later to see what kind of a flight plan they had been able to file, and to settle takeoff time.

By then it was seven forty-five in the evening. In Scorzè itself shops were still open. He asked Praxi what her dress and shoe sizes were, and she told him, glumly, with no enthusiasm. It took him almost half an hour, a great deal of embarrassment, and many oohs and aahs from salesgirls, to buy a conservative, navy blue suit, plain, no frills underwear, panty hose, shoes, a shoulder bag and toiletries for them both. He paid for the whole lot with an AmEx card in his Bunyan identity, and walked casually back to the parking area where he had left the van.

Praxi did not seem to have moved. She appeared to be detached, impervious to anything he said. She did not even thank him when he told her about the clothes.

They drove on towards Quinto di Treviso and found a motel about five miles from the airport. It was clean, and had a small restaurant attached. The manager at reception, a thin lugubrious, harassed-looking man, appeared to be delighted that they had another couple of guests for the night—"Around here we do little business in the winter," he said. "A few truck drivers, but it's hardly worth opening. All the major traffic goes by the A4, or the A27. I'd close the place, but my wife comes from Treviso, and we manage to scrape by."

Bond nodded sympathetically, but the man was piling it on. They obviously had regulars, for there were three TNT trucks parked outside, not to mention another five private cars. He took the keys, inquired how late the restaurant stayed open, and drove over to park outside the ground-floor room: a pleasantly large bedroom, with bathroom attached. There was no TV. The manager had apologized about it. "We're refitting all the rooms. The rental place we used to do business with has closed. If you come back in a week we'll have everything, including the Sky Channel and BBC's World Service."

They wouldn't be looking at TV anyway, he told the manager with a broad wink, and the Italian had nodded, knowingly.

He hurried Praxi inside, clutching the carrier bags with one hand. Then he closed the door and told her she would have to shower, get the fresh clothes on, and make herself look respectable. When she opened her mouth, as if to start haranguing him again, he took her by the shoulders.

"Praxi," his fingers dug hard into her flesh. "I feel as bad as you do, but we have to make an effort. You were the driving force of Cabal for years. London and Washington relied on you . . ."

"And look where it got me . . ." she began.

"That doesn't matter . . ."

"It got me nowhere. We were compromised all the way. That's been made very clear in the past few days. . . ."

"Stop it!" He was near to slapping her face to haul her out of this slough of despair. "You, Praxi Simeon, worked for us. You showed courage, discipline, devotion and all the other things it takes to do a job like that. I know, Praxi, I've been there before. Don't let it all go now. Get yourself a shower. Change your clothes, and we'll have a meal, and grab some sleep. At least we deserve that."

She glared at him and, for a few seconds, it seemed that they were locked in a long struggle of wills. Then her face sagged and her body seemed to drain of the tension that had inhabited it since Bruin's death. She turned away, sorted through the carriers, found the toiletries and walked slowly towards the bathroom. As she reached the door, she turned.

"I'm the only one left now, James. You realize that? I'm the only member of Cabal left alive. How long do you think *I've* got?"

"All the time in the world," he said, then immediately regretted it as a bolt of anguish came out of nowhere and struck him like a knife. There was another time and another place. A time when he had said those very words to another woman whose memory still clung to him: sometimes, if he woke in the night, her memory was so strong that he could swear she lay beside him in the dark. For some incredible reason and for a fragment of time, Easy had banished that guilt and pain which still lay just under the surface of consciousness. Now it was back, and he felt an almost superstitious shiver of horror. Had he sealed Praxi's own fate by simply repeating those words, like a terrible curse of death? He sloughed the foolishness from his mind.

There were five rounds left in the magazine of the ASP, and one spare magazine which he had salvaged from Weisen's Venetian home. That was it. Fourteen 9mm Glaser slugs, and a girl with a "Baby Beretta" pistol. She had held it in one hand from the moment he found her with Bruin. The only time she let go was for a few minutes while he clasped her hands in his.

She had even taken it into the bathroom, as if it were a talisman to wear and fend off the evil spirit of that revolting hairless tub of a man whose power did, indeed, seem boundless.

All the depression that had swamped Praxi seemed to fill his body now. He dropped heavily onto the bed, the ASP pistol in one hand, and allowed the exhaustion to take him down into a deep pit of unknowing.

Seconds later, it seemed, Praxi was shaking him by the shoulder. "James? James? Wake up! Oh, please wake up!"

He grunted, felt the day return, squeezed his eyelids a couple of times and propped himself on one elbow. "Praxi . . ." he began.

"God, you gave me a fright. I thought, for a moment, you were dead, like all the others."

"I'm sorry." His mouth tasted vile. "I must've been more tired than . . ."

"Of course you were. Don't you think we should eat? You said that's what we needed, and deserved."

He swung his legs off the bed. She wore the smart navy blue suit, had redone her makeup and hair, yet she still clutched the "Baby Beretta."

She must have seen the look in his eyes and nodded. "You have taste, James. It's a perfect fit. And the shoes also. I feel better, thank you. Thank you very much. You can depend on me now."

Yes, he thought, you feel better, but it is really only skin deep. You are putting on a good front. Well done. He touched her shoulder lightly. "You look terrific," he smiled at her. "Let me get myself together."

She leaned forward and kissed him: a peck on the cheek, but he had the distinct feeling that she wanted to move to his mouth. He stood, grabbed the bag with the razor and other toiletries he had bought, and headed for the bathroom. In less than twenty minutes he had shaved, showered, and dressed again. He had nothing new to wear, but that did not matter. He brushed the dust from his blazer, combed his hair and went back to the bedroom.

Before they left for the restaurant he called Aereo Tassì. They had filed a flight plan which meant leaving a little before dawn, but it would get them into Calais by ten-thirty. "There'll be a lot of traffic in the area tomorrow." For some reason Bond could not explain, the familiar picture of Cold Claude and Big Michelle in the car came into his head with the unsolved spoken sentence still just out of reach.

He said they would be there by five in the morning so the flight would be able to leave on time. The Aereo Tassì operator rechecked the American Express number Praxi had used from Weisen's place, and said the company looked forward to flying them.

"Okay, let's get some food." Bond replaced the receiver and rose. "We've got an early start, and you need sleep."

"Look who's talking?" She did not quite laugh, but there was a trace of smile on her face.

The food was run-of-the-mill, though the menu gave few choices. They settled for the conservative dishes: good solid minestrone, spaghetti and savory meatballs, followed by chocolate mousse. A drinkable house Chianti helped, and the coffee was real: certainly not gourmet, but neither was it a greasy spoon. "When we get to London, I'll take you to one of the best Italian restaurants in the world." He smiled at her over the table with its chi-chi candle stuck in a bottle, and the red-and-white checked cloth and napkins. He thought of the other place now, in Marylebone High Street and, for a moment, longed to be in dirty old, crowded, unsavory London. He even smelled its familiar scents and heard the sounds he had loved for so many years.

"You went away again, James," she said. "Where this time?"

"Oh, just showing you my city. It's like everywhere else nowadays. Expensive, crowded, dangerous."

"You weren't thinking about Wolfgang?"

"I'd almost forgotten him."

"How could you forget?" It was a half laugh, full of cynicism.

"I'd put him away for the night. Tomorrow's another day."

They went back to the room and booked a wake-up call for four-fifteen. "You have the bed, Praxi, I'll sleep across the door."

She came close, almost thrusting her body against him. "You don't have to, James."

"No, no, I . . ."

"Please. If nothing else, I'd like to be held by another human being. Just for a while. It wouldn't do you any harm either."

He hesitated, then kissed her, feeling her need transferred to his loins, knowing that she was offering not simply lust, but companionship and a cave in which they could both hide for a few hours.

"I'm still wearing Monika's things," she giggled as he began to undress her. Then, as they slid between the sheets, she pressed a small package into his hands. "Nowadays, you can't be too careful," she whispered. After that, the night dissolved into whispers, sighs and moans, and the world shrank, as some poet once said, to hot flesh straining on a bed.

Now, the gleaming wing of the *Gulfstream I* dipped as the sun came up, glancing off the metal skin like a fireball reflected in a mirror. "All the time in the world," he thought, still nervous at having uttered the words out loud. He closed his eyes. Perhaps what had passed between them in the soft, beautiful, loving night had been all their time. If that was so, nothing would be the same ever again.

He sank into a light doze, the words of an old blues repeating and entwining in his mind:

> *Baby, oh baby, won't you answer me please?*
> *Baby, oh baby, won't you answer me please?*
> *All day I stood by your coffin tryin' to give my poor heart ease.*

He knew it was *Coffin Blues,* but it had come, without warning, as he dreamed he was back in London, sitting in a restaurant with a woman, though he could not see her face behind a flickering candle. In the dim background, a man was saying something about standing room only. Then he woke to hear their pilot saying they would be landing in ten minutes.

Praxi was awake, and he asked if she was all right, then glanced out of the window. It looked cold down there—a clear autumn day. The water of the English Channel gave off little glitters as the sunlight seemed to leap from ripple to ripple.

Calais was on their side of the aircraft, and he could see the great scar that was the huge new terminal at Coquelles to the west. The place seemed busy, even though the Eurotunnel would not be in service until next year. It was like looking at a well-made model—the roads and rail tracks snaking from platforms, ramps and loading bays, into the wide rectangular mouths of the tunnel entrances. A lot of cars, he thought; and a lot of people out in the new Terminal. Then, it struck him as though some invisible, magic bullet had ripped into him. "There'll be a lot of traffic in the area tomorrow," the Aereo Tassì operator had said, last night on the telephone.

His stomach turned over, and for a second he thought he might stop breathing.

At last, his mind grasped the missing sentence. He was back in the Faubourg St. Honoré, crushed next to Cold Claude Gaspard in the Japanese car.

He heard Big Michelle, in the recent past, say: "We would rather you didn't stay in the country any longer. I would prefer you to be out by tonight, but I have an unfortunate tendency to be soft-hearted."

Then the man he now knew as Claude Gaspard began to speak: "Particularly with *Misanthrope* coming. . . ." He had seemed to bite off the sentence, as though he had crossed an invisible line.

Misanthrope. Oh, my God. He thought he had said it aloud.

"James, what's the matter?" Praxi grabbed his arm, her eyes wide, and concern written across her face. "What's wrong?"

"What's the date?" He could not even remember what day it was.

"October fourteenth. Wednesday. James . . . ?"

"God help us." He sounded as though he really was praying. Then he looked at his watch. Ten-thirty. They might just be in time. In his head he saw the pink file on his desk back at the Regent's Park Headquarters. It was flagged Most Secret, and there were only half a dozen names neatly initialed on the cover. The cover also said *Misanthrope*. No wonder something had clicked and jangled when Gaspard nearly bit his tongue out. It was not surprising that, since the moment in the car, Bond had constantly searched his mind for what the Frenchman had said.

The Eurotunnel, running under the English Channel, would not be in service until well into next year, 1993, but it would see a train pass through it today. This morning. At eleven o'clock. *Misanthrope* was the operation's cipher, and it would have remained secret until the previous night, October 13. A news bulletin was to be issued during the evening, to give the press and television just enough time to get crews there. That was why the pilot had known, when they talked on the telephone, that there would be a lot of air traffic around Calais.

It had been decided not to announce the European Community leaders' short train ride through the tunnel until hours before, as a tight security measure. The press would have time to get there, but no terrorist organization would have time to set up any complex operation—except for Wolfgang Weisen, of course. He had known, probably from one of his intelligence sources.

The train leaving the Coquelles Terminal for the British Terminal near Folkestone, would have around one hundred people on board: all the heads of the twelve countries which made up the EC, together with most of their ministers and members of their cabinets, advisers and closest confidants. Prime ministers, Presidents, Chancellors. Ministers, Cabinet ministers. Even M was supposed to be traveling in the British PM's party, together with the Director General of the Security Service.

A gala day. The first train to travel through that extraordinary feat of engineering—in fact three tunnels—which now ran below the English Channel. Below the sea itself, for fifty kilometers, the train would bear the leaders and governments of Europe from France to England and back.

Now Bond knew, with a terrible thunder in his head, that somewhere in the tunnel Wolfgang Weisen's men and women waited. Maybe Weisen himself would be there, to see the total leadership of Europe die in one awful moment deep below water.

As he unbuckled his seat belt, he had already begun to yell at the two pilots who were concentrating on landing at the small airstrip east of Calais.

21

Death Under Water

The narrow door to the flight deck had remained open for the entire flight. The *Gulfstream I* is not a large aircraft, and on charters the two-man crew did not have to worry much with security matters. Bond leaned in, shouting his message, and the captain in the left-hand seat moved his head slightly, annoyed at being interrupted during the most crucial stage of any aircraft operation: the landing.

Even with the engine noise, he could hear the constant chatter emanating from the headsets of both men. The second pilot, who looked young enough to still be in school, turned, one hand lifting the left pad of his earphones.

"You're in contact with the tower?" Bond shouted.

"But of course." The pilot looked as angry as the man who was actually flying the plane. "If you would sit down . . ."

"I've got to get a message to Coquelles. To the Eurotunnel Terminal. Security."

"We'll be down in ten minutes. Can't . . . ?"

"No, it can't wait! Get the tower to call up Terminal Security. I am an officer of the British Intelligence Service. Tell them to check with Admiral Sir Miles Messervy—he should be with the British PM's party. Message from Predator. Abort *Misanthrope*. Urgent and essential. Use those words, please. If the Admiral isn't available, get Colonel Tanner. Say Predator needs to be picked up at the airfield. Again use the words 'Urgent' and 'Essential.' "

The young man appeared to be taking him seriously for he was scribbling on a clipboard. "I'll do what I can, sir. It might have to wait until we're down, though."

"Send it now." Bond looked at his watch again. Ten thirty-five. "There isn't much time."

"If you'd go back to your seat, sir."

He nodded and returned to Praxi, who looked bewildered. "Please, James, what is it?" She clutched his arm as the aircraft gave a little buck, hitting some kind of thermal as it began the long descent on finals.

"It's Weisen: or maybe just his people. Every single ruling member of the EC is going to be on a train, going through the tunnel in about twenty minutes from now. Wolfgang knew, and he was due to come here for it. He might even be here." His hands rose and fell in a gesture of hopelessness.

Praxi said something which was lost in the noise from the engines, and the gear coming down with a whine and thump.

"If he's planning to do what I think, there'll be chaos in Europe. Every single major political figure in the EC'll be wiped off the face of the map. I can't think of a worse situation . . ."

He remembered Wolfgang Weisen's words. Only yesterday he had said, "Tomorrow, the whole structure of Europe will be changed. Altered out of all recognition."

If the train entered the Eurotunnel, it would be changed: blown apart. There is nothing more dangerous to a country than a political vacuum, he thought, and Weisen was attempting to create the ultimate political vacuum. Tiny fingers of ice crept up the short hairs on the nape of his neck.

They touched down at ten forty-one, and the co-pilot came back, stooping as he walked towards them along the narrow aisle.

"You'll be picked up." He looked at Bond with a hint of suspicion. "They told me that you are both to remain by the buildings until somebody arrives for you."

"Who did you speak to?"

"The tower passed a message to Head of Security at the terminal. They *are* coming to get you, sir. You and the lady."

Bond nodded, peering out of the little window. The airstrip which serves Calais looks more like a flying club than a full-blown airport, but he could clearly see a row of important-looking aircraft lined up near the low, white buildings. The leaders of the European Community had flown in only a matter of hours before. They expected to be flying back to their various capitals very shortly. He prayed they would need the aircraft in which they had arrived.

By the time the *Gulfstream* reached the little cluster of huts, with its engines stopped and parking brakes on, it was eight minutes to eleven. Outside, despite the bright sunlight, it was a cold morning, and as they left the aircraft, both passengers and crew hunched their shoulders against the chill.

Bond thanked the crew, and the co-pilot again stressed they were to remain outside. He paced around, not speaking to Praxi, except to make the occasional "Where the hell are they?" remark. He felt impotent, his nerves strung out, and a growing sense of desperation invading mind and body. It was like drowning in anxiety, he thought.

She tried to calm him, but it was no use. For once in his life, James Bond had lost complete control of the business in which he excelled. At two minutes to eleven a little French military helicopter came in low from the west. It hovered on the edge of the field to allow a Cessna to come bustling in, then it dipped, heading towards the buildings, chopping in, sending a wild downdraft of air which made both Praxi and Bond turn their backs as the rotor blades wound down.

"James? Everything okay?" Bill Tanner, M's Chief of Staff, dressed in the Whitehall uniform of dark suit, white shirt and

281

regimental tie, climbed from the helicopter with a cheerful grin. "It's good to see you. Quite a surprise."

"Did you stop the bloody train?" Bond hurled the words at him, as though speech could kill.

"Stop it?" Tanner's eyes opened wide.

"I sent a message. Abort *Misanthrope*. Weisen. He's on the loose, and his people're in the Tunnel."

"Abort . . . ?"

"You didn't get my signal?"

"Just your codename. Reference to M, and that you needed to be picked up here."

"I sent you an 'Urgent and Essential'." He looked around to see the younger of the two Gulfstream pilots coming back towards the aircraft.

"I said they'd pick you up."

"Did you not send the signal as I instructed?"

"It was probably garbled, but yes. I said you needed picking up; I gave the funny name and the bit about an Admiral . . ."

Bond felt the color drain from him, as though he had become a ghost in less time than it took to click your fingers. Suddenly he was awash with the fatigue of the past few days. Like the previous evening, part of him was saying forget it. Give up and get some sleep. Then the old adrenaline pump took over. "Bill, for Christ's sake, stop the bloody train from leaving, and get us all back to the terminal."

Tanner stood for a second, then he saw the look on Bond's face and turned back to the helicopter, calling to the pilot who reached out to fire up his radio and began talking rapidly.

"Get in!" Tanner shouted, and they started to climb aboard as the rotors turned. The Chief of Staff always went straight to the heart of matters. He did not even ask Bond about the exact situation. After their long association in the British Intelligence Service, he did not need a lengthy briefing. Talk about detail was simply an unnecessary waste of time.

The helicopter shuddered, then rose smoothly, dipped its

nose and began to hustle its way west. They had been airborne for just over a minute when the pilot turned his head and said something to Tanner.

"The train's gone!" Tanner yelled into Bond's ear.

"Then get the bloody thing back. Stop it!"

Bill Tanner began to shout the instruction at the pilot when Bond cut in—"No, don't bring it back. Just stop it. Cut the power to the rails if necessary, but just stop the thing dead."

His mind was covering all the basics. It was safer to simply get the train to a standstill than reverse it from the depths of the tunnel. He did not know if Weisen's men would even be in the tunnel, so there was a possibility that the train itself had been rigged with some kind of bomb. What would he have done in Weisen's shoes? The best way to blow the train and its precious passengers to kingdom-come would be an explosive device with a mercury-activated trigger. The bomb would become active after the vehicle had moved over a certain distance: a mile or so. Then there would be a point of no return: a specific amount of time—two, ten or fifteen minutes—before it exploded.

"Stop the train. Cut off the power and instruct the VIPs to leave and walk back through the tunnel. It's the only safe way."

Tanner nodded and shouted to the pilot, who again began to talk into his headset. Through the bubble they could see the Coquelles Terminal coming up fast. Images blurred in Bond's mind. He saw a military band, standing around at ease near one of the long platforms, talking, laughing, looking at their instruments. He was aware of one of the branch lines and the great slab-sided rolling stock that would eventually transport heavy trucks from Britain to the Continent and back again. Another line held sleek passenger and private car carriages.

For centuries, he thought, Britain had been in many ways protected by the English Channel. That short strip of water had stopped Napoleon from invading in the early nineteenth century, and again it had been the sticking point in 1940, when Hitler and his legions had overrun the rest of Europe. At the

Channel, Hitler paused, then lost the battle for air superiority, and had to abort his Operation Sea Lion—the full-scale invasion of the United Kingdom.

Many people in Britain regarded those twenty-five miles or so of water as a natural barrier, a defense against aggressors, but in spite of history, the political leaders of France and Britain had set in motion something which had been on the drawing board for decades: a tunnel, linking Britain to the Continent. In December 1987 ground had first been broken, and within three years the British and French tunnelers met, carving their way through the rock and clay underwater to form the first-ever land connection on December 1, 1990. Since then the whole face of the European transport system had been changed. This was certainly an historic and momentous day, even though the best part of a year still had to pass before any regular service would be established.

If ever, Bond thought. If today exploded into a moment of wrath and terror, the result could be far worse than anything that had happened in war-torn Europe during this century—or any century in its long history.

The pilot shouted something back at Tanner, who craned forward to listen.

"The train is stopped." He cupped his hands around Bond's ear, and the words seemed to lift a great weight from him: as though his entire body had been released from gigantic pressure.

The helicopter nosed down towards a landing pad, around which a gaggle of Special Forces troops were drawn up near two dark grey, squat, ugly-looking armored Saviem/Creusot-Loire paramilitary vehicles.

At least the French had been prepared, Bond thought. These were GIGN Special Forces troops: members of the elite, low-key, anti-terrorist unit, trained in all types of overt and covert operations. As they touched down, a young officer ran, crouching, to the door, which he wrenched open, calling up to Bill

Tanner. "Colonel, you are required in the Operations Room. I am to take you and your colleagues there immediately."

As they trotted past the GIGN men, Bond saw they appeared to be preparing themselves for some kind of move. "The train *has* been stopped?" he called, asking the young Frenchman.

"But yes, it has been stopped." The man turned to take a curious, long look at him. "You are Captain Bond, yes?"

Still at a trot, he nodded.

"We received your signal, via Colonel Tanner, from the helicopter. It came in at almost the same moment as the train was stopped in the tunnel."

"*Was* stopped?" His heart skipped and his stomach turned over.

"*Was* stopped, sir. Yes, and there is more. The entire carriage crew—the attendants who should have been on board—have been discovered in the crew facility. All ten of them. Dead. Shot to death. Left naked. I personally viewed the bodies just now. Horrible. Dreadful."

The Operations Room, high up on top of a great skeletal structure, had been designed like an airport control tower. Through the tall glass windows its occupants could view the entire terminal, and, on two of its sides, desks and electronic arrays winked as information was displayed on VDUs and CRTs, similar to those in Air Traffic Control Centers.

Several men and women sat at the displays, and in the middle of the room, a six-foot, uniformed Colonel of the GIGN was talking quietly to a small man in a white coat. The Colonel vaguely resembled the late Charles de Gaulle, hard-faced and with a stubborn jaw.

Bill Tanner introduced Colonel Henri Veron, who looked at Bond with piercing light-blue eyes. The skin of the Colonel's face was like well-tanned leather, his hands were strong and scarred, and there was a worm of distrust stirring deep in the eyes. His right hand constantly hovered over the big, holstered 10mm automatic at his hip.

They shook hands, but the Colonel did not smile. "I'm told you think you can tell us what is going on?" The voice was sharp, and he spoke as though every sentence was an order.

"No." Bond had already made up his mind that he would be the one to settle old scores. He was not about to let the Colonel take that away from him. "No, Colonel. I *know* who's behind it. He might even be there, in the tunnel, and I should tell you that he has a large following, and plenty of arms at his disposal. If you'd care to brief me, I can tell you what *should* be done."

Veron gave him a long hard look, then, with a small shrug, told the story so far. The train had traveled some twenty kilometers when it stopped. "There, you can see exactly where it is, on that display." He pointed to one of the screens which showed a long, thin rectangle of light against a map of the tunnel systems.

The driver had reported a malfunction, and asked that all power to the rails be turned off. About the same moment, word had come that the crew of train attendants had been found dead. "It was, of course, obvious to us that we had a serious terrorist action on our hands. We waited for some word from the driver, and when he last came on—five minutes or so ago— he managed to give the code word for hijack." Colonel Veron had exceptionally disconcerting eyes. He gave the impression that he could see deeply into Bond's mind.

"So," he snapped. "We have a hijack, and I am personally mortified. You see I've been responsible for all the security systems and procedures on the French side of the tunnel. A hijack was always a possibility when the regular service began, but today? The place has been sealed off like a fortress. I would not have thought it possible . . ."

"With respect, Colonel." Bond had now assumed his own sharp and clipped manner. "You have *not* got a hijack situation. If you're waiting for these people to make demands, you'll wait till Hell freezes over. This is a multiple assassination. Until last night I had the man responsible. I was in the process of taking him to England, when he was rescued. He's ruthless in the extreme, and knows exactly what he's doing. Now, sir, what are *we* doing?"

Colonel Veron was in no way shaken by the Englishman's assessment. "Yes, we had considered this possibility, and we're ready to move now."

"With what kind of plan?"

"As you can see from the display, Captain Bond, the train is in the first northbound tunnel. Between the north and southbound tunnels there is what we call a Maintenance Tunnel. This has a number of uses. The air-conditioning units can be serviced from this middle tunnel, for instance. Men and equipment can be moved along it and into the tunnels on its right and left, through metal doors and connecting chambers set every kilometer. These access chambers are also there for safety purposes. In the event of a serious problem, passengers can be got out of the trains and brought into the relative safety of the Maintenance Tunnel, and so ferried back here—or to the British Terminal."

"Not if they're in small pieces they can't."

"There I would agree with you. That is why we must go now. You can see from the display that the train is lying between two of the access chambers." He pointed to the screen. "We plan to perform a kind of pincer movement. Half of my men will enter by the furthest chamber, the other half by the near one. In that way we can surprise and confuse . . ."

". . . And maybe even precipitate whatever they plan to do." Bond frowned. "I know this man, Colonel. In all probability he's not there—not in the tunnel itself. If that's the case, his men, and women for all I know, will have very clear instructions. If attacked before they're ready to act, they'll sacrifice themselves.

"Even if he's with them, the man concerned will almost surely allow himself to be killed also. He's a crazy, Colonel—a political crazy—and I suspect he imagines he is not as other men. In other words, I think there's the distinct possibility that he thinks he's immortal."

"Then you were very careless to lose him, Captain Bond."

"I lost a number of very good friends as well. You control the power and lights from here?" He turned to a white-coated man who, so far, had not been allowed to speak, and now was able to introduce himself as M. Charles Daubey, Chief of Operations, Coquelles Terminal.

"Yes, Captain Bond. We control the power along the central rail, and the lighting. Also emergency power."

"And, presumably, there are safety locks on the train doors?"

"They are operated from the driver's cabin and from large rubber buttons outside each set of carriage doors."

"Not from inside?"

"Yes, but the driver can disengage that function. . . . He probably . . ."

"We presume that has already been done." Veron was grabbing the initiative again.

"We have radios?" asked Bond.

"Of course. I suppose, as you have some personal score to settle with this man, you wish to come with us?"

"I don't wish to come, sir. I am coming."

"Under my command only, Captain Bond."

He nodded, and Veron looked grimly happy. "Very well. You're armed?"

The ASP was in his hand. "The radios, sir."

The French officer pointed to a Motorola HL-20 radio, complete with earpiece, being held by Charles Daubey. These were the same small radios used by people like the American Secret Service, whose main occupation is a twenty-four-hour guard on the President and Vice-President of the United States, together with visiting, and other, political VIPs. The HL-20s were exceptionally reliable and could stand up to practically any mishandling short of a direct missile hit.

"Might I suggest," Bond touched the radio with the fingers of his right hand. "Might I suggest, that we have a special series of click codes."

The French colonel smiled. "We were just finalizing that

288

when you arrived, Captain Bond. Two clicks, cut off the lights. Three clicks, resume power to the rails. Four clicks, cut power to the rails again. Five, turn on lights only."

"And one click?"

"Restore power to lights *and* rails. You can remember all that, Captain Bond?" The Frenchman was already striding towards the door. "If you're coming, you'd better hurry."

"I need a radio," Bond was at the Colonel's side as he went down the stairs two at a time, calling back to Praxi: telling her to stay where she was.

"You shall have one."

"How do we go in?"

"You are familiar with our VAB IS vehicles?"

"Yes." The ugly-looking, grey armored cars he had seen as they landed were known as VABs. With their six-wheel drives, heavy protection, searchlights, missile launchers and twin machine-guns, the VABs could carry twelve men, including the driver. Sturdy, and exceptionally constructed, the VAB is one of the best anti-riot, anti-terrorist, vehicles in the world.

They were ready, with motors running, when Veron and Bond reached the helicopter pad. Veron led him to the first vehicle, opened the rear hatch, and told the men inside to look at Bond. "He is with *us*. Remember him." He asked for a spare radio which Bond clipped onto his belt, running the earpiece up the inside of his blazer and into his ear. Deafening static blasted into his ear as soon as he turned it on, and he saw Veron give a supercilious little smile as he twisted the squelch to reduce the noise.

They went to the back of the second vehicle, where Veron gave the same little speech to his men. It was as though he was telling them to look after their civilian colleague.

"I am in the first vehicle," the Colonel told him. "You will travel here, in the second one." He introduced the young lieutenant who had first broken the news on the helicopter pad— André Bucher. Only fifteen minutes ago, Bond thought, looking at his watch.

Veron gave his orders, signals, and other necessary information, speaking in the same clipped French. Bond heard him use a number of single words that were obviously coded instructions, used for speed and secrecy among the unit.

While Bond did not like the man, he at least conceded that he appeared to be an efficient and well-organized soldier. He would give the same orders to the men in his own VAB when they were on the move.

Bond climbed into the back, heard the clang of the armored door coming down, and nodded to a grim-faced little tough who moved up to let him sit on the hard metal bench with the other five men. A similar seat ran down the opposite side of the vehicle, and he noticed that the five men across from him gave him knowing winks and smiles of welcome.

The engine purr rose, and they began to bump forward.

"Bonne chance!" he said, and felt the atmosphere become more friendly as his new comrades in arms called, "Good luck!" and "Cheers!" in English.

It took almost twenty minutes to get near the rear access chamber. After ten minutes. young Bucher ordered one of the men to man the roof turret. Ten minutes or so later, they rolled quietly to a stop, and Bucher nodded, indicating the rear hatch should be opened.

Bond climbed out, behind the officer. The sides of the tunnel were still in their natural state, and it was lit by high-powered bulbs set at intervals, in a maze of wiring, into metal reflectors with thin grilles as their only protection.

He saw the big steel door to the chamber as soon as his feet touched the floor. It lay only five or six paces away, and he was just about to move towards it when the explosion ripped through the tunnel.

For a second, he thought it was the VIP train, but the sudden hot blast on his face, and the magnified rattle of machine-gun fire which followed the blast, made it plain that they were under attack.

An image of Weisen went through his head. He saw the

290

pudgy little man, drumming his feet on the floor and laughing with glee, like some monstrous overgrown baby. Wolfgang, he thought, had considered everything. Somehow he had found a way to infiltrate the terminal and take out the train attendants—which meant there were only ten of his men and women on the train itself. He had also preempted the only chance of rescue by putting some of them in the Maintenance Tunnel. Unless he had somehow managed to get more people into the tunnel system, this meant that the ten who had traveled on the train were now split into two groups—one section with the VIP train, the others here, waiting in ambush in the Maintenance Tunnel.

The other GIGN soldiers were piling out of the VAB, and the cannon in the turret had started to rap into life. Peering around the side of the vehicle, he could see about half a kilometer up the tunnel.

Colonel Veron's VAB was on fire, shattered and burning, slewed side on. There was no sign of life, but the ammunition had begun to explode, and he thought he could see movement behind the smashed and crumpled death trap. No explanations were necessary. The VAB had been hit by a high-powered anti-tank missile. Where there was one, he thought, there would be another.

Without waiting for young Bucher, he shouted to the men to get away from the VAB, but nobody moved. These soldiers only took orders from their own: After all they spent years of training as a team, knew each other's ways, understood particular orders given in single-word commands.

He knew none of them, but he was not about to hang around with these undeniably brave men. He lunged for the chamber door, slammed down on its long metal handle, and pulled. The heavy slab of steel swung back easily, and he was just stepping inside when the second missile hit.

He almost believed he had seen the thing streaking through the flames and explosions of the first wrecked VAB; for a few moments he even imagined that he was in the center of the blast, which threw the armored car back for some five yards as it exploded and burned with a white heat. Then he realized he had only imagined the horrors of the direct hit. The door was closing as the missile struck, and he merely experienced a vivid mental picture of what was happening as his ears were clapped by the violent crump, the whump of flame and the other dreadful sounds that followed. He heard pieces of metal clang against the door, and it was a good thirty seconds before he truly knew that he was alive.

His ears still rang, and he thought he might be slightly wounded, for his body ached from the sudden onset of tension in his muscles. He was in a narrow chamber. At the other end, a door—twin to the one he had just come through—stood shut against the main northbound track.

Gently he pushed down on the handle. It slid easily in his hand and the new, well-oiled door swung forward, sending him sprawling into the vast tunnel.

"Oh, look. Captain Bond, how nice of you to join us. We're just putting the finishing touches to a lovely big firework. You can enjoy it with all your friends."

Wolfgang Weisen stood, with four other men, behind the sleek French train. In the seconds that passed, Bond saw the Uzi in one man's hand, the square package they were fixing to the back of the last coach, the wiring running forward from the package, and, fleetingly, some of the imprisoned people within the train. Helmut Kohl and the President of France were certainly there, in the rear carriage, their faces white and drawn.

"Just put the gun down very carefully, James. We really don't want that going off, do we?" Weisen wore the uniform of an SNCF attendant, as did the four other men, but on him it looked ridiculous, making him seem even more bizarre than ever. "Oh, I'm so glad you're here, somehow it makes things complete." He continued, "Though I'm cross, very cross with you. In fact, I'm only just feeling better. You gave me a very bad hangover, you know. I've had to drink gallons of coffee. The gun, James. Down, James. We haven't got much time and I, for one, would like to get clear before I detonate this train."

Slowly, Bond let the pistol's butt drop into his left hand, then he held it flat, as he bent his knees, not taking his eyes off the group as they huddled around the carriage. He kept his feet well away from the rails, and, as the pistol reached the ground, so his right hand touched the send button on the HL-20. He pressed it three times—three clicks. Restore power.

For a second nothing happened, then the five men, with Weisen in the center, began to go through a terrible ballet of smoking death.

He had seen that Weisen had one foot on the center rail, and was steadying himself by holding onto the arm of the man with the Uzi. The other three were crouched, fixing the package of explosives directly under the coach. They were all in contact with each other, and at least two of them were kneeling on the center rail.

The whole group seemed to freeze, as though petrified. Then Weisen appeared to almost levitate as each of them began to tremble, shaking violently. There were sparks around their legs, and a horrible burning as they performed this puppet-like movement, arching their backs, shivering, their arms waving like branches in a gale. All wreathed in blue fire.

Weisen's face became a twitching macabre mask, eyes bulging out of their sockets, lips drawn back from his teeth, the pudgy fat around his jaw vibrating.

Smoke began to come from the men's hair, and the most revolting thing of all was the burning of Weisen's bald scalp. It looked as though someone were slowly melting a kind of black wax across the pink little head. The skin wrinkled, and, in a few seconds, the baby face turned into the visage of a mummified head.

He did not know how long it lasted. Only that by the end, they were burned and charred, the remains still jerking when he pressed the send button again. Four clicks, asking for the power to be cut.

To himself, Bond muttered, "An absolutely electrifying experience."

Then he retched and vomited as the stench of death hit his nostrils.

22

R.I.P.

Many things happened in the hours following Weisen's death. One at least was miraculous. A team from the British Special Air Service had been alerted by the French, and began to sweep the Maintenance Tunnel from the Folkestone end.

They took three of Weisen's men, killing the other two, and retrieved a number of weapons, including four LAW80 short-range anti-tank systems. Two had been fired—the LAW80 is a one-shot, disposable weapon—and two were intact.

As they moved forward to the burnt-out shells of the two Internal Security vehicles, they were amazed to find six of the French GIGN Special Forces men still alive, including the redoubtable Colonel Henri Veron. He was badly wounded, but Bond visited him in hospital the next day and he still had the hard, uncompromising glint in his eye.

At the end of the visit, the Colonel grasped Bond's hand. "I understand you put an end to things, Captain Bond." The eyes softened. "Thank you. On behalf of my unit and the French people, thank you."

"Luck. Getting to the right place at the right time." Bond made a gesture which, from any other man, would have meant "It was nothing." 007 was too much of a realist to indulge in that kind of phony heroics. He really meant it *was* luck, more than skill. Luck and quick thinking, though when he heard the truth of things, he put it down solely to Dame Fortune, and thanked whatever God or saint had been looking out for him.

The facts were that Weisen had attached no less than five hundred pounds of a Semtex-type plastique explosive, in fifty-pound packages, to the underside of the train. All ten bombs were interlinked with electronic detonators. When Bond arrived in the main northbound tunnel, they had been fixing the final bomb to the back of the train. They had yet to attach its detonator, together with the prime detonator for the first bomb in the chain, under the engine itself. Had the detonators already been attached, the huge pulse of electricity which had killed Wolfgang and his cohorts would have also set off an explosive reaction which would have not only destroyed the train, and everybody in or near it, but also smashed through the tunnel wall.

They found the detonators, and a remote-control unit, in an armored case, lying only a few yards from where Bond had entered the tunnel. Weisen, they deduced, had intended to activate the bombs from the Maintenance Tunnel, then make his escape in the confusion which would have undoubtedly followed. It was later revealed that they had taken the explosives, and weapons, aboard the VIP train in champagne crates and assorted boxes which should have contained food.

M told him that he was one of the luckiest men alive.

The official story, released to the press within an hour of the bloody incident, was that a terrorist group had penetrated security at the Coquelles Terminal and made an unsuccessful assassination attempt on the European leaders. Nobody had yet claimed responsibility.

The dead train attendants, and those soldiers of the GIGN who had given their lives on that fatal morning, were buried at a military funeral near the French Terminal four days later. Neither Praxi nor Bond was allowed to attend. It was essential that both the agents should keep low profiles from now on. Weisen still had many followers on the loose in Europe, and an international alert was out for Monika Haardt and the woman they knew as Michelle Gris.

The captured members of Weisen's crew were in for a long interrogation, as were Praxi Simeon and Bond. Both British and American authorities needed names, and descriptions, of men and women who had sided with Wolfgang Weisen's organization after the reunification of Germany and the collapse of Soviet Communism.

Praxi and Bond were allowed to make one short visit to the United States, so that they could attend Easy St. John's funeral in the small town of Culpepper, Virginia. It was a sad and moving occasion for all of them, and Bond was asked to read a few lines from one of Easy's favorite poems. He knew it well enough, for it was declaimed at Armistice Day ceremonies each November throughout the United Kingdom. His voice cracked only once as he spoke:

> *They shall grow not old, as we that are left grow old:*
> *Age shall not weary them, nor the years condemn.*
> *At the going down of the sun and in the morning*
> *We will remember them.*

They flew back to France, where combined French, German, British and American interrogation teams were debriefing everyone concerned with the last days of Wolfgang Weisen.

After that, they were taken to London, spending some four weeks in a safe house while inquisitors from Bond's own Service probed their minds for more facts, and more information.

So it turned out, on a raw December evening, they were told to report to M's office where the Old Man had particular news for them.

The French government had awarded each of them the Croix de Guerre, and, at the British Prime Minister's request, HM the Queen wished to make James Bond a KBE and Praxi Simeon an honorary DBE. With great respect, they both refused the latter honors. The French medals, however, were presented to them there and then in M's office by the French Ambassador. After the short ceremony, Bill Tanner took Bond's citation and medal from him and locked the items in a safe which contained many such awards, earned in secret. The Brits still cling to their secrecy with the fanaticism of an arcane religious sect. Later, Bond said he thought being an island race had something to do with it. In private he wondered whether, with the advent of the Eurotunnel, they would ever regard themselves as an island nation again.

That evening they dined, as he had promised, at the Italian restaurant in Marylebone High Street where the *padrone* and his partner, Umberto, were pleased to see him and fussed over the pair, constantly referring to Bond as *Dottore*.

It was well after ten at night when Bond told the taxi to drop them off in the King's Road—some ten minutes' walk from the tree-lined square and the Regency building in which he owned a ground-floor flat.

It was force of habit. He rarely drove, or was taken, directly to his front door. It was always preferable to be dropped some small distance away—a routine security adhered to by most active members of the Service. It allowed people like Bond to check there were no unusual cars, vans or people parked, or loitering, nearby.

Some of the lower windows of houses around the square were lit up with early Christmas decorations: a tree twinkling with lights in one, another decked out with spray frost on its windows and a holly wreath on the door.

He had telephoned May, his fussy elderly housekeeper, from headquarters, so knew there would be a fire in the book-lined living room, that the curtains would be drawn, and the bed made up. It was good to be home, and he watched Praxi in amusement as she admired the ornate Empire desk, the other antique pieces, and the rows of books, many of them rare first editions which he collected as a hedge against inflation or hard times.

She was particularly interested in the misty-bright painting over the mantelpiece which so captured the light of Venice burning off the mist of an early morning. "It can't be." She turned to him, one eyebrow raised. "Is it?"

"Is it what?"

"A Turner. This looks like a Turner, James. It must be worth a fortune."

"It could well be." His mouth twitched into a half smile, and he was about to tell her that, in certain circumstances, he might even be able to pass the painting off as the real thing. For a second, he deliberated as to whether he should show her the back of the picture, and the words written on it: LOVEJOY FECIT—a joke appended to it by his doctor friend who was also a very accomplished forger, as a pastime, naturally, not as a way to dupe members of the art world. The good doctor had learned his art from one of the greatest art forgers who ever lived.

He took a step towards the fire, his arm rising to the gilt frame when, with no warning, the long red velvet curtains drawn across the windows which looked out on the square, suddenly parted and a hellion leaped into the room, launching herself towards Bond, taking him completely by surprise.

Praxi screamed as a second figure hurled herself from behind the curtains covering the other window.

It took him a few seconds, struggling with the woman, to realize that he was face to face with Monika Haardt. He had seen her once only, on the day of her departure from Venice, but the thing with whom he now wrestled, looked nothing like the original. Her hair had been dyed a jet black and the face seemed older than he remembered. Now, close to his own face, Monika Haardt's features had become wrinkled, gouged with deep lines around the eyes and mouth, as though the events in France had prematurely aged her.

She was fit, though, and she held the glittering silver dagger low, in the classic knife-fighting position: the haft in her right hand, blade protruding from the thumb and first finger side of the clenched fist.

"Hold her. We'll deal with that little slut when I've ripped this bastard apart," she hissed towards the other figure. Out of the corner of his eye, Bond had seen the second woman spin Praxi around and hold her, right arm across the neck, the hand grasping her own left biceps, and the left hand to the back of the head. It required only a quick, strong tightening of the muscles to break Praxi's neck. He had resorted to that hold himself, many times in the past.

Monika made two quick upward jabs, which he parried with his arm, then she turned, the blade moving at lightning speed. As he stepped back, crouching, with his right hand scrabbling for the Sykes-Fairburn Commando dagger strapped to the outside of his right calf, he heard the blade as it whistled past his face, barely an inch from the skin.

He felt his legs touch the back of the beautifully restored leather, buttoned settee which stood side on to the fireplace, and with a feint to the right, he put all his weight on his left hand and vaulted backwards over the piece which now stood between him and Monika.

It gave him a moment's advantage: time to draw his own blade, adopt the bent-kneed stance, and circle the piece of furniture. Monika did not take her eyes from him. She crouched low, thrusting with quick short jabs across the settee, keeping him just far enough away from the obstacle as she tried to edge around it, and so come in close to him again.

Just as she jabbed, so Bond parried, stepping closer, using the same tactic to keep her from the edge of the settee. It was like a terrible, deadly game of tag, and it seemed to go on forever.

"Come on, brave Mr. Bond," she said, her mouth twisting into a red gash. "You were courageous enough to kill my Wolfie. Can you not bear to meet me face to face?"

He did not waste his breath. This was not a gentle, quiet business. Each movement had to be fast, drawing on maximum energy, as they both used every variation of the feint, thrust,

300

and parry, trying to break the deadlock forced upon them by the piece of leather furniture between.

Now he began to increase the pace, his steps to left and right becoming faster, feet dancing across the carpet: first to the left, then another to the left again, followed by two quick steps to the right. If he could wear her down, tire her, or even force her into a moment of extreme frustration, Monika Haardt might make a fatal move.

Yet she kept up with him, dancing to and fro, skilfully moving her feet and body. She was good, knew all the thrusts and parries, every move and counter-move. She had been taught by an expert in the field. Bond knew there were few really good knife fighters left these days. It was fast becoming a forgotten art which he had learned from a wizened little Spaniard who, it was said, had fought three hundred duels with the knife and won every one of them.

While Bond had tried to quicken the pace, Monika now upped the stakes by moving even faster than him. After some ten minutes, he was aware that she could possibly tire him: that she was at least as good, possibly better, than him. Already his breathing had become heavy, and he felt as though the room was a steam bath. Sweat trickled from his hairline, down onto his eyebrows, then into his eyes, distracting him from the target.

The first law of knife-fighting is never to lose concentration: Always keep the whole of your opponent in view. Your eyes should not simply watch the knife hand, but take in the face, eyes and feet all at the same time, for it is often a hand or foot movement or a sudden shifting of the eyes which signals your adversary's next maneuver.

Monika Haardt gave no such signal, and if she did, Bond missed it because of the sweat now making him blink constantly to clear his eyes. With no warning, Monika, while moving fast to her right, suddenly pushed off, springing into the air, doing a forward roll like a diver going off the top board, then extending her legs, smashing her feet into his face before landing, squarely, on his side of the settee.

She wore neat, flat black shoes with ridged rubber soles, but they caught his face like a champion boxer's pile-driving straight right. He knew his nose was broken before he slammed back into the wall, now blinded by pain as well as the sweat.

He was aware of a scuffle to his right, but tried desperately to regain balance. His head still swam from the blow, and he was almost down as the silver blade of Monika's dagger curved towards his throat in a long, slamming stroke.

He rolled to one side, face contorted with fear as the blade swept in with the speed of a jet. Somehow he knew this was the end, and, in that last moment of desperation, Bond reversed the direction of the roll, thrusting out his own hand, twisting his knife so that it became the tip of a spear at the end of his rigid arm.

The pain went through his left shoulder like a great lance of fire. Then he felt the sudden weight of the body, heard the terrible gurgle of pain and death as Monika, moving fast and out of control, impaled herself on his dagger. His right hand even sank a short way into the wound, so revolting him that he let go of the knife, struggling to his feet, pushing the writhing thing away.

She was pulling with both hands at the hilt of the Sykes-Fairburn as her entire body gave a reflex twitch, jack-knifing to the tune of her death rattle.

He rolled clear, his hand going for the ASP to deal with Michelle Gris holding Praxi. Michelle was not there. She lay on the carpet, with Praxi bending her right arm almost to breaking point, her own right hand holding the "Baby Beretta" which had belonged to Gus, ramming the barrel into the back of the fat girl's neck.

There was blood, damp on his left shoulder, and the Haardt woman's dagger still protruded from the wound, the pain shrieking through him.

"I thought I'd better do something about Big Michelle,

James. You going to be okay?" Praxi did not loosen her grip on the girl, but her eyes reflected the concern of her words.

"I'll live." He struggled to the telephone and dialed the number which would put him through to the duty officer at that tall headquarters building overlooking Regent's Park. He told them to send a cleanup squad as quickly as possible, and a doctor. He also said they should let themselves in.

The last thing he remembered saying was, "May they all rest in peace." He saw Praxi's mouth move, and could have sworn she was saying she loved him.

When he came round, in the hushed hospital room, she was the first person he saw. Behind her, M's and Bill Tanner's heads seemed to be floating in space.

"You're going to be fine, James," M said.

"It's a nasty wound and you lost a lot of blood. Up and around in no time." That was Tanner's voice.

He thought he should ask Praxi how she had turned the tables on Monika's partner, and exactly what she had tried to say to him in his sitting room, as she knelt on Michelle's back. Then he changed his mind. Tomorrow would be soon enough, so he closed his eyes and slipped back into a peaceful, drug-induced sleep, where there was no death and no violent endings.